TO SAVE THE MAN

ALSO BY JOHN SAYLES

Pride of the Bimbos

Union Dues

The Anarchists' Convention

Thinking in Pictures: The Making of the Movie Matewan

Los Gusanos

Dillinger in Hollywood

A Moment in the Sun

Yellow Earth

Jamie MacGillivray

A NOVEL

TO SAVE THE MAN

JOHN SAYLES

TO SAVE THE MAN

First published in 2025 by Melville House

First Melville House Printing: November 2024

Melville House Publishing
46 John Street
Brooklyn, NY 11201
and
Melville House UK
Suite 2000
16/18 Woodford Road
London E7 0HA

mhpbooks.com
@melvillehouse

ISBN: 978-1-68589-141-1
ISBN: 978-1-68589-132-9 (eBook)

Library of Congress Control Number: 2024942353

Designed by Beste M. Doğan
Printed in the United States of America

1 3 5 7 9 10 8 6 4 2
A catalog record for this book is available from the Library of Congress

To Maggie

_________ is back from Outing, a failure.
We are ashamed to print his name.

THE MAN-ON-THE-BANDSTAND

TO SAVE THE MAN

THE BOY CRAWLS OUT FROM BENEATH THE GONDOLA LEFT orphaned on the siding, bending low as he scurries across ballast and track to the westbound freighter with its engine snuffling and throbbing beneath the rickety water tower. It is an isolated, jerkwater stop, a single lantern hung from the spigot for the boilerman to see by, and the boy keeps to the far side of the boxcars till he finds an unlocked door, sliding it open, slow and steady, till there is space to haul himself in. The smell of candle wax. He slides the door shut and sits on the floor in absolute darkness.

He doesn't feel like he's alone.

Metal slamming as the couplings engage, one after another, and the train huffs into motion. A scratching noise, flickering light, and a scrawny white boy is seated on a crate with a lit candle in his hand.

"You weren't invited," he says.

"If the door's not locked, it's up for grabs."

The white boy seems to accept this. "You nailed a rattler before."

"Been doing it a couple weeks. Where'd you get the candle?"

The white boy shifts the flame to reveal an open crate beside him, packed with rows of glistening white tapers.

"This car is lousy with 'em. Nothin' to eat, though."

He stretches the candle forward to get a better look at the newcomer. "You're an Indian."

"You win the cigar."

The boxcar rocks as they take a curve, the train almost up to speed.

"What kind?"

The new arrival peers into the rest of the dim interior. "Ojibwe," he answers. "You probably heard us called Chippewa."

The white boy lights a trio of candles already stuck to a crate top with drip wax. The Indian boy can see now that they sit in a little clearing between dozens of crates stacked nearly to the roof.

"So the Chippewas—they still, like, hunt and fish—"

"Plenty of that, yeah."

"Take a few scalps—"

The newcomer gives the white boy a level gaze.

"Anyhow, you people go back a long way in this country."

"That's what I'm told."

The white boy grins. "My old man, he only come over twenty years ago. Stumbled off the boat and somehow dragged his carcass to Chicago."

"I went through there a couple days ago," says the Indian boy. "The yard I was in, there was ten, fifteen tracks laid out side by side."

"That's Chicago. What's your name?"

"You mean my Indian name?"

"Yeah—"

"You couldn't pronounce it."

"But what's it mean in English?"

"Walks Far—but Would Prefer to Ride."

The white boy smiles again. "Me too. I already walked holes in both my shoes."

There is a single blast of the whistle from up ahead. The boys listen for a moment.

"Maybe something on the track."

"It was too dark to read on the side of the cars," says the Indian boy. "Got any idea where we're headed?"

The white boy shrugs. "All I know is we're going north."

"Good."

The Indian boy leans back against a wall of crates, closes his eyes for a minute. He is dressed in what looks like a uniform, elbows and knees scuffed and soiled, shoes battered from hard travel.

"You run off from the Army?"

"Not exactly."

"Cause you're not, like, a wild Indian."

He opens his eyes. "I used to be, up till the Sisters of Perpetual Adoration got hold of me—"

"That's nuns—"

"A whole tribe of 'em, hooked up with the Benedictines. They started me out on the righteous path, and then I got shipped east to the Indian school."

"Indian school." The white boy grins. "Where they teach you how to shoot a bow and arrow."

"No," says the newcomer wearily. "That's not what they teach—"

SEPTEMBER

MUSKRAT, IF YOU DO A DECENT JOB WITH THE SKINNING, scraping, and tanning, will bring you fifteen cents a hide at the mercantile over in La Pointe. Catching them is the easy part. Antoine sees his father standing on the shore, hands cupped around his mouth to call out.

"How'd we do?"

Antoine lets the canoe drift, grabs one by its excuse for a neck to hold it up.

"Got five in the traps!"

They carry the canoe from the water, carefully turning it over to rest on an old stump, and lug the chunky rodents by their tails, the footpath through the red pines just wide enough for two. Antoine's father works something over in his mind before he speaks.

"I talked to the government fella about this Dawes Act."

"Where they take our land."

Antoine has heard some about it from Père Etienne and some more from the Indian agent himself, a man everybody calls the Swamp because of his foul breath.

"They take it from the *tribe*. And then they give some back to the head of each household. Call it an 'allotment.'"

"How much?"

"A hundred sixty acres."

Antoine, always good at numbers, tries to imagine this, but can only see the clearing where their cabin is, see the fishing hole and the bank where they put in to harvest rice. All on what he thinks of as their land. "Do we use that much?"

His father looks away. "How it goes," he says, "is from father to son. Least that's what the Swamp tells me—"

"Yeah—?"

"So if your father was French like mine was, you're not considered part of the tribe unless a man who *is* has adopted you in."

"So?"

"Nobody ever done that for me, not on a piece of paper."

"But you always lived with—"

"They say it don't matter how you *live*, it's what's on paper. They got people coming up all the way from Milwaukee, look like goddam squarehead Swedes, with papers saying they're Ojibwe and they should be on the roll."

"That isn't fair."

"That don't matter either."

The muskrats are feeling heavy now, and Antoine shifts the biggest from one hand to the other.

"It don't matter that your *maman* goes straight back to old Chief Buffalo—the government says Jacques LaMere don't qualify for no allotment."

They walk a moment in silence. Antoine's father seems more embarrassed than angry when he speaks again.

"But then I was talking to Père Etienne and Sister Ursula, and they say how if you got one of your children at this Indin school back East, it means that according to this Senator Dawes *you're* an Indin."

Antoine stops in his tracks, looks at his father.

"I don't want to go to school in the East. Send Pascal or René."

"You're the one I can spare the most. You're the one who's good at school, the one who reads English good and who knows what to say to those people."

Antoine hears a woodpecker hammering, high in a tree up ahead. He waits until his father will look him straight in the eye again and speaks forcefully in Ojibwe.

Does my mother know about this?

AT THE CABIN Antoine's father stays outside, unhappily yanking muskrat hides off their bodies.

Antoine's mother watches a lump of lard melt down in a hot skillet, speaking to him in Ojibwe.

There are too many white people to shoot them all.

It is the closest she comes to cursing, in any language. Antoine stands behind her, awaiting the verdict.

I've been to enough school, he says.

Père Etienne says it's the only way.

I thought you never listen to priests.

Antoine's mother dips her fingers in a bowl of water, flicks droplets into the skillet, where they pop in the spreading grease.

Because they lie. The earth—our earth—is the white man's paradise, and money is his only god.

She deftly places small balls of dough from a floured board into the skillet, sizzling as they begin to fry.

I haven't done anything to make you punish me like this, says Antoine.

If we were in a flood, would you bring a boat to pull us from the water?

Yes—

If a bear attacked the little ones, would you try to kill it?

Yes, but—

This is what you can do to save us now.

Tears form in his mother's eyes as she stares at the frying lumps of bread, then she turns and puts her arms around him.

Don't ever forget who you are.

YOU'D THINK THE WHITE PEOPLE had never seen an Indian sit in a passenger train before. But Antoine has the ticket stub in his pocket and his Sunday church clothes on and deals it right back to them, stare for stare, even when he opens the window and learns about the cinders and smoke flying in and they all shake their heads and harrumph. Hank Downwind was off to Red Cliff with his wagon so Antoine's father had the Indian agent send a wire for the train to stop at the water tank on the rail that runs through Lester Cadotte's old patch, only a couple hours' walk through the woods from their cabin. His father didn't talk much on the way.

"We do good with the rice this year," he said, "maybe we can send you money to ride home for a visit."

It is the rice harvest he'll miss the most, the job he took over when Pascal and then René got on at the sawmill, poling the canoe through the high stalks while his mother taps ripe grain off the heads with wooden knockers. There is a rhythm to it that he loves, *chock-chock, chock-chock*, like there is a rhythm to this train as it rolls over the joins in the rails.

At first it is only thick woods to be seen out the window, now and again pointed stumps and a beaver pond, then some open spaces and a few unpainted shacks. Though there's no reason to be tired, the side shimmy of the car and *kathunk-kathunk-kathunk* of the wheels below lull him to sleep for a spell, till there is the whistle blasting from ahead and the man in the blue uniform shouting.

"Five-minute stop, folks! Stretch your legs."

The train slows, passing a pyramid of dark-stained railroad ties, then stops, hissing in a cloud of steam at a platform with no station house on it.

Antoine stays glued to his seat, not wanting to chance being left behind, while a good number of the white passengers get up and move to look out the windows on his side of the aisle. A bony, stern-looking white man stands on the platform, towering over perhaps a dozen Indian boys and girls, most of them younger than Antoine. They are dressed in dusty buckskins and scraps of cast-off cotton clothes, most with blankets draped over their shoulders, looking like they're about to be hanged. Antoine turns to stare like the other passengers do, but declines to point or mutter as the children are marched into the car by the white scarecrow man and deposited into empty seats. The oldest of the boys is pushed down next to Antoine.

"You try and run again, Imonna have to *tie* you to this seat."

When the scarecrow moves to the back of the car to keep an eye out, Antoine asks the boy in Ojibwe who they are and where they come from. The boy acts as if he doesn't hear.

The man in the uniform calls out again and some bags are hurried aboard, then the whistle is pulled and the train jolts back into motion. There are telegraph poles alongside the track here, evenly spaced, and Antoine thinks that putting them up would not be such a bad job, pacing off the distance, digging a hole, setting a pole in, pacing off the distance . . .

White people at the front of the car lean out into the aisle to look back at the newcomers. The boy next to Antoine pulls his dusty blanket up to hide his face.

It is past noon when Antoine realizes what the scarecrow is up to when he escorts each of the Indian children to a door at the back of the car, waits for a bit while they are on the other side of it, then takes them back to their seat. All but the boy next to Antoine. Some of the white men in the car go back there, and finally Antoine gets up the nerve. It is a small closet, smaller than the one at the mission school, and he can see railroad ties flashing underneath through the hole in the box you sit on.

So whatever you do is left behind on the tracks.

When he is finished Antoine goes back and takes the arm of the boy at his seat, motions for him to come along. The boy resists, but Antoine smiles and nods with his head and finally the boy agrees to come along. Antoine takes him back to the closet, the scarecrow watching them suspiciously, and shows the hole in the box and makes signs with his hands before leaving the boy inside and shutting the door. The boy stays inside for a good while, Antoine wondering if he might be thin enough to fit through the narrow hole and drop under the train.

Which would surely kill you.

When he finally comes out they go back up the aisle, the boy grabbing the backs of seats to keep his balance. He waits for Antoine to sit by the window, then slides in and covers his head with his blanket again.

They change trains once, the scarecrow motioning to Antoine to come with his group, and then it is night and they are all given a square of dry corn bread from a basket. Antoine sleeps again, waking whenever they stop at stations with lights and noise and black men in uniforms on the platform, pushing carts piled with bags and trunks.

"Just stay put," says the white scarecrow man, standing in the aisle and holding his hands up. "We got a ways to go yet."

One of the little girls is crying most of the night, but nobody comforts her or tells her to be quiet.

At the speed that they roll and the time it is taking, thinks Antoine, he is already impossibly far from home. Sister Bernadette, who is in charge of teaching numbers at the mission school, is fond of posing travel conundrums. If the train makes forty miles every hour, and runs for six hours only stopping to take on fuel and water for thirty minutes, how far is it to Bemidji? Antoine was adept at these once he discovered the trick of how the changeables—time, distance, speed—related to each other, and there is always a trick of some sort, like what his father says about signing the white man's paper.

"You think you smell dinner," he'll say, "and then them iron jaws snap shut on your leg."

Antoine's father is very clear that he is not half white, he is half *French*, considering that a tribe like the Ojibwe or the Potawatomi.

"The things they *done* to our people," he complains, and you can't tell if he means the local whites scheming to steal their land or the ones he calls *les mauvais anglais* up across the border.

It is dark and quiet, except for the crying girl, for a long time, then the sky lightens to a grayish rose color. More and more stations now, more and more white people, new ones, more people in and out of this one train car than Antoine has ever met in his life. At one of the last stations a young Indian woman dressed in white comes aboard, slight and frail-looking with a beautiful, sad-eyed face. She stops in the aisle to speak in an almost-familiar tongue to some of the blanket children. When she comes near Antoine he gathers his nerve to call to her.

"Do you know them?"

"No," she says. "But I know who they are."

"We're going to the Indian school." It shakes him a little, that "we."

Even when she smiles she looks unhappy. "As am I."

"They take us as old as you?" he asks, and immediately regrets it. She might not yet be twenty.

"I'll be teaching there."

"Sorry—"

"At the school I'll be Miss Redbird."

The boy sitting next to him is staring at her, and she says something in his language. He replies angrily and she touches his shoulder with her hand, speaking softly. The boy does not seem comforted. The young woman turns back to Antoine.

"Try to look out for him," says Miss Redbird before walking back to sit next to the white scarecrow man. "If you can."

When it says CARLISLE on the station sign they all get out, Antoine realizing that there have been Indians in the other cars as well, more than a hundred of them spilling onto the platform. He doesn't hear any Ojibwe. Some of the arrivals are dressed like he is, in Sunday pants and shoes; some, both boys and girls, in uniforms; and some, like the blanket wearers from his car, still dressed Indian and with hair even longer than his own. Uniformed boys his age and older are there to greet them, shouting and waving to herd the crowd into a long double line, and soon they are following the white scarecrow man, who Antoine hears the cadets call Mr. Skinner, away from the tall town buildings they passed by on the way in and down a road that parallels the tracks. They walk for a spell beside a high wooden fence and then come to an arched entrance, another of the uniformed boys, blue jacket, gray pants with stripes down the sides, standing stiffly beside it. He swings the metal gates open and Mr. Skinner waves the parade through, hovering near to look each of them in the eye as they pass, a look that Antoine feels it is not a greeting but a warning.

And then there are the buildings.

It resembles some of the forts in Père Etienne's picture book about the white people's Civil War, an enormous rectangle of a parade ground surrounded by huge white wooden or redbrick buildings, some with long balconies running along the front of the second floor, and in one corner a white-painted bandstand flanked by a white-painted pole on which their flag hangs limply. More boys and girls, some in uniform, all in white people clothes, have gathered near the entrance to watch the newcomers enter. Antoine fixes on an oversized older boy who is being led by, or possibly dragging, two uniformed cadets on each side, crossing their path toward an old, low rectangular building made of round stones.

"New fish to fry!" calls the oversized boy at the newcomers, a huge grin on his face.

"Imagine that," says one of the older cadets walking near Antoine, "Induction Day and they're already stuffing Sweetcorn back in the can."

Sweetcorn is pushed into the stone building and one of his escorts hangs a heavy lock on the iron ring, jamming it shut.

There are a half dozen older girls clustered ahead, laughing and waving and pointing at various of the arrivals streaming by them. All wear what seems to be the big girls' uniform, gray wool despite the heat of the day, long sleeves, skirts to their ankles, except the tallest of them, a girl in a light green dress with a tiny silver cross hung on her neck and hair plaited into a single braid that hangs down her back. The tall girl meets Antoine's eye as he comes near. He can't look away.

"Hello," she smiles. "Welcome to Carlisle."

He is in love.

It is Induction Day on the parade ground and all the new ones need to be photographed, with Mr. Choate expecting Leslie to arrange the blanket Indians. Never mind that Leslie doesn't speak their languages—not a single Puyallup among last year's newcomers—it's clear the photographer would rather keep his distance till they've been through the hair cutting and bug killing and fitting of uniforms. Leslie takes the new boy, hollow-chested and terrified, by his skinny arm, leads him to the chair in front of the bandstand, which Mr. Choate always calls "the gazebo," and sits him down. He unpins the paper tag that has been stuck to the boy's sleeve.

Ascención Viajero, it says. Papago.

Leslie believes those come from somewhere down by Mexico.

"You see the camera?" he says, pointing back toward Mr. Choate, who is extending the bellows for a single portrait. Leslie walks back to the device, taps his eye, then points at the lens and calls to the Papago boy.

"Right in here—that's it—"

Mr. Choate crouches to look through the finder. This one must be dark enough, because he hasn't told Leslie to screen the sunlight off his face. Captain Pratt uses the before-and-after photographs to raise money for the school, and maybe the people who donate really think that five or six years' instruction here will lighten your skin. For the graduate portraits they always shoot inside and train a bright light on the students' faces, and if that doesn't work Mr. Choate will have him dodge around the face during the exposure so it comes out just on the living side of ghostly. And of course their hair has been fixed by then and they've got a clean dress uniform on and are told to strike a college-boy pose, legs crossed and arm over the back of the chair, or knees together and hands neatly folded in the lap if they're girls. Working in the darkroom is Leslie's favorite part—the quiet, the little plashing sounds the liquid chemicals make when you lift a photograph out, the magic when the exposure first appears. There is a holy feeling to it.

"Right here," says Leslie, circling the lens with his finger, and the boy looks into it, suitably miserable, and there is the wonderful little crunch of the iris and the plight of this bewildered wild Indian has been captured forever. Who wouldn't feel sorry for such a wretch, who wouldn't agree that anything would be an improvement over his present state?

"I've got that," says Mr. Choate. "You can bring in the group now."

Leslie copies the boy's name onto the work chart, then goes to pin the name tag back onto his threadbare cotton shirt. He motions for the boy to stand, points to the hospital building, where more of the blanket boys are lined up waiting for their haircuts.

"You go over there now. Go."

He gives the boy a gentle push and Viajero starts uncertainly for the hospital. That was never me, thinks Leslie, who came here from the mission school in Tacoma already speaking English and knowing how to deal with white people. He had sat in the chair in front of the bandstand after getting off the train, exhausted from days of train travel, and asked Mr. Choate if he could have a copy of his photograph to send home to his parents. Choate was amazed that any Indian knew you could make more than one print from the same negative, and invited him to look through the finder.

The Apaches are sitting on the ground. There have been so many of them the last few years, sullen and underfed when they arrive, looking ready to bolt. Leslie motions for the group, mixed boys and girls, to follow him, leads them to stand in front of the bandstand. Captain Pratt is there now, up on the platform just out of camera range. He is tall with a long nose, eyes that miss nothing, motionless as a statue.

"Our new postulants," he smiles.

"Yes, sir."

"We have our work cut out for us."

Leslie has spoken with Pratt only a few times, mostly about his progress as a photographer, and the Captain always talks about "we," meaning all of them at Carlisle—students, instructors, even the warrant officer and the dinner matrons.

Leslie guides the boys and girls into position as gently as he can, hoping they don't really have fleas like the Sioux cadets claim they do. Several of the girls, placed in the front row, hold hands with each other, but none utters a sound. Only a few have moccasins, the others barefoot, wearing scraps of this and that, many of the boys with vests and rope belts, all with hair hanging past their shoulders. He wonders if it isn't cruel not to tell them about the cutting about to happen, but of course that would lead to more runaways on the trip here. There are nearly a dozen, and it takes some effort to get them all looking to the lens at the same time. Mr. Choate makes two exposures to be sure he's got it, and Captain Pratt beams down on the process, standing behind and just out of the picture. Most of Leslie's friends here say that Captain Pratt has to be the Man-on-the-Bandstand who writes the little mystery messages in *The Indian Helper*, but their School Father is away in Washington so often, pleading for more government support, that he can't possibly be spying on students in every dormitory and classroom.

"Children of nature," muses the Captain, "awaiting the blessings and bruises of civilization."

Leslie has the Apaches stand where they are until he has copied the names pinned on their backs to a sheet of paper, making circles to indicate the order of their heads from left to right, girls in the front row. Most will be getting new names, the old ones corralled between parentheses on the before-and-after postcards the school sends out. Ga-yar-lay becomes William Black, with short hair parted down the middle and a brighter if not happier countenance.

"You lead the boys over for their haircuts," says Mr. Choate when Leslie has all the names recorded. "We don't want anybody wandering off the reservation."

Leslie performs in the sign language he uses for all the blanket Indians, and the boys follow him toward the shearing.

The bruises come first.

It is Induction Day, and the bony man from the train, Skinner, is leading a younger white man through the boys' infirmary where the barbers are set up.

"In some of the tribes you only lose your braids if someone close in your family has died," he explains. "You should hear the caterwauling they set up."

Antoine submits patiently to the clipping—the nuns were always after him to cut his shorter, saying that white men's hair was "more manly," and both René and Pascal had theirs lopped off before they applied to work at the sawmill.

"It takes a while for some of these new ones to understand it's just a haircut," adds Skinner as he passes with the new teacher. "They take one step toward being civilized, and we solve a health problem."

Nobody has explained anything to the boy who sat beside Antoine on the train, whose name, written on the tag on the back of his shirt, is Makes-Trouble-in-Front. When the scissors, gripped hard, chop off the first handful, he is up and out of the chair, hollering, and it takes three of the older cadets to wrestle him back into it, one of them lecturing him in Sioux. He sits with his hands covering his eyes, cheeks wet with tears.

"You're finished," says the barber, whipping the sheet off and dumping Antoine's mess of hair onto the pile on the floor. A younger cadet, maybe ten years old, plows by with a push broom, gliding away with a mound of loose black hair and ropy braids. The barber points to a wall of white screens at the end of the room. "Bug station next."

Antoine passes three more unhappy boys being scalped, careful not to step on clumps of hair, and peeks behind the screens. A man with a mustache wearing rubber gloves is roughly sudsing the head of an Apache boy who was ahead of Antoine in line with a gooey, brownish salve while another white man, standing on top of a stool, crooks a finger at him.

"Step over here," he says, "and bow your head."

In Mass you do things like this, thinks Antoine, but always kneeling. The man on the stool, also wearing gloves, pokes at what's left of his hair for a moment.

"You're good," he announces. "Out the door and turn left."

It is Induction Day, and as they wait in line on the stairs, girls who stayed over for the summer catching up with those who got to go home, it is apparent that Wilma Pretty Weasel has grown at least two inches since Grace saw her last. Wilma's uncle, an important man in the tribe, died in June, her family scraping the money together for the train fare to Crow Agency and now back East to school.

"I didn't know if you were going to come back."

"The agent said I had to," says Wilma.

"But your parents must want—"

"They don't have a say in it."

Wilma has a good heart, but is still a bit lost in the classroom, left back with children younger and smaller than she is.

"How was it to be home?"

Grace has only been back to Green Bay this one summer since she was enrolled, but her older brothers, both Carlisle graduates, write often, and Sister Claire always sends news of her parents with her beautiful, slanted penmanship, in violet ink.

"The people made fun of me," Wilma grumbles. "Said I'd forgot how to talk proper Absaroke."

"But it came back pretty quick—"

"Not really. Every time I said something I felt I was going to be punished."

"Well, the rule here—"

"Do you remember any of your—what is it—?"

"Oneida—it's a kind of Iroquois."

"Could you say something right now?"

Grace makes sure no instructors or matrons are near, then takes Wilma's arm, looks her in the eye, and tells her she is so very happy to see her again.

"I can't tell if that was any good."

"It was fine. I practice."

Wilma waits till Mrs. Fish, the sewing instructor, passes them up the stairway, then lowers her voice. "Really?"

"At night in bed I whisper it, like I'm telling my parents everything I did that day."

Wilma grins. "You're a wicked girl."

"And then I say my prayers in Oneida."

"If the Man-on-the-Bandstand ever hears you—"

"Men aren't allowed in the girls' dormitory."

Just then Miss Ely comes down, followed by Miss Burgess.

"Miss Ely," Grace smiles. "Miss Burgess—"

"It is so nice to have you back, Grace," says Miss Burgess without looking at Wilma. "You'll be in the same room."

"That's wonderful."

"And how was your visit home?" Miss Ely is a good twenty years older than Miss Burgess, and it is known that the two have shared quarters since they came together to the school, that they walk arm in arm when on chaperoning excursions, that they have been overheard using pet names for each other.

"It was good to see my family."

"No pressures, chastisement, temptations—?" Miss Ely serves mostly as an Outing agent, checking up on the girls when they stay and work with farm families, and one of her nicknames is the Bloodhound.

Grace holds her ground. "We're very civilized up in Wisconsin."

Miss Burgess puts a hand on Grace's shoulder. "We're expecting great things from you this year," she says, and the two continue downstairs.

"And they don't expect nothing from me," says Wilma when they are out of earshot.

"Of course they do."

"I think it's one of them—the Man-on-the-Bandstand. Either Miss Ely or her young wife."

"Wilma—"

"I bet they sleep in the same bed."

"Now who's being wicked."

"They expect us to be so perfect," says Wilma resentfully. "But white people aren't even *good*. Not the ones I seen in Montana, not even all the ones here. I smelt whiskey on Dr. Hazzard's breath."

Grace wants her roommate to be happier. Last year an Arapaho girl down the hall, Minnie, got so low she hid behind the laundry and swallowed a cupful of lye and was too far gone to save when she was found. Their part of the line has reached the top of the stairs now, and Grace can see into the classroom where the new clothes are piled on tables, several girls already trying garments on for size.

"Wilma! We're getting *capes* this year!"

Miss Burgess loves Induction Day. The excitement, the sense of beginning, the opportunity to restore order after the lassitude and backsliding of summer. Even her parents, more devoutly Quaker than she, would agree that there is great value in the military structure of life that Captain Pratt has established here, the days evenly sectioned by bugle and bell, a proper procedure for every function, a benignly ordered world for these children of chaos. She unlocks the printing shop and enters, leaving the blinds down on the windows. She loves it at its busiest, machinery clacking, boys scurrying about with layout scissors, reams of paper, trays of lead type in hand, but this private time is equally blissful. The smell of ink and ammonia. Every afternoon work session here ends with cleanup, while the one field trip she arranged to the *Carlisle Herald* in town was, despite their impressive modern equipment, a disaster—how anything worth reading could emerge from such clutter and pandemonium remains a mystery.

"This would never do at a Philadelphia newspaper," she sniffed to the boys, though she has never had the opportunity to visit one.

Miss Burgess sits at her editor's desk, arranges paper, pen, inkwell, and ponders for a moment. *The Indian Helper* is Captain Pratt's messenger, of course, not only to the students but to the world, supported as it is by caring citizens who, depending on the efficiency of their local postal service, receive it weekly, but it contains another voice, a moral undertone one might say, spiced with a bit of mystery and humor. When her father was the Pawnee agent in Nebraska, she'd discovered how those miserable, primitive people loved a touch of the unknowable, the keepers of the various medicine bundles afforded extra respect. Why not an all-seeing trickster at Carlisle, but one dedicated to the righteous path instead of transgression? And if it be clandestinely female—

Things I See and Hear, writes Miss Burgess in her strong, clear hand. *By the Man-on-the-Bandstand.*

It is Induction Day, and the man in charge of uniforms tells Antoine he may keep his clothes from home. He makes a sack with his shirt and carries the bundle from station to station, an older cadet at each to size him up and thrust some article of clothing into his hands.

"Try this on."

The pants and shirt feel stiff and itchy to his skin, made worse by the late-summer sun spilling through the open window. Each newcomer receives two pairs of woolen socks and instructions about when they are to be left in the laundry hamper, and a white flannel nightshirt, which they are ordered to wear after lights-out. They are allowed to sit to try on new shoes, none of which have laces yet. Makes-Trouble-in-Front and a boy with a long Spanishy name have been relieved of the clothes they arrived in, and Antoine shows them that there is indeed a left shoe and a right shoe and pushes his thumb down on the toes to be sure they haven't chosen too big a pair.

"Laces at the next table," says the white man in charge. "See if you can teach them how."

"When do we get our rifles?" Antoine asks, and the man gives him a long look before answering.

"You'll be issued those when it's time to drill," he finally answers. "They're made from a block of wood and don't shoot bullets."

Makes-Trouble and the Spanish-named boy both look too small for the clothes and grip their name tags tightly in their hands now, as if that is all that remains of their true selves. They watch Antoine lace and tie his shoes and carefully try to do the same. The darker boy, Ascención, seems unsteady when he tries to walk with the shoes on his feet.

"Caps come last, don't let them cover your eyes," says the man in charge. "Then outside and muster for room assignment." He gives the boys a last look, speaks to Antoine. "And get them to button their flies."

Antoine helps the boys try on kepis, his own feeling way too big with his hair gone, even if it looks fine in the mirror. Makes-Trouble seems stricken by what the mirror reveals, uttering one contemptuous sound. Antoine leads them outside, Makes-Trouble having some difficulty going down the steps, and they join the crowd of new boys waiting there, all sweating in their blue woolens. A boy holding his own bundle approaches Antoine.

"You got to keep yours too."

"Even my old shoes."

The boy shifts his bundle, holds out his hand to shake. "Moses Smoke," he says. "Cherokee."

"From the Territory."

"Nawp—Carolina. We're the ones that hid out when the rest got pushed west."

They shake. "Antoine LaMere."

"You think they'll make us live with all these blanket Indians?"

"I got no idea. You smell something burning?"

Antoine steps around the corner to follow the cooking odor. A black man pokes at a smoldering bonfire with a long rake. Antoine has to step closer to see that what is burning is the clothes taken from the new arrivals, a lot of it buckskin or cowhide. A white woman uses a pair of sticks to lift a colorfully beaded dress out of a pile waiting for the fire, holding it up to examine and finally laying it on a table on top of a few other skirts and dresses with intricate handiwork.

"You! Private!"

One of the older cadets is shouting at him from the corner of the building.

"Get back with the new meat!"

Every Induction Day there are a handful you can't accept. Dr. Hazzard knows the verdict with this one even before the auscultation—the boy hollow-eyed, pigeon-chested, manfully attempting to breathe normally and not to cough. One of the new crop of Apaches, he exhibits the usual adverse reaction when the bell and diaphragm are pressed to his bare, hairless chest—is there not a stethoscope to be had at the San Carlos Agency? A quick listen confirms that the upper lobes are seriously impaired, that the consumption is well advanced, and that this is material unsuitable for the school's mission. Dr. Hazzard sighs, looks down the line of equally emaciated, shirtless boys waiting for his examination. He takes the boy's bony wrist and pulls him out of the line.

"This one's too far gone," he says to Nurse Tucker, most efficient and least favorite of his helpmeets. "He'll have to be sent back."

He thinks of whatever poor, failed bastard is sweating it out at San Carlos, ordered no doubt to reduce the number of mouths to feed, with no hope of profit from the sort of bribes the government beef inspector enjoys. They don't call it Hell's Forty Acres for nothing.

"He'll never survive a train ride to Arizona," says Nurse Tucker with her usual note of accusation.

"Well, we don't want him dying *here*, do we?"

On Induction Day the blanket Indians are reborn.

Makes-Trouble-in-Front listens but does not understand, remains wary, but sees no escape. It seems that in this place women tell men what to do. Two of the younger white women seem to be in charge of this square room with smooth black rock lying flat against one of the walls. One of the women, making noises he can't understand all the while, gives him a long stick and motions for him to step to the black rock, which has swirly patterns of white on it, too irregular to be designs. It is humiliating to be here in these clothes and with his head shaved naked, but if he hits the woman with the stick and tries to run they will surely kill him. And where would he run to? The long days on the rolling rooms that swayed but never tipped over have left him only with the knowledge that his people are an unimaginable distance from here. The woman takes the stick and demonstrates hitting the white snake patterns with it, then hands it back to him. He hits the white with the point of the stick and she smiles and writes something on a piece of paper and puts it folded in his hand, making more sounds.

Miss Cutter turns to the next one, takes his name tag, tries to read it.

"A-sen-kio—no, *see*yone—"

"Ascención," says Miss Low, reading over her shoulder. "It's Spanish."

"Via—jayro—"

"You say it Via*hay*ro—"

"I'm certainly not remembering all of that. Write down 'Asa.'"

"That's good," says Miss Low, writing the name, folding the slip and handing it to the boy. "The simpler the better."

It is Induction Day, all in uniform by now, new students keeping their faces blank and their movements cautious, silent, stomachs knotted.

What will they do to me next?

Antoine follows at the rear of the group brought up to the second floor of the large boys' dormitory, pausing as the two older cadets, who have introduced themselves as Clarence Regal and Jesse Echohawk, master sergeants, deposit other newcomers into rooms four at a time. It takes a good while, Antoine hearing a horn being blown outside, hard footsteps above them on the third floor, where the same process is underway. Finally there are only two left by the doorway to the room at the end of the hallway. Jesse Echohawk reads from a list in his hand.

"Antoine LaMere."

Antoine raises his hand slightly. "That's me."

"La Merde," says Clarence Regal.

"I been called that."

Clarence glances at Jesse's list. "Chippewa."

"Yeah—"

"I'm Sioux. My grandfather and yours used to go after each other with war clubs."

Antoine has been told the history. He makes a show of looking the tall sergeant up and down.

"What are you gawking at?"

"This is the first time a Chippewa ever seen a Sioux from the front."

Echohawk has to laugh. Clarence Regal points inside. "You'll be in this room. Who else?"

"Moses Smoke—"

The Cherokee boy steps closer.

"Smokey," says Clarence after a once-over. "Do you speak English, Smokey?"

"Pretty good."

"Cherokee," reads Jesse Echohawk.

"You from the Territory?"

"Carolina."

"One of the holdouts—"

"We didn't *run*."

Clarence indicates the room. "You're here with La Merde," he says as two more bewildered newcomers are hurried down the long hallway by a younger cadet. "And these two blanket heads."

Echohawk checks his list as the boys arrive. "Ascención Viajero. Papago."

Clarence looks the boy over, tilting his head to one side. "Papago is what the Apaches call you people. Bean eaters. I'm going to call you Bean Boy." He points. "You're in here, Bean Boy."

"He doesn't speak any English," says Antoine.

"Then he'd better learn it damn quick, hadn't he? And the last one—?"

"Makes-Trouble-in-Front. He's—"

"He's Sioux," says Clarence Regal, stepping close to tower over the boy and repeating his name in Lakota. Makes-Trouble-in-Front looks spooked.

"What's this?" Clarence pulls the folded paper from the boy's hand, reads it. "Percival? All the names you could have picked off the board, and you point to *Per*cival?"

"You should talk," says Jesse Echohawk. "*Cla*rence."

"He looks like just plain Trouble to me," says Clarence Regal, pushing the boy in through the door. "In here, Trouble."

Clarence turns to Antoine and Moses Smoke. "We hear a peep of anything but *Eng*lish from this room and you will be up on charges. Court-martial session on the parade ground every Saturday!"

They leave the new boys. Antoine steps into the room, puts his bundle of home clothes on a little bed with a metal frame. Four beds, two desks, an electric light dangling from a cord overhead that can be guided to the various corners of the room by pull strings. One window. Antoine crosses to look out the window down to the parade ground. The tall girl he saw before, now wearing a school uniform, passes underneath with an even taller girl. He wonders if she got to keep her real name.

It is Induction Day for Miss Redbird as well.

The surprise upon entering through the gate was how much more interesting the school grounds are than the town itself. White-painted buildings clustered around a vast, grassy parade ground, leafy trees among the former barracks made into dormitories and classrooms, the fanciful bandstand that seems to anchor it all. And then her eye followed the plank fence, at least ten feet high, that runs around the circumference of the institution. A fort after all, she thinks, its walls in this case meant to keep the enemy on the inside.

Her room, though fully carpeted, is as cell-like as she imagined. The two windows that should open to the parade ground, veiled with yellowed muslin curtains, seem to be painted shut at the moment, and Miss Redbird wonders who she will find to remedy that. Her violin case and small suitcase full of clothing take up very little space. A small table, two stiff-backed chairs, nothing hung on the walls. She knows that white people prop photographs of their relatives up on desks and end tables, but her mother will turn away at the sight of a camera. Her mother lives in a cabin now, a poorly made box at the edge of the reservation, and cannot understand why her daughter has left her again. The original desire to go to the Labor Institute in Wabash had been a misunderstanding, little Zitkala-Sa, as her mother called her, dazzled by Quaker missionary stories of a place where shiny red apples were always available for the picking, a gateway to further wonders. Once confined there her wounded pride overcame her misery, the shame of returning to Yankton in defeat not bearable. The apples proved to belong to proprietary white neighbors who sold them by the roadside and eventually put up unscalable fences to protect the trees from Indian atrocity, but finally the music kept her there, an unknown tongue that she understood almost immediately. And eventually their spoken language became hers as well, its power when used in a certain way, its subtleties, till she could stand before a white audience where opponents held up placards mocking her and regularly best them in formal debate.

SQUAW ARGUE WITH FORKED TONGUE was the placard held closest to the stage.

A discrete knock on her door, and Miss Redbird opens it to an intimidatingly tall, gray-haired man holding a straw boater in one hand. Despite the civilian clothes she knows this is the Captain.

She puts her small hand into his huge one and can sense what he is thinking—so tiny, so frail.

"So you're the little Indian girl who created such a fuss among the college orators."

"That was some time ago—"

"I just wanted to welcome you to our family here at Carlisle."

"Thank you—"

"Is there anything more you require for your comfort here?"

He is looking past her into the room, a tight fit for a man of his stature.

"I'm quite fine, thank you."

"You came to us from the Yankton Agency."

"Where I was born, yes—"

"We have several students from there."

"I met a few of them on the train."

"We of course discourage our young men and women from returning home during the summer, and only those who can afford the fare do so, but there is such a wonderful *en*ergy each September when academic classes begin again."

"The new students—the ones who have just come from the reservation, must feel—well, I went through the same thing when I was eight."

"Drawing out the process of immersion is no kindness." The Captain frowns. "In that regard I am a Baptist—once we've got the Indian under the rules of our civilization I believe in holding them there till they are thoroughly soaked."

She wonders if it is meant as a joke.

"In my first week at school I was convinced I would be murdered."

"Yes—you were at the—?"

"Just a little Quaker school in Indiana. But you don't understand a thing that's happening, English words are just noise—"

"And therefore you must sink or *swim*. You'll see, Miss Redbird." He smiles. "These children have an amazing ability to adapt to circumstances. Convocation in an hour—you'll hear the bugle call *Assembly.*"

He is gone, and Miss Redbird sits. She hasn't been well. She'll be teaching music, speaking in English even with the ones who know Lakota. A more familiar face, she hopes, an ally, *giv*ing them something instead of taking something away—

But already she feels like a traitor.

Early evening, Induction Day, and the small boys test their new, hard-soled shoes on the stairs as they climb to their beds. Miss Burgess and the newest matron, whose name is Fannie Noble, follow them up, Miss Burgess raising her voice above the assault.

"Most have never worn real shoes before!"

"It's quite a racket."

"Don't let them play marbles on the floor up here—nobody on the first floor will be able to think."

"There are so many of them," observes the younger woman. "Do they ever get to sleep?"

Miss Burgess smiles. "Oh yes. We make it a point to wear them out."

They reach the dormitory, a row of beds spaced three feet apart along each long wall and one down the center, over a hundred in all. The boys rush to claim their own spot, bigger ones pushing smaller ones away.

"Boys!"

The voice freezes them for a moment. Miss Burgess holds up her list, fastened to a clipboard. "You will be as*sign*ed your sleeping accommodations! Please come forward when your name is called. Arthur Arcasia—"

No boy moves. Miss Burgess turns to the new matron. "They still have their tags on. See if you can find young Arthur—"

Captain Pratt's Induction Day welcome is held in the new auditorium. Formerly the recruit barracks, the building was converted to classrooms by his first cadre of students, most of whom had been his prisoners in St. Augustine. Excellent carpenters, as it turned out, once they'd had the training. Then just three years ago the center of the building was rebuilt to add offices and this spacious assembly area—no more huddling in the old gymnasium in the dead of winter. The captain has worn his uniform for this occasion, an extra touch of gravitas, the buttons and epaulets gaudy enough against the somber Army blue that his few campaign decorations have been left in their jewel box. He is struck, as always, by the pleasing symmetry of the display before him—boys to the left, girls to the right, ranging back from the smallest to the largest, the white faces of staff members on one wing, those of benefactors and honored guests on the other, Mr. Skinner and his assistant disciplinarians in the aisles and rear, ready to quickly remedy any lapse of decorum.

"The Bohemians in Chicago, the Italians, Turks, Greeks, Germans, even the Russian Jews when they come here—all of them learn English, put aside their foreign ways, and become—if not in the first generation, surely the next—self-supporting American citizens," he tells the rows of children in blue and gray, the instructors and disciplinarians and support personnel, the benefactors in their city finery. "Why not the Indian?"

He lets that vital question hang in the air for a weighty moment. For Pratt had first dealt with the red man as a second lieutenant with the Colored Tenth at Fort Arbuckle in the Territory, shortly after the end of the great and terrible Civil War. Finding no lack of intelligence or initiative among his Negro cavalrymen, many of them former slaves—they were, in fact, altogether less prone to slack and disruptive behavior than the white soldiers of the same era—he was further pleased to discover the same admirable qualities among the Cherokee, Caddo, and Wichita scouts he commanded. That the former should be banished to segregated units and denied officers of their own color and the latter condemned to dwell on prisonlike "reservations" seemed an intolerable abrogation of the safeguards of the American Declaration of Independence and Constitution.

All persons born or naturalized in the United States, and subject to its jurisdiction, are citizens thereof.

Indeed.

"In my many years of military service, encountering dozens of tribes," Pratt continues, "I grew to realize that the obstacles to this end were not lack of innate ability or intelligence, but merely those of culture and environment."

Père Etienne uses words like this in his sermons sometimes, but in French. Antoine looks across the boys in his row. The Papago boy they are calling Asa appearing as uncomprehending as Trouble next to him, Clarence Regal with arms crossed on his chest, faintly smiling, Smokey surreptitiously picking his nose, the other privates at least attempting an attitude of grave attention. He makes an impressive figure, the Captain, tall, broad shoulders, a man who has never allowed a doubt to linger in his mind. *Mashkawizi*, they would say at home.

"Here at the Carlisle School we take the Indian child out of that culture, out of that environment, away from the obscenity of the reservation system that has been imposed by politicians who've never been west of the Mississippi"—the Captain seems to expand his chest with umbrage at this concept, brass buttons gleaming in the new electric footlights—"and immerse them in a system that is *or*derly, that is disciplined, that is pro*gres*sive—that being the world of the white man, or perhaps an idealized version of it—and there attempt to bring out that which is *best* in him. There are no halfway measures at Carlisle—to save the man, we must kill the Indian!"

A mutter of appreciation among the benefactors. Clarence Regal nudges Trouble and whispers a translation.

Save man. Kill Indian.

He draws a finger across his throat, and the boy is duly impressed.

"The buffalo are gone," intones the Captain, "the vast plains breached by iron railroads, the days of the tipi and the roving hunter gone, gone forever."

Miss Redbird has heard this poetry before, most often expressed in a wistful manner by those who were principals in the slaughter. She is flanked by the Misses Burgess and Ely, who make small humming noises of approval as Captain Pratt holds forth.

"On the miserable reservation land left to him, the Indian has only the shameful indignity of government beef, vermin-infested blankets, the debauchery of liquor and prostitution."

The Captain lets this sit, panning a steely gaze across the rows of listeners.

"His only way out, save ex*tinc*tion—is to throw down the blanket, turn his back on the government handout, and step forward into the light of progress and civilization!"

A smattering of applause from the staff and benefactors. Trouble wonders at the noise—is there a spirit they are hoping to scare away? He wishes he knew what the School Father is saying will be done to him, and be better able to avoid it.

"To you students, especially to those who have only just joined us—I understand that this is not an easy road to travel. It is *work*, and it cannot be mastered all at once. Stick *to* it, I say, only stick *to* it and you will be astonished by your own accomplishments!"

The School Father takes a step back from the wooden box and again people strike their hands together, as do even many of the Indians around him dressed in the white man uniforms. It sounds like hard rain to Trouble, the sort of rain that can tear a camp down.

Clarence Regal motions that they are to stand as Miss Hyde's chorus of older boys and girls, nearly twenty voices, begins to sing—

Mine eyes have seen the glory of the coming of the Lord;
He is trampling out the vintage where the grapes of
wrath are stored—

Excellent singers, thinks Miss Redbird, feeling dwarfed by the sturdy pair at her sides, and wondering if the students understand the provenance of the lyrics. Her own first triumphs in the English language were sung, the words somehow easier to pronounce when matched with a specific note.

He hath loosed the fateful lightning of His terrible
swift sword:
His truth is marching on!

Antoine again looks down his row, the cadets all standing now. Clarence Regal is singing along in full voice. Smokey moves his lips, but they don't quite match the words.

Trouble holds his hands over his ears.

Having survived Induction Day, they are left, strangers, together in the small room. The Sioux boy, already barefoot, stalks around it—the four beds, sink with wash pan, small table, and few chairs—stopping at a corner to put a hand on each wall.

This is what the white people put their cattle in before they kill them, he says in Lakota.

This is your new home, Clarence Regal reminds him in the same tongue as he appears with Jesse Echohawk, standing in the doorway. You had better get used to it.

Trouble steps to the one empty bed, his roommates watching him, and lifts the white nightshirt that has been laid across it.

You have to put that on before you go to sleep, Clarence tells him.

It's for a girl.

Clarence laughs, switches to English. "You'll look like an angel."

He steps in to look the boy in the eye, changing back to Lakota.

If you speak our tongue again, you'll be whipped.

The older cadets leave. The three roommates look on as Trouble sits on the bed, still clothed, wraps himself in the top blanket, and lays down with his face to the wall.

Clarence and Jesse Echohawk descend to the first floor.

"That Trouble looks like he hasn't eaten in a month," says Echohawk.

"They put us on half rations."

"*Us*?"

"Last year the government chopped Sioux country into six smaller reservations, gave everybody three hundred acres of scrub and hard rock, and told them to learn to farm," says Clarence. "People are starving."

"That much land, people ought to be able to grow *some*thing."

Clarence turns at the bottom of the stairs.

"You ever been to the Bad Lands?"

Jesse Echohawk, a Pawnee, has not.

They hear the bugler play *Taps* out on the parade ground. Clarence raises his voice to shout up the stairwell—

"That's lights-*out*, gentlemen!"

There are still oil lamps instead of electric lights in the small boys' dormitory. Fannie Noble screws down the wicks one by one, the eyes of some of the tucked-in boys following her, others already asleep or making an attempt at it. She reaches for the next lamp, pauses her hand—a furry lump on the nightstand leaps at her and then races in jerks and starts across the floor.

Her shriek is met with a chorus of giggles. She strides to catch up with the still-moving lump, stomps on it, bends to look it over, then finally holds it up to the final glowing light.

"Very amusing, boys," she says. "I trust you will apply as much enterprise to your studies."

Later in the carpeted room that serves as a teachers' lounge, she dangles the dead mouse from its string to show Miss Burgess.

"Ah—I neglected to warn you. With Miss Patterson they employed a rat. I'm afraid her nerves never recovered."

"There are *rats*?"

"Back in the first years of the school, yes. The barracks had been abandoned since General Stuart burned them during his march to Gettysburg. But Captain Pratt offered the young men a bounty on the creatures, and the problem was quickly solved."

Fannie sits across from Miss Burgess, thoughtfully twirling the dead rodent by her ankles. "When the light went out there was a great deal of weeping."

Miss Burgess smiles. "Little warriors. They hold it back until no one can see them."

THERE IS A CLOUD ON THE HORIZON, just one, distant and holding no promise of rain. It does not move. And then there is Walker Lake, which in this bone-dry, yellow-brown wasteland is evidence of powerful medicine.

But sitting in the simple wickiup made of woven tule rushes that the Fish Eaters—the Northern Paiute—build to live in, the seeker from the Cheyenne is struck by how few *things* there are—no trade blankets or buffalo robes, no beaded shirts or moccasins, no modern rifle to hunt or make war with, not even a small pot to make coffee. The visitors are fed, though, as they sit on the ground around the Messiah, by a woman he does not introduce, a meal of mashed seeds and toasted pinyon nuts and the meat of a jackrabbit. There are five of them, all from the other side of the great mountains, including the young son of the Arapaho chief Left Hand and another prominent member of that tribe, who are good friends to both the Lakota and the Cheyenne.

When they have finished eating, the Messiah asks them how their journey has been. Each has a somewhat different story, for travel now, long travel, is controlled by the white man, permission from the Indian agent on your own reservation required to leave, questions from the agents on the other reservations you must cross, many stories to invent if you don't have papers in their writing that say you are allowed to go from one place to another. None of them admitted they were coming here to see the Messiah, and each needed the help of many people to gather enough money to pay for railroad tickets—there is no longer freedom to ride across the great land on horseback.

When these stories have been told there is a long silence, and it is Grant Left Hand, the Arapaho chief's son, who asks the Messiah if he will tell of his vision, and politely asks if he may write that which he speaks down in the white man's language so that it may be shared with many people. The Messiah says that this is a good idea, but first he wishes to show them something.

He is a poor and simple man, yet tall and powerful-looking, past his thirtieth year, with a soft, confident voice. It was a surprise when they entered the wickiup to see the Messiah dressed in white man's clothing, somewhat worn, with a large, black, round-brimmed hat that he has placed on the ground before his crossed legs. He has worked for much of his life on a ranch owned by a white man named Wilson, and the white people who know him here call him Jack Wilson. He has heard all the stories from the Bible that the holy white men on the other side of the great mountains love to read from, and he says there is much of value in those stories, but only red men can know their true meaning.

There are two other men in the wickiup with them, interpreters who understand the Paiute that the Messiah speaks, and also have been to the eastern side of the great mountains to learn the language of signs that is used on the plains there. But both words and signs have many shades of meaning, so the tale that the seeker from the Arapaho understands is not exactly the same as the one understood by the seeker from the Cheyenne, or any of the other seekers.

Let me show you something first, says the Messiah, and begins to pass an eagle feather over the crown of his large round hat, speaking words so softly in Paiute that the interpreters cannot hear to make them into signs. Finally, he lays the feather down and turns the hat over and tells them to come forward, one at a time, to look into it.

The seeker from the Cheyenne sees something black inside, maybe moving, maybe not. He is disappointed—medicine men of his own tribe have shown him much stranger things. But when the seeker from the Arapaho stands to look into the hat he sees that there is no bottom to the hole within it, and feels himself losing his balance, as if he might fall up into a starless night sky and keep falling, falling forever.

When all have looked in the hat, Wovoka, for that is the Messiah's Paiute name, puts it back on his head.

I keep the world in there, he tells them. At least the part of the world that is west of the great mountains. I can make it mist or fog or rain, or even drop hail in the desert. But I could not do these things before I came back.

The two interpreters, a little behind and to the sides of the Messiah, make their signs, and every once in a while it is as if they are one person in two bodies, hands moving in unison. But the rest of the time their stories are slightly different, so that the seekers quickly choose to look at one or the other, but never both at the same time.

Will you tell us of your journey? asks the son of Left Hand.

Most of the reservations on the Plains have a few of these young men and women now, who have been to the white man's school for Indians far to the East, who can speak and read and even write in the white man's language. With so many tribes desperate and seeking, it is good to have one tongue in which the Messiah's words can be recorded, though it is a poor one, he believes, for expressing many things.

It happened to me when the sun died, says the Messiah.

This had happened on the other side of the great mountains as well, on the very first day of the white man's year. The sky going black, dogs howling while the birds went silent, medicine men chanting, children crying—many were certain, after all the bad things that had happened since the white man had come into their lands, that the Creator of All Things had decided to destroy the world.

I also died, says the Messiah.

I died a shuddering, twitching death, and all was black, as black as what you have seen by looking into my hat. But then I awoke, and I was no longer in this world, but in the place where the Creator of All Things dwells, and all the Paiutes who have lived before, many of whom I knew personally, were there to greet me, living in a green, forested land full of beautiful streams and animals to hunt, which they did the ancient way, with bows and arrows and spears.

Were there white men there? asks the seeker from the Cheyenne.

No, says the Messiah, the Creator explained that he had only made them as a test for the red man, like a great storm or a fire, and that like those things they are not meant to be constant. The Creator told me that I was to be a messiah to my people, that I must go back and tell them to be good, not to drink alcohol, not to fight with each other or even with the white man, for soon there will be a great upheaval.

Each of the interpreters pauses to think for a moment before they make a sign for "great upheaval," then exaggerate with their gestures to convey just how powerful this event will be.

The earth will open up, says the Messiah, and out from it the buffalo will come back to the land, great herds of them that will cover the plains as before, and behind them, when their dust begins to clear, will come all the red men who have been before, riding upon spirited ponies. And in the places where there are white people, because they are not needed anymore, some will be swallowed by the earth and others buried by mountains falling upon them, all of them will be buried deep beneath dirt and rocks. The world will be again how it was before the whites came.

There are some soft, thoughtful *Hos* of appreciation when this is signed by the interpreters, whose hands describe the earth lying flat and heavy upon the whites.

It will be better even, says the Messiah, because nobody will ever again become ill or age or die.

The seekers can hear the sound of Left Hand's son scratching across the paper with an ink pen, trying to catch up to these wonders they have been told.

Is there anything we must do to prepare? asks the seeker from the Arapaho, who is still feeling dizzy from his glance into the sky below.

There are five songs the Creator taught me, which I will pass on to you, and a dance that must be done with the songs. The dance must be done for five days in a row, and then some time to wait for certain signs, and then done again for five days. The more red men who do these things, the sooner the time of the great upheaval.

Must the songs be sung in Paiute?

The Creator of All Things created speech, says the Messiah, and so understands every tongue. I will tell you the songs, which are very simple, and you will find your own words for them.

Be good people, says the Messiah, and do this dance, and you will help bring the great upheaval nearer.

But it will happen soon? asks the seeker from the Cheyenne.

Yes. The Creator of All Things said "soon."

Good, says the Cheyenne, whose people at home are dying of a disease they have never known before.

Before we are all gone.

WHEN *REVEILLE* SOUNDS Trouble leaps to his feet, crouching, ready for an attack. Jesse Echohawk's voice booms out in the hallway—

"Out of your racks, people! Into your clothes and on the parade ground! Let's *move* it!"

Antoine rises, grabs his uniform shirt from where he left it folded on top of his footlocker, then mimes putting it on for Trouble and Asa.

"Do what I do."

"It's still dark out," observes Smokey.

The sun is attempting to light the eastern sky when the boys stumble out onto the parade ground, herded with barked orders and small shoves into a three-row formation in front of their dorm, most still tucking and buttoning.

This is A Company.

Clarence Regal strides along the front row, inspecting dress and tonsure as Jesse Echohawk stands before them reading the roll from a sheet of paper, the experienced cadets knowing to answer "present" when called.

Clarence stops in front of Trouble, fingers his misbuttoned tunic, then looks to Antoine beside him.

"La Merde—work with him till he gets the hang of it."

"Smoke!" calls Jesse.

"Present!" answers Smokey.

"Viajero!"

"*Aquí!*"

Clarence looks from Asa to Antoine. "And straighten out Bean Boy too."

"Percival Makes-Trouble-in-Front!"

Antoine kicks the side of Trouble's foot, hisses a whisper to him. "Present—"

"Prezza!" calls Trouble.

Captain Pratt does his paperwork after morning drill. When the students are outdoors or assembled for whatever reason, he likes to show himself, the School Father watching over his charges. The most effective officers, in his experience, were always those who were most *present*. If the "Old Man" sequestered himself in his quarters, rarely left his tent when in the field, or, like one troubled colonel he served under, always traveled by ambulance, he quickly became more of a rumor than a leader. Soldiers, black, white, or red, understand their duties, but profit from constant supervision.

The first day of classes and already there is a discipline problem. Herbert Sweetcorn has never been a good fit at the school, a scofflaw and a stirrer, and would have been sent home years ago but for the government's conviction that his continued presence at Carlisle is a vital factor in keeping his father, a notorious war chief in the '60s, planted on the reservation. Captain Pratt understands that this sort of hostage arrangement was key in the Army's decision to allow him to begin the noble experiment at Carlisle, ceding the ruined barracks and allowing him to petition Congress for operating funds. But the Sweetcorn boy, almost a man now, is disruptive and intransigent. He's been sent off on the Outing program several times, and though a strong and able worker, his attitude has always run afoul of his host farmer's patience. And his years of transgression and consequent punishment seem to have inured him to both thrashing and incarceration.

When Captain Pratt was at Fort Griffin on the Brazos his scouts were Tonkawas, of a pariah tribe rumored by their Indian enemies, fairly or not, to engage in cannibalism. Too small a group to defend themselves against the Comanche and Kiowa, they lived in close proximity to the fort, with the usual deleterious effect. With bootleggers impossible to completely eradicate, there was much drunkenness, the tribe's elderly chief being the worst offender. On arrival the Captain saw this as a sorry model for his scouts, and proceeded to attack the problem. Discovering the Tonkawa chief passed out at the side of the road, Pratt had him transported to headquarters, and upon waking explained to him through Jones, the able interpreter, what was to be. For this first offense he would be pardoned, and when he could walk, allowed back to his dwelling. But the next infraction would bring him seven days of guardhouse duty—like the black soldier within sight of his office, shoveling horse leavings into a wheelbarrow while shadowed by a corporal with a rifle equipped with fixed bayonet.

"You will sleep in a cell and be required to work like that man every day," he told the chief, "and then you'll be released. If there is a further incident of public drunkenness you will receive four*teen* days punishment"—Jones made use of his fingers to show the number of days, as the Tonkawas had not yet adopted the concept of weeks—"and if there is a next time it will be twenty-eight, and then fifty-six, doubling each time till you won't be able to get drunk because you'll be living full-time in the guardhouse."

The chief said he understood, said whiskey was a very bad thing, and left for home. It was less than two weeks later that the Captain came upon the chief and another important leader of the tribe, drunk beyond reason, with the chief about to have his brains dashed out by a large stone. Pratt dismounted, wrested the stone from the other tippler, and had both of them transported to headquarters. There he explained to the thwarted murderer that he was receiving the first-time indulgence but would in the future live by the same rule as the chief, and let him go. The chief went to the guardhouse, and once sober enough to function, was turned out in the fort and its environs to collect horse pucky. Almost immediately a delegation of Tonkawas arrived, complaining that it was demeaning for their chief to toil like a lowly Negro private.

"But he re*quest*ed the assignment," the Captain explained through Jones. "I told him what would happen and he became intoxicated again. As you know, I'm a man of my word."

This delegation left, somewhat mollified, but was soon followed by nearly a dozen of the women, stating that it was a disgrace for the young men of the tribe to see their chief humiliated so.

"And what sort of exemplar for his tribe," he asked them, "gets his brains dashed out by his best friend while both are in a drunken stupor?"

The women retreated, not happy but accepting his authority, the Army being their only protection from the wrath of enemy raiders. And when his week of chastisement had ended, the old chief came to speak with him.

"I will drink no more forever," he said.

And he was good for his word.

There is no equivalent to that kind of corrective power here at the school, of course, the students, once habituated, knowing well that the neighboring townsmen and farmers are not out to kill and mutilate them, that the ultimate punishment is only expulsion and a return to the blanket.

Perhaps Herbert Sweetcorn is worth one more try.

Jesse stands by the clock on the mantel in the large boys' library, moving the hands as Clarence explains.

"Whenever the bugle is blown," says Clarence, "you must react promptly and in an orderly fashion. Six o'clock, *Reveille.* Six fifteen"—Jesse slides the minute hand to a quarter after—"*Assembly* call. Six twenty-five, *Mess Call.* Seven thirty, morning work detail—those daily tasks will be assigned to you later today. Eight thirty"—Antoine can tell that Trouble is lost. With Asa it's hard to know, as the Papago boy seems not to be altogether *there*, a faraway look in his eyes, his expression vague—"classes begin. Today you'll be separated according to degree of previous schooling, rather than age. Eleven forty-five, *Assembly* again and then we march to the dinner hall. Afternoons will be dedicated to industrial training—you'll be matched with a trade after dinner today. Five thirty, back on the parade for flag salute. Six o'clock, supper call."

Jesse continues to move the clock hands as his fellow master sergeant outlines the day.

"Seven thirty to eight thirty is evening hour—special activities, clubs, study, leisure time."

At home, thinks Antoine, no day is quite the same as another. Even at the mission school they were not tied to the clock, and at the end of instruction he'd walk the three miles back to the cabin, sometimes stopping to fish or check a trapline. This bugler who wakes them up here must have been given a pocket watch.

"Eight forty-five, evening roll call and prayer. Nine thirty, quarters, room inspection on a regular basis, then ten o'clock, *Taps* and lights-out."

Clarence does not ask for questions.

"Until you learn this, just look around and see what everybody else seems to be doing."

Jesse lifts the clock off the mantel and carries it to Trouble, demonstrating. "Hour hand—minute hand—"

Clarence snorts. "Good luck explaining *time* to an Indian."

Uniformed students, one line of boys and one line of girls, stand waiting on the long porch of the school building. Miss Cutter, backed by Miss Burgess and Miss Ely, waits until the majority of the students have assembled and straightened their ranks. Miss Burgess gives her the nod.

"You may come forward now," she says, "and receive your placement."

The lines move slowly, the two older instructors checking their lists and assigning students to the various academic levels, subgroups forming on the porch. Antoine sees Asa and Trouble and several of the new Apache boys shunted off with the small boys and girls, while Smokey is assigned to a middle group behind Miss Cutter. He becomes aware that the girl is waiting almost parallel to him with the other females, and that at least these morning classes will be a mix of the two sexes.

"LaMere—" reads Miss Ely. "Six years with the Catholic sisters."

"Do you speak English?" asks Miss Burgess.

"English, Ojibwe, some French—"

Miss Burgess points to a balding teacher who wears glasses, a dozen students already behind him.

"You join Mr. Gertz."

He crosses to stand with the group, watching, hoping, as the girl steps up to the white women.

"Grace, you know where you belong," says Miss Burgess.

Her name is Grace.

And she's walking toward him—

Class time, Basic English—

Miss Low well remembers her first day of schooling. The portrait on the wall of the kind-faced man who was later identified as Benjamin Franklin, the metal-lined fireplace that bore his name, the long, uncomfortable benches that made it near impossible to doze, her teacher's lovely Spencerian script on the blackboard—what a sense of orderliness for a child. They sat in rows by age as the children here do in assembly, the smallest in the first row, with the teacher often setting a unique task for each row while pausing to warn the older boys misbehaving in the rear. Here at Carlisle, thankfully, the students in each classroom are all roughly at the same learning level, although ranging from six to nearly nineteen. Miss Low does not seat them by age but alphabetically—spelling their new Christian names will be an early, diminutive mountain to climb, and the English alphabet, emblazoned on a strip above the chalkboard, one of the basic principles to be mastered. This seating lends a somewhat disorderly aspect to the *look* of the class, small ones hidden here and there behind big ones, requiring her to be constantly moving so that none is forgotten. Miss Low does not banish dullards to the rear or irritants to the front for closer supervision—

for the large ones, especially the boys, their mere presence here mixed with those on their first set of teeth is sufficient humiliation.

Look how far behind I am in the race of civilization.

Miss Low calls out the names—from American Horse, Bear Shield, Couteau, down to Makes-Trouble-in-Front, Viajero, and White Bird—as the children stand in an uncomfortable scrum at the rear, assigning them seats, having each remain standing till all have been classified and put in their place.

"We may now *sit*," she says, demonstrating with her own chair, which has been pulled out from behind her desk, understanding that wooden furniture may be foreign to some in the room. She has her instructional properties in hand.

"This is a sheet of paper," she says, holding it up. "*Pa*-per. Repeat, please."

A few respond, and she keeps at the word till all have uttered the syllables a few times.

"And this is a *pen*cil."

Class time, Reading—

"We shall begin on page thirteen," says Miss Cutter, and Smokey paws through the reader till he is there. His slate is full of writing and he doesn't like what he sees. He always tries to make the swoops and loops of the letters look like they do on the chalkboard, but his fingers won't obey. At school in Carolina when he was asked to remember and repeat anything he was one of the best in the class, but *read*ing—

His band had been saved partly through the help of William Thomas—a white man who'd been adopted into the tribe. He was a successful trader who bought up land for them before the rest of their people were forced to walk to the Territory, fought in the white man law courts to keep the Qualla Boundary, and even led Smokey's father and other young Cherokee to fight for the Confederates in the big war. He was pardoned by the president for that, but went crazy and is locked up in Raleigh.

"So that's why we need a white man," his father told Smokey.

"But I'm not white."

"If you learn how they do things it will be the same. You will come back and be our shield against their trickery."

"Please stand when you are asked to read," says Miss Cutter, "and speak out with brio!"

There were always so many things that needed doing at the cabin, especially after his father lost the toes. Out hunting racoons with Gil Youngdeer—who could have known the temperature would drop so quickly in September? At first they took the shimmering green light in the northern sky as a good omen, so beautiful, but it was actually a warning. Hobbling home down the mountain, his father saw dozens of birds that had frozen and fallen from the trees, but was too worried about what he'd see when he took his boots off to gather any for the pot. The tip of old Gil's nose had turned gray, but his feet were fine. Smokey's mother was not sympathetic.

"It's what you get for playing around up in those woods," she said.

That was when it was decided young Moses needed to learn to hunt, and his father gave him the old Winchester and taught him how to stalk. In the warm months he'd wear moccasins, easier to move without making noise, and sometimes they'd sit in a hide for hours, just watching animals come and go. Smokey got so he could hold on the buck for a full minute, if need be, breathing deep and slow, the sight held steady, then think the bullet through the deer to its heart. He would think the words the old Cherokee men had taught him, thanking Deer in advance for—

"Moses!"

The whipcrack of his name startles him back into the classroom. Miss Cutter and the other students are staring at him.

"Are you with us? Will you stand and read for us, please?"

Smokey stands, lifts the book, lost—

"See the frog," says Miss Cutter.

He quickly finds the passage with his finger. Somehow the letters never seem to sit still, attaching themselves to the next word or the one before, sometimes whole words hopping out of line and butting in somewhere else. He takes a deep breath—

"See the fr—see the frog—on a log. Rab sees the frog," he reads. "Can the frog see Rab? The do cang—no—the frog can see the dog. Rab ran at the frog—"

Class time, Mathematics—

The dilemmas that Mr. Gertz presents are not moral, not the thorny choice between telling the truth and betraying a friend that Père Etienne would challenge them with back home, but only Sister Ursula's complicated ciphering stories, and Antoine, standing to answer, has always been good at these.

"So would you prefer to have two slices each from three different watermelons, or one slice from each of four different watermelons?"

There is already something about Mr. Gertz that Antoine doesn't like, a little too delighted when a student fails to answer correctly. And he can feel the girl, Grace, watching him, two rows to the left.

"I suppose I'd want one each from the four."

Mr. Gertz raises his eyebrows. "Are you certain of that?"

"Yes, sir. I don't much care for watermelon."

The others laugh, even the ones unable to do the calculation, and Mr. Gertz narrows his eyes, taking stock.

"That's very clever. You may be seated."

He is not here because he wants to be, and they should know it. When he asked Clarence Regal what it took to stay in the school, the master sergeant smiled and said, "Better to learn what it takes to get *out*." Antoine steals a glance to Grace.

She is looking at him, but not smiling.

"Miss Kills Swiftly," Mr. Gertz continues, turning to a Blackfoot girl, "would you rise, please?"

There is no instruction in the guardhouse, no clock on the wall.

But Sweetcorn knows the unvarying bells and bugle calls—wake up, get dressed, out and be counted, into your classes, dinner, off to your trade, supper, go to sleep. He watches the other measure of time slant through the high, narrow slits in the walls, his entire cell a sundial, and on cloudless days he knows the light will touch a certain crack in the floor a few heartbeats before the bugler blows morning *Assembly*. When he lived with his parents on the reservation you could tell the time in the morning by the shadow of a willow tree that crept up the eastern wall of the council house. The old people used to have sayings about what time of year it was that had to do with the height or color of the prairie grass, but after the buffalo were gone you didn't hear them anymore. The people at the mission church and even the Quaker agents seemed to build their idea of the year around Christmas, as if a number on a calendar in the dead of winter might be something to celebrate. At least they considered that day sacred, and would always pass out their charity gifts to the young children, mostly clothes that had been worn by white children before. Government Issue Day, on the other hand, was supposed to happen twice each month, but this was not so reliable and it never came early.

Sweetcorn stops pacing and lies back on the bench, staring up at the guardhouse ceiling.

They were brought in to the agency to learn to plant and to plow from the white "assistant farmers" hired by the agent. On the Santee they mostly grew corn, which took some real work at planting and harvest, and then the rest was waiting. Waiting for the commodities issue. Waiting to die.

His father, who had been in the uprising when they were still in

Minnesota and knew some of the men who President Lincoln chose to hang, did not love the plow. He understood that it was more efficient to plant in even rows, that you could walk between the tall stalks filling baskets during the harvest, but nothing in Nature, he warned, grew that way. He insisted for years that they live in a tipi, when most of the people living close to the agency were in square or rectangular huts or dugouts—bad spirits became caught in those sharp corners, he warned, and could not find their way out of your dwelling. He borrowed horses from his brother one day and rode out with Sweetcorn to what he said had been the path of the great herd. What they found was a jumble of white bones on the ground as far as you could see from horseback.

"If this were closer to the railroad," he said, "even these bones would not be here. White people would have piled them into wagons and taken them to a place where they are ground into dust. They want us to believe that we were only dreaming, that there never were any buffalo."

A finger of sunlight touches Sweetcorn's cheek, and sure enough there is the bugle call for dinner. He will be brought his bread and water from the dining hall after the others are finished. He is not tired or bored enough to sleep, so he tries to open himself to a visit from his spirit animal. This is another thing the old people talked about a great deal, never revealing their own, but telling stories about Dakota men long dead whose spirit animals had protected or guided them through some perilous situation. He was thirteen the year before he was sent to Carlisle, and had never dreamed of animals in a special way—he rarely dreamed at all. But then one very hot day, waiting at the agency for the annuity payments that were long overdue, there was shouting and running among the people and Sweetcorn watched as a patchy, long-legged coyote, crazy-eyed and rabid, wandered crookedly down the street. Lightner, who was Indian agent then, had just stepped out from his office when the coyote stopped in front of it, leering, drooling, panting rapidly in the heat. The diseased animal and the Quaker agent stared at each other for a long moment, then Lightner quickly backed inside and the coyote continued its aimless trot till Wesley Thunder put it down with his shotgun.

When Sweetcorn reported that the coyote had looked deep into his eyes, that he had found his own spirit guide, his father said he would have to think about it.

It was a week before his father, Sees Far, having discussed the matter with some of the older, wiser men, told him the Mad Coyote was not inherently evil, but was a restless, unpredictable spirit. It was not the guide for someone who wished to follow the white man's road, as they were told daily was their only option, or the guide for a man wishing to live a long life. But, if the animal had sought him out and looked into his soul—

There are three days left on Sweetcorn's punishment. The letters from the Santee Agency since he has been here—six years in all—have not been full of good news. His father has fallen ill and rarely rises from bed. Chief Wabasha has died, and two years ago the tribe members voted not to follow chiefs anymore. The annuity and commodities issues have been inconsistent, his mother and sisters hungry much of the time, and then there was the Great Freeze of '88, when much of the livestock owned by Dakota people died in the cold.

He is not learning anything new here at the industrial school, and he has been warned about his inattention in class, his forbidden night visits to the town, his taste for alcohol. If he runs away again, like he did in his first year here, he will be a fugitive from the law, his photograph sent to federal employees and railroad workers. But if he is ex*pelled* by the Captain—

Nobody wants a mad coyote in their camp.

End of class time.

The bugler, a thin Walla Walla boy, wipes the mouthpiece of his horn with a handkerchief as students pour out of the classroom building and are formed into their companies. These first days it will be a bit chaotic, he knows, till the newcomers learn the drill and move to their ranks without thinking, smalls in front, each company a bit taller than the next—

"Column of two!" shouts Jesse Echohawk. "Dress it up there—keep your spacing—"

Antoine gently pulls Trouble into the formation next to him, signs that nothing is wrong, that they're going to be fed, as the dozen members of the brass band pound out *The Thunderer* at the front of the mess hall.

The girls' companies move first, their drill sergeants trying to get them all to step in unison, left, right, left, right, and Clarence Regal strolls in front of Antoine's group, digging into them with his glare.

"Cadets—when we move, you will step in *time*, and you will not tread upon the *grass*—"

They are marched in through a different entrance than the girls, each company of twenty assigned one of the long tables, and told to stand facing across from each other, ten and ten, behind their chairs. Antoine can see the girls already ordered and at attention on the other side of the hall, but can't find Grace among them.

"Eyes forward!" barks Clarence Regal.

Nobody speaks and then the last footstep is heard.

Mrs. Bakeless, the supper matron standing at the head of the room beneath the American flag hung on the wall, lifts a small bell and rings it.

Jesse Echohawk catches Antoine and Trouble by the elbows as they begin to sit.

"Not yet."

The ones who've been here before have pulled their chairs away from the table and again stand at attention. Antoine thinks of the agency trader's dog, which will sit when the man snaps his fingers.

Mrs. Bakeless rings the bell again, and the students all sit and pull themselves in snug to the table, the veterans folding their hands and bowing their heads. Antoine nods to Asa and Trouble to do the same.

"Miss Cloud," says Mrs. Bakeless, nodding to a prim-looking Oneida girl.

Lizzie Cloud rises, rolls her eyes Heavenward.

"Thank you for our food, we pray, may we in turn do good today."

Mrs. Bakeless rings her bell a third time and suddenly everyone relaxes as a squadron of female students in aprons appears bearing platters and pitchers of food and drink. There is a low murmur of talk as they spread out to serve the tables, Antoine relieved to hear it. Père Etienne tells stories of the silent orders, priests and nuns who never utter a sound unless in prayer, and he had worried there might be a similar ban here.

At the girls' table closest to Mrs. Bakewell, a scrawny Apache girl, who has been given the name Evangeline, just manages to cover her mouth with her handkerchief as she is wracked with a coughing fit. The matron notes this, writing on her seating chart, but does not intercede. When the girl pulls the white handkerchief away from her mouth there is a tiny spot of blood on it.

Grace appears at the A Company table, leaning in between Trouble and Antoine to lay down a platter of boiled potatoes.

"No watermelon for you," she says without looking at him.

He can't tell if she's teasing or disapproving, and then she is gone. Trouble seems lost beside him. Antoine taps his fork on his plate, then signs, *you*, *watch*, *me*, and begins to spear potato, greens, and bread from the platters nearby. Trouble watches, readjusts his grip on his fork, and manages to impale a potato. Antoine can hear bits and pieces of conversation, all of it in English, and notices that all the other new boys in the company are mute, watchful till they've figured out all the rules.

"Excuse me!" calls Lizzie Cloud, addressing the whole room, Grace standing next to her now.

"The Susan Longstreth Literary Society is sponsoring a recitation for the Thanksgiving exhibition, and we are in desperate need of a young man"—laughter here from some of the older boys—"a young man to portray one of the important roles. A firm grasp of English and a manly demeanor are required."

Grace waves a sheet of paper. "We will leave copies of the text of the reading at the entrance to the large boys' quarters for anyone who wishes to audition," she announces. "Thank you."

Antoine watches Grace return to her serving. She seems so content, so—so at *home* here.

"If you put it on your plate," says Clarence from the head of the table, "you had better *eat* it. We have no waste here at Carlisle."

They sit about the round table in what is termed the "teachers' lounge." Miss Ely, Miss Burgess, and the new instructors they have invited to luncheon, all of them female. A trio of girls from the school in aprons and caps silently serve—cream of barley soup, roasted hothouse chicken, brussels sprouts—a reward for the skill they've shown in domestic training. A slight breeze rustles the lace curtains, silverware and fine china tinkle discreetly as the two older women take turns explaining the dos and don'ts of the Carlisle Industrial School.

"There is no smoking or drinking allowed, of course," Miss Ely informs them, "the Captain himself being unusually abstemious for a military man—"

"We must at all times remember that we serve as models for these unfortunate children," adds Miss Burgess.

"And a special emphasis, when in public," continues Miss Ely, "should be placed on courtesy and manners. One of our tasks here is to train the young men to treat their women with the same gallantry and respect accorded to their more favored white sisters."

Miss Redbird, nibbling without appetite, attempts to recall instances of gallantry among the white men on and around the Yankton reservation. The one her mother claimed had fathered her, some sort of French, was gallant enough to abandon them in midwinter of her second year. The one-eyed trader who lived just on the other side of the river thrashed his equally white wife with a hickory switch till she met a Mormon pushcart pilgrim come from Belgium and ran, or at least walked, off to Utah Territory with him. And the soldiers—

"Miss Noble," says Miss Burgess, turning to the young woman seated next to Miss Redbird, "your work with the small boys is of tantamount importance. Controlling their more boisterous outbursts, initiating them into the mysteries of personal cleanliness—"

"And discouraging salacious nocturnal habits," adds Miss Ely, her gaze averted from the others at the table. There is an uncomfortable silence as the act she refers to is imagined.

Miss Redbird has done this before, dressed the part, handled the teacups, behaved with grace and modesty at the receptions after her debating triumphs or her violin performances. She is naturally soft-spoken if not angered, and knows what is expected of a virtuous young woman. She will not be the one to venture down the road Miss Ely has warned them of.

It is Miss Noble who picks up the standard. "What attracted you to this work, Miss Burgess?"

Burgess has a round, doughy face, and thick, squared-off fingernails, Miss Redbird has noticed, tinged with black at the cuticles.

"I must admit that I was *born* to it," she answers. "My father ran the Indian agency among the Pawnee, along with my mother, of course." She looks fondly to Miss Ely. "And that's where Annie and I became acquainted."

"I had requested a teaching mission from the Friends' Society," Ely explains, "and they sent me to Nebraska, where the Pawnee were then situated—"

There are so many *things* in the room, none of them useful. Paintings of horses grazing in bucolic settings cover much of the wall space, a tall cabinet with glass panels is near bursting with ceramic knickknacks, while another displays Indian handicrafts garnered from a half dozen unrelated tribes. The effect of a Navajo blanket laid over an intricately patterned Persian rug nearly made Miss Redbird swoon upon entering the room. The tipi she lived in when she was small had designs painted on the outside, and she loved when the sun was so strong that you could lie on a sheepskin inside and see them outlined. Her moccasins were always beaded, the deerhide satchel her mother made was fringed and decorated with porcupine quills, but there was none of this col*lect*ing, this drive to fill every space, that she discovered when she came east. At home if you wanted to see horses in bucolic settings, you stepped outside—

"And when I saw the *fruit* of my parents' efforts, both bitter and sweet," says Miss Burgess, glowing with the memory, "I thought, 'Is not here an opportunity for Christian enterprise?' Energizing these extremely dormant minds, influencing them to abandon the twisted path of barbarism and walk with a sure step along the pleasant highways of civilization."

Wilma Pretty Weasel leans between the teachers to pour tea, wishing she could spill some on Burgess, feeling worse every moment, keeping her face placid and movements precise. "Service is not merely laying items on a table," they have been often told, "but the art of being both industrious and in*vis*ible at the same time."

"We have our failures, of course, disappointments, but there are so many rays of hope, paragons of transformation and accomplishment"—Miss Burgess turns to smile at Miss Redbird—"of which Miss Redbird, though not a product of our particular institution, is such a sterling example."

Afternoons are for Industry.

Grace sits at the edge of a hospital bed, her arm being bandaged by Nurse Tucker as a half dozen other girls wearing starched white caps look on.

"We must be sure not to wrap it too *tightly*," says Nurse Tucker. "This is a dressing, not a tourniquet."

It feels warm and reassuring, like a loved one holding her arm there. Grace remembers when she was small and fell out of a tree, the saving warmth when her mother picked her up and held her. It didn't heal the scrapes, time and a balm her grandmother made up did that, but her ragged breathing slowed to normal, the insult of the hard ground swiftly fading. She remembers some people shaking their heads when her grandfather was dying and asked for a visit from Old Crooked Nose and the man, who she knew as one of her grandfather's gambling friends, wearing the wooden mask carved on a living tree, came to blow tobacco smoke over his body and sing healing songs. Her grandfather died the next day—he was a very old man—but he was so peaceful after the visit, he slept so well. It isn't all cleanliness and chemists' tinctures.

Nurse Tucker instructs Lizzie Cloud to bandage Grace's other arm.

It was Lizzie, who practically lived at the Episcopal church back home and there learned the stories of Florence Nightingale—such a beautiful name for a white person—who convinced Grace to apply for the nursing program, and it has given her stay here at Carlisle purpose.

She rolls her left sleeve up so Lizzie can get at the bared forearm.

"Depending on the nature of the injury," says Nurse Tucker, "the wound would first be what?"

"Washed thoroughly with carbolic soap and hot water," say the nursing girls in unison.

"*Gen*tly and thoroughly," adds Nurse Tucker. "But what comes before that?"

A hesitation. Grace speaks—

"Wash your own hands with the soap?"

Nurse Tucker pats her on her already-bandaged arm. "Very good, Grace. The first principle of antisepsis is to create a barrier against—?"

"Germs!" cry the nursing girls.

"And germs are—?"

"*Ev*erywhere!"

"As Dr. Lister informs us."

Even though she has seen them through the microscope, Grace finds this hard to envision. Her grandfather, whose name meant the Owl in Oneida language, said that there were unseeable spirits everywhere, good ones and bad ones. Grace can barely see pollen in the air when the sun is shining through it, and germs are even smaller, bad spirits that you can breathe into your lungs or that will rot your flesh. Good spirits—Grace knows they are real, though they aren't taught by Nurse Tucker—also exist. The warmth of the sun. Healing love. She wants to be a nurse who understands both the science of healing and its spirit.

"Where conditions are not sanitary," Nurse Tucker continues, "it will be your responsibility to *make* them so."

From the state of the children who have been sent directly to the infirmary upon arrival, it is clear to Grace that their "conditions" are not ideal. Most look as if they never get enough to eat, and a few have been isolated by Dr. Hazzard for fear they'll spread consumption. At home, *filth*, as Nurse Tucker always calls it, is not a problem, at least not in any of the dwellings Grace has been inside. The ones who have failed at farming, like her father, complain about the weather—the short growing season, crop-killing droughts and cold snaps, how much firewood they went through in the winter of '88. Or contention with their neighbors, like her father's resentment of the important families like the Wheelocks and the Corneliuses and the Archiquettes, who he claims have gotten all the good land up by the ridge road, or his worry that the white people in Green Bay are planning to steal everything out from under the tribe once the Severalty Act comes into effect next year. Grace was shocked on her visit home this summer to see how much of the woods around her house are gone—not cleared for farming but for the timber itself, acres of stumps, even down along Duck Creek, where she remembers stands of white pine and the black ash that people use to make baskets, the places where her grandmother has her gather wormwood and mugwort and other medicine plants, all gone. It started, her father says, a few years before she was born, when the city of Chicago burned down and needed lumber to rebuild, and though logging is how he now earns a living, he prefers to hire out up in Canada.

"They'll cut it all down here, sooner or later," says her father, "but I don't have to help."

There is plenty of *dirt* at home, and piles of rotting wood chips, but nothing Grace imagines as filth, though she suspects that when Nurse Tucker thinks of Indians on a reservation that is the first word that comes to her mind.

Lizzie finishes wrapping her arm, tying off the gauze neatly and tucking the ends in. It feels too tight, but she'll tell her friend later.

"How does that feel, dear?" asks Nurse Tucker.

"Fine." She bends both arms, flexes her fingers. "Not too binding."

Her hands are always chapped now since she's taken to washing them with the carbolic soap several times a day, a habit she picked up here and can't seem to stop. Now that she knows they're all around it's hard not to think about the germs. When she was home for the summer her mother took it as an insult, a comment on her housekeeping, till Grace told her it was only practice for the nursing.

"It is an exacting profession," she told her mother, in English, which her mother understands perfectly, the skill going back in their family all the way to New York and the American Revolution.

It is a profession, they have been told, that can be practiced anywhere, and Grace has dreams of moving from reservation to reservation—she has met so many fellow students here from different tribes and different parts of the country—and being of service to the people who live on them. It is not just a trade but a spiritual calling, she believes, as it was for Florence Nightingale.

"Now then, Priscilla, if you would take those dressings off," Nurse Tucker instructs. "And let's imagine that Grace is in a great deal of *pain*."

Industry is learning a craft—

"You shall be trained to become both skilled cobblers—repairers of footwear," says Mr. Woodcock to his shopful of tyro apprentices, "and to be *cordwainers*—or shoemakers, if you prefer that rather prosaic term."

Most of this is lost upon them, he knows, even those with the English tongue, but he hopes to impart a sense of the history and dignity of the profession before they get down to the physical actions. They are, if properly motivated, capable of being wonderful artisans, though working quickly does not appeal to them, a trait his own father shared that condemned the family to long periods of financial embarrassment.

"I ask you to regard your own feet for a moment," he says, pointing to the school-issued clodhoppers worn by the nearest boy on the bench. Most look at that boy's shoes, a few at their own.

"These were handed to you yesterday, chosen rather carelessly, and are no doubt less than comfortable, no matter what you are used to wearing at home. By the time this school year is ended, you will have, with your own hands, made a pair of Derbys tailored to your own pedal extremities, and I promise you they will fit like a *glove*."

He means a fine kid glove, of course, something these fellows may not have encountered. But the point here at Carlisle is to introduce these people to that which they do not know, to create in them desires beyond a warm campfire and a belly full of buffalo ribs, for it is desire of betterment that drives the successful worker.

"The process you will master is many-faceted—there will be steaming, soaking, shaping, stitching—and you will not be trained as cogs in a factory process but as *crafts*men, able to create the whole from the most basic elements. I will of course explain everything to you, but your principal organ of understanding will be your *eyes*"—here he taps on the lens of his spectacles—"the particular technique first demonstrated, then attempted, and repeated until performed correctly and consistently. Gentlemen," he says, spreading his arms out with a smile, "I welcome you to an old and honored brotherhood."

The *zapatero*—Shoe Man—talks and Asa smells leather. There are different-shaped pieces of leather piled in wooden boxes all around them, and different tools and machines, which the Shoe Man points to as he talks. It is clear to Asa that he and the other new ones in the room have been brought here to learn how to make white people shoes. The ones they've made him wear feel heavy and confining, like they're meant to keep him from running away. At home he either goes barefoot or wears the sandals his mother makes from the fiber of the yucca plant, or from rawhide when they can get some. Asa can't tell yet if this work the Shoe Man is explaining is a punishment or just to pay for their food and lodging at the school. If it is a punishment he's not sure what it could be for—the Tohono O'odham have never made war against the Americans and even helped them fight against the Apaches. There is a new school for them in Tucson, with room for only a few students, but it was decided after the arrest that Asa be sent farther away. On one of his runs he had found a spot where the peyote cactus carpeted the ground, and his best friend Julián told him how the buttons had magical powers. Some of the other young men they knew were interested as well, and he and Julián gathered a satchelful and they began to meet at night and try eating them. Some of the young men always had to vomit first, but it only made Asa feel like his stomach wanted to float out of him through his throat, and the first time when he only ate five of the buds he laid down and closed his eyes and ran one of his favorite paths, which took you through a mountain pass and into land they said was actually Mexico and then looped back—all in just a few hours instead of taking half a day. He was barefoot then, and despite how much cholla and horse crippler were on the trail his feet weren't bloody or even dirty when he woke and looked at them. He always prayed when he ran, mostly for rain, as his sister, the best runner in the village, had taught him, and soon he was eating the peyote buds before his longer runs and no longer felt he had to pray. The path spoke to him, the rocks, the lizards and rabbits and snakes, the tall saguaro men twisted their bodies to watch him pass by them. The heat and the noise of the insects were like a solid thing that he was partly made up of, and sometimes he could hear the footsteps of people long dead running behind him, telling him to *keep going, keep going*—

Then the Indian agent heard about it and came with soldiers and said that as the ringleader Asa would have to be sent far away.

The Shoe Man talks, pointing to tools, pointing to machines. It was nine days on the railroad train to reach this place from Tucson, and Tucson is two days from Asa's home. The train ran so much faster than Asa, and he can't imagine how far away home must be. The Shoe Man is holding up a pair of wooden blocks that look like a person's feet without the toes. It is unclear whether they are meant to make these wooden feet as well. If your feet were wood, thinks Asa, you wouldn't need shoes. There is a window in the wall next to him and through it he can see the branches of a tree, branches so covered with green leaves you can barely see through them to the sky. This is a place where nobody needs to pray for rain.

Industry speaks to the world—

Sheets of printed newspaper roll off a drum-cylinder press powered by a compact steam engine as more than a dozen boys, shop aprons over their uniforms, hurry from station to station, seeming to know what they're doing. Antoine is impressed—he has seen books in school and Bibles in people's homes, but never thought of how they were made. He wonders why he is the only new boy to be sent here for industrial training.

Cato Goforth, a Peoria boy who looks more white than Indian, has to shout over the rumble and clacking of the roller.

"This is the best trade we offer. Anywhere you go, except maybe back on the reservation, they need printers."

Antoine picks up a copy of a newspaper from a pile. Though smaller, it looks not unlike the ones he saw being sold in the eastern railroad stations on the way here. He scans the front page—Père Etienne said he was the best reader he'd ever taught, and Antoine has gotten so he doesn't have to linger on every word to know what a block of text is about. He wonders if this thing—reading and writing—explains why the white people always win. Though the Ojibwe have never really fought them on the battlefield, they've witnessed the fate of their enemies the Sioux when they angered the Great White Father, and have not been able to avoid being pushed onto less and less land—

"We put out *The Red Man* every month," says Goforth. "That's where the Captain takes on his opponents in print, and there's news of what's happening at the Indian agencies all around the country. And what you're holding, *The Indian Helper*, goes out weekly and is more for the students—"

"Who's this 'Man-on-the-Bandstand'?"

"*That*, young man," says Miss Burgess, stepping in behind Antoine, "is the great *my*stery."

Cato Goforth, behind the instructor's back, taps his head, points at Miss Burgess and mouths, *I think it's her.*

"You're LaMere." She stands close, looking him in the eye. Antoine has gotten used to this with white people, knows that it is not always a challenge.

"Yes, Ma'am."

"You told me you speak English."

"And some French too—"

"That won't be needed here. How's your spelling?"

"The sisters drilled it into me pretty good."

Miss Burgess nods. "I'll put you on correction and typesetting to begin with." She looks to the Peoria boy. "Our Mr. Goforth here will be in and out—he is going to apprentice with the *Sentinel* in town."

A much younger boy approaches, holding up ink-stained fingers.

"The rollers are sticking again, Miss Burgess."

"I'll take a look at them." She turns back to Antoine. "Cato will show you what to do."

She moves away with the young boy, Cato stepping closer to Antoine, though with the racket of the printing machinery he can't really lower his voice.

"Miss Burgess says she learned printing from her father, who was a newspaperman before he became an Indian agent. She runs the shop, edits the papers—"

"The students don't write for it?"

"Oh, they write," says Cato Goforth with a small grin. "Then Burgess *re*writes."

Who can this Man-on-the-Bandstand be?

—teases the poem in *The Indian Helper*—

—as little Evangeline pushes the treadle of a sewing machine with her foot, then jolts back, almost falling out of her chair, startled by the sudden motion and sound. The white woman makes noises at her, then presses the treadle down with her own foot to make the machine chatter again. Evangeline covers her mouth with her hand before she coughs. The white woman reaches into a bin full of clean rags and hands her one—

> *Is it a ghost or a goblin or shrew*
> *With an ear that is always ready to hear*
> *And an eye that is ever on you?*

—as Grace Metoxen makes beds in the infirmary. She is good at the hospital corners, enjoys the smell of starch and the symmetry of the two long rows of beds, only a few occupied at the moment. At the far end of the room Nurse Dantley is holding the mask of a nebulizer over the face of a young Kiowa girl, and the mint smell reminds Grace of one of her grandmother's curing teas. It is so quiet in here, so peaceful—

> *Is it woman or man, or spirit unseen*
> *Who ferries the dark into light?*

—as Ascención Viajero presses down on the leather with an awl, tracing around the edges of the shaped piece of wood they have given him, as do the other new shoe boys at their benches. Hand strength is required, but no particular skill yet, and misshapen uppers can be trimmed later. Boys who have worked in the shop for a year or more apply themselves to other aspects of the process, as Mr. Woodcock strolls among them, hands folded behind his back, humming as he occasionally bends to examine someone's work. Asa leans back so that the sun coming through the narrow window hits the side of his face. He takes the wooden shape away and sees the outline of what he is supposed to cut out, switching to the small, wood-handled knife with the curved point. There is a pair of heavy scissors on the table beside him, an implement he has not encountered before and doubts he will be able to use properly. He begins to cut through the leather, still surprised that the white people let them hold anything sharp—

Or a firm guiding hand dedicated to steer
Young minds to the path that is Right?

—as Moses Smoke uses both hands to work the wooden paddle, stirring the flour and water together into a thick paste that becomes harder and harder to move, while one of the veteran baker boys sifts another cup of white powder into the tub. He has seen his mother make bread, but never paid much attention till it was out of the oven or the skillet and ready to eat. The ovens here are huge iron things on short legs, fed six logs of raw dough arranged on a flat, floured wooden peel and later scooped out when they've become a fused rectangle of baked loaves. The chief baker, who assigned the new boys their tasks for the day, said they'd learn from watching and from their fellow students. He was eager to point out how nearly self-sufficient the school was, student trainees making their uniforms, hats, shoes, helping to maintain the heating systems of the buildings in the winter, working on the school farm, publishing the newspaper, painting, doing carpentry, roofing, and even making some items for sale like carriages and wagon wheels.

"At the Carlisle Indian School, however," said the baker proudly, "there is no basket weaving."

The older boy helps Smokey lift the tub up onto its side, and he begins to scrape sticky dough out to be kneaded—

Or just anyone, who happens to see
A thing that is worthy of note?

—as Wilma Pretty Weasel, who put a dead horsefly in Miss Burgess's barley soup at the teachers' lunch, yanks a tangle of wet, steaming linen from the metal boiler, pivots to dump it into the hamper. After cleaning up in the teachers' club there were still two hours of Industry left, and this year they have assigned her to the laundry, a step down, maybe even a punishment, from last year, when she was in dressmaking. She can't tell if there is sweat running down her forehead or if it's only the steam that hangs in the room turning back to water. She wheels the hamper over to the huge mangle—it is run by electric power now, with leather belts hung from the ceiling turning the gears, replacing the crank that was used when she arrived six years ago. Gussie, a sullen Paiute girl who was also demoted this year, is at the big metal sink with the washboard built into it, scrubbing stains out with a cake of lye soap. Wilma turns her back to it, the odor of the soap making her want to vomit ever since her first year when she was caught speaking Absaroke to another Crow girl and had to hold a wet chunk of it in her mouth for five minutes. The disciplinarian sat her in front of a clock and said it would also serve as a lesson in telling time.

There is a boy on the floor today, a new boy who looks to be about ten, moving from task to task with the process—here, everyone knows, because he piddled in his bed and was caught at it. The supervisor, Miss Hemphill, shadows him, making sure he doesn't stick a hand where it will be crushed or sliced off.

Wilma feeds sheets into the mangle, water streaming out of them as they squeeze through the roller. She wonders if an entire white woman, a fairly plump one, could be passed through the machine, and what would come out the other end—

And gossips a bit of the good and a bit of the bad
Reporting the news that's afloat!

—and finally, as Make-Trouble-in-Front waves flies from his face, standing just inside the open door of the barn with the others, studying the animals. They are mostly wagon horses, nothing a bold young Lakota would steal unless times were desperate and it was meant to be eaten. The ones kept locked up in here, eight of them, are too big and too slow-looking to be fit for anything but pulling a heavy load. Still, they are members of the Horse Tribe, friendly relatives gifted by the Thunder Beings—Trouble will have to find out if they are worth knowing or have been so broken by the whites that they only hang their heads and obey when the horn is blowing.

The Horse Man speaks words in the white tongue, but Trouble only watches as one of the boys they've kept here for many years demonstrates what the jobs will be. Walking the horses outside but not riding them, bringing them to water, keeping their coats clean. They are kept here in a wooden enclosure with a roof like the bluecoat soldiers use—easier to be sure they are not stolen, but horses like to move a bit at night, to graze when they are awake, to know the security of the rest of the herd all around them. In here they are separated from each other by low wooden walls. The boy is showing off the tools now—the white people nail iron rims onto the hooves of their horses, but that is because they make them run on streets made of hard stone or small, sharp rocks.

As Trouble was growing up in his uncle's lodge, they had only three ponies, his uncle who always boasted more than twenty when he was young. Some were killed by snakes, he said, one gored by a buffalo, and the rest taken by the bluecoat soldiers when Gall had enough of starving in Canada and they followed him back down across the freezing plain to surrender at Fort Buford. His father, who had been a shirt wearer among the Hunkpapa and therefore must have been a great warrior, had been killed charging up at the cannon on Wolf Mountain, where Crazy Horse left his heart. Trouble could not yet walk on his two legs then, and knows only the stories.

When he was old enough to climb on its back by himself, Trouble was given the smallest of his uncle's remaining three ponies, a mare with large brown and white spots and two white forefeet. The way his father began to ride as a small boy was to rub an old buffalo hide over his pony's head to make it unafraid of the smell, then follow along on the hunt, no weapon in hand, both he and his pony learning how to gallop with the stragglers of the herd once it had been spooked into motion, staying just behind the shoulder of the chosen bulls, away from the horns.

But there were no buffalo left, even in Canada, and none when they were sent to Standing Rock to live, though there they pitched their camp as far away from the agency and the stink of white men as was allowed.

At first Trouble used a small saddle, made from pieces of wood and part of an elk's antler, but soon rode her next to the skin, with only a bison hide halter and the mare's mane to hang on to. He fell off more than once, and the mare would only step away a bit and search for something to nibble at on the ground, never looking at him as if to avoid the embarrassment. Trouble's people did not push pieces of metal in their horse's mouths or feed them wet grain in a trough, as if they were ancient men with no teeth at all. There was respect between the Hunkpapa and the Horse Tribe.

Trouble watches the trained boy make motions as the white man talks, showing that each day they will have to clean the shit and the piss-soaked hay out of the walled-in spaces they keep the horses in, which would not be needed if they'd just hobble them out on the big grass in front of the buildings every night. The boy shows them something you push a rod into, miming that this sprays something that will kill the flies. If it kills the flies, thinks Trouble, what does it do to the horses and the people who come in to care for them?

Trouble was known as an excellent rider on Standing Rock, proud to have his own pony when many of the boys, with no Crow or Shoshone nearby to steal mounts from, had none. When Trouble's father was young he was known for being bold, he and a friend spending a month away from camp and risking their lives and coming back with more than thirty good ponies, many of which they gave to poor widows to keep or sell, making the two boys greatly admired within the band. Trouble's uncle told him these stories and said he must learn to be a daring rider because some day the buffalo would come back, and his skill would be needed. But in the last few years his uncle said less and less, waiting with the other defeated people for the white man goods that were never what had been promised, with even Sitting Bull back from Canada now and brooding in a cabin by the Grand River. His uncle and his mother began to go to the church where the Black Robe named Craft, a rude and impetuous man, taught them about the white man's God, and whenever they did Trouble would climb onto his mare and ride angrily, aimlessly, over and around the low hills near their camp. The Indian agent, McLaughlin, wanted them to move in closer to his white wooden buildings, wanted them to live in cabins instead of tipis, wanted them to scratch the earth with plows or sit idly waiting for handouts as if they were Loafers and not Hunkpapa.

Then the betrayal.

Some of the important men had given their children away to be taken to the East, claiming they would be taught there to travel down the white man's path far enough to know how to survive, claiming that this was not surrender but only being wise—if there are no more fish in a river, you move to another river. The Black Robe wanted Trouble sent to his school on the reservation, but Gall, who was still their chief and a respected man, was in a struggle with Agent McLaughlin, afraid that he would be sent away to prison, and felt he had to make a sacrifice to show that he was not "hostile." So when School Father Pratt came looking to steal children, Gall asked Trouble's uncle for a favor. The Black Robe was angry, and his uncle was ashamed, but when he asked Trouble to do this for his people, Trouble accepted. If his father could ride straight into the mouth of a cannon, was he not brave enough to be taken away to face whatever torture the whites had planned for him?

The Horse Man, smiling, shows them the fire that heats the metal to put on the hooves of the wagon horses, shows them the hammer that is used to shape it—

Trouble's mother has scars on her arms from when Trouble's father was killed. As a shirt wearer he was honored by the entire band, his body sewn into a buffalo robe, then laid out on a high scaffold, the old way. His favorite pony, the one that he rode to his death upon, was killed and left beneath the scaffold, its tail tied to a post. The day Trouble was taken away, his mother only wept and fingered the beaded necklace the Black Robe had given her, mumbling prayers he did not want to hear. There was time enough before the wagon came for him for Trouble to ride his pony to the top of a ridge overlooking their camp and the barren land surrounding it, land where he had never seen a buffalo. He got off the pony and held its head for a while, speaking in the language they had together, and then he shot it behind the ear with the pistol his father was said to have won at the Battle of the Little Bighorn.

Industry ceases when the bugle blows.

The watch comes with the position, as does the vest to carry it in. The regulation boys' uniform at the school does not include a vest, so Willy is the only student who wears one. He has a feel for the days here, and finds he takes the watch out and snaps the hunting case open to read the face only five or six minutes before the next call. Time to excuse himself from classroom or Industry—he is in the carpentry shop—and hurry to his spot at the base of the flagpole, bugle ready in hand. After *Taps* every evening Willy hands the watch to the head disciplinarian, Mr. Skinner, who winds the stem exactly thirty-six half-turns and keeps it for the night. Willy then hurries to his room and winds his own two-bell alarm clock, the only one allowed in the boys' dormitory. His roommates have trained themselves to sleep through that noise, though he often opens his eyes just before it sounds and cancels the alarm. Skinner must have an alarm clock as well, because dark or light, fair weather or foul, he is always waiting by the flag with the pocket watch offered in his hand when Willy races out to play *Reveille.*

Willy has not allowed himself to be ill since he was given this responsibility.

Though he spoke English fairly well when he arrived at the school as a small boy, the others made fun of him because he said he was a Walla Walla, a tribe barely represented here that few had heard of, deciding he must have a stutter and calling him Willywilly. Two years ago this became Bugle Boy, or, to the bold ones, God-Damned Bugle Boy. Willy checks the time, slips the watch into his vest pocket, and brings the instrument to his lips—

Assembly at this time of day means that industrial training is done and they are at liberty till called to dinner. Willy blows, and before the echo off the high fence around the school has died the students are pouring out of the trade buildings, out of the laundry and the stables and the hospital, assembling on the parade ground. There are six companies of boys this year, five of girls, the ranks eventually tightening into proper shape with the officer cadets shouting instructions. Willy, standing at attention with his instrument held against his chest, feels like a general who has summoned his own personal army.

The girls, as always, are allowed to march to their dormitory first, and those of them who venture outside during free time will stay on their own side of the parade ground. At the mission school in Pendleton they were all thrown together, but that had been only one drafty building and nobody slept over at night. Willy is in the band as well, first cornet, comfortable now with *The Gladiator March*, *Semper Fidelis*, *The Washington Post March*, *The Thunderer*, *El Capitan*—any of the Sousa marches—and much of the German pomp as well. Whenever he is off traveling with the band the stubby little Ottawa boy will take over the pocket watch and attempt to bugle for the day, with Skinner supervising every call, wincing at the sour notes. Willy went home this summer, and the most difficult thing—besides some of his friends making fun of how he spoke Wallula—was dealing with unmeasured time. The days oozed like sap down a tree trunk, often seeming like they weren't progressing at all. With so many foggy days it was hard to use the sun or the moon for guidance, and with the spring chinook and coho already gone, he became what Mr. Skinner would call "a very lazy Indian" until the steelhead run finally charged down the Umatilla and time was not measured in hours and minutes but in pounds of fish to be gutted, filleted, and dried.

The boys' companies are marching now. Willy will wait till all are in, then follow them to enjoy what he always thinks of as Almost at Liberty—none of the other students at Carlisle will be looking at a timepiece. There are boys and girls from every tribe you can think of here, there are scholars who will continue their learning at white schools, there are notable athletes and clever debaters. But there is only one God-Damned Bugle Boy.

Free time is for special activities—

Antoine cautiously enters the music room. Lizzie Cloud is at the piano, playing scales on the keys and then singing them with *aah*s, going higher and higher. Grace sits nearby, reading something in her lap. Antoine clears his throat and Grace turns her head to see him—

"Oh—hello—"

Antoine holds up the paper with the poem printed on it.

"I came for this."

"You want to be Hiawatha?"

"I'm willing to read it out loud for you—"

"You're the only one."

"The only one—?"

"To volunteer."

"Oh."

He wonders now if this is not a huge mistake, if there is some unwritten but never violated rule among the boys here never to—

"I thought there'd be more," says Grace Metoxen, standing and smiling at him.

"I'm sorry—"

"Do you think you can stay out of trouble until Thanksgiving?"

Is she teasing? You don't get much time alone with girls who aren't close relatives back home—they're with their friends or some older woman you can't be normal in front of or already supposed to marry somebody—

"I'll give it a try."

She looks him over, evaluating.

"We'll have to rehearse it a few times. Memorize all the lines."

"Sure—"

She nods to Lizzie at the piano. "With a teacher or at least one of the girls from the society present."

"To protect your reputation?"

"Or yours."

Is she *flirt*ing? He knows the Oneidas were eastern Indians once, in tight with the Mohawks and Senecas and that bunch, but has no idea what their girl-and-boy rules are. Or maybe this is part of trying to be white—

"So I read—?"

She nods to the paper he holds.

"The sections in bold print are Hiawatha's lines. You read them, and then I'm Nokomis and Minnehaha."

He's trying, but it's hard not to stare at her. She looks a bit like the Indian maiden on a calendar he saw at the general store in De Pere.

"I'm Antoine—"

"I know."

Of course she knows, they were in the same classroom when the roll was called.

"So I should—?"

She hands him some more papers. "Here's the rest of what we'll be doing. You can start memorizing—"

"All this?"

"You should see the full version. It's a story, really, and once you understand the story it will be easier. I'll let you know when we're ready to have a rehearsal."

"All right. I'll—I'll study it—"

Grace holds out her hand to shake.

"I'm Grace."

He takes her hand. "I know."

The Ojibwe boy backs out of the room making apologetic noises, and when he is gone Lizzie begins to play *Beautiful Dreamer*—

"Stop."

"Will you have him pick you up in his manly arms? I forget how the poem ends—"

"Stop, Lizzie. He's the only one who showed up."

Lizzie stops playing. She has an angel's voice, singing soprano with the Episcopal choir back home, Christian songs translated into Oneida. She and Grace have been friends since they could talk.

"Well, you could have done a lot worse," she says.

Free time is for sporting endeavors—

Asa sits on the grass of the parade ground and watches boys running and jumping and throwing things. They wear a different kind of shoe, cut more like a moccasin, and tight-fitting pants. Some boys race each other, but stop almost immediately, which seems like a waste of effort. A javelina could run that far, that fast, maybe faster, and you'd never catch it. But if you know where its holes are and either stop them up or have friends waiting near to scare them away, you can run a javelina to death. His uncle Eusebio is well known for bringing in javelinas dead but without a mark on their bodies.

Some boys have set up a bar on posts that they try to jump over, often knocking it down, and another boy has set up a number of lower bars, evenly spaced, and runs fast, vaulting over each one when he comes to it, graceful as an antelope. Two of the bigger boys play with what looks like a heavy metal ball, heaving it ahead of them and then walking to where it rolls to a stop and then heaving again, working their way across the grass. And some boys are running to a rope laid across the ground in a straight line and when they reach it jumping as far as they can. Sometimes they walk carefully back from where they land to the rope, one foot in front of the other, as if measuring.

A boy comes up to Asa and says something, maybe a question by the music of it, but he doesn't understand and shakes his head. The boy goes back to running, but he doesn't go anywhere, just moving his legs really fast with his knees kicking high.

What interests Asa the most are two boys who look somewhat like he does—wiry, narrow shoulders—who run along the inside of the tall wooden fence that surrounds the school grounds. They lope along at a good pace and never stop, and he can follow their progress when a building doesn't block them from sight. Though they seem relaxed, it reminds him of a wild mustang he once saw in the hours after it had first been corralled, running around and around, hoping to come to an opening and freedom. Asa runs in a loop at home, never coming back the same way he went out, and each time it is a different path, chosen as much by whim and weather as by design. The few times he's raced with other boys, trying to win, a course has been laid out with markers—usually different-colored rags you have to pull off a stick and show when you come to the finish line. He always gets ahead right away and wins, not liking to follow anybody and spoil the view.

A boy has appeared with a spear in hand, and a couple of the others run ahead to tell the boys out on the grass to get out of the way. Finally the boy runs, does a complicated little dance with his feet, and heaves the spear as far as he can, the point of it breaking the turf first but not sticking. You'd be crazy to throw at an animal that far away with a spear, thinks Asa, and wonders if this is just for another kind of contest, like the boys seeing how far they can jump. The two boys running along the fence appear again, holding the same pace, and Asa is tempted to run after them, but sure that if he leaves his new heavy shoes behind, somebody will steal them.

Dinner—

Knowing that he helped to make it doesn't make the bread taste any different, but it makes Smokey feel useful, like the first time he brought a deer back home all on his own. Shooting it had been easy, the big doe downhill and upwind from him, paused with head erect and one foreleg raised, ears twitching. *Here I am.* He had a good sharp knife and gutted it easily, wrapped the heart and liver in leaves and stuffed them back into the body, but then the real work began. He got the forelegs and hind legs tied together, realized it was just too heavy to carry, and then broke and sawed off enough willow branches to make a kind of mat you could slide it on, looping his belt tight around its neck and using a fallen sapling with a bit of root that served as a hook at the end of it to pull with. Down the foothill, across the gulley, uphill again, several hours of hauling till he dragged it into the clearing in front of their cabin. His father had nothing to say but "She's a fat one," and helped to hang it from the big elm to bleed out the rest of the way before butchering. His mother came out to look, and you could tell she was happy too, giving the haunch a little push and leaving it swinging. It was the first time he killed something bigger than himself.

The dinner monitor, a white man he hasn't seen before, walks up and down the aisles as they eat, and there is a matron doing the same on the girls' side of the room. He wonders if there's a special white way of eating they'll be taught, as he's never sat down to eat with just white people. Of course some of the blanket heads from out West, like Trouble sitting across from him, don't really know how to use a spoon and a fork, whereas civilized tribes like his Cherokee were living in cabins and farming well before they were forced to leave for the Territory, his father saying that some even had black slaves like the Confederate white people did. His father said the chief of the ones who left, Ross, could have passed for a white man, and that those who went had their own little civil war, which the eastern band didn't have to get involved in. Some of those first Territory Cherokee could even write books in English, and Smokey's mother says he has to pay attention and learn here—there's no telling when their white neighbors might decide to push them out, and that usually begins with words on paper. If you can't read and understand those words, says his father, you're as helpless as a beef cow waiting slaughter.

They think he has trouble reading because he isn't trying hard enough, and that the white teachers here will make sure he does.

The bread Smokey helped make, in fact, doesn't taste like much of anything, but it fills your stomach and Clarence Regal says they can have it toasted in the morning, with butter and maybe even blackberry jam. By the end of the day in the bakery Smokey's face and hands were covered with flour, and Lincoln Wahoo, a Cherokee from a place called Tahlequah, joked that he'd only been at the school two days and already looked like a white man.

Counting around and then multiplying by the number of tables, Smokey thinks there are almost six hundred boys and girls in the big dining hall. He wonders how many deer you would have to kill to make them all venison stew—

Dinner is simple but there is enough bread to make you full, just like lunch, and Antoine feels some of the tightness fall away from his arms and chest—he's not starving here and so far nobody, teacher or student, has even tried to hit him. In his whole time under the nuns he only got one swift rap on the knuckles from Sister Ursula, who carried a wooden yardstick she used to point out things on the chalkboard and to deal out punishment. Getting along with white people, his father says, is like canoeing down a fast river. You have to watch ahead, know what to paddle through and what to steer around. Antoine has always been good at this, unlike his brothers or his best friend, Charlie Tetrault, who fought the sisters every day for three years till they could raise red welts on his body but not hear a whimper out of him, and Père Etienne stepped in to call it a draw, suggesting that Charlie end his academic training and apply himself to something that paid a wage.

After being assembled in ranks again and then let go, Antoine finds the library on the ground floor of the large boys' dormitory, securing a chair covered in cloth with a soft cushion under his tail, and starts on the long poem, softly reciting the words to himself—

> *"Smiling answered Hiawatha*
> *'In the land of the Dakotahs*
> *Lives the Arrow-maker's daughter*
> *Handsomest of all the women—'"*

"I'm surprised I never met her," says Clarence Regal, somehow appearing over his shoulder.

"Right—you're a—"

The master segreant snatches the paper from Antoine, glances at it—

"It's for the—"

"I know, you want to impress that Oneida girl. 'Minnehaha' has no meaning in Dakota."

"I figured—"

"*The Song of Hiawatha*, by Henry Wordworth Whitefellow—a prime example of trochaic tetrameter."

Antoine has never met anyone like Regal, seemingly smarter than even the white teachers here. Clarence hands the poem back to Antoine and strikes an orator's pose as some of the older boys in the library room begin to gather around to watch.

> *"In the woods of Pennsylvania,"* he orates—
> *"By the tiny town of Carlisle*
> *Stands a noble institution*
> *For the dregs of evolution."*

Antoine realizes Regal is reciting in a singsong rhythm that is probably what the trochaical thing means, something almost like a steady drumbeat—

> *"Cropped of hair and dressed as soldiers*
> *We must learn to wield utensils*
> *Eating oatmeal and molasses*
> *Or be belted on our asses."*

The older boys laugh. Regal must have performed the real poem at some point during his stay here. He breaks the pose, looks back to Antoine.

"We could use you in the club."

"Club—"

Jesse Echohawk is there. "The Invincible Debating Society."

"As opposed to our rivals," says Clarence. "The Standards."

Jesse sits on the broad arm of Antoine's stuffed chair. "We're given a resolution to support or oppose, then each team has three members argue the case in a fixed amount of time."

"Miss Burgess heads the judges."

Antoine is flattered to be asked to join something, but wary. He looks to Jesse—

"Like what kind of resolution?"

"Our first one this year is—Proposed: Should the Indian be Exterminated?"

"We're in favor," says Clarence. "They're against."

Trouble, wearing only his undershorts, eases out of bed and pads to the window, the other boys already asleep. He bends to look out the window, finding the moon first, then looking down to the parade ground. He sees an older boy in uniform crossing on the walk. Of course they will have sentries posted around—otherwise, who would not run? Trouble hears a train whistle, approaching. It is the sixth one he's heard since sunup, smoke from their locomotive chimneys visible over the tall wooden fence, slowing to stop at the edge of the white people's town. On the journey here, when they were going so fast and he glanced out the window, he thought they were flying, some witchery of the white people, and he couldn't bear to look. Now he has seen that the train rolls on metal-and-wood rails, that one long road may join with another going in a different direction, like rivers and streams. He has seen the sun set behind the tall fence and knows which way is west. If you could hide near a rail, pointing to the west, and a train was just leaving the station, you might be able to run and climb onto it without anybody seeing and ride its back till—till it stopped rolling in that direction. And then you'd have to find another. His uncle said that on long hunts he always used to travel with three horses, one to find the herd, another, the fastest and cleverest, to race in among the buffalo and do the killing, and one that was only good for carrying hides and meat. He claimed he could pull a pony up alongside while riding another and switch to its back without stopping to get off and on like white men always do. White men who don't even know which side of a horse to mount on.

The train whistles again, calling to him—

—and to Miss Redbird, who can't sleep in her little room. She sits up and reads for a spell, then dresses again and steps outside.

A nearly full moon, crickets.

She strolls out onto the parade ground, immediately running into one of the boys with night sentry duty, who touches the bill of his cap when he sees her, looking embarrassed. Miss Redbird walks to the bandstand, climbs up, and takes a seat. Another train whistle—probably a freight at this hour, passing through, slowing but not stopping.

That will be me, passing through, thinks Miss Redbird, who can't imagine making a career at this school. She is the only Indian instructor here, an item to show off and brag about, the proof of the Captain's premise.

See what we've made her.

She heard the band play during the assemblies today, very tight, very accomplished, lots of brass and drums and martial spirit. An insistent kind of music, *Here we are, get out of our way.* Miss Redbird plays the violin, plays music written by white Germans and Frenchmen and Italians long dead, and can move herself to tears with it. A wonder. It never seemed foreign to her, never seemed *other,* but was like the sound of a river she'd never sat beside before, new but familiar at the same time. White babies, she has discovered, sound the same as Indian babies when they cry, although they seem to cry more often. She has read the Captain's manifestos, and he never seems to say that Indian culture is wrong or even inferior—only that it is *over,* of no practical use in what the world has come to be. She has always been struck by how much white people leave behind when they move from a place, and she has heard stories of thousands of buffalo left to rot with only their tongues and their hides taken. Her mother, before she moved to the little cabin, would carefully pack everything in bundles, roll up the tipi skins, balance the loads on the back of a horse or a mule, and carry their whole life from one camp to the next. Leave it behind, the School Father says, leave it all behind, join the human race before it's too late.

Miss Redbird has always been slight, even now barely coming up to her mother's shoulder, and her mother is not a big woman. She sits in the white-painted bandstand, listens to the crickets, the now-fading train whistle, and has never before felt so small.

The Captain watches the Indian girl from the porch of his house. Writer, orator, musician—if he succeeds here at Carlisle there will dozens of Miss Redbirds. This girl seems a wan shadow of the other Lakota women he's encountered, hard to picture her plowing through snow drifts with a heavy bundle of firewood on her back, or skinning a bear—

Mrs. Pratt retires promptly at eight, and the Captain uses his remaining waking hours to plan the next offensive. There is no resting on laurels for the school, its yearly funding depending on the whim of the U.S. Congress and the continued benevolence of certain Quaker ladies. And so the endless articles, the speeches, the trips to Washington, a campaign not of territory won or enemies slain but of perception—for the battle is with prejudice and ignorance. The majority of his fellow citizens, having no personal experience with the red man, prefer to believe in the dime novel version—vicious and underhanded in war, prone to sloth and drunkenness, inferior in intellect to the white man. The Captain still bridles at the memory of the article that appeared in *The Atlanta Constitution* after the special train bearing seventy-two Indian prisoners-of-war under his supervision passed through that city late at night. No permission to interview was requested or granted, and in any case not one of the Kiowa, Cheyenne, Arapaho, and Comanche hostiles understood a word of

English—yet here was a reporter quoting from a half dozen shackled ringleaders, all speaking in fanciful chop suey. "Me killum heap white man, takum women, scalpum head." No wonder the Eastern reading public hold so little sympathy for the plight of the Indian, reduced to a fraction of their former numbers, incarcerated on reservations—

And those in the West who've suffered at their hands, even if it be only the loss of some livestock, wish them all dead.

With the prisoners in Florida he at least had superior officers who had known the tribes in their natural form of life, men who had seen firsthand the double-dealing of politicians and government contractors charged with honoring peace treaties. There had been a thought to bring the raiders to trial—they were after all wards of the state who had quit their reservations without permission, off to perpetrate murders, thefts, kidnappings, terrible atrocities—but as neither the civil nor the military courts wanted to face their own culpability in the situation, the warriors were relegated to a Limbo of exile with no fixed date of sentence. St. Augustine seemed far enough away to discourage even the most hardened from dreams of escape and return to their families, and the old Castillo de San Marcos was chosen because—well, because it was already there and would cost very little to garrison. A square fort of coquina blocks on a peninsula, complete with a flooded moat and drawbridge, dungeon-like casemates within the walls to stuff the prisoners into, the terreplein and surrounding low parapet affording a view of both the sleepy town and the ocean inlet. It was, he thought on first view, a miserable post even when the Spanish built it in the 1600s. But with his colored troops now left behind at Fort Concho in Texas and no orders but to continue in charge of the miserable hostiles, there was nothing to do but make the best of it.

Captain Pratt lights a cigar. He does not like the students to see him smoking, a vice, though it is a minor one, they can do without. Tobacco has a holy place in most of their cultures, and those are meant to be forgotten here.

The courtyard was only one hundred feet square, the casemates—even with the barred doors left open—sweltering hovels with rough plank floors and a scattering of hay for bedding, and not a window to peek from. Piles of ancient cannonballs on the ground had rusted into solid pyramids. The open sky above was merciless upon their arrival in midsummer, and several of the men died in the first few weeks. The Captain began by having the prisoners brought up several times a day in groups of six to take a circuit around the terreplein and breathe the ocean air. His troop of guards were the dregs of the Army, barely worth the court-martial they deserved, so he requisitioned Army uniforms for the prisoners, gave them the pride of shiny brass buttons and shiny leather shoes, and within a year they were not only drilling in close order but serving as their own guards. He brought workmen in to teach them the basics of carpentry, and they used the skill to build themselves a long barracks up on the terreplein—better air and bunk beds. Discovering a local tourist industry, they first were set to the task of polishing sea beans, a popular novelty for northern visitors, then to the manufacture of souvenir bows and arrows, packing oranges in crates, clearing scrub, and even the digging and sifting of local ancient shell mounds, sending skulls, axes, and other artifacts to Dr. Boas at the Smithsonian Institution. The money earned was split—half sent for the relief of their families back on the reservations, the other half held in individual accounts and drawable to buy personal items or food from the town. An uneasy mix of tribes, without families or pagan ceremony, there was no giving away of goods on momentous occasions, no primitive barter system. Cash money was put in their hands at the end of a job well done, or only shown and kept in security.

Make them capitalists and you're halfway there.

A number of good ladies, both locally born and seasonal visitors from the north, volunteered to teach English, and soon that tongue became the lingua franca between Kiowa and Cheyenne, between

Comanche and Arapaho. Some of the younger men, whom Captain Pratt had always considered only soldiers guilty of obeying the orders of their war chiefs, were even writing, supplementing the picture stories that passed back and forth from their relatives in the West.

"We have thrown our mad away," wrote Squint Eyes to Washington, "and buried the war axe so deep it may never be found," pleading to have their families transported to Florida or another neutral place. There were frequent visitors, military and civilian, with Mrs. Stowe, of *Uncle Tom's Cabin* renown, becoming an ardent supporter in print and on the podium.

Discipline was required of course, but as with his Indian scouts during the prairie wars, nothing more than what would serve for white troops. Always Sitting in the Wrong Place, a Comanche ringleader, was the first to receive and then alter his Army uniform, cutting the legs off to refashion them as leggings—brought before the assembled prisoners, his punishment was to be publicly upbraided for destruction of Uncle Sam's property. A rare Indian who does not prefer physical pain to humiliation. The Kiowa planned a harebrained escape at one point, but this was detected in time and nipped in the bud, the main pair of plotters suffering a few weeks of confinement but eventually rejoining the guard, somewhat reduced in rank. There were inspections—shoes polished, pants creased, personal items stowed away properly—and bricks from toppled outbuildings used to build a bread oven, two prisoners trained to bake the daily ration. The men learned to relish oysters, something they'd never encountered before and were at first a bit squeamish about, and soon became enthusiastic harvesters of the local beds. The St. Augustinians were at first more curious than fearful, appreciated the business when prisoners were allowed into town to make purchases, and were won over on the late night of the fire that threatened the town, when Captain Pratt led the lot of them in a bucket brigade that kept the disaster from spreading.

At the end of three years, the government, perhaps more conscious of the expense of keeping them prisoners than impressed by their strides down the white man's path, declared an end to their incarceration in Florida—and sent most of them back to the relative bondage of the reservations. But more than a dozen, almost all of them young men, requested they be allowed to continue to learn the white man's language and ways, preferably with the guidance of Captain Pratt.

If it could work with known marauders in a dilapidated Spanish prison with extremely limited resources, think how much more could be done with younger, more pliable minds, on a larger scale. It wouldn't have to be Florida, but distance would be part of the cure—trying to reform Indians on a reservation was akin to reforming drunkards in a saloon. There was an Army barracks in Pennsylvania, lying unused since the Confederates had put it to the torch—

The Captain watches Miss Redbird leave the bandstand and cross the parade ground, retiring for the night. He draws on his cigar, listens to the crickets. The campaign is really just beginning, last year their very first graduating class, this year another chance to show the skeptics, the haters, that the Indian must not be exterminated but ab*sorbed*, woven into the American fabric as the Germans and the Irish and now even the Italians have begun to be, with the Negroes, having the advantage of the English language, not far behind. Americans all, and Christians, with a few exceptions, those of Indian blood with no more relation to the life of Geronimo or Sitting Bull than a modern Athenian has to Achilles or Odysseus.

Until that day, he thinks, we will create something in between the animist savage and the white citizen.

Carlisle Indians.

EVERYONE IN THE territory assumes the Ethnographer is a spy. He is employed by the Institute in Washington, of course, but his visits to the various tribes garner the interest of any number of military officers, Indian agents, and even a few of the more responsible newspaper scribblers. But because of his audience with the Messiah, the chiefs and even the normally antagonistic medicine men have welcomed those visits, eager to touch the hand that touched the hand.

He has resolved to tell every one of them literally what he has seen and heard, reserving his own opinion for eventual publication by the Institute.

The Kiowa, like most of the Plains tribes, have had a rough go of it in the last few years—the epizootic killing off of their horses and cattle, a drought, a run of scarlet fever—and they are ripe for salvation. The Ethnographer has approached them with his usual honest entreaty, a desire to learn about their culture, their history, their lives, and casually let it drop that he had made a similar visit to the Northern Paiute in Nevada. Yes, as it happened, he *did* visit with the Messiah, who asked him to pass on his message to all who are interested.

And then he has the photograph.

The Kiowa are familiar with photography by now, of course, the important men of the tribe willing to look stern and noble in what finery they have left if sufficiently flattered. He shows them a photo from the Institute, taken of a delegation to Congress several years ago, a group of chiefs including one of the most important men, since deceased, of the Kiowa. This is passed around the cabin for careful study, several stories about the man related. The Ethnographer follows with several high cards—photographs of Little Raven, Chief Joseph, poor Spotted Tail—and then, offhandedly, Wovoka standing in front of his wickiup.

There is one man among them, a visitor from the West, who has made the pilgrimage to Walker Lake and can verify that it is indeed a photograph of the Messiah, and then it is studied with intense interest and much comment.

"He gave me this," the Ethnographer tells them, producing the block of dried ocher paint, reputed to ward off sickness, prolong life, help induce trances, "to show to his followers."

Roughly the shape of a bar of soap, he does not allow them to pass it around but to come and rub their fingers on it, gently, please, as they mutter and nod.

"With the proper ceremony and seriousness," he tells them, "you can make your own sacred paint to adorn yourselves with—at least that's what the Messiah says."

Given the vagaries of translation and distance from the source, it is no surprise that each tribe has its own version of the Messiah's prophecy, its own variation on the dance. The Ethnographer speaks Cherokee very well, can divine a good deal from the Plains sign language, but never makes a visit without first procuring the service of that necessary evil, an interpreter. On this occasion it is a young white man named Edwin Burgess who seems to have grown up with the Pawnee, his parents being Quaker missionaries and rather unsuccessful Indian agents to the tribe. Burgess has a relaxed, confident proficiency with the sign language, able to banter quickly with the men in the room, hands chopping out words and concepts as he makes small grunting noises for emphasis.

The dancing is not a new story. There was Popé, of the Tewa, whose vision helped foment the Pueblo Revolt in 1680, there was the Delaware Prophet in 1762, and shortly after there was Tecumseh and his brother the Shawnee Prophet, then the Kickapoo Prophet, and of course, moving far back in time, the Hebrew Messiah who Wovoka has obviously been taught something about, and before him Moses bringing the Red Sea crashing over the heads of the pharaoh's army—

Human beings long for earthly deliverance at the least, and if possible, eternal life in a Great Good Place.

The Ethnographer, raised poor and Catholic, never dipped into the Book of Revelation till a few years ago, and was struck by the parallels of its imagery to that of the various apocalyptic visions of the red man.

The earth is too old, the most deferred to of the Kiowa medicine men tells him through Burgess—it must be renewed. A new layer of earth will slide over the present land, while all the red people will be lifted into the air by the sacred dance feathers in their hair, then set down on this new earth, where they will sleep for four days. When they awake the buffalo will have returned, and all their dead friends will be there—

Heaven will have been joined with earth so there is room for all, adds another man.

"And the white people?" asks the Ethnographer.

The answer comes without hesitation, and the Ethnographer can read the signs without his interpreter's aid.

A great wall of fire will precede the new layer of earth, signs the medicine man, and drive the whites back across the Great Water to where they came from.

He has found that the tribes living near lakes are more likely to believe it will be a flood, those near tall mountains predict a world-shattering earthquake, but here on the tinder-dry southwestern corner of the Territory it will be fire—

The Shawnee prophet told a very similar story, also insisting that the new things the white man had brought—his metal tools and weapons, his manufactured cloth, his inebriating spirits—must all be discarded. But the added, surprising caveat from Wovoka has been the warning not to make war—not against the whites, not against each other. The warrior ethic is so deeply ingrained in so many of these cultures, thinks the Ethnographer, that they must be truly desperate to entertain laying aside their weapons forever.

Interesting to see how this will sit with the Lakota.

"The Messiah wishes to know," says the Ethnographer, "if the people on this side of the great mountains are doing the sacred dance as he instructed."

Of course we are, comes the response from several of the men. You can watch this evening and see for yourself.

But no photographs, signs the medicine man almost apologetically. Those who have not heard or do not believe the Messiah's words are likely to make up a bad story from the pictures.

The Ethnographer agrees that this might happen.

"So you've met the Dreamer," says Eddie Burgess as they climb the hill from which they'll be allowed to watch the dance.

"I have."

"What did you think?"

The young man seems to be something of an adventurer, passing through the Territory on his way to appear in a Wild West extravaganza as the "White Chief of the Pawnee." The Ethnographer well knows that rumors, especially among the Western tribes and the white men who have chosen to control them, are like wildfires, easily ignited and impossible to control. Sitting Bull, always more medicine man than war chief, is already talking about "the return of the ghosts" from his anxiously observed compound at Standing Rock.

The Ethnographer answers cautiously.

"I found him to be absolutely sincere. He accepts nothing more than a handful of pine nuts from his acolytes, he seems to be content to stay right where he is, and I think he believes every word he utters to be the truth."

"Ah," smiles the interpreter. "A dangerous man."

It takes a while for the blessing of the four corners, objects placed to the north, east, south, and west of a recently cut tree that has been propped up in the middle of the ground—fires will be lit on the periphery when it grows dark, but fire is not central to the dance. People begin to arrive in clusters, men and women, young and old, with the youngest of the children left at home and those who have been brought along consigned to spots near the piles of sagebrush that will be lit at dusk. The medicine man the Ethnographer spoke with is much in evidence, placing sacred objects, organizing the dancers into a ring, man-woman-man-woman, and with no great fanfare they are holding hands and moving in a circle while chanting a song. They will go on for hours, he knows, but there is none of the drama of the hunt and war dances he has witnessed. Perhaps half of the men are wearing "ghost shirts" made of buckskin, most with some sort of eagle drawing on the back, none with any metallic ornament attached. Both men and women have applied red paint to their bodies and faces, and a few have feathers in their hair—the great transformation is expected in the spring, still months away, so no means of flight to rise above the new layer of earth will be needed this evening. There is one man sitting by the central tree, beating a simple rhythm on a drum.

The Ethnographer, already distressed by his tour of the Kiowa Agency, too similar to the other miserable reservations he has visited, is filled with a weary sadness.

Even without the interpreter's aid he can understand the words of the first song, chanted over and over, so similar to what he heard among the Arapaho—

My father have pity on me!
I have nothing to eat
I am dying of thirst
Everything is gone!

TWO WEEKS NOW, and they're almost presentable.

Jesse Echohawk stands with his hands on his hips facing the vague rectangle made by A and B Companies, four rows, twelve across, dummy guns in hand, half asleep.

"Fall in."

Bodies adjusting, the mass taking a more geometric shape. The parade ground grass is wet with dew—all those shoes will need buffing and shining afterward.

"Tailor your lines—parade rest—"

Rifle butts to the ground, feet spread slightly apart—even the new privates who don't know the words yet know most of the drill. Monkey sees, monkey does.

"Atten-shun!"

The boys snap to with exaggerated rigidity, eyes forward, seeming to look past him. Jesse often thinks of his father, a trader licensed by the Pawnee Agency, raised in the shadow of a series of hastily built forts, and consequently eloquent in his low regard for soldiers.

"Shoulder arms!"

Up go the rifles, this morning without anyone being poked in the face by the barrel of his neighbor's weapon. Jesse hears Clarence echo the command off to the left, now in charge of C and D. They try to alternate their orders to avoid confusion—there has been enough of that with the green troopers mixed in.

He is grateful they are not actually heading to war.

Jesse was present at one bloody battle, if it could be dignified by that name, though still in his mother's belly. Miss Burgess was a young woman then, teaching alongside her mother, her father the Indian agent when the Pawnee were still in Nebraska. Quakers. The government issue had been late as usual and people were hungry, people were sick with one of the white man diseases that killed so many, and word came that a buffalo herd had been sighted just above the reservation land. The men dogged Agent Burgess until he reluctantly allowed an off-reservation hunt—Jesse's mother says that more than three hundred left, packing up their tipis, wives along to deal with the kill, children along to be with their mothers. His father followed a day behind with a wagon full of provisions, ready to buy the hides fresh off the backs of the kill.

The party had already had some success, skinning felled buffalo on the west side of the canyon that runs to the Republican River, when the Sioux attacked. Sky Chief was one of the first killed, surrounded and shot full of arrows, and Jesse's mother remembers screaming, screaming and running, pregnant, dragging his sister, in her second year, by the arm as she ran for a place to hide. She was able to reach a thick stand of timber and struggle through it, cut and bleeding, till she was too far in for the raiders to bother to come find her. The rest of the day was spent listening to whoops and wails and gunfire that never seemed to quite die out, holding her hands over the ears of her terrified daughter.

His father arrived the next afternoon, filling his wagon with the bodies of the dead and dying, numb with the fear that the next corpse he'd turn over would be that of his wife or daughter. Nearly half the Pawnee party were killed, many of their bodies mutilated, some of the men burned while still alive.

Spotted Tail, whose children came here to Carlisle for a spell, was one of the leaders of the Sioux party. It is a bitter joke between Jesse and his Lakota friend Clarence Regal.

"First two rows, column right!" calls Jesse Echohawk. "Double file, *march*!"

The first two rows take a quarter turn and head off together, gradually stepping in unison, with the next two rows waiting till the last pair passes—"Second two rows, column right, *march*!"—and then turning and hurrying to fall in step behind them.

Jesse was born during the period of mourning, when the people told Agent Burgess they wanted to go—to go anywhere away from the Sioux and the Cheyenne. A few parties were sent to scout in the Indian Territory, and Burgess passed their plea on to the powerful white men in Washington who controlled their movement. So Jesse's first memories are from the Territory, the tribe squeezed between the Osage, the Sac and Fox, and the Creek Nations. His father struggled to reestablish a trading post, while his mother washed the clothes of the Burgess family to earn extra food money. But the Quakers and other religious orders who'd volunteered to minister to the red man had lost the confidence both of the government and of the "pacified" tribes themselves—too lenient for the whites, too docile and easily bullied by crooked government suppliers for the Indians. Jesse's mother talks of cattlemen boldly standing on the scales when the inferior Texas beeves they'd delivered were weighed, pistols on their hips, smirking at Agent Burgess and his assistants all the while. The Quaker family was soon gone, the new agent no great improvement, but at least they were no longer at war with their neighbors. The tribe's new home was a tiny parcel of land, and there were only a few thousand of them left.

"We have been thrown away," his mother often says. "Put where we cannot be seen or remembered."

"Watch your spacing!" Jesse calls to the formation, moving now parallel to but in the opposite direction of Clarence's companies. "Left, right, left, right—keep your cadence, people!"

Living within sight of the agency buildings, it was no sacrifice to go to the little school there, picking up the white people's language, even learning how to play baseball. He was eight years old when Miss Burgess reappeared, on a recruiting trip for the school. She remembered his father and his mother, made her case.

"This land has become a den of wickedness," she said.

Bad men of every color and mix used the Territory as a hide-out and pleasure resort—stealing cattle in Texas and selling them in Kansas, stealing them in Kansas to sell in Texas or Mexico, bootlegging liquor to the various Indian nations, robbing trains—and deputy marshals had a long, long ride to capture bandits and carry them back to their hanging judge in Arkansas.

"There is no future for him here," Miss Burgess said to his parents. "There is no future for the Pawnee."

His mother told him that when she was a small girl the future was nothing more than the next turn of season—you smoked meat or fish, you dried fruit, you sewed together warm clothing for the coming winter, and then in winter you watched your flesh fall away and listened hopefully for the mighty cracking of the river as ice began to break up. The future was very much like the past—children were born, there were fights with enemies, young men strove to be brave and earn the right to take a wife, women hoped to marry a good provider and a man well regarded by all. There was not a master plan, only the knowledge of how to best deal with things that had been happening, in their season, as far back as people could remember.

Leave him here, Miss Burgess warned his mother, speaking her excellent Pawnee, and he'll become an agency layabout, a drunkard. Let me take him to the famous school in the East, to learn the white man's path and become a good Christian.

Jesse sees that Captain Pratt is sitting on the bandstand, as he often does during morning drill. He wears civilian clothes except for formal occasions, but his size and his broad shoulders always remind you that he is the commanding officer here.

"Column left—*march*!"

LaMere is one of the two lead boys, and though a first-year private, misses nothing. He does a quick turn, reaching out with his free arm to snag the Papago boy beside him and pull him along to the left. The next four in line, veteran marchers, know enough to step to the pivot point before they turn and change direction, the rest of the column following their lead. Once they understand the patterns they are making, drawing designs on the parade ground, most of the boys accept the drill. They are dressed like white soldiers and white soldiers stand in lines and then march to wherever they are going, so it must be done.

The Captain is leaning on the white-painted railing of the bandstand, smiling—

"To the left—sa*lute*—"

A few of the boys haven't mastered this, one knocking his cap off and leaving it behind for later retrieval, but the Captain seems pleased. He knows Jesse well after so many years at the school, nearly its whole existence, and often asks him what his plans on graduation are. Jesse knows that the Captain's desire, repeated in his many speeches and lectures, is to see them go forth into the white world to become tradesmen, educators, doctors and lawyers even. And Jesse will tell him that he is still deciding, that Carlisle has opened his eyes to so many fields, so many possibilities in great white America.

He hopes to graduate, to leave this place where he has spent more than half his life, next year. He will go home to his mother and father in the Indian Territory.

The Pawnee will have a future.

"Column left—" calls Jesse Echohawk, "*march*!"

The sun is midmorning height in the sky when Sweetcorn is released from the guardhouse, Mr. Skinner posing his question.

"Have you learned your lesson?"

The same question he asked after the first time he thrashed the boy, when Sweetcorn was twelve years old and new at the school and did not understand the words. Skinner used a cane then, which the Captain later amended to a leather belt, not out of sympathy, Sweetcorn believes, but because he realized some of the boys were strong enough to take a cane from the disciplinarian and beat him senseless.

"I don't want to be sent back into the guardhouse," he answers.

"You won't be." Skinner has no hair on the top of his head, and doesn't wear a hat to hide the fact like most white men do. "For the next serious infraction you'll be expelled from Carlisle."

This is not necessarily as good as it sounds. Last year a boy who decided to run away stole a bicycle in town and rode it so badly he was immediately caught, tried, and sent to prison. It has been explained to Sweetcorn that his choices are Carlisle or the Santee Agency, where the Indian agent has made it clear his presence is not wished for.

"You are not citizens," Captain Pratt has explained to them in his talks, "you are wards of the state. This is unfair, and I am opposed to the situation, but it is currently the law of the land. Should you renounce your membership in your tribe, however, forfeiting all annuities and territorial rights that come with it, and locate yourself at some distance from the reservation you've been assigned to, you could indeed come to be considered a citizen—sink or swim." The Captain always smiles at this point.

"Here at Carlisle we're teaching you how to *swim*."

Sweetcorn and Skinner are walking together, no student guards on their heels, toward the old army building that has become the steam-heating plant, and Sweetcorn feels a vibration in the ground before he hears the furnaces inside.

"You'll start classes again tomorrow," says Skinner, "but today I thought I'd introduce you to your new trade."

Steam fitting is one of the trades they reserve for older boys. Sweetcorn was a baker last year, hot work and tedious once you learned it, but not the worst they could deal out. There were a few good fights, slinging doughballs—

Skinner opens the door and the heat rushes upon them. Voices, echoing, and Sweetcorn is led down to face the open maws of three huge furnaces. Two men, stripped to the waist and glistening with sweat, heave shovelfuls of lump coal into the fiery vaults. One of the men is black-skinned, the other white, though he is so begrimed with coal dust you can only tell this from the yellow hair sprouting from his squarish head.

"Gentlemen," says Skinner, shouting over the roar of the fires, "I'd like to introduce you to your new apprentice—this is Herbert Sweetcorn."

The men glance at him, barely pausing as they feed the iron beasts.

"This isn't steam fitting," says Sweetcorn.

"No, but it is a *trade*. And I'm certain that Mr. Gamble and Mr. Pryzylowski will train you well."

"Stosh don't talk English," says the black stoker. "But the man is a *mule* for work."

Trouble turns to look back at the marks the Papago boy is making on his little rock board. The boy is copying the marks the white woman made on the big rock board in front of them. Trouble recognizes some of the shapes now—

A, the tipi with the sides pulled up on a hot day—

C, a bow with no bowstring—

D, a single, strung bow—

B, two strung bows, one on top of the other—

Somehow the white people mix these shapes together, changing the order of them, and it tells them what sound to make.

But Trouble doesn't know what those sounds mean, whether they are sung or only spoken.

You rub the piece of chalk on the rock board and it makes a mark, and then if you don't like it you can rub the mark away. His mother makes marks like that before she cuts rawhide to make things from it. Once the thing is made you no longer see the mark, like a belt to keep your buffalo robe tight around you in the winter. But there are other marks they make here, with black water on pieces of paper, that cannot be rubbed away. This is the way the white man keeps his stories. Their lives are so complicated, it must be hard to remember it all, and so they make the shapes on paper that become sounds that are the words of the story.

At home everybody, but especially the old men, remember the stories, and tell them again and again so that if they die the stories won't be lost. And one old man, who they call Long Sleep, paints pictures on a doeskin of what has happened in the last year, and each year's story is then rolled up and kept with the stories of earlier years. If Trouble came and asked, "What happened to our band the year that I was born?" it might be remembered that he was born in the fall of the year that the grizzly bear ran into camp and killed some dogs, and so that roll of painted pictures would be found and an old man who had lived through that year would read the pictures out loud, elaborating on the stories for the crowd that was sure to come and listen. Even Trouble, who is not an artist or a storyteller, can tell the difference between a dead Blackfoot and a dead Pawnee in a picture by the colors used or how their hair is drawn. These shapes and sounds the white men use might be just as good for remembering stories, but Trouble doesn't care to learn those stories. All he wants to know is when he can leave this place.

The white woman sings out a number of sounds, and the others in the room continue to copy the shapes that are on the big rock board. Trouble begins to mark with his piece of chalk. It is a drawing of his pony, the one he left lying on the ridge for the buzzards to eat. In the drawing the pony is running to the west—

—while Smokey stands, holding the essay he has written, the other students and Miss Cutter watching him. It took him a long time to write, crossing out words, writing in new ones, but then Antoine read it before lights-out and said it was fine, the class wouldn't laugh at him. Antoine is good at all the classroom business, and sometimes even pretends to know less than he does if it means they'll leave him alone for a while.

"Moses, you may go ahead," says Miss Cutter.

He takes a deep breath. She doesn't make you read in front of the others for punishment, though it seems like that. When you read something out loud, she says, your ear catches mistakes that your eye might not see.

"Christopher Columbus," he says.

There is a town called Columbus back home, well south of the mountains, that is probably named after this man. Antoine told him that how you write an essay is to read the story you're writing about just once, then try to explain it in your own words, like you were passing it on to a friend. Antoine had him tell the story out loud, writing it down so he could copy it in his own hand. Antoine says this is not cheating but just learning more gradually.

"Columbus got a job sailing for the Queen of Spain to find America. He had three ships and none of them sunk on the way."

The book he learned the story from had a map that showed Spain on one side of the blue and then the island Columbus landed at on the other and a dotted line connecting them. Only there wasn't any dotted line floating on the water, so it was really just an accident that he got where he did. Antoine suggested he leave that part out of the essay.

"If not for Columbus, nobody would know about America except the Indians, and they wouldn't tell—"

—and Antoine sits in Mr. Gelder's class, learning about white people killing each other. This, as it turns out, began long before they crossed the ocean to kill Indians. What is truly surprising is the *number* of each other they kill in these wars. Whenever Antoine raises his hand to ask, Mr. Gelder has a casualty figure for the engagement—Hastings, Culloden, Waterloo—to go with the date he chalks on the blackboard. It amounts to a lot of dead white people. Antoine thinks of his father's story of the last great battle between the Ojibwe and the Lakota—the Lakota thinking they could surprise the La Pointe band camping next to the Brulé, but Chief Buffalo, a great-uncle of Antoine's mother, warned in time to set a trap for them, the Lakota chest-deep in the water when suddenly surrounded, at least a hundred of their warriors slain.

One hundred men, in a white people war, is barely worth mention. But for the Lakota it was a disaster, encouraging them to move west and make life miserable for the Crow and the Pawnee.

"It was a long, hard winter at Valley Forge," says Mr. Gelder, in the midst of the American War of Independence. "Supplies were low—food, clothing, firewood—the men were dressed in rags, boots worn through, those that even *had* boots. And why? Politics. Contention and neglect at the Continental Congress—"

Antoine's father and mother are old enough to have been at Sandy Lake in the winter of 1850, when the American government changed the rendezvous for receiving annuity payments and commodities from La Pointe to a little agency all the way back in Minnesota. Most of the bands made the long journey and arrived by November, then waited for weeks for the federal agent to arrive. When he did, he told them the government had been unable to send the annuities and supplies, and they could either go back home or wait for them to be delivered. The people waited. A small fraction of the annuity money arrived, but there was nothing in Sandy Lake to buy, and when the goods came most of the food was spoiled. People died of dysentery, people died of measles, people froze and starved to death. More died on the long trip home—

"The ground at Valley Forge froze so solid the deceased could not be buried," says Mr. Gelder. "By the time the Schuylkill River thawed, thousands had died."

Thousands. Compared to that, thinks Antoine, what are four hundred men, women, and children, Indians at that? For the first few hours of his journey here he was impressed by the train, which he had seen only from a distance but never ridden before. Then the towns and then the cities, each larger than the next, the *scale* of it, brick and stone buildings seemingly piled one on top of another, smoke from factory chimneys blotting out the sun—the people who created these things have the power to make a speech or write on a paper in Washington and other people hundreds of miles away lose their homes, lose their lives.

The mighty thunderbirds of the Ojibwe seem feeble beside them.

"But that willingness to sacrifice, that unshakeable perseverance, proved greater than the might of the great British Empire," says Mr. Gelder. He looks as if he might weep. "There was indeed a forge in that little Pennsylvania town, and on it was stamped forever the *character* of the American citizen."

Miss Redbird follows Nurse Tucker down a long row of beds in the girls' ward of the infirmary, most of them occupied. Some girls sleep, a few read, others just stare with feverish eyes. Miss Redbird wants to cover her mouth and nose, afraid of whatever they're sick with, but restrains herself.

"Once, before my time," says Nurse Tucker, "they had to use the old chapel to quarantine some of the children. Thank God we haven't had that kind of emergency lately."

"But children die here."

Nurse Tucker shoots her a look, then leans closer and lowers her voice conspiratorially—

"We've lost so many of the Apaches, especially the girls. I don't know if it's the climate here or if they come to us already infected—"

"Nurse Tucker?"

One of Miss Redbird's music students, Oneida, she thinks, sitting on a chair with a nurse's cap on her head, holding the hand of a young girl barely peeping out from under the white hospital sheets.

"Did Doctor release Hannah?"

There is an empty bed, stripped of linens, on the other side of the Oneida girl.

"Hannah was so ill that Doctor sent her back to Alabama, Grace."

"But it's just a prison there—"

"It's a fort—"

"It's a fort where they're holding people prisoner."

"It's where her people are."

"And who's this?" Miss Redbird asks Grace, the Oneida girl. A violinist, she remembers.

"Her name is Evangeline. Her father was killed in the fighting and her mother is at the San Carlos Agency, in Arizona Territory."

Miss Redbird moves closer, lays a hand on the Apache girl's bony shoulder.

"Has she written to her mother since she's been here?"

"She doesn't write—and I'm pretty sure her mother doesn't read."

"You could write a letter for her."

"I don't speak any Apache. What would I write?"

Students are meant to write a letter home once a month. They are often read by instructors before sending, ostensibly to correct mistakes in spelling and grammar, but Miss Redbird suspects that any grievous complaints don't survive the process.

"Think of your mother at home the first year you were here," she says.

Miss Redbird's letters to her own mother during her first year at the boarding school were full of lies, her pride preventing her from revealing how miserable she was. It had been her desire to go, after all—

"What would your mother want to hear?"

"Should I say that she's sick?"

The Indian agent at San Carlos will probably be the one to read the letter out loud, an interpreter by his side, and he'll no doubt do his own revising.

"Of course. But say that she hopes to be better soon." She turns to the little girl. "Evangeline, what is your mother's name?"

The girl has beautiful black eyes, huge now in the drawn face. No comprehension.

Miss Redbird pulls out the pad and pencil she carries and swiftly makes a simple drawing of an Indian woman holding a baby in her arms. She shows it to the girl, pointing to the baby—

"That's Evangeline—" she says, then points to the mother, "and this is—?"

"Nahii," says the dying girl, her black eyes brightening.

Captain Pratt leads a group of philanthropic Philadelphians, including a most proper Negro gentleman and his wife, on a tour of the classrooms while they are in session. Some benefactors, he knows, come expecting Bedlam, while others will be disappointed it is not more like Penn Charter. But there is something comforting to the generous mind about young people uniformly dressed and seated in rows, so far removed from the scaremongering headlines issuing from the Western states and territories.

"We make our own uniforms, shoes, serving utensils, pots, and pans," he informs them, "our own bread. Our nearby farm produces milk and vegetables, and we even sell some of our surplus items from the trade classes, such as harnesses, wagons, carriages, to the Indian agencies throughout the nation—"

Congress, already stingy and resentful of the various annuities it must pay out to tribes each year as part of the peace treaties and land grabs it foisted upon them, has appropriated only the bare minimum for the experiment here at Carlisle, so these guided tours, as well as the lectures and church events that constantly pull him away from the school, are a necessity. He pauses in front of a door—

"Don't be surprised by the incongruity of the students' *size* in some of our classes," he warns them. "We must group them by their intellectual rather than their chronological age. I dare say if it were the Greek language being taught, we should all be placed with the toddlers."

A few giggles from the ladies, and Pratt leads them into Mr. Drinkwater's bailiwick.

"A basic grasp of geography," Mr. Drinkwater declaims from the chalkboard, "is the foun*da*tion of an understanding of history. Mr. Viajero"—he turns now to a skinny boy Pratt recognizes as one of the new students from the Southwest—no, not Apache, but possibly Papago or Pima—"indicate for us, if you will, where your people dwell."

The boy, standing beside a large pull-down map of the United States, is clearly befuddled.

Drinkwater raises his voice a tad, pointing at the map.

"Show—where—Papago—live."

A few titters from the students more proficient in English. The boy ponders for a moment, then moves to the board and takes up a stub of chalk. He draws a large square, then carefully makes an X in the center of it.

"Tohono O'odham," he announces.

"Our red brethren's view of geography," says Captain Pratt, smiling, "with their own tribe located at the exact center of the universe. When we all know that to be in Philadelphia."

The visitors, and even a few of the students, laugh. Drinkwater sighs.

"Perhaps we should start from the beginning," he says, moving to the handsome globe tilted on its stand, and slowly revolving it. "We live on the earth, which far from being a square, is *spher*ical."

Trouble watches the white man spin the painted ball around. He knows the talking is about where things are, the man having pointed to a spot on the flat picture and said "Carlisle," which is the name of the school. The spot was not so far from the Great Water, which is always painted blue. Trouble has stood close to that picture and studied the thinner blue lines, which he has decided are rivers, and found the widest one that runs from north to south, and from that found others that he has made camp beside. The picture is what an eagle very high in the sky would see, so high it can even see where the great rivers begin and end. Trouble knows where west is when they stand on the field of grass in front of the buildings before marching, knows that if you keep looking to the left on this eagle-picture you come to a second Great Water. What he would like is for the eagle to draw him a picture that shows all the rails that the rolling houses move on, one leading to the next leading to the next till they reach Standing Rock—

"And I must say," continues Mr. Drinkwater, "that if anything is *central* in this situation, it is the earth's molten core—"

—as Wilma throws an armful of dirty uniforms into a vat of steaming hot water. She pulls her apron up to blot the moisture off her face. There is a hard rapping at the window. Wilma crosses to it, wipes a clear circle into the steam-fogged pane, and gives a little hoot of surprise. A tall, black-faced man is standing outside, staring in at her.

But when he smiles she recognizes Sweetcorn under the layer of soot. He points at her, then clutches both his hands to his heart. Wilma giggles, flattered.

Sweetcorn is out of the can.

THE GENTLEMEN OF THE PRESS have convened on the ivy-covered porch of what they have christened the Hotel de Finley, the finest, and only, rental accommodation on the Pine Ridge Reservation. Fortunately, Al has had the foresight to pack adequate refreshment all the way from Rapid City, a suitcase full of it cushioned by his extra socks.

"One can never bring enough socks." He winks as he passes the elixir to the rest of the gang, each with their cup ready in hand—for they are newshounds, not mule skinners, and would never consider drinking straight from the bottle. The men sip politely, savoring the vintage, whatever it might be, and look across to the low, drafty barracks that serves as the agency's administrative office, police station, and medical dispensary. A half dozen blanketed Sioux wait by the outside door of Agent Royer's office, one on the back of a dozing pony, the others cross-legged on the cold ground. Waiting, perhaps, for something to happen.

"If Remington was still here," says O'Brien, the AP stringer, "he might make a painting of that."

"If Remington was still here he'd cut his own throat with a butter knife," grumbles Will Cressy, the least patient of the correspondents "I've seen more action at a Lutheran funeral."

"Patience, my boy," advises the one they call Professor, who is, in fact, a geologist when not filing for the Chicago-based *Inter Ocean*. "'Tis but the lull before the storm."

"You read Will's copy you'd think it's a hurricane," says Boylan of the *St. Paul Pioneer Press*. "And that we're risking life and limb just poking our heads outside of Mr. Finley's little fort here."

The hotel is a one-story affair made of peeled logs, with only three available bedrooms. Two of the intrepid journalists are sleeping head-to-foot in each of the beds, with a third, and at times a fourth, enjoying a bedroll on the floor. By the second day of this Mrs. Finley had had enough, fleeing to relatives in Kansas City, leaving Big Jim to assume her usual duties in addition to running his general store. The logs, they have been assured, will afford greater protection come the reckoning in lead that all expect than the flimsy side planks of the agency buildings.

"If you think Will is ballooning in the *Bee*," says Charles Allen, who lives in Chadron but is here filing for *The New York Herald*, the *Omaha World-Herald*, and *The Duluth Weekly Tribune*, "you should read the Dakota papers."

"I would, but the ink comes off in my hands."

The men laugh. It is an old joke, and none of them are from either of the newly minted states.

"I do not b-b-bal*loon*," objects Cressy, who tends to stutter when excited. "I simply rep-p-port what I hear."

"One who packages hot air and sends it aloft is a *balloonist*. Especially if he fails to consider the source."

"I work with the sources available. General B-B-Brooke won't talk to us, getting a quote from Agent Royer is like p-p-pulling teeth—"

"He *is* a dentist—"

"—the Indian p-p-olice pretend they don't speak English, and the hoi polloi"—here he waves his hand vaguely toward the hundreds of tipis clustered on the flat ground and low knolls that surround the agency buildings—"pretend that they *do*, only I can't unscramble a w-word of it."

"Paleface write-um story with forked pen." Al retrieves the scotch, pours himself a few more fingers of joy. "Pull buffalo robe over reader's eye. Mrs. Finley absquatulates to visit her family and you write 'White Residents Flee Pine Ridge!' in scareheads."

"She was afraid—"

"Afraid of dealing with a cabin full of underpaid inkslingers, not of losing her hair to a hostile. She rode down to Rushville with the postman in a *car*riage. There might have been a parasol involved."

Cressy scowls. "I s-suppose your editors aren't crying for b-blood?"

This draws a rare moment of silence. They arrived shortly after the ghost dance was spotted on the reservation, and mere tension is difficult to transform into newspaper circulation.

"And at the *Bee* the paper we use is *w-w-white*."

This is aimed at Charles Allen, whose own *Chadron Democrat* is printed on yellow stock. But Allen is the most connected of the scribes anchoring the porch chairs, having worked at Pine Ridge as a freighter in the early days of the agency, and even witnessed the near uprising when Red Cloud chopped then-agent Saville's flagpole into pieces.

"My editor has me down to twenty-five words a dispatch," Allen admits, "but I don't use them to stir up trouble where there isn't any."

"*I have tramped the Bad Lands o'er and o'er*," croons Buckskin Jack, the visiting veteran scout and doggerel-demon—

"*and camped on Wounded Knee.*

But my heart grows faint at the warriors' paint
And the lurid hue of the savage Sioux
As they charge—in the Omaha Bee!*"*

Cressy does not join the laughter. It has been a frustrating assignment for all, rumor unchecked and true action rare as hen's teeth, the boys reduced to collaborating on the invented *Bad Lands Budget*, taking turns to see who can write the wildest misrepresentation in the most tortured prose. At least the hotel has a nice, well-lit dining room and more than decent chuck, even with Finley's wife absent, and Big Jim Finley lets them use the long counter of his trading post to shuffle their notes and compose their tales on after he closes shop.

"I wish someone on this agency could tell me a story above which the halo of truth will linger for even fifteen minutes," laments the Professor.

"And here we sit," says Seymour from the *Chicago Herald*, "waiting for the Messiah to appear."

Tibbles and his Indian wife stroll past then, Tibbles wielding a walking stick and nodding to them.

"Gentlemen," he says.

Kelly, young and new at the trade, removes his hat for the lady.

"I wonder how the grub is in their cabin," wonders Al when they are out of earshot. Tibbles and his wife, whose byline, depending on their editor's whim, is either Susette La Flesche or Bright Eyes, are staying with a Sioux acquaintance, said to be a Christian, in a log house within sight of the agency office.

"If it's what they hand out on the issue day, I wouldn't touch it. Strictly USIC." That being the army shorthand for "Inspected and Condemned," a tag they also hang on copy posted by their more inventive brethren. "Have you seen the flour? I don't recall that it's supposed to look and feel like beach sand—"

"If they knew how to *bake* that might matter," says Cressy. "From what I've seen they just dump it in a skillet, m-mix some creek water in, and lay it on the stovetop."

"I read one of her pieces in the World-Herald," says Kelly, watching Mrs. Tibbles walk away. "Not bad at all."

"You think she really writes them?"

"Well it's a sure thing that *Tib*bles doesn't," says Charley Seymour. "He's not a writer, he's a—what would you call it?"

"A stump preacher."

"Exactly. With an inflated vocabulary."

"He was quite the abolitionist in his day," says the Professor. "Fought side by side with old John Brown in Bloody Kansas, lost a chunk of his ear—"

"And I thought Bright Eyes had nibbled that off—"

She has been a disappointment to the men unfamiliar with her photographs. Hoping for a fiery, braided squaw, they have encountered a pleasant, round-faced Christian woman, a wearer of modest dresses and author of balanced prose. It does not help that the couple enjoy access to the native population that most of them have been unable or too lazy to establish.

"Did he kidnap her off some reservation?"

"No, the former Miss La Flesche is a lace curtain gal. Private academy, music lessons, that sort of thing. I saw them speak together when they were in Chicago, trying to help the Poncas get their ancestral land back."

"We took that too?"

"Took it and gave it to these wild Sioux," says the Professor. "The poor Poncas had to walk two hundred miles to some patch of scrub that was left unclaimed up in the Territory."

"How'd the Sioux manage that one?"

"Ask General Custer. These chiefs have learned that the bigger pain in the caboose they make themselves, the more attention they get."

"Only this time they'll get more than they bargained for."

"We shall see about that," says O'Brien, the AP man.

"But *when*? My editor gives it till next Friday, and then I'm back to St. Louis."

"You poor fellow—clean sheets, cold beer—"

"Please—no mention of beer, at any temperature."

The gentlemen of the press had not understood just how tightly prohibition of alcohol was enforced on the reservation, and only Al has taken precautionary measures. Big Jim Finley has been offered a small fortune to smuggle something in, but has professed to value his trader's license too highly to take the risk.

"Hey—no booze, no drunken Indians."

"Worse—no drunken *reporters*."

The men laugh, Kelly of the *Nebraska State Journal* getting up to stretch his legs.

"I was talking to the post office fella today—"

"The half-breed—"

"I don't know how he's bred, but he speaks their lingo and ours both. Even reads and writes letters for folks that can't—"

"A window into the soul of the heathen—"

"He says doesn't anybody care for Agent Royer, who only got this post cause the Democrats won and had favors to pass out."

"Hope they never do me any favors," says Burkholder. "I mean, what if you had to *live* in this place?"

Carl Smith, another writer for the *Omaha Daily*, steps out from the agent's office and crosses toward the vine-covered porch of the hotel, flanked by a pair of Indian police.

"Smitty!" calls Charles Allen. "Any troop movements we should know about?"

"Son of a bitch just run me off the reservation," Smith snarls, snaking between them. "I got to clear out my room and sleep in the guardhouse tonight."

"What?"

"*Slan*der, he says! The man's an incompetent ass and all I did was to state that fact in print, plainly and clearly."

"Did you remind him that we have freedom of the press in the United States?"

"We're not *in* the United States," Smith mutters, and stomps into the hotel.

"I get his spot in the bed," declares Albert, who pronounces his name the French way.

"Who says?"

"I've been on the floor since I got here."

"Fine. I hope you get bedbugs."

"Smitty must have lit into Royer pretty good—"

"Hey, I've written several times that people in the know here question his abilities," says Will Cressy.

"Only to refute such accusations in the same paragraph."

"And then stick a few incendiary quotes into his mouth—"

"I may sh-sharpen the gentleman's pronouncements, but I do not inv-v-vent."

"Now you've got him all upset—"

"Smitty wrote that he was a dilettante and a bungler."

"Did he really use the word *dil*ettante?"

"What's wrong with it?"

"Is there anybody in Omaha who knows what it means?"

Only half the men laugh at this.

"Listen, Mr. New York know-it-all—"

"Smitty's really getting booted because he's been lifting military orders."

They all look to Kelly.

"He told me. He used to be a telegraph operator, so when he goes down to the office to file his copy he can just watch the man tap the key and know what's being transmitted. That's how he got all Royer's telegrams begging for more troops."

"The sly little bastard. And didn't share with any of us."

"You could make *up* some troop movements, Will. Nobody'd know the difference back in *Bee*-land—"

"That's because they're a bunch of dilettantes," says Charley Seymour.

Kelly recognizes one of the waiting Indian policemen as George Sword, captain of the reservation force.

"Sword, you must know what's going on. Agent Royer and Smitty had words, did they?"

"Agent Royer is plenty mad," says Sword, smoking a cigarette. "And General Brooke don't like him either."

"And there's a lesson for us all, boys," says the Professor. "In this situation you can unload on the Indian Bureau hack or on the military headman, but don't get them *both* riled at you."

"What about the Indians?"

"Call them anything you want," says Will Cressy, "they can't read."

A moment for them all to consider this, then Kelly turns to the police captain.

"That true, Sword? Nobody here reads a newspaper?"

Sword looks the men over. The ones who ask him questions in broken English he doesn't answer, and those he does talk with are told whatever is the least likely to get him in trouble. Agent Gallagher did not always do what was the best for the Lakota, but at least he didn't think they were savage wolves that should be hunted or poisoned. But this new one—

"We have boys who come back from white school in the East," he tells them. "They can read what you've written and tell it to us."

"And what do the people think of it?" asks Will Cressy, already grinning.

Sword ponders for a long moment before he answers, a Lakota trait the newsmen have struggled to get used to. "We have liars here at Pine Ridge," he says finally. "But their voices don't travel so far as yours."

Then Smitty comes down with his bags and goodbyes are exchanged, his brethren commiserating that he is the victim of thin-skinned injustice. The other policeman carries Smitty's suitcase for him as they cross back to the agency barracks.

"If you're joining me tonight," says Cressy to Burkholder, suddenly very annoyed, "you'd better go wash your *feet*."

IT IS CLEAR TO CAPTAIN PRATT that the reporter has already written his article, at least mentally, and is only trying to provoke him into saying something outrageous. Two can play at that game.

"If I had my way there would *be* no Carlisle School," the Captain tells him as they walk briskly toward the trade buildings. "These young men and women should be placed in white communities with white families, attending local schools—im*mersed* in our culture."

He maintains a pace that the newspaper man, a stubby little fellow, struggles to match.

"Then why aren't you doing that?"

"Because it is, unfortunately, impossible, especially in the West, where more recent hostility between the races has left prejudices firmly entrenched and tempers aflame."

"With great justification—"

"What we offer here at Carlisle as an alternative is our Outing program—students board at area farms, living and eating with the families, earning their keep through domestic or agricultural labor—"

"Very courageous of their hosts."

The reporter is from a news journal that once criticized the Captain for "attempting to revive a savage and, one must say, justly exterminated race." The Captain assumes their editorial policy is unaltered.

"The hosts are chosen as carefully as the students. We visit the home, assure ourselves that the cleanliness and moral standards are acceptable—"

"And these students are able to speak—?"

"Some are still struggling with the acquisition of our tongue. They must be *shown* their tasks as well as having them explained. You'll see the same principle applied to some of our boys in the carpentry shop."

The newsman raises a hand before Pratt can open the door to the shop. The sounds of hammering and sawing, the music of industry, always comfort him when he looks in here.

"This so-called ghost dance that has the Western tribes on the warpath—"

Ah—the point of this inquisition.

"What of it?"

"Any stirrings of unrest among your charges?"

"What you refer to is an unfortunate but understandable delusion that has affected a relative handful of those held on our reservation prisons. They dream of otherworldly deliverance just as a convict dragging a ball and chain might dream of escape. It will come to nothing, and has no bearing on our mission here." He throws the door open to offer the full cacophony of woodworking noises. "Shall we observe something con*struc*tive?"

The Man-on-the-Bandstand notes with pride the pristine condition of our lawns and walkways. We are judged not only by our personal appearance, but by that of our habitat, indoors and out—

—out on the parade ground, boys who have received demerits for tardiness, slovenliness, or failure to complete written assignments police the grounds, raking fallen leaves into cloth sack—

Only through discipline, constant, unswerving discipline and vigilance of behavior, can we hope to be the persons who will succeed in the world—

—and on the grass next to the infirmary Miss Ely demonstrates how to play croquet to a dozen Carlisle girls, while in the new gymnasium a dozen Carlisle boys face Jesse Echohawk, mirroring every move he makes, each waving a pair of five-pound wooden Indian clubs—

—whether at work or at play there is a standard of comportment that we must always maintain—

—and in the room set aside for photography Leslie John moves a front light closer to shine on the Papago boy's face. Mr. Choate says it works better than makeup for the "after" pictures, and the boy, Viajero, Asa, already looks a different person then he did on admission, sitting now in front of the pastoral backdrop in his uniform, hair cut short, leather shoes glossy with polish. The same mournful expression maybe, but when the two shots are married side by side on a postal card they will tell the appropriate story. A loud pop and a searing flash of white light as the chlorate powder in Mr. Choate's tray is set off—

—if we are to achieve the level of civilization we aspire to, say to yourself, I am getting better every day—and then strive to make that a reality—

—the print shop in full clatter, belts humming, inked sheets rolling and quickly stacked for folding, as little Tecumseh Starr sets lead rectangles of type into a composing stick and Antoine reads backward to decipher the words they add up to—

"I am getting better every day."

"What?"

Antoine points to the wall next to him, where the phrase is on a banner in ten-inch capital letters—

I AM GETTING BETTER EVERY DAY

"Do you think that's true?" he asks.

"Absolutely," grins Cato Goforth as he enters the shop, "and I've been here seven years. Just think how bad I must have been when I came."

"What's the news from the world?"

"White people getting nervous," he says. "Some crazy Paiute down in Nevada has got everybody on the reservations doing ghost dances."

"People are dancing?"

"Dancing, chanting, hopping around a fire all night. You know—how the old-timers do."

"Not my people," says Tecumseh Starr.

"Well, *some*body's making them nervous." Cato unfolds his copy of the day's *Sentinel* and points to a headline.

MESSIAH MISCHIEF

OCTOBER

"AT THE FEET OF LAUGHING WATER," ANTOINE DECLAIMS, right hand over his heart, chin in the air—

"Hiawatha laid his burden,
Threw the reindeer from his shoulders—"

"It's '*red deer.*'"

He drops his hand from his heart. "Other places he says 'reindeer.'"

"I know," says Grace. "But here it's 'red deer.'"

"What's a 'reindeer' anyhow?"

"It's another word for caribou," says Miss Redbird, sitting at the piano and writing a letter. She has been tasked with chaperoning the rehearsal. "They look more like elk than deer to me, and they live way up in the northwest."

"You've seen them?"

"I saw one stuffed, in a museum."

"You shouldn't just stand like that," Grace tells Antoine. "You should act it out."

"Carry a deer?"

"Pre*tend* to carry one."

"Won't that look stupid?"

"Not if you do it well."

Antoine thinks about this. He is pretty sure he remembers a part where Hiawatha gets to carry Minnehaha.

"Will we have a tipi?"

"We can make something that looks like one. And Mrs. Pratt has a collection of clothing from different tribes."

"I thought the Captain disapproved of—"

"Remember, we're just pre*tending* to be Indians."

"Even though we really are. I'm even Ojibwe, like this Hiawatha—"

"Who was Mohawk," says Miss Redbird without looking up from her letter. "Or maybe Onondaga."

"Hiawatha was real?"

"Not the one in the poem, but, yes, there was a Hiawatha. He helped form the Iroquois Confederacy."

"So the poem—"

"Takes poetic license."

"You mean he just made it up."

Miss Redbird smiles. "A white poet's dream of the noble savage, far back in the mists of time."

"It ends with a priest coming—a Black Robe," says Grace.

"Of course it does."

Antoine decides that if he was not in love with Grace he would be in love with Miss Redbird. Back home boys and girls his age don't get to be in a room together and talk like this, or if they do it is a scandal. His father's stories of what he went through to court his mother, leaving gifts to see if they'd be accepted, speaking to her parents to make his case, dancing near but never with her at ceremonies—

At Carlisle there is gossip, he has discovered, even scandal. But there are no parents.

"So I've got the red deer on my shoulder, which is heavy—"

"Not for Hiawatha it isn't—"

"—and you—Minnehaha is sitting in her tipi—"

Grace carefully sits on the floor, hugging her knees. "It's a *wig*wam."

"Do I bring it in?"

She considers this. "Let's say she's sitting near the opening of the wigwam where she can see him, so he lays it down just outside."

"*At the feet of Laughing Water, Hiawatha laid his burden,*" says Antoine, miming a load on his back and going to one knee. "*Threw the red deer from his shoulders—*"

"*And the maiden looked up at him,*" says Grace, looking first at the spot where the imaginary deer has landed and then up into Antoine's eyes—

"*Looked up from her mat of rushes,*
said with gentle looks and accent,"

—and then, in a normal voice, as if just talking to a real person, says—

"*You are welcome, Hiawatha.*"

Antoine, eyes locked with Grace's, has no idea what comes next. He would absolutely go find a deer, or even a caribou, and kill it for her.

"Are you just going to stay out there?" she asks.

"Oh, right"—he stands, then pretends to duck slightly as he steps into her dwelling—

"*Very spacious was the wigwam,*
Made of deer-skins dressed and whitened,"

—Antoine turns in a circle as if viewing the inside decorations—

"*With the Gods of the Dacotahs,*
Drawn and painted on its curtains—"

Trouble sits in the sloyd class with the little boys, watching Mr. Kersey explain with his hands. The white man uses words too, but mostly he shows them, picking up the wood, picking up the tools, showing the pieces and then how they are put together.

Trouble knows what they are up to, knows what this means.

When he was a small boy he and the other small boys had small bows, and were shown how to make arrows with blunt ends for killing very small animals. They practiced with these, hitting a spot on a tree or shooting through a rolling hoop or shooting at squirrels and chipmunks and rabbits, bragging that they were the best and having contests to see if it was true. They are making him a small boy again, telling him that the old ways are gone and that he'll have to start learning like a colt just up on its feet does, learning to do the white man's kind of work. He knows some of their words for things now—"bed," "window," "desk"—even some of the things in this room—"wood," "metal," "knife." They have put him with the small boys but they know he is not small, almost ready to be a warrior—

So it is a surprise when the white man, Kersey, passes a basket full of wooden sticks with a knife blade stuck in the end around to the boys and does nothing when Trouble takes one. He looks Trouble in the eye, yes, but it is not a challenge. Kersey shows them a finished example of what they are meant to carve—a wooden stick with a metal hook in it, the stick curved so that their uniform clothes will hang from it. He shows them the stroke, steady, gentle, always away from the body, that they are to use, then passes another basket, this one with long blocks of soft, yellow wood for them to shape.

It is a good knife, with a very sharp blade, the yellow wood curling away as you cut it with long strokes. Trouble has made countless arrow shafts, has cut designs in leather and bone, and finishes well before the small boys. Kersey says something to him, smiling, then lifts the uniform hanger up for the other boys to see, holding the empty basket in front of Trouble without looking at him.

Trouble puts the knife back in the basket.

Next they'll learn how to twist the metal to make the hook—

Miss Burgess opens the top crate and there they are. She has waited all day for this, telling the boys to go enjoy their free time and leave her to close up the print shop. They were good about carrying the crates in, curious, but content to hear "A mystery that shall be revealed" from her. They fit in two rows of three, each ten copies deep, front covers up—

STIYA

A CARLISLE INDIAN GIRL

AT HOME

She bends down to breathe it in. New-print smell, all the sweeter because she is the author. And the photograph of the little Apache girl, though not a Pueblo like the title character, captures admirably that forlorn longing for a better life. For Stiya is not meant to be only a Pueblo but any Indian girl on a degraded reservation yearning for deliverance from filth and savagery. Miss Burgess will send several copies to her parents tomorrow, imagining her father's pride, her mother's sense of vindication upon receiving them. For this is not romance, the stuff of calendar art and swooning poetry, but a clear-eyed moral tale, *founded*, as the inscription on the title page declares, *on the author's actual observations.*

Her mother, long-suffering, wrenched from a comfortable life in the East to serve as a model of behavior at the raw agency outpost, ridiculed, misunderstood, eventually revered. Her mother, who took a stand, who set a bar for civility, insisting that the Pawnee men must don a shirt to enter the agency building to receive their government handouts, and the proudest of them, a recalcitrant old pagan, only holding out two months before he conceded.

The book will touch hearts and alter attitudes, she hopes, as has the work of her hero, Mrs. Stowe. Would that it be as widely recognized—and not for personal glory. The author is listed as Embe, and only the cleverest cryptologist will find a connection to M. B. and therefore Marianna Burgess. Her mother's dilemma, attempting to civilize children who every evening returned to dens of ignorance and superstition, must not be allowed to continue. *Other seeds fell among thorns, and the thorns grew up and choked them*—

Miss Burgess pulls out a single copy, admiring its modest girth, the font she has chosen, and again the smell of it. I will sit now, she thinks, and compile a list of everyone who must read this—

On Friday nights Reverend Talmadge leads a Bible study class for the students who are either pagan or rather hazy as to which denomination they subscribe to, boys on one side of the aisle, girls on the other.

"Isaac and Rebekah had two sons," says the reverend, standing behind the pulpit, "the elder named Esau, and the younger Jacob."

There are a few of the Roman persuasion among them, he knows, and hopes to make a convert or two before the good fathers at St. Patrick's discover their presence at the school. Catholics, as a rule, have very little knowledge of the Old Testament—

"Esau was a man of the woods, and fond of hunting with his bow and arrow"—of course the Book does not elaborate on what exact weapons Esau carried, but one must make the stories *real* to these children of darkness—"while Jacob was quiet and thoughtful, staying at home and caring for the flocks of his father."

Trouble sits in the big room with the benches and boards that you have to kneel on sometimes, vaguely listening to the sounds the white man makes and turning the papers in the thick book he has been given to hold. There are drawings in it, and some of them seem to tell part of a story—

"Isaac, the father, loved Esau because he brought home that which he had killed for the table—"

Trouble turns the paper and there is a drawing of a terrible creature—something like a man, but with a bright red hide, with horns and eyes like a mountain goat, hooves like a deer, and the long, black, forked tongue of a snake. Trouble is so shocked by it that he makes a sound and has to look up to be sure the white man behind the long box did not hear him.

Asa, sitting beside him, sees the drawing of the creature and leans close to whisper in his ear.

"*El Satanás*."

There is a name for it. The white people must keep it somewhere, maybe chained around the neck like their vicious dogs, to kill their enemies, tearing them apart—

"But Re*bek*ah," says Reverend Talmadge, "loved Jacob, because he was wise, and diligent in his work—"

A few minutes before *Taps*, Trouble is still pacing the room like a trapped coyote, telling them something important in Lakota. His roommates hurry to take their uniforms off, worried that the sound will carry. Trouble has been upset since he came back from Bible study, throwing his shoes against the wall when he pulled them off, waving his arms as he shouts.

"*El Diablo*," Asa explains to Smokey and Antoine. "*Él ha visto el Diablo en la biblia*."

"*Diablo* is devil," says Antoine, who recognizes it from *le diable* in French. "Was the reverend going on about the devil?"

"He's talking about the hunt."

Trouble stops abruptly as Clarence Regal steps into the room.

"He's bragging about how he killed his first and only buffalo in the White Mother's country—that's Canada. It was only a calf, but he brought it down from horseback, with one shot, and then cut its liver out and ate it while it was still hot." Clarence moves to stand directly in front of Trouble, who seems ready to fight if need be. "I left home before I got the chance to kill mine."

Regal puts a hand on Trouble's shoulder, looks him in the eye. That tongue is forbidden here, he says in Lakota. You have to learn—

The mornings are starting to be chilly. Willy Lavadore hurries out with his bugle in hand and finds Mr. Skinner at his post beneath the flagpole, watching one of the new boys, a Sioux, standing in the center of the parade ground holding two thick Bibles straight out from his shoulders. His arms are beginning to shake.

"What did he do?"

"Broke the language rule."

"How long will you keep him there?"

"Student discipline. It's up to his officers."

The boy's arms falter, then straighten. Willy has never been disciplined, learning early what the infractions are and steering clear of them. With only one other Walla Walla here and that not somebody he likes, there has been little opportunity or temptation to speak Wallula. The boy's arms begin to sag.

"Maybe it's just till *Reveille*," Willy suggests.

Skinner grins. "Then you'd better blow your horn."

Antoine sits in history class with Grace just across the row from him. He can feel her nearness in his stomach. Cato Goforth stands reading from their textbook, *A History of the United States* by Horace Scudder, while the instructor, Mr. Gelder, stands at parade rest by the columns he has written on the chalkboard.

CIVILIZATION	SAVAGERY
FAMILY	POLYGAMY
CLEANLINESS	FILTH
PRIVATE PROPERTY	SOCIALISM
INDIVIDUALISM	TRIBALISM

"*—and they died out rapidly under the cruelty of the Spaniards,*" reads Cato.

INDUSTRY	LAZINESS
AGRICULTURE	HUNTING
WEALTH	POTLATCH
CHRISTIAN	PAGAN

—read the columns. Antoine broods over the word "savagery." He remembers Sister Ursula using it, describing the Slaughter of the Innocents by King Herod—

"*Negroes were brought from the coast of Africa, and though at first few in number, their labor was found so profitable that the number was constantly increased. At last the Indian disappeared—the hardier Negro slave had taken his place.*"

"Very well put, Mr. Goforth," says the instructor. "You may be seated."

It is very quiet in the classroom. Antoine glances to see Grace, her face impassive. Mr. Gelder spreads his arms the way Jesus does in pictures of Him addressing His flock.

"History," he intones, "is the story of man's progress from savagery to barbarism, and then from barbarism to civilization."

Antoine raises his hand, a first for him here at the Carlisle School.

"What is it?"

"So are we savages or barbarians?"

Most of the class laughs. But Grace, he can see, is shocked—

"You, Mr. LaMere, are im*per*tinent. Present yourself to the disciplinarian."

Sweetcorn is always seated at the rear in secondary English. He knows it's because he has grown so large that his presence is intimidating to the teachers. Or embarrassing. Still in what they're calling the sixth grade, boys and girls who barely come up to his chest in some of the other seats, all struggling with the same tics and twitches of the white man's language.

"I go to *the* bank," says Miss Vetch. "We mustn't forget our articles."

Students do not go to *the* bank, actually. The money they earn from their trades, from their farm wages when on Outing, are received by the school. Some of this is sent to their parents, if they have parents, and the rest kept in an account they may draw from at the school's whim. Sweetcorn, constantly on discipline, has barely been allowed to touch his for the last two years.

"When you leave you'll be happy we've held it for you," he is told.

There are two good things about this class. The first is that Wilma Pretty Weasel is in it, only four seats in front of him. The other is that Miss Vetch has to turn her back to tap with her pointer at what she has written on the chalkboard.

"And of course it is '*I* go to the bank,' not '*Me* go to bank.'"

She turns to the board and Sweetcorn pokes the boy in front of him, handing him the note he's written. The boy quickly passes it forward, the note deftly hidden just before Miss Vetch turns to them again. It is the wonder of writing, thinks Sweetcorn, the most valuable thing he has been forced to learn here. That a young Lakota man can communicate in a common language with a young Absaroka woman, without either uttering a sound—

"We say '*He* gave *it* to *me*,'" says Miss Vetch, turning back to the board and tapping words with her pointer. "Let's look at the order in that sentence—"

The note is passed up to Wilma, and he can see her glance at it. A simple question, and she'll either be there or she won't. What they started before she went home for the summer—

"And conversely, '*I* gave *it* to *her*—'"

Sweetcorn remembers when his oldest brother was after one of the Iron Eagle girls. Wasaka would wrap himself in a buffalo robe, for it was winter, folding it over his head and around his face so only his eyes were uncovered, passing, late in the evening but before the light of their fire had gone out, by the tipi she lived in with her parents and sisters and leave something he had trapped or killed just outside the flap, brushing slightly against the skins of the tent so they'd know it was there. He'd crouch behind another tipi close by then, stones in hand to discourage nosy camp dogs, and wait. Sometime before the sun dropped completely below the horizon her father would come out, stretching his arms and legs and yawning, then feign surprise at the dead animal at his feet. He'd turn to send a question inside—Someone has left us a gift. Should we accept it?—and there would be female voices inside and some giggling as the younger sisters teased the eligible one. When the girl did not protest, her father would pick up the beast by the legs or the tail and bring it inside. A brace of prairie hens before snow covered the ground, several rabbits, a marten with a glossy pelt, a small deer. Sweetcorn's father, badly wounded while raiding the Crow, was no longer able to hunt, and as Wasaka was responsible for feeding the family he was constantly out looking for game. For her part, the Iron Eagle girl spoke to him only once, at the edges of the firelight during a dance the whole band were present for, her face as hidden by her blanket and shawl as his by the buffalo robe.

She told him she wasn't getting any younger, and that her father kept telling the story of offering a full-grown bear, killed by him with arrow and lance, to win the first of his wives.

Wasaka convinced his best friend, Chapa, to go on a raid with him. They had done this before, but never in the winter, when it would be so easy to follow their trail. They told nobody of their plan, just went missing from the camp one morning, and Sweetcorn remembers slogging on snowshoes to check the trapline Wasaka had laid out, and having to kill a furious badger with a club that seemed far too small for the purpose. The young men returned after several weeks, the snow beginning to melt, with eight horses stolen from the

Crow. Wilma's tribe. The entire band came out to honor the two young warriors, who looked like skeletons, and that night Wasaka, with no robe covering his face, led the finest of the Crow ponies to the tipi of his intended, both her mother and father stepping out to accept it, calling him son and settling the marriage.

Sweetcorn remembers it as the hungriest winter.

Miss Vetch demonstrates possessive pronouns. Wilma doesn't turn in her seat. It is a very simple sentence, falling under the heading of what the instructor would term "the inquisitive."

Same place—tonight?

Captain Pratt stares at Antoine from behind his massive desk. Antoine can feel the disciplinarian's breath on his neck.

"Mr. Gelder confirms the boy's version of the incident," says Skinner.

The Captain lets Antoine stew for a long moment before speaking.

"Irony," he says finally, "is beyond the grasp of most of our students here—I am impressed with your command of the English language."

Antoine looks straight ahead the way Clarence and Jesse have taught them. Superior officers are not to be stared at—

"Why have you come to Carlisle, Mr. LaMere?"

The way the Captain says it, it sounds like a real question, not an accusation. Antoine proceeds cautiously.

"So my family will get the land they deserve. My father is half white—"

"*My* father was murdered, returning from the California gold rush, when I was nine years old," says the Captain. "I went to work to support my mother and younger brothers."

Antoine has no answer for this. The Captain stands, looking down at him now, then crosses to gaze out his window at the parade ground.

"Do you believe that your people should continue as they did a century ago? Living in darkness, slaughtering their enemy—"

"You people done some slaughter to each other."

It is out before he can consider his situation. Pratt turns to look at him again, eyebrows raised—

"You are correct. I fought at Chickamauga—and hope never again to witness such tragic *waste* of life."

With the nuns, thinks Antoine, punishment was swift and uncomplicated. Their world was not a subtle place, with room for debate—

Who made the world?

God made the world.

Who is God?

God is the creator of Heaven and Earth, and of all things.

What is man?

Man is a creature composed of body and soul, and made to the image and likeness of God.

"An injustice concerning your land allotment has occurred, perhaps," says the Captain. "Nevertheless, here you are and here you shall remain. The only question being—what will you make of your time at Carlisle, young man? And more importantly, what will you make of your *life*?"

The change-of-class bell echoes across the parade ground. Captain Pratt sits down again and looks to the papers on his desk.

"Attempt to harness your wit when questioning your instructors, Mr. LaMere. Dismissed."

Asa works the crank with one hand while guiding the section uppers leather under the needle with the other, following the line he has drawn on it. He has always been good with his hands, carving, tying knots, thatching roofs. Not so adept as his mother, who can weave baskets of yucca and devil's claw with beautiful designs—leaping deer or desert runners or just repeating shapes—without an array of tools like those that surround him. Asa snips the leather free, ties the thread off, then takes up his cobbler's hammer to gently tap the new seam flat on the anvil. He has a picture of all the various pieces in his head now, heel, sole, insole, uppers, and how they will come together. One day Mr. Woodcock ranged them in a long line, assigning each boy one task of the many needed to fix a heel to a sole, the pieces moving front to rear from one boy at his station to the next. Asa soon tired of his part, tapping tiny nails in, but at the end of the session they had quite a pile ready for the next stage of the process.

"You now have a taste of manufacturing," Mr. Woodcock told them before the bell rang, one of the Pueblo boys later translating it into Spanish for Asa in a whisper. "But here I train *art*isans."

White people love shoes, he now understands, even nailing iron ones to the hooves of their horses and mules. He has seen *rancheros* ride by on beautiful horses, always wearing beautiful boots, with spurs that shine like silver attached to the heels. Every time he picks up the wooden lasts, one for the left, one for the right, he thinks of the story his father told him of the Pueblo people to the east of the Tohono, who rebelled against the rule of the *conquistadores*, chasing them from their land for a spell. But then the *españoles* came back with more soldiers, and as a punishment, the right foot of every Pueblo man and boy able to lift a weapon was cut off, leaving them a nation of *cohos*, limping men.

It is the worst punishment short of death Asa can think of.

Mr. Woodcock, the Shoe Man, has shown them pictures of the various styles that are made for white people, including the strange-shaped, brightly colored things their women put on their feet. Asa still dislikes the ones he is required to wear, the soles and heels too thick to properly feel the ground beneath him. But now that he has seen the hard stone streets in the town on the other side of the high fence, he understands the need for them, and is happy he is learning to make something useful.

Asa picks up the vamp and the toe cap he has cut, folding them over the wooden last to see that they will fit together without further trimming. Time passes rapidly when you've been put to building the whole thing yourself, whereas the trade period in which they were made to do only one task over and over seemed never to end. He has helped his father put up lodges several times, and there it is the task you are doing at the moment as well as the picture in your mind of what must come next, and then next, and then next, till the structure is sturdy enough to stand before the wind. They worked together at the same careful, steady pace, and Asa feels a regret that this is such a solitary trade, each boy at his own little bench, only the instructor allowed to speak and he more likely to demonstrate with his hands. Asa has spent long hours watching ants build their homes, carrying bits of this and that, only occasionally bumping together and touching the tiny sticks on their heads, unaffected by the desert sun at its most brutal. But ants seem to be of one mind, whereas here at the school he is as alone among the throng as if he were lost atop a great mountain, seeing much, but too far away for anyone to hear if he should cry out. The English words, one by one, are beginning to have meaning, Smokey and LaMere regularly holding things up and saying the name of them for him. At night before he can sleep he tries to picture everything in the room and whisper its English name.

Asa stares at the toe cap and vamp, trying to envision the way they are supposed to be joined together.

Shoes. He can say "shoes."

Free time.

Jesse Echohawk cradles the football in his arms. He has seen several games at Dickinson College in the middle of town and has memorized the rules. Mr. Gault, the athletics instructor, has begged from that institution the little equipment Jesse and the other boys carry on their way to the playing field between the dormitories and the trade shops, stating that it is "an all-American sport" that they should learn to play. Jesse loves the combination of strength, speed, and strategy the game requires, loves the rough-and-tumble of it, so like the games he and the other little boys used to invent back home, games where a scraped knee or bloody nose was a badge of honor, games the Quaker agents had discouraged. He likes the smell of the cowhide ball, likes the satisfying crunch when he puts his shoulder into a running opponent, likes the way the ball spins end over end when it is kicked through the wooden uprights of the goal. A player from Dickinson, their best running back, is coming by today to give some pointers.

They come upon Clarence Regal and some of the other older boys choosing lacrosse sticks from a pile.

"Care to try a man's game?" he calls to his friend.

"Too much like war for me," says Clarence.

The football boys move on. Clarence sees the sullen Lakota boy in A Company, Trouble, watching them shyly, sitting on the grass by the small boy's dormitory. He waves his stick, calls out—

"You play, Trouble?"

The boy considers for a moment, then stands and walks over to take the stick, hefting it in both hands.

"Trubba play," he says—

—while Antoine sits on the edge of the bandstand, watching the boys at their liberty spread out on the parade ground, brooding over his talk with Captain Pratt. They are great ones for planning, white people. He has not, as a matter of fact, given a thought to his future, only to surviving this place day by day, and to spending as much time as he can with Grace Metoxen, even if it means remembering poetry. He sees the two boys who always run go by in the distance, moving at a good pace next to the high fence—and today there is a third, only a few strides behind them. It is Asa, gliding along effortlessly, running in bare feet with his shoes tied together and hanging around his neck.

Afraid somebody will steal them.

If an Ojibwe boy marries an Oneida girl, Antoine wonders, and they aren't Hiawatha or Minnehaha, where do they live?

Grace is not thinking of marriage, but of croquet.

Her favorite thing is the sound the ball makes when you hit it with the mallet. Wood on wood, satisfying chock! Miss Ely taught them the game, which she said was both engaging and ladylike. Grace tries to think of where you could play it at home, but the idea of a flat lawn dedicated to croquet somehow doesn't fit. Wilma doesn't like it because she is so tall and she says the mallets are too short, making you bend over. Wilma says she thinks she would be good at baseball if they'd just let her try, but girls playing baseball is one of the things that "just isn't done." Lizzie Cloud sends a good, strong shot toward the middle wicket, rolling short but coming to rest just touching Grace's yellow ball.

"You're mine," says Lizzie.

Lizzie is very sweet but she loves to win. She places her foot on top of her orange ball and gives it a tremendous wallop, sending Grace's ball skidding across the grass, then rolling over the walkway to rest on the edges of the boy's playing space.

"You're heartless," Grace says to her friend. In the spring at home as a little girl there were chasing games and dolls and a game where you made a hoop and kept it rolling with a stick. But her favorite thing was night fishing on the lake, their entire village out in sturdy canoes, each with a flaming torch or two carried in the boat, which both attracted fish and kept people from bumping into each other. She loved the stars above in the black sky and the reflection of the torches on the black water, loved the joking and shouting from boat to boat, the cheering when someone would spear a walleye. When she was old enough Grace was given a paddle to help steer around the edges of the lake, and sometimes when they already had plenty of fish two canoes would just be pulled alongside each other for a visit. The spearers had to be careful because the water was still really cold, and the big fish would be boarded writhing and flapping on the spear, so you had to be ready to duck.

Lizzie takes her second bonus turn but only hits the edge of the wicket, so it is Grace's turn again. Some boys on the lawn beyond her are playing a rough game of lacrosse, and she watches for a few moments before addressing her ball. If you swing too hard you're likely to mishit the ball and it won't go straight or far. The best technique, she has found, is to choose the exact spot on the side of the ball where you want the center of the mallet head to hit, and then keep looking at that spot even after the ball is knocked away. If you look up to where you want it to go it will never get there. It is a special kind of concentration, like how her brothers showed her that in spearing fish in the shallows in the daytime you had to know how the water could trick you at certain angles and the fish actually be inches ahead or behind where it seemed to be. She swings her mallet back, then drives it through the ball, staring at the spot where it used to be. When she does look up it has traveled across the walk, rolling to a stop only a few feet in front of the center wicket. She strolls back to where it lies, pleased with herself, her mallet resting at an angle over her shoulder—

—as Trouble snatches the ball from the air. He is unclear about which of the boys are on his side and which are not, all of them from different tribes yet wearing the same uniform clothes, so he only runs not to be knocked down. Runs and ducks and dodges and feints and changes speed, pressing the ball in the netting against his chest when he has to slam into someone sideways, once even faking like he is going to pass it to another, evading them all until he comes to the walkway at the end of the grass and hurls the ball straight up into the air.

There is a cheer from the girls' side of the parade ground.

Trouble leans on his stick, breathing hard, feeling good for the first time since he's been here. Clarence Regal retrieves the ball and flips it back to the others, shooting him an amused look. On the far side of the fence, a train, westbound from the way the sound curves, blasts its whistle as it pulls out of the station—

People still respond to the uniform, especially here in the East. Though the Captain occasionally discovered white Southerners under his command after the Great Tragedy, the average Virginian, say, would rather swallow arsenic than serve under "the Yankee flag." Some wounds run deep, and he has been encouraged here at the school by how quickly students from tribes that are sworn enemies come to tolerate or even befriend each other. The Sioux, because of their number, have formed a bit of a clique, as did the Kiowa back at the Castillo, but here they fraternize only in the English tongue or are punished. Perhaps if white children of the two sections, north and south, could somehow be brought together under the same roof—

No—it will take a common enemy.

The Captain checks himself in the mirror they brought up from St. Augustine, the imperfections of the glass kindly softening his facial crevices. The dress coat still fits him without having too much alteration, though he is grateful he'll have the pulpit to stand behind tonight. He was not trained as a speaker, was, in fact, rather critical of those officers inordinately fond of their own voices, and it has been a necessarily rapid study, rather like a drowning man learning to swim. His greatest skill as a military officer was always his attention to detail, leaving nothing to discretion—make the rules clear and enforce them with neither fear nor favor. He did, unlike many of his military peers, ex*plain* to his soldiers, black and white, and to his Indian scouts, the reasoning behind their orders, often boiling it down to, "If you don't do this properly you won't *eat*, or you'll freeze when winter comes, or you'll end up dead and mutilated on the prairie"—which during the various tribal uprisings was no exaggeration.

Explain, but never apologize.

The Captain is still troubled by the Ojibwe boy brought to him today. Obviously very clever, with real academic potential, but intent, it seems, on swimming against the current. He'll make a point tonight to observe that *selfishness* is one of the habits the Carlisle School is hoping to inculcate in these children, coming as they do from a culture not especially acquisitive, unless it be in the glory associated with stealing the enemy's horses. A culture in which land, until the Dawes legislation takes full effect, is not surveyed to fix boundaries and passed from father to son. The white mind struggles to comprehend a concept of land held not by recorded deed but by habit and force of arms, with all members of a tribe free to roam about it at whim. Territory was not won during the Indian wars as it was during the Great Tragedy, with generals of the Grand Old Army sure to garrison prized southern ports and cities before moving on, and the red man's lifetime of pulling up sticks to pursue war, better weather, or the whim of a passing buffalo herd was key to their early advantage. Their inevitable downfall was that they were fighting against soldiers who were far from home and hearth, most of them without children, and therefore only vulnerable for their own lives. Sand Creek, the Washita River, Camp Grant—unconscionable slaughters, but no doubt lessons impressed on the savage mind. *These people will kill us all if they need to.*

But the sound of cannons will be absent tonight. The speech must befit the audience—one for his military brethren, one for railroad barons and politickers, and one for those gentle citizens with minds open enough to reconsider their idea of the red man and his worth—and, perhaps, the cynical naysayers at their elbow.

As his Pawnee scouts used to say, even those who stop their ears with dirt can see your lips move.

Mrs. Pratt calls from the next room that Jasper is waiting with their carriage. Time to shake the money tree.

Seven o'clock, the sun down an hour ago, Antoine stands at attention next to the stone guardhouse with four of the other A Company boys.

"Night guard is very simple," Clarence Regal tells them. "Nobody unauthorized enters the school grounds or leaves them. Any students caught away from quarters after lights-out are to be apprehended and reported for court-martial."

He does the little stroll past them, chin lifted, that he uses for inspection. Antoine doesn't suspect the older boy of enforcing school rules just to be cruel, but he certainly seems to be*lieve* in them, being extra tough on the Sioux boys like Trouble—

"I will be checking you at your posts," says the master sergeant. "Remember that you will be allowed to sleep late tomorrow. I want to find you awake, a*lert*, and standing on two feet. *Vig*ilance, people. To your posts!"

Antoine walks to the old gymnasium building. They have been given heavy old Henrys to carry, real rifles but with the triggers removed to discourage playacting during their watch. Without more specific orders, he decides to walk his post between the gymnasium and the carriage house to the rhythm of trochaic tetrameter—

"*Laughing answered Hiawatha*," he utters softly as he paces, rifle shouldered—

"*For that reason, if no other*
Would I wed the fair Dacotah,
That our tribes might be united—"

—while Miss Redbird sits amidst the sympathetic citizens, listening to the Captain hold forth from the pulpit. There is a Presbyterian sparsity to the religious decoration, no saints bleeding on the walls or window glass, and the bare wooden kneelers look suitably punishing. The pulpit is raised from the floor, augmenting Pratt's command of the high ground, a sounding board above him to enhance his baritone. He is a direct and self-confident speaker—

"I am often asked my opinion of the Dawes Act," he says, "and I do believe that the allotment of parcels to individual Indians is preferable to *tri*bal ownership of the land."

Will they really allow her mother to choose her eighty acres of land, most of which is fit only for grazing, from what is left of the reservation? And if they check the birth records and discover that Miss Redbird's blood quantum is half white, will she be "detribalized"? All she is certain of is that the law will eventually lead to Indians losing half or more of the wind-scoured wasteland they've been pushed onto.

"But better still would be *no* free land for the Indian until he masters the act of modern agriculture! Too often the allotted terrain lies unplowed, unused, until the law allows its lease to white men. This may seem harsh, but only when the Indian strikes *bottom* will he lift himself up!"

Were I prostrate on the ground, thinks Miss Redbird, and Captain Pratt resting a foot on my back, I shouldn't be able lift myself up an inch. Merely the weight of one booted foot—

"Our mission at the Carlisle School is to baptize the Indian youth in the waters of civilization—and to hold him under until he is thoroughly soaked!"

Miss Burgess, sitting alone in the first row tonight with Annie off on Outing business, is relieved to hear the laughter. Though well-heeled, few of those in the audience tonight will have sent their own offspring away to boarding schools, their flesh and blood too precious to banish for much of the year. But if they understand the pernicious environment her students have escaped—in fact, if they had read her *book*—

"We must wean our students from the degrading socialism of the reservation system and awaken his *wants*—we not only give him *pockets*, but the desire to *fill* them!"

Another appreciative laugh from the listeners. Miss Redbird looks around at them—more women than men, devout, she is certain, in a very public way, who might as well be thrilling to a tale of Sumatran tigers, though the subjects of Pratt's peroration dwell just on the other side of that ten-foot wooden fence—

"Only that kind of individual thinking, that kind of *self*ishness, will give him the motive to compete in the greater society which he can no longer avoid. Does it work? Living in Philadelphia today are three of our alumni, one a printer, one a boilermaker, and one an apothecary with his own business—and all, I might add, happily married to white women."

Miss Redbird savors the audible gasp from the congregation. Ladies are bewildered. The Captain shows them no quarter—

"Let me remind you of the long tradition of white trappers and traders taking a squaw as a wife—the chiefs of many of the so-called Five Civilized Tribes being the descendants of such unions."

Miss Redbird wonders if her own father, a man she has no memory of, thought he was "taking a squaw." Still, this Captain Pratt is a rare one—

"For are we not all brothers, created by the same Lord?"

—even Mrs. Gutchel, obese and narcoleptic, who snores. Each evening she sits in a rocker under the dim but steady electric bulb, new this year in the girls' dormitory and so much safer than the old gaslights, the same copy of *Hidden Hand* in her lap, fingers of her right hand holding her place as she first closes her eyes, then lets her massive gray head loll back into slumber. She is usually sawing logs before the young ladies on her floor can fall asleep, leading to a great deal of giggling and some unauthorized visiting from room to room. Tonight it is Wilma, boldly padding around the matron on her way to the already half-open first floor window. If seen she will only ask the matron, politely, to muffle her thunder—the young ladies muster at the crack of dawn and need their rest. But she reaches the window undetected, takes a look outside, eases it up a few more inches, and slips out into the night—

—as the small boys sit cross-legged on the floor, Fannie Noble reading to them with a trio of candles on a low stool lighting the text. It is past their lights-out, but there was a surprise inspection this evening, which, though they passed with flying colors, pre-empted their usual story time. Miss Noble is amazed at the condition of their teeth—though none confess to have either brushed or rinsed them with vinegar before coming here, there is none of the rot you'd see among boys of similar age at a city settlement house. When she worked at the Home for Little Wanderers the children were required to wear their toothbrushes around their necks on a string, allegedly to keep them from being lost or stolen, but she suspects it was meant to advertise their wretchedness, the way you'd tag a sick cow to keep it separate from the herd.

"*From some distance we saw a boy trying to leap a pony over a gate: the pony would not take the leap,*" she reads softly, "*and the boy cut him with the whip—*"

Perhaps a third of them have no English at all, she knows, but they follow her every word. She has shown them the little cameo of Black Beauty on the cover, and they know that it is the autobiography of a horse "Translated from the Equine." One of the boys, called Jefferson here, has told her that his real name in Osage means Black Pony and that he is closely related to the Horse Tribe—

"*—but he only turned off to one side. He whipped him again but the pony turned off to the other side. Then the boy got off and gave him a hard thrashing—*"

—and Antoine can see the faint glow of those candles in the second-story window of the boys' dormitory, but assumes it is the matron's doing and not his responsibility. He pivots, heads back toward the gymnasium, still muttering in cadence—

"*After many years of warfare*
Many years of strife and bloodshed

There is peace between Ojibways
And the tribe of the Dacotahs—"

If those old wars he has heard about from family and learned of in the classroom were still inflamed—Seneca and Delaware, the Creek and Choctaw, Ojibwe and Lakota, the Comanche and almost everybody—there could certainly be no peace here at Carlisle. When Smokey asked him what the word for just plain "Indian" was in Ojibwe, he could not think of it. If a white man was to lump Ojibwe people together with Ottawa or Potawatomi people, it might be acceptable, but to consider his mother as a sister to a Mohawk woman—

Somebody is moving behind the girls' dormitory. He considers calling out, then lowers his rifle to port arms and hurries, crouching slightly, to catch up with them.

A girl, wearing a cape like a shawl to cover her head, strides quickly to the carriage barn. A crack of dim light as somebody opens the door to let her in.

Antoine hugs close to a utility shed, lowers himself to one knee, planting the rifle butt in the ground in front of him to lean on. He'll wait—

—as Wilma steps up onto the seat of the open carriage. A lit lantern, partially hooded by a scrap of old leather, sits on the driver's bench. Sweetcorn bars the door, and comes to join Wilma, nestling close and putting his arm around her.

"How do you like my wheels?"

"It doesn't have any."

The carriage body, nearly finished, rests atop four wooden crates.

"Even better," smiles Sweetcorn. "We won't have to look at the back end of a horse."

They had come together at the end of the last school year, meeting twice in the bakery after hours, when Sweetcorn had stolen a key. Wilma sat on a cloth on the edge of the big roll-out table and they kissed and talked and kissed and almost did more. She was terrified she'd get telltale flour marks on her uniform, no amount of cleanup after the workday able to deal with all the fine dust that hung in the air and settled every night. There were stacked bags of flour on the floor to lie on but they were like boulders—nothing nearly as comfortable as the cushioned seat they share at the moment.

"I missed you."

He may have missed her, but he certainly didn't *write*, though that is not surprising. Mail in and out of Carlisle is not private, and Wilma carefully folds and stashes the notes he has passed her, including today's, in her most secret hiding place.

He kisses her again—she had forgotten about the tongues.

"What did you do all summer?" she asks, pulling her head back for a moment.

"Worked on a farm near here," he says. "Got in a little trouble."

"Of course you did."

"And I didn't look at a single girl."

She has to laugh at this. He is unbuttoning things, much quicker and adept at that than she is at buttoning them back up again.

"It was bad at home."

"They made fun of you for coming here?"

"No—just the reservation. People don't know how to be."

Sweetcorn shrugs. "Take it one day at a time."

"You haven't learned anything here."

"Not from the teachers."

Sweetcorn has learned quite a bit in a very short while from the black stoker, whose name is Otis Gamble and who never stops talking as he flings coal into the furnaces, thrilled to have an audience. He has learned where in town the house where you can pay for girls is, and how much it costs for what, learned some of the best things to say to the girls who you can't pay for but can maybe have, learned that if you just keep *at* it "they likely stop sittin' on it and get busy."

"Mmmm," he says. "You grown in all the right places."

It's not that it doesn't feel good, doesn't make her head spin. But the things that can happen—

"I hate it here," she tells him. "The minute I walked over from the train and saw these buildings again—"

"Ask to go on Outing. You've never done that before."

"But I'll be far away."

"Not so far I can't find you. You think I'm going to last another year here?"

Sweetcorn has been on Outing often and always they said he is a good worker, some even saying if he comes back unconnected to the school they'll raise his wages. It will really be his own money then, all of it, to do whatever he likes with. And if he doesn't get along with a farmer he can tell him to go eat alfalfa and then take to the road. If he renounces his tribe, the new law says, at least the way he understands it, he gives up whatever sorry patch of stinkweed they'd allot him back home and the government will owe him nothing—but he'll be an American, even if not a white one.

"Is the work hard?"

"For girls? No. You might have to learn how to milk a cow."

She is in his lap now. The other girls say things and shake their heads when he walks by, but she knows they think he is the handsomest, the strongest—

The light from the lantern flickers, goes out. It is very dark. It will be easier, she thinks, the first time, in the dark.

Miss Redbird is taking her time walking back from the church, mulling the evening's entertainment, when her name is called out. A liveried black man at the reins of an open, two-horse phaeton, and yes—that is Captain Pratt seated shoulder to shoulder beside him.

"Would you care for a ride back to the school?"

The Captain reaches to help her up onto the carriage step, and she finds herself sitting on plush leather next to Miss Burgess. The phaeton begins to roll.

"Our boys made this rig," the Captain calls back to her.

"Very impressive."

"I thought it went swimmingly tonight, don't you?"

"There were donations?"

"Very handsome, very generous."

"Then it was a success."

She remembers her last trip home, riding a hay wagon half a day from the train stop and her mother coming to the door of her little shack, long-faced and not taking a step to greet her till she could explain in Lakota that no, the wild-haired, gap-toothed white man of indeterminate age on the buckboard beside her was not her new husband, merely an employee of the feed store paid to bring her to the reservation. That ride, made over rutted roads, cattle trails, and dry washes, had hammered her spine unmercifully, whereas this feels like they are floating.

"It's so smooth," she calls. She can only see the backs of the two men through the front opening, lamps mounted on either side of them.

"Double set of springs," calls the Captain. "Laminated."

When Miss Burgess joins the conversation there is an edge to her voice.

"Do you think it wise, Captain," she asks, "in that particular setting, to so emphasize the aspect of race mixing?"

"The boys have married well—what of it?"

"I think you may have upset some of our supporters."

"If there is to be any progress in this country," he says evenly, without turning, "they'll have to accept the inevitable. These terrible things I read of lynchings in the South—"

"Those men committed outrages—"

"*Pos*sibly. But how many white men have violated Negro women over the years, and gone without the least punishment?"

Miss Burgess is shocked, Miss Redbird fascinated—

"But when we sent those Shinnecock children home—"

"It was because they were too Negro in physical aspect. It had nothing to do with their value or capabilities. We are the Carlisle *In*dian Industrial School. Had they appeared too white I would have sent them away as well."

Miss Burgess is not mollified, but concedes the round. "You've given me something to think about, Captain."

Pratt turns then to smile in at them. "Then I shall consider my little peroration a success."

Antoine can see the cracks between the boards in the carriage barn, and then he can't when the light inside goes out. He hears, no, *feels* something behind him.

"You're out of your sector, private."

It is Clarence standing over him, hands on hips. Antoine hurries to his feet, fumbles as he shoulders the rifle. Whoever is in the barn, they're in the master sergeant's hands now.

"I was just—just—"

"Rehearsing your lines. I heard you."

"There's so much to remember. And I've never been up in front of a lot of people before."

"You'll be the noblest of savages," says Clarence Regal, then turns and walks away from Antoine, walks away, knowingly, from the carriage barn and whatever is happening inside of it.

Smokey has taken to calling him the Great Mystery.

THE PINE RIDGE SIOUX, being the most recently aggrieved, have taken to the prophecy most aggressively. Pressed, and finally giving in last year to relinquish half their lands, their bands then relegated to six different reservations, they have much to be angry about. McGillycuddy, despite his constant sparring with the formidable Red Cloud, built an efficient Indian police force here and never in his seven-year tenure as agent suffered an outbreak or called for bluecoat soldiers. But when the Democrats took Washington in '86 he was replaced by Colonel Gallagher, under whom the morale of the Indian police and the well-being of the general population deteriorated slowly but steadily. Though not personally responsible for the late or nonpayment of cash annuities, the cutting of food rations nearly in half, and the shoddy nature of many of the commodities issued as per treaty—bacon, beans, beef, coffee, sugar, flour, salt, soap—Gallagher failed to become their advocate. As Indians may not vote, Congress feels no responsibility to deal fairly with them, so when northern beef was replaced with Texas steers, weighed to meet the contract limits prior to being driven from that state and then losing hundreds of pounds on the journey, he urged his charges to make do. And now even Gallagher has resigned and been replaced by the regrettable Royer, who the Sioux here have quickly saddled with the moniker *Lakota Kokipa-Koshkala*—Young Man Afraid of Indians.

Miss Goodale, as fetching and as oblivious to her own charms as ever, was here on an inspection tour when the Ethnographer arrived, and took him aside for a warning.

"This new one is a disaster," she said, "and the people are destitute."

But he is here for observation, not politics.

The medicine men have regained some of their prominence, of course, now that redemption is rumored to be in the hands of higher powers, and the old rituals are observed with their former care. The men have fasted for a full day, then retired to sweat lodges built of willow branches, covered with blankets now that buffalo robes have become so rare, the crawlspace meant for entry and egress facing east with a buffalo skull set just outside of it, an offering of tobacco hung on a pole, sage grass covering the floor. Medicine men and their apprentices are waiting to ferry in fire-heated rocks, which are quickly transferred into a hole dug in the center of the lodge and water poured over them to make steam. The Ethnographer has survived one such experience, feeling, once the fear of suffocation had abated, both physically and spiritually cleansed.

Once the purification has been achieved, the men come out to have their foreheads and cheeks anointed with sacred red paint—circles, crescents, and crosses representing the sun, the moon, and the morning star. Thoroughly rubbed with sweetgrass, they are ready to don their ghost shirts.

These have evolved as the Ethnographer has traveled eastward. As deer hide is now a rare commodity, most are fashioned from cloth, the rougher the better, it seems, sewn together with sinew, as the white man's thread reeks of manufacture. The shirts are decorated with random eagles, arrows, symbols with personal significance, and worn all the time, whether under other clothing now that it is winter or out for all the world to see.

The Ethnographer sits on a camp chair next to William Selwyn, the very able Yankton Sioux postal officer recently dismissed by Royer in the usual purge of employees when parties switch position in Washington. That none of the new appointees have a whit of experience, or, from Miss Goodale's perspective, *in*terest in the job, is sadly typical of the Indian Bureau.

The opening formalities have begun. The dances on Pine Ridge have mostly been here at No Water's camp on White Clay Creek, the Ethnographer invited to observe after an interview with Short Bull and Kicking Bear, Brulé apostles who have come over from the Rosebud Agency to spread the gospel. Short Bull, who has visited the Messiah twice now, has had a few tense confrontations with Wright at Rosebud, the agent wishing to remove him as well as Crow Dog as bad influences. McLaughlin at Standing Rock wishes Sitting Bull transported to Florida, and Palmer at Cheyenne River complains about Big Foot's coterie of "irreconcilables." Royer, it seems, would be happiest if all six thousand of his Oglala wards succumbed to whooping cough, la grippe, or one of the other deadly diseases that have so reduced their number in the previous decade.

The bole of a tall tree, stripped of branches, has been propped up at the center of the ground, with an American flag rippling atop it. The Ethnographer guesses this is an appreciation of the bright hues on the cloth rather than the nation it symbolizes—on other reservations colored streamers have been used. It is just past noon when the medicine men prompt a young woman with a small bow to shoot four sacred, bone-tipped arrows to the cardinal points—east, west, north, south—while another maiden stands holding a sacred redstone pipe, pointed west, as she will throughout the ceremony. The medicine men arrange themselves around the base of the center pole, while the celebrants, perhaps even more women than men, have formed a loose circle around the center, sitting and passing two wooden bowls of sacred food around to share.

At least an hour or two of movement and song generally precede the convulsive frenzies, trances, and reports of visions, each seeming to trigger other expostulations, the experience having no fixed time but brought to a halt when the medicine men feel the spirits have been sufficiently honored. The Ethnologist has attended a Free Methodist service in Kentucky that took a fraction of that time for the congregants to be rolling on the church floor and jabbering in tongues, but the seriousness of the enterprise was no less intense.

And there is no hurrying Indians.

They can be provoked, though. The Ethnographer is not the first to spot Royer and an assistant standing atop a wagon on the other side of the creek, the Indian agent watching the preparations through binoculars. There are young men hanging about the periphery of the ceremony, and though no weapons, especially those designed by the white man, are allowed in the hands of the dancers, these outliers openly brandish their rifles and seem extremely tense. Until he arrived here, the most striking aspect of the Messiah's creed was the admonition against violence—any violence. For men whose highest ambition has always been to follow the warrior's path, this has seemed to be a very bitter pill to swallow, but swallow it they did. Now, among the Sioux, a new belief has been added, stating that the dance will render the white man's weapons impotent, that his bullets will lack the force to penetrate a ghost dancer's bones, even that the mere attempt at attack will cause a bluecoat soldier to fall into a heap on the ground, as if he has no bones. All this is most likely prompted by the knowledge, verified by Selwyn, that Agent Royer daily sends telegraph messages to Washington pleading for federal troops.

At a signal from one of the elder medicine men the postulants rise, joining hands. Without winter layers over their ghost shirts, the Ethnographer can see how thin they have become.

A drum begins to beat. Psalm 30:11, he thinks, *You turned my wailing into dancing; you removed my sackcloth and clothed me with joy—*

JESSE ECHOHAWK LEADS half of A Company down a country road through maples and birches in full autumn color. No rifles for this march, just a haversack with lunch in it, which the boys take turns carrying. There's a pump at the farmhouse, nice cool well water. He has purposely not told them what the detail is about, and they are lagging.

"We're awful far off the reservation, Master Sergeant."

La Merde. Of course.

"The faster we move," he calls back to them, "the sooner we get there."

"Get where?" asks Smokey.

"Watch your spacing, people. This is a march, not a stroll in the country."

Actually, it *is* a stroll in the country; any day you get off the school grounds a good one in Jesse's opinion. And there is so much more shade here than there is in the Indian Territory—

"Why walk straight if nobody's looking?" Smokey mutters to Antoine.

"No talking in the ranks!" calls the master sergeant.

They slog, in weary cadence, around two more bends and there is the school farm, looking just like it does on the postal card. Jesse strides past the yard pump to the barn, pulls the doors open. The cadets form around him to see what they're in for. The barn floor is piled halfway to the rafters with newly picked corn.

"Here we are, gentlemen." Jesse points. "That wagon gets filled, husks and cornsilk go in that corner. Grab a stool or a milk can and strip 'em down!"

Miss Ely stands under the portrait of President Harrison in the girls' reading room, a dozen young ladies seated with their hands folded in their laps facing her, each wondering why they, of all the older girls, have been pulled out of their Saturday activities to receive this lecture.

"*Chas*tity," says Miss Ely. "*Char*ity. Monogamy, temperance, honesty, pure thought and speech—"

Wilma wonders if somebody saw her go to the carriage house, or if Sweetcorn has been bragging. She remembers this talk from last year, and the year before, almost the same exact words.

"—these add up to what civilized persons regard as *char*acter. Boys, unfair as it might be, are not held to as strict a standard in some of these matters. But once a girl loses her good name—"

Grace Metoxen hasn't been brought here, or her little angel friend Lizzie. It's like they think that if you're good in class, you're *good*.

"—loses her *vir*tue, there is no return to decent society. No return."

It is cool in the barn, and not especially hard work, Antoine quickly getting into a rhythm, bracing each ear on his thigh and yanking the husks down, peeling twenty before he stands and tosses the shuckings into the growing pile in the corner. Asa has been assigned to collect everybody's denuded ears and lay them in the wagon, which keeps him constantly on the move. The master sergeant is stretched out on a horse blanket laid over a hay bale, staring up at the dust motes dancing in the rays of sunlight angling down through the rafters. Women would do this task at home. No special reason that Antoine can think of—if he pictures shucking corn, women are doing it, unless it's him and his friend Charlie stealing ears from old Nestor's field and roasting them later at their hideout. Stolen apples, especially if they're hard to get away with, always taste the best. He would never, however, steal from somebody who was hungry, the way the people in charge of government issue back home do—

Jesse Echohawk has said the boys can talk if they want, but only one out of three in the barn have enough English to bother. So there is mostly the wet ripping and tearing, occasionally a sneeze, till the master sergeant calls lunch.

He does a count as they fill their cups at the hand pump.

He goes into the barn, comes back out.

"Has anybody seen Trouble?"

The boys look at each other, doing their own count.

"I saw him come in the barn with us," says Smokey.

"Did anybody see him step *out*?"

Silence. Antoine sees that Asa knows something and isn't going to share it.

"Shit on a saltine," says Jesse Echohawk.

Once Trouble is clear of the trees he looks for high ground with none of their houses on it. There was a knife with a curved blade lying on the hay bales, now feeling heavy in the pocket of his uniform jacket. He knows which way the railroad tracks are, knows which way is west, toward home, but that will have to wait. He needs guidance. As his uncles always say, if your future is unknown, is maybe full of danger, give yourself up to the Great Mystery and wait for guidance. The fasting is easy, as he carries no food, and he has taken a box of the white people's fire starters and some tobacco from the stubs of cigars he found behind the wooden house of the tall man who brought him on the train, Skinner, the one who will beat you for discipline. One of the ways they punish you is to make you roam around and pick up small things that have been dropped on the ground. There are different kinds of trees here, but he thinks he can make something like a sweat lodge. At home there would be one of the old men who knows medicine, who has gone to meet the Great Mystery many times before, to help him.

Instead, there is a dog following him.

It is a happy dog, ears up, tail swishing, a dog that wishes to play. It is free, like a camp dog, no leather or metal fastened around its neck the way the white men do to make them slaves. The Dog Tribe and the Lakota have been related forever, dogs helping to warn against enemies and to carry things during a move long before the people saw and learned to ride the *sunka wakan*—the big dogs—that escaped the white people. But he needs somebody who knows medicine, not a dog.

It even looks like a camp dog, one ear crooked, thin tail, alert to every sound and opportunity as it stops and sniffs and snorts and then trots to catch up with him. A dog that is not lost, just—free.

He has yelled at the dog in Lakota, which they all understand, and even stopped to throw stones at it, which it seemed to believe was a kind of game. It got close enough to touch the back of his leg with its nose once, and he kicked at it, so for now it stays a bit behind no matter which way he walks, like a nervous shadow.

To the north Trouble can see a line of thick green trees and some willows among them, sign of a river or at least a good-sized stream, and beyond that the land rising to what is almost high enough to call a mountain.

He is a Lakota boy in a blue uniform, and knows that the white people who live near the school will try to catch him or at least set up a cry if they see him. They are all together against you, the whites, they must sit together in council to plan strategy. So Trouble does not walk straight across open ground, but moves from tree to tree, taking his time to watch for movement on the ground or smoke in the air before he continues.

The happy dog follows.

Tom Skinner finds Chester dozing in his seat at the railroad telegraph office.

"Slow day?"

"This time of day is always slow," says the operator. "Unless there's some holdup with the three ten."

"We've got a runaway."

"I heard. You've looked in all the usual hideouts?"

"No sign. This one's a real wild Indian. I had to near hog-tie him to get him here from the reservation."

There are Wanted posters papering the walls in the little room. Joseph and David Nicely, thieves and murderers, are drawn together, having escaped from the Somerset County Jail. Skinner thinks he heard they've already been recaptured.

"I remember you had that one—what was, it—eighty-six? Got all the way down to Gettysburg."

"Alonzo Jackson," says Tom Skinner. "St. Regis Tribe—they're Mohawks, up by Canada. He headed off in the wrong direction."

Chester snorts a laugh. "Don't you teach geography over there?"

"Oh, they look at a map, but still they've got no idea—"

"Heap big country."

"And they forget about the singing wire."

"Right," says Chester, taking up his notebook and pencil. "Give me the particulars."

"Indian boy, fourteen years old—"

"Born the year they scalped Custer—"

"Five feet, six inches, dark complexion, black eyes, black hair—"

"Wearing the uniform?"

"When last seen, yes. Understands very little English, Indian name translates to Makes-Trouble-in-Front."

"That's a good one," says Chester, still writing. "But he'll have to change it to Caught-Dingus-in-Wringer—"

She must be beyond suspicion here, thinks Antoine, to be allowed with him in the music room with only Lizzie Cloud sitting at the piano. Lizzie plays on the keys, sometimes a bit of a song, something flowing and romantic that embellishes the growing love between Hiawatha and Minnehaha, as Grace waits for her cue.

But today he can't remember the words.

"*As unto the bow the cord is,*" he begins, "*So unto the man is woman—*"

And then the creek dries up.

"Think about a bow and arrow," she says.

"We have rifles now," he says. "Great new invention."

"Yes, but you know how a bow and arrow *work*—"

"You pull back on the bowstring—"

"And what happens to the bow?"

"It bends?"

"*Though she bends him, she obeys him*—" she recites from memory.

He has no idea what comes next.

"*Though she*—'?" she prompts.

"She shoots the arrow?"

"You're worried about your friend."

"Friend—?"

"Your roommate."

He *is* worried about Trouble, who has not been found yet, but that's not what is interfering with the words to the story. He keeps thinking about the girl, whoever she was, and the boy in the carriage barn, and what they must have been doing in there together. Nobody dragged her in there. Is that just a certain kind of girl, who goes willingly, who wants to, or do all girls, even Grace, or even Lizzie Cloud sitting over there on the piano bench, who the nuns back home would have made a pet of—

"They'll find him, won't they?"

"They always do," says Grace, who has been at the school for six years now.

"Nobody gets away?"

"That's what the telegraph is for. He'll learn."

She sounds like Miss Burgess at the print shop. Like the Man-on-the-Bandstand, sees all, knows all, keeping the team in harness—

"You've read this whole poem?"

Grace nods. "A few times. But we're only doing—"

"You read the part about Hiawatha's childhood—"

"*Of all beasts he learned the language*," she quotes—

"*Learned their names and many secrets,*
How the beavers built their lodges,
Where the squirrels hid their acorns,
How the reindeer ran so swiftly,
Why the rabbit was so timid—"

"What do you think would happen if the Black Robes got ahold of Hiawatha when he was a boy and sent him here to Carlisle?"

Grace takes a moment to think about this, and Lizzie Cloud stops playing.

"I think," says Grace finally, "he'd feel like a prisoner."

Not what Miss Burgess would answer.

"*So Though she bends him, she obeys him*," Antoine remembers, "*And Though she draws him, yet she follows, Useless each without the other!*"

Grace smiles.

"Do you think that's true?" he asks.

Lizzie Cloud answers from her seat.

"Maybe not," she says, "but it's how it should be. It's a *poem*."

It's hard to know if it's an insult to the Great Mystery to try this alone, or if his cry for guidance, being so desperate, will be better heard. What Trouble has built from branches and sticks hardly looks like a sweat lodge, but more like a beaver's den, the stone face of a cliff providing its back wall. He has done as much of the ceremony as he knows, laying the tobacco in the center, marking the four directions with poles dug into the ground, each wrapped with a rag of the proper color—black for the West, white for the North, yellow for the East, red for the South. He has climbed far enough to find this spot where he believes no one will see the fire when he lights it, or if they do they won't worry about something so far away.

The dog has not left, watching each part of the ceremony, tail still swinging as if mocking him. A real camp dog would have given up on him by now, no food or encouragement, and there must be something wrong with this one, something strange about it being here. Trouble wonders if the dog is a message. A message that he will become the white people's dog, following them everywhere, sitting or lying down when they signal, begging for scraps. Or maybe it is an evil spirit having nothing to do with the whites, only waiting for him to fall asleep—

It is dark enough now that he can barely make out the shapes of the trees on the slope below him, can see the dog only when it shifts position, watching him from less than a stone's throw away.

Trouble lights the pile of sticks and dry moss he has gathered, adjusts the branches above and around him till the smoke is drifting out through the proper opening. He has dry wood piled against the stone of the back wall, and will be able to feed the fire all night. The structure is close enough, tight enough, that he is already feeling very warm. He is hungry, no food since breakfast the morning they left to husk the corn.

Trouble sits, cross-legged, eyes closed, trying to open himself to the Wakan Tanka. He hears the dog creeping a bit closer to the tiny lodge.

But he will not sleep.

There are only eight in what Mr. Ellenbee chooses to call Classics, seven of the older boys and a Mohawk girl whose father served on General Grant's staff during the Civil War, with Clarence the only among them who came to Carlisle with no English. Mr. Ellenbee is a chipmunk-like man, quick of movement, puffy of cheek, enraptured by Shakespeare.

This year they are working their way through *The Tempest.*

"A combination of the sort of royal skullduggery we find in *Macbeth* or *King Lear*," chirps Mr. Ellenbee, "with the farcical antics of spirits and fairies so beloved by the Elizabethan groundlings."

Clarence finds no utility in this study, agreeing with the critics of the school that their purpose should be to train the red man in skills that might earn him a living, and suspects that it is encouraged by the Captain for its novelty interest—their public recitations much like the trained dogs he has seen at the carnival in town, walking one behind the other on two legs rather than four, earning applause not for themselves but for the mastery of their trainer.

But he loves the stories.

When he reads the harangues of Prospero, Clarence pictures Captain Pratt. For what is Prospero but the triumphant white man, using his superior, mysterious arts to control the island he has been marooned upon, sitting high in judgment over all he surveys?

And who am I, thinks Clarence, as Ellenbee continues to chitter, but his Ariel, scurrying to do his bidding, ears open for murmurs of rebellion, eager to torment his enemies. And Trouble, poor clueless Caliban, not yet resigned to the loss of his former domain—

They're now using a pack of bloodhounds, borrowed from the Eastern State Penitentiary, to find the boy's trail.

Clarence can't imagine that Ariel takes any pleasure in his mischief, acting not on his own whim or strategy but only to weather the great magician's darker moods, to earn his approval, to perhaps even be released, someday, from servitude.

The Crow scouts who helped the bluecoats defeat his people were at least working against their old enemy, paid for their expertise, and served only for the period they had signed on for. Ariel is in a strange sort of bondage, freed by the great magician from one form of captivity but kept in another, trusted as Prospero's angel of wrath, but never his equal.

There are worse things, he knows. You could be stuck on Pine Ridge at the mercy of an Indian agent with the brain of a hummingbird and a heart like a shriveled pea. You could be bound in a tree for eternity, or a hunted fugitive like Makes-Trouble-in-Front, dogs at your heels—

Mr. Ellenbee has ceased his enthusiastic noise and is looking right at Clarence.

"Mr. Regal," he says, "if you would be so good as to render us this passage—"

He is on his feet before he can think, years of military training infused in his limbs by now, holding the text open in two hands.

"*All hail, great master!*" he reads. "*Grave sir, hail! I come*
To answer thy best pleasure. Be 't to fly,
To swim, to dive into the fire, to ride
On the curled cloud, to thy strong bidding task
Ariel and all his quality."

On the third morning Trouble decides it is over. He is sore from barely moving, and though not really hungry, knows he should find something to eat. The smoke has kept the insects away, and finally, this sunup, the dog is gone. Last night—he thinks it was last night—he could see its amber eyeshine outside, reflecting the flames of his fire. It is a relief, because it is so clearly a white man's dog that has run away, safe to roam in this tame country. Trouble has not heard a coyote or a wolf since he came to the school, only roosters, and where there are roosters strutting around announcing themselves there can barely be foxes. Probably after they killed all the red men who were here the whites killed all the wolves and coyotes.

Trouble is wearing only his underpants, shivering slightly in the morning cold as he walks unsteadily to where he remembers seeing water trickling down the rock face.

It is still there, tasting like moss and stone. It is hard to know what was real sleep and what only the state of sitting and doing nothing for so long. At first he was very aware of time being different, no bugle calls, no bells chopping the day into lengths. None of the animal spirits visited him—not Mica the coyote, or Mató the bear, or even Iktomi, the mischievous spider. The spirits of wind and fire and thunder were absent. He thought he might dream of dogs, but no, as much as he can remember he dreamed only of trains, trains that were long, hissing, drooling animals, trains that huffed like a tired horse galloping up a steep hill, trains that screamed before they ran over your body.

When Trouble gets back to the tiny lodge the dog is waiting for him, and it has brought him a bird.

It is a ring-necked pheasant, a large male, and the dog must have shaken it to death because the skin has not been broken. Trouble thanks the dog, which stays several arm's lengths away, swishing its tail and watching as he pulls the feathers out, then guts it with the curved knife and begins to cook it, impaled on a stick. The dog quickly gulps the innards down when Trouble throws them at its feet. The smell of the cooking bird makes him feel a little dizzy, but he concentrates and tries to think if anything has been revealed to him. At home, of course, there would be the older men experienced in medicine to help, who would talk through the experience with you and help draw out meaning from what had been revealed.

A dog that might only be a dog.

Trains.

He knew before that he could not hope to walk or to ride a stolen pony all the way home, that at some point he would have to find a train heading where he wants to go and cling on to it, have to ride on the backs of a series of the snorting beasts till he began to recognize the country and could leave the iron road. Trouble eats most of the bird and gives the happy dog the rest to chew on, the dog holding the carcass still with one paw and pulling bits off with its teeth. Trouble puts his pants and socks and shoes and an undershirt on, rolls his matches and his knife in his uniform shirt, and heads down toward the stream and the rails he knows run parallel on the other side of it. The dog follows him.

Sunday.

Antoine has always loved the secret language.

> "*Credo in unum Deum,*
> *Patrem omnipotentum,*
> *factorem cœli et terræ*—"

He even understands what some of the words mean as the priest drones away.

> "—*visibilium omnium et invisbilium,*
> *Et in unum Dominum Iesum Christum,*
> *Filium Dei*—"

He and Charlie Tetrault would pretend to talk at each other in front of the pagan boys sometimes, bits of phrases they could remember or sometimes just making it up. It gives all the sitting and kneeling on hard wood some mystery, some ceremony—

"—unigenitum,
et ex Patre natum—"

Both his father's parents were Catholics, and his mother's mother, Memengwaa, had taken it up when she had her third child. Antoine's mother goes to Mass, but still does all the old Ojibwe ceremonies and talks to the Indian spirits.

"—ante omni sæcula. Deum de Deo—"

The Carlisle School Catholics sit together in the left rear pews, boys and girls allowed to pray together here. Antoine peeks down the pew in which he is kneeling and yes, Clarence Regal is still there, though sitting up and looking uneasy. Antoine has never been able to lose himself in the Mass the way he did the few times he was brought along to the all-night Ojibwe dancing, jumping and chanting in rhythm with everybody else till you feel joined into something, feel just one part of it and not Antoine any more, till exhausted and allowed to wander back from the fire and find a place to sleep. There are so many parts to the Roman liturgy, building finally to the Mystery of the Eucharist, a moment where he, Antoine alone, kneels before the God of Judgment and takes the Host.

"*Ça ne peut pas faire de mal,*" his father says when asked about his wife honoring both creeds. It can't hurt.

People have slaughtered each other over differences of faith, and Antoine is careful not to talk about beliefs with the other students. He has only just begun to realize that somebody *start*ed each one, whether it came to them as a revelation or was written on a stone tablet—somebody gathered other people around and told them, "This is how the whole thing came to be, this is how it works." Christian Apostles wrote books, and Ojibwe storykeepers passed on tales, generation after generation, that somebody observed or invented way back when.

Like the story sweeping through the reservations that Cato Goforth talks about at the print shop when Miss Burgess is out—

ON WITH THE DANCE
HOW INDIAN BRAVES ARE WORKED
INTO A FANTASTICAL FRENZY

This Wovoka, who they say started it, must be a Christian, or at least was given the teaching, because sometimes he talks about Jesus, or says he *is* Jesus. The other part of the story, buffalo returning, white people buried under rocks and earth, sounds like the tales his mother's father, Mishoomis, would tell around a fire late at night, details changing slightly every time.

"—*lumen de lumine, Deum vero de Deum vero*—"

Antoine wonders if, liking the Catholic ceremony but only half believing in it, it is acceptable for him to pray for Trouble.

Sunday.

Miss Redbird sits alone at the piano, plinking out melodies on the keys, wondering which of the staff here it will be to confront her. It is Sunday again, and she has not gone to any of their churches.

She always went to services with the other children when she was at the boarding school, marched in by the teachers and doled out among the pews. At first she didn't know there were so many different kinds of Christians, not just Catholics and Protestants, and until she went to New York to play music onstage she thought Jews were only ancient people who had died out during the Bible days. When she left the reservation as a little girl the few Lakota who followed the Book were considered damaged, like old Wiyaka-Napbina, who you knew was crazy because he couldn't take more than five steps before turning quickly to look behind, certain that an evil spirit was following him.

But on her last visit home the belief had spread like a pox, with even her mother keeping a well-worn Bible on a shelf, and inviting her lay preacher neighbor, who used to be Two Cuts but now went by Isaac, to try to save her soul.

"You seem like a good young woman," he told her, "and it hurts my heart to look out upon those who come to hear the Word each Sunday and find that you are not among them."

He explained to her, as if to a small child and calling her "cousin," as was polite, that there is one God, a God who gives reward or punishment to the race of dead men. In the upper region, he told her, the Christian dead dwell in unceasing song and prayer. While in the deep pit below, the sinful ones dance in torturing flames.

"Look around this reservation," she said to him evenly. "Hasn't this God punished us enough? And now he's going to torture us in the land of the dead?'

Forgive my daughter, her mother told the believer, speaking Lakota. She's been educated.

"Think upon these things I've told you, cousin," said the man, seeming more sad than insulted, "and choose now to avoid the after-doom of hellfire!"

She hears steeple bells from town. There are seven of the Protestant denominations with churches in town, and there is St. Patrick's. They all have their own bells, which heard from the school are staggered just enough to make counting the chimes useless for counting hours. There is Chapel one weekday night, which Miss Redbird is required to attend as a girls' supervisor, though the girls are never any trouble. The chapel at the boarding school she attended had only simple crosses on the walls, but in one of the texts there was a color picture of Christ suffering, with the nails in his hands and feet and the crown of thorns and spear wound in his ribs, that haunted her. She knew there was such a thing as torture, but why keep a picture of it? Why wear a metal figure of the poor twisted man on a thin chain around your neck like a few of the girls at her college did? You'd just as well wear the hair of somebody you killed in battle on your belt.

When she first encountered them, Miss Redbird thought white people something special, something above the natural order. They knew things, could do things, *had* things that nobody else did. She now knows they are only members of the tribe of two-legged human beings, no more different from other mortals than any one of the ivory keys on this piano, white or black, is from the next. Strike each, and it will sing, but with a slightly different note—

"Miss Redbird."

It would be her.

"I see you're back from early Mass." Miss Burgess, standing to look in from the doorway.

"I didn't go to Mass."

Give her that and nothing more.

"Ah," says Miss Burgess, smiling tightly, and moves on.

Miss Redbird picks out a melody. Black keys and white keys, arranged left to right in an ascending scale.

And a few are out of tune.

Sunday, in the infirmary.

They're not supposed to use their own language, even for singing. But Nurse Tucker isn't sure it isn't Italian or German or something else they do in opera. She knows that the girl, Grace, is a music student and very talented. She certainly has a beautiful voice. Nurse Tucker has stopped just short of the doorway to the infirmary, listening. When she peeks in she can see Grace sitting beside the little Apache girl, the one, according to Dr. Hazzard, who isn't going to make it, holding her hand and singing what sounds like a lullaby.

Nurse Tucker leans against the wall, closes her eyes, listens. It's like being in church.

Night. At the school Trouble would know the white people's name for the day, know if it was a day to sit on hard chairs in classrooms or to sit on hard benches while their holy men talk. But he has lost track of their time, and it is only night. He is at the edge of another white people town, smaller than Carlisle and a long walk to the west of it. Trouble sits in the woods by the track until he sees the lights go on at the railroad platform. The dog, patient, has been sitting close by his side most of the day, waiting, ears up to listen for anyone coming near. They rise together, Trouble walking carefully on the wooden ties so as not to crunch on the stones, the dog following a little behind and on the cleared margin beside the rail, alert. When they are close enough Trouble moves to crouch behind a pile of debris and watch the track, the dog moving behind him to stay out of sight.

The train, eight cars long, sits on the track, the engine under the lights of the platform, rumbling as if just waiting to roll. It is facing west.

The cars are different shapes, some higher, some long and low, and none are the rooms with windows like the ones he was brought to the school in. There are no people in sight, but he knows that the train will not lay there forever, that at some point white men will come and climb into the engine and it will scream and hiss and roll away.

Trouble crosses to the side of the train away from the platform, bending low and lifting his feet carefully, the dog slinking behind. There is a metal ladder on the side of one of the tall wooden cars—he knows he can't ride on the part that links them together or he'll be seen. He climbs the ladder quickly, and only when he is up on the roof and laid out flat on his belly does the dog begin to speak.

It is a loud, insistent complaint, high-pitched like the camp dogs use to warn of a stranger. Trouble has nothing to throw at it, and he doesn't want to call for it to be quiet and reveal a human voice. He decides he will have to climb down and catch it and break its neck, but then hears crunching on the stones and a white man hollering. Two white men. The car he is on is very high, and maybe they will be lazy, so he presses his face to the roof and tries to think himself invisible. Patience and calm can save you. His cousin caught an eagle once, lying on his back and covered with earth for nearly a full day, a dead rabbit laid on his chest. He gave the feathers to a medicine man whose daughter he wanted to marry.

Trouble feels the footsteps on the wood before he hears them, sees the spill of yellow light from a lantern—

"Hey, you!"

He rolls to the edge, throws his legs out, hangs, holding on for a moment—and then somebody grabs the back of his belt and yanks him down to the ground, quickly pinning his arm behind his back.

The dog finally stops barking. The dog is part of the white man's medicine, sent to watch him and make sure he neither starved nor escaped them. A lantern is laid on the stones by his face, close enough that the heat of it hurts him.

"That must be him."

Trouble is yanked to his feet.

"Come on, chief—back to the reservation."

One white man on each side, he is dragged around the train and up onto the platform. Before they pull him into the little shed he manages to look back and see the dog, sitting right next to the front of the engine.

Laughing at him.

THE TWO APACHE boys, cousins, stand before the court-martial officers and the assembled boy's companies, both shivering. Captain Pratt and the disciplinarian, Skinner, stand to one side, watching. Clarence Regal levels the charge—

"Duncan Hunterboy and Job Toprock, returned from their Outing residences without permission. How plead you?"

Antoine has never seen the two before, and has been told they've been at the school for three years.

"Guilty," say the Apache boys in unison.

Captain Pratt speaks up. "Do you understand what a poor decision it was, if you were going to desert your farm situations, to return here?"

This last farmer had said they smelled bad, and made them take all their clothes off while he stood up on a bench and threw buckets of cold water over their heads. Another time Job saw him watching them work in the truck garden with his hand down his pants. They are too ashamed to speak of this, even to each other, but agreed to run away back to Carlisle together.

"I guess we didn't think too good, sir," says Duncan.

"You certainly did not." He turns to the ranking cadet officer, Wesley Cornelius. "Sentence?"

"Six days in the guardhouse, prison rations, loss of privileges."

Pratt adds nothing to this.

"Percival Makes-Trouble-in-Front—*run*away," announces Clarence. "How do you plead?"

Trouble, a few feet to the right of the Apache boys, realizes he is supposed to respond. Everybody is looking at him.

"Trubba run," he says.

Tom Skinner speaks softly into the Captain's ear. "What do you think?"

"If we give him a thrashing now, we'll never win him back."

"But this Trouble—"

"There's a time for the rod and there's a time for reason."

Wesley Cornelius says, "Six days in the guardhouse, prison rations—"

"If I may?"

The court-martial officers look to Captain Pratt. Antoine can see Trouble trying to hide his fear. For all he knows he'll be hanged—

"Yes, sir?"

"This is a new boy," says the Captain. "No serious offenses on his record. Let's make it three."

Cornelius nods. "Three days confinement, prison rations, loss of privileges. The prisoners will be escorted to the guardhouse."

Antoine, Asa, and Smokey join three boys from C Company to flank the guilty parties, all following Mr. Skinner down the walk. Antoine moves up so that Trouble can see him, points to the sun, then shows three fingers. Trouble nods.

Word spread quickly when Trouble was brought in, veteran students impressed by how far he'd gotten. Clarence and Jesse were relieved at the capture, as he is from their company, but Clarence asked permission to go to the train station when he arrived in handcuffs, and later reported to his boys.

"A couple bruises from the yard bulls," he told them. "He's lucky he didn't steal anything or hurt anybody. Those real jails are no place for an Indian."

There is some saluting and then the unlocking of the door to the guardhouse. Antoine is able to give Trouble the Ojibwe sign for "be strong."

The door closes and they hear it being locked. It is a narrow room with only slits, high up on the wall, for windows. The Apache boys immediately sit on the bench and begin to whisper together in their tongue, looking as if they've been here before. Trouble moves as far as he can from the bucket for prisoners' waste, sits on the floor with his back to the wall. He closes his eyes, vowing that he won't eat again till they let him out. If the Great Mystery has a message for him, stone walls mean nothing—

Clarence Regal is waiting when they get back to their room, sitting on Trouble's bed.

"I need you three to help him," he says, but is looking only at Antoine.

"When he gets out."

"The quicker he learns English, the better off he'll be. He's going to learn it faster from you than he will in class."

"We point to everything in the room," says Smokey, "and tell him the words."

"Window," says Asa, pointing to the window, surprising both his roommates. Asa never talks.

"He doesn't want to be here," says Antoine.

"The best thing he can do to change that, and you can help him understand this, is to pay attention here and learn how the white people run things. If you're going to defeat your enemy, or even just avoid getting killed by him, you'd better know how he operates."

It's what Antoine vowed to do when he got on the train in De Pere.

"You're a Catholic," he says to Clarence.

"I go to a different one of their churches every few weeks." Clarence gets up and moves to the door. "Good to keep them guessing."

"But you *go*."

Clarence shrugs. "Our magic stopped working—might as well try the white man's." He strikes his orator's pose, falls into Hiawatha cadence—

> "*Stalwart Captain Pratt, the Founder*
> *And his band of bookish Christians*
> *Struggle earnestly to teach us*
> *What the Holy Bible preaches.*
> *Lost to progress, near extinction*
> *Keen to learn the path to wisdom*
> *'Not a problem,' says our head-man,*
> *'But we first must kill the Red Man!'*"

Smokey looks confused—

"*So in Army blue we muster,*" Clarence continues—
"'*Neath a flag of stripèd glory,*
Vagabonds from reservations
To salute the best of nations.
Bless us with thy holy knowledge
Dress us in thy manly garments
Tie our hands and bind them tighter
If you must—to make us whiter."

Even Asa, who didn't understand a word, seems awed by the master sergeant's bitterness.

"You don't like Carlisle?"

"That, La Merde, is beside the point. We are *here*—hostages to progress."

He pulls a letter from his jacket pocket, wiggles it at Antoine. "The Invincibles meet in an hour. Be there."

Grace and Lizzie Cloud sit with Wilma in their room, helping with her request.

"*I want to go out to the country,*" Grace reads from a form she got at the administrative office. "*I promise to abstain from drinking alcohol or smoking*—"

"I'll promise anything to get out of that laundry."

"You know," says Lizzie, "they send you all the way to Chester County, or even out of state. And your—your *friend* will be back here—"

"He's not my friend," huffs Wilma. "He's my in*tend*ed."

Grace has given Wilma a few books to help her with her reading, books she knows she would like, about poor girls who almost choose the wrong man and then go back to the good one.

Who turns out to be wealthy.

"Whatever he is," explains Lizzie, "you won't be able to see him."

"Maybe, maybe not."

"You're not planning anything crazy, are you?"

"I'm planning to stick my arm in the mangle if I have to stay here."

"It can be lonely."

Grace did an Outing two years ago, a stay through the summer with a farm family. She had loved helping take care of the animals, didn't mind all the household chores, and the family brought her to church with them on Sunday, proud of her voice when the hymnals were picked up. But the farmer's wife only spoke German, and her twin girls were silly, talking without cease and about nothing. The farmer, Mr. Muller, called her "our girl" when talking to friends and was surprised she knew how to eat soup with a spoon.

"I feel like I can't breathe here," says Wilma.

"You'll have to go to the public school there—*if* there is one. "

"I'll make money—"

"You work for two weeks," says Grace, "and then *if* they want to keep you, they get in touch with the school and propose a wage. If you don't think it's enough—"

"I don't care how much it is. It will be *mine*."

"Half of it you keep, yes, but the other half comes here and goes into your account—"

"If they don't steal it."

"Now you're being mean, Wilma—"

"Well they might—"

"You'll get visits from a field agent. Probably Miss Ely."

Wilma makes a horrible face. "How many visits?"

"Every month, maybe every six weeks."

"Do you want to be a domestic servant?" asks Lizzie. "That's what your training will be."

"Nobody I know back home has servants."

"*White* people have servants."

"But they're Negroes—"

"Not all of them."

Grace raises her hands in surrender. "She's made up her mind."

"I have."

"Just between the three of us," says Lizzie, "does Sweetcorn *know* he's your intended?"

Jesse Echohawk looks out onto the parade ground—nothing moving, with the cold and wind driving all the free time activities indoors today. He shuts the door, steps back in.

"All clear."

Clarence Regal holds the letter, standing before the other Invincibles scattered about the large boys' library room. He begins to read, keeping his voice low—

"*I was not home for more than an hour when I despairingly discovered I no longer spoke my own language. My father lamented that the whites had bewitched me, but the words have since been coming back, like a powerful dream remembered—*"

"Grant Left Hand," Jesse whispers to Antoine, seated on the arm of a plush chair. "His father is chief of the Arapaho in Colorado—"

"*Sitting Bull tells us that the Great Spirit sent the whites to punish us for our sins, but that since we have suffered so deeply the day of deliverance is at hand.*"

"He went here?"

"Only a few years ago. He was master sergeant of my company—"

"*Though we are few in number now, soon the ghosts of all our people who ever walked the earth will join us, driving before them herds of buffalo and fine horses—*"

"And he believes this?"

"*Listen—*"

At the far side of the parade ground, by the disciplinarian's house, two Lakota boys rake leaves into a pile, heads down, one muttering what he has heard in their forbidden language—

—while in the stairwell of their dormitory a Pueblo boy has stopped Asa to relate the news in Spanish, that the whites will soon be smothered under a great landslide, will be buried under sod and timber—

"—and those who escape will turn into little fishes, pulled away by the current in the rivers," Sweetcorn explains to Otis Gamble as they thrust shovelfuls of coal into the maws of the insatiable furnaces. "But to make this happen we got to turn away from the white man's things—his clothing, his liquor, his religion, his language—and go back to the old ways."

Otis considers this for a few sweaty heaves, coal dust lingering in the air, flames flickering red on his naked torso.

"Them old ways," he says finally, "you still get to dip it in the honeypot?"

"*The Great Spirit, if we keep dancing, if we keep singing for his intervention,*" reads Clarence Regal to the Invincibles, "*will rob the white man's gunpowder of its strength to drive a bullet through a red man's skin*—"

STANDING ROCK RESERVATION lies on land only a herdsman could love. A herdsman or a hunter. Mostly flat, wind-scoured, the soil unpromising for anything beyond the roughest fodder—Father Craft tugs the reins to keep Pinch at a nervous trot. No need to arrive too soon, with his acolytes clattering in the wagon a mile or more behind. The circuit of mission stations and Indian camps he rides on Standing Rock is a three-hundred-mile trek, and this may well be his last time around. The sun is peeking over the horizon just behind him, pheasants scoot out from the underbrush, and he keeps the Grand River to his right, having forded a bit south of St. Elizabeth's, the good sisters packing the remains of a schnitzel for his post-Mass restorative.

Pinch skitters off the road and the father wrestles him back onto it. The bay stallion has a rebellious streak, but he can't imagine another steed equal to the weather and the distances they face on this reservation. Asked why he hasn't had the unruly animal gelded, Father Craft answers that in a horse he values spirit over obedience.

Would that the bishop and the director of Indian missions felt the same about their field workers.

Extraordinary circumstances require extraordinary measures, and yesterday's intercession at Flying By's settlement—performing a baptism, confession, marriage, and last rites within an hour and for the same treacherous sinner, might be something of a record. But old David Comes Last professed to desire conversion, legitimacy, and absolution in his last hours, and his pulse was weak and erratic, his breathing shallow—an opportunity to snatch a soul for the Lord. His consort, however, a formidable creature with "Satan's mother-in-law" stamped upon her wrinkled phiz, wanted nothing to do with a Black Robe in her tipi, the telltale signs of the father's competition—tossing stones for divination, wild sage, the tobacco board, and the medicine drum with a horned demon painted on it—had only been moved to one side when he entered. Some contretemps between the loving couple in Sioux, which they assumed, mistakenly, that he did not understand, the upshot being that it was Davey's dying wish for the future Mrs. Comes Last to hold her nose and endure the sacraments. Father Craft had already sprinkled the tipi, outside and in, with holy water, reserving some for the baptism, Comes Last croaking that he was more than happy to finally renounce Satan. Confession proved to be a somewhat truncated affair, the ancient reprobate assuring Father Craft that he had done many bad things in his life, too many to remember and too awful to reveal to a *wasichu*, holy man or not. But they got through it, a death rale in the man's chest by now, and moved on to the peremptory matrimonial rite—a suitably pious neighbor, Martin Catka, popping his head in to witness, the newly wedded Mrs. Comes Last somehow repressing her tears of joy. Much of the color had drained from Davey's face, and the father felt the need to hurry, granting a plenary indulgence and then donning the stole for Extreme Unction, anointing the old man's forehead with blessed oil, then helping him sit up to receive the host. The communal wine Father Craft offered to quell the choking fit this brought on seemed to revive the afflicted sinner, to the point that when it was time to leave, Comes Last got to his feet and saw the priest out to his tethered stallion, saying that if he had a recurrence of the symptoms they should do the whole thing over again.

Out of the depths I cry to you, oh Lord!

This low comedy, so typical of his hiatus here among the ignoble former savages, was put into perspective by his next visit, to the bedside of sweet Cunegunda, already at twelve determined to take her vows and be named, in absentia, Sister Mary Aloysia, a considerable comfort to the girl as she lay in death's doorway. He began with his medical assessment, concurring with Dr. Caskie of the agency that her case was hopeless, the child at this point too weak to withstand more opiates. A sip of brandy and water, then they spoke in near whispers, her father, Black Bear, in and out of the cabin, already grieving. There was a brief confession—what could such a pure soul have to reveal?—then an act of contrition interrupted by her hawking cough and a bout of spastic retching. Father Craft's status as both a medical school graduate and a holy man has always fit well with the Sioux concept of "medicine," though he is saving souls for the Sacred Heart of Jesus, while his rattle-shaking rivals are merely dragging their people closer to eternal damnation.

She left this world, he is satisfied to think, absolved and blessed. Black Bear rushing outside to wail and strike himself, Father Craft was left alone with the body, feeling as low as he had the day the Society of Jesus chose to exclude him from their righteous army. I am unworthy, he thought, a convert, a pretender, a rank failure as a fisher of souls.

As a penance then, he took up and swallowed what the poor child had coughed and vomited into the emesis basin.

I feel no ill effect, he thinks as he rides, no nausea, no fever. Whatever the power of infectious disease, it is no match for True Faith.

It is a chilly morning, Father Craft in his overcoat, but always sure to wear the missionary cross and his Sons of the Revolution medal hanging on the outside of it. The crucifix, big as a big man's hand, to advertise his mission here—when one of the wags at Fort Yates suggested it served as a sort of magical shield protecting him from superstitious natives, he retorted that it made a better target, and that though his hair might now be safe in all of the settlements, his life was not. When the movement to have him removed from Standing Rock, instigated by Sitting Bull, in concert with, if he's not mistaken, Agent McLaughlin, was put into action, he bought a bundle of arrows from one of the carvers outside the walls of the fort and rode into the camps, offering them to all.

"If you want to be rid of me," he announced, "you'll have to use one of these."

Few of the younger men these days could hit the side of a New England barn at ten paces using a bow, but he felt the traditionalist touch was appreciated.

The Sons of the Revolution medal is to declare that he is an *American*, only one out of ten Catholic priests in the country being native-born. The Germans and Swiss who preside over St. Benedict's mission, though dedicated, are as stolid as cattle, their Irish counterparts manning St. Xavier's up in Cannon Ball predictably slow-witted, and the reservation has been mercifully spared an infestation of French clerics, despite their stranglehold on the faith just above the border. Father Craft rather regrets he was not born when noble families sent their second or third sons into the priesthood—the quality of blood should match the glory of the mission.

He dismounts, standing beside the river to rest his spine and wait for Emeran White Boy and his saved-today-lost-tomorrow cousin to catch up in the wagon. He's wearing his white pith helmet today, souvenir of his stint as an *homme de guerre* in Belgium, confident that should Sitting Bull poke his nose out of his cabin to gaze across the river, it will gleam as a reproachful beacon. Bishop Marty and Father Stephan have ordered him to meet them in Chicago, and there is no telling if he will be able to return. Stephan, a German of limited abilities, was once the agent here, before his obduracy led to his replacement by the genial but Machiavellian McLaughlin, and now that Stephan is director of Indian missions for the church, his jealousy of Father Craft's successes here will be unchecked. And the Swiss bishop Marty is more politician than ecclesiast, no doubt under pressure to do something about this Messiah business. Father Craft's own strategy, to place his life on the line in opposing devil worship wherever it may appear, is perhaps too contentious for their taste.

So why not raise the flag one last time?

There was some idle belief when Father Craft was banished from Rosebud and sent up here that he was the very man to confront and convert the notorious medicine man and cavalry slayer Sitting Bull, a task anomalous to St. George vanquishing his dragon—and just as unlikely. Sitting Bull, recognizing someone he could neither hoodwink nor intimidate, took an instant dislike to the father, an animus that only deepened when Craft lent his support to General Crook's commission in '89. Father Craft, consulting with a lawyer acquaintance, discovered that the federal government could, indeed, eject the Sioux from *all* of their territory, and therefore urged those chiefs and respected men under his influence to touch the pen before the offered redistribution was rendered even more in their disfavor. During the last frantic moments of the counsel, when the progressive tribe members were ready to either sign or bolt, Sitting Bull arrived with a cadre of his followers on horseback to make a boisterous demonstration outside the building. Agent McLaughlin sent Captain Bullhead and his Indian police out to chase them away, which they accomplished without shots being fired, and the agreement was duly accepted by the required two thirds of eligible enrollees. Father Craft's thanks for his service was to be accused by Sitting Bull, in a series of poison missives to state and national government officials, of unspeakable crimes. Though these were eventually judged to be without merit, his person and his mission were placed in doubt, and mountebanks such as Father Stephan encouraged to further mischief. Stephan, who takes credit for establishing the Benedictine mission here, as if Philadelphia's Miss Drexel and her millions had no part in it—

Father Craft has time, thankfully, for a cigarette before the wagon comes into sight.

The site is just around the bend, and his acolytes understand what must be done. Belly Fat is waiting for them with more than two dozen of the occasionally faithful, attracted to the supply of tonics, phosphates, castor oil, laudanum, and medicinal brandy always packed in the wagon, Dr. Caskie's visits this far south as rare as his own. Oh, and yes, concerned about the fate of their immortal souls. Only a month ago half his bush congregation was lured away, in medias res, when a decidedly hostile neighbor set up an impromptu *wakicagapi* upwind of them, cooking a quarter of a steer over a flaming pit. As an Indian's thoughts tend to be centered in his stomach, there were few celebrants left by the time he got to "*Ite, missa est.*"

The boys set up what Father Craft thinks of as his wilderness chapel—they've brought the four notched sticks to drive into the ground, the two long-barreled rifles to lay as cross-supports—symbolism is never wasted on the red man—a rectangle of canvas, and then the altar cloth laid across the table these make, a pair of number six candles lit on either side, and then his big crucifix hung on a pole just behind the improvised altar, lest anybody forget why they have assembled.

Smoke rises from the cabins and tipis just across the river, and

Father Craft can see a few of Sitting Bull's idolatrous pagan outfit wandering down onto the bank to look across. Belly Fat has a big, pleasing bass, and will lead the hymns today. The sweet sound of holy prayer will, *Deo volente*, penetrate the lair of that most recalcitrant blasphemer, that peddler of self-serving visions and prophecies. There is no hiding place from the Lord.

Emeran White Boy and his cousin kneel, facing the altar, right arms free from the blankets draped around them. Father Craft meets the eyes of those who have come, all of them kneeling on the ground, then turns his back on them to place the veiled chalice on the center of the altar, drops to a knee, and makes the sign of the cross—

NOVEMBER

IT IS A PITCHOUT AROUND THE RIGHT END, JESSE TUCKING THE ball and putting his head down, seeing that the corner hasn't been fully blocked and planting his foot for a sharp cut back in, knee locked when the player, a Mandan from D Company, puts his shoulder into it. Everybody on the field can hear the snap and then Jesse is down and screaming, still holding the ball clutched against his belly as he lies on his back, undamaged leg bent and pushing at the ground, the other twisted at an angle that is hard to look at. Antoine, who had been watching idly from the sideline, is one of the three who lift Jesse up and carry him, gasping the same phrase in Pawnee over and over, toward the hospital. Someone stuffs a rolled handkerchief in his mouth to bite on, and Jesse makes rhythmic noises through his teeth as they hurry along.

Clarence comes in to wait outside the examination room with Antoine and a few of the other boys, Captain Pratt arriving a few minutes later, saying nothing to them. When Dr. Hazzard comes out he looks grave, speaking only to the Captain.

"Compound fracture, torn ligaments—he might lose that leg."

Pratt nods grimly, turns to the boys.

"That is the end," he says. "There will be no more football at Carlisle."

The tall white man, Skinner, is standing in the doorway, waving with his arm.

"Come on out. Your time is up."

Trouble looks to the two Apache boys, who smile and make shooing gestures to him. It is just as cold outside as it is inside the guardhouse, not a leaf left on any of the trees, a stiff wind blowing from the west. Skinner takes him straight to the spray bath, where water shoots down from above when you turn the metal, and waits on the other side of the low wall, not looking, as Trouble lets it fall on him and uses the soap, careful to keep it from getting into his eyes. When he is done there is a towel hanging over the low wall and a fresh set of uniform clothes sitting folded on a chair. His old clothes are nowhere to be seen. Skinner leans against the wall, arms crossed in front of his chest. When Trouble is all buttoned in, Skinner walks him to the entrance of the large boys' dormitory, and watches him climb the stairs, not another word passing between them.

The others are still at class when Trouble comes into the room and lies down on his bed. He is hungry, and will go out to muster when the bugle blows for dinner. In the guardhouse he kept thinking, maybe even dreaming, about his father's horse. His cousins told him it was the envy of all the small boys, who bragged how they were going to find and steal a horse like that from their enemies. After his father was killed, the horse was prepared with special paints, special designs, feathers woven into its mane and tail, all the while being told what was about to happen. His cousins said that when the horse was led to his father's scaffold to be killed, it pranced and held its head high, displaying its pride at the honor.

Trouble lies on his bed and pictures the horse, wondering if when all the Lakota who have ever been before return to the land of the living, chasing after the great herd of buffalo, his father will be riding on its back.

Miss Redbird has suggested that the students rehearsing for the Thanksgiving celebration be allowed to do so in the assembly hall this evening, so they have a sense of its size and of how powerful a voice will be required to be heard by all. She sits in the extreme rear row as Lizzie Cloud stands on the platform that will be expanded into a stage, singing *Love's Sweet Song.* Grace and Antoine sit in the first row, waiting their turn, Grace with her eyes closed and her lips moving as she goes through her lines.

"He'll be on crutches for who knows how long," says Antoine, "but they're not going to amputate."

Grace opens her eyes, looks annoyed.

"And you were in on it."

"I wasn't even playing."

"But you were *there.* Wasn't there something in the newspaper saying the football boys were getting out of hand—"

"You always follow the rules—"

"I att*empt* to. Did you ever work on a farm?"

"What does that have to do with anything?"

"Did you?"

"A couple times, for wages—"

"How did you like it?"

"Not much."

"If you don't do well with your schoolwork, if you make yourself a nuisance, they'll send you for an Outing. Maybe permanently."

"Not until I'm here for two years—"

"For you they might make an exception."

"And you'd miss me terrible, wouldn't you?"

Grace has to smile at this. "I doubt I could bear it."

"Your roommate, that Wilma, she went—"

"She went because she thinks the teachers are all against her."

"Do you think that's true?"

Grace considers—

"Not all. But enough."

Lizzie has stopped singing and Miss Redbird is telling her how to stand to get more from her voice.

"I would, really," says Grace, looking away from him. "I would miss you."

THE FLIES ARE THE WORST OF IT. Big, lazy, biting things, they should be dead from the cold by this time of year, but in the closed barn the heat from the cows is likely keeping them alive. There are at least a half dozen of them worrying each drowsy heifer's swinging tail, another few crawling on their faces. Wilma's favorite activity on the farm so far is killing them, a swatter made from a stick and a patch of wire screen always at reach. She tries to get five—*whap! whap! whap! whap! whap!*—before she even thinks about her other chores.

Today is Saturday and the farm mother's sister and her family are coming, which means a hen for dinner, and the birds are running around up in the loft. Wilma climbs the ladder and it is a worse smell than the cows or even their old wagon horse, a sharp smell, and she croons to them in Absaroke as if she's just come for eggs. She knows which one she wants.

She hadn't really thought through a hard winter when she signed on for Outing. They have a good, deep well here, and it's her job every morning to go out and drop the bucket down, tilting it just right so it will crack through the layer of ice that forms overnight, then let it sink till it fills and haul it up hand over hand. Then pour the bucket into the pails, one, two, three, and bring the pails in for the morning's cooking and cleaning. One time she got the bucket trapped under a thicker than usual layer of ice and Mr. Hauptman had to come to yank it free. There is a crank pulley over the well opening, but it's broken and Mr. Hauptman hasn't gotten time to fix it yet.

Wilma turns quickly and snatches the hen, a surly barred Plymouth Rock with one eye pecked out, holding it upside down by the legs, the bird gibbering and flapping till the blood goes to its head and it becomes dead weight. Then she quickly flips it up, grabbing the neck in two hands to give a hard twist—

The other chickens complain and flutter back into their roosts, feathers left hanging in the air, and Wilma backs carefully down the ladder, taking up the flyswatter again when she reaches the bottom. There were always flies around the camp ponies when she was a little girl, but those were kept away from the tipis, hobbled so they could move to graze but not easily run away, and she used to love to watch the boys and young men run out to catch them in the morning, the animals making a kind of game of it. She envied them so. Her father had several horses and she knew each by its spots or blazes, even by their gait, but he and her brothers were the ones who got to go catch them, to ride them. The closest she got was helping her mother load everything on their backs when they moved camp, and then the flies seemed to understand when you had too much in your hands and couldn't drop it and they were free to bite you at will.

Wilma flops the bird onto the block, whacks its head off with the cleaver, swiftly guts it with the knife Mr. Hauptman keeps extra sharp, and hangs it on a hook over the enamel basin to bleed out. She listens for a moment, hears nobody crunching over the ground outside, then pulls the rag out from her blouse and lets a few drops fall in the center of it. She carefully wads the rag up, stuffs it back into her blouse, and heads back to the house where things are boiling.

The water in the big pot on the iron stove is starting to roll and will be ready to scald the bird for defeathering. She walks through the house quickly, noting that Mrs. Hauptman is sitting by the fireplace darning socks, then goes out the side door toward the woodshed, a good-sized fire already set under the washing tub, which is filled with a heap of sodden overalls and a few of her own unmentionables. She pulls the bloodied rag out and tosses it in, grabs the paddle and gives the wet clothes a stir around, using all her strength

Still doing laundry.

She watches the rag swirl around, ready to pluck it out when there's still a pinkish stain in the center. It's only the second one she's missed, so it might not be the worst, but she knows they—or at least the missus—are watching her. No word from or sign of Sweetcorn. She doesn't even know if he's still at Carlisle.

Wilma dips the paddle to pull the rag out, letting it steam in the air. She's been given her own little clothesline on the side of the house where Mr. Hauptman and the boys don't often go—"privacy for your ladies' items," Mrs. Hauptman called it. But Wilma knows there is no hiding from the school, that the Man-on-the-Bandstand is probably up on a tree limb watching her right now, and she wants to be sure the missus sees the rag and its stain hanging out on her line, telling its story, like one of the foreign flags they were shown in geography class—which one was it?

Maybe Japan?

THEY'VE BEEN CALLED TOGETHER for a "special demonstration," thirty of the older new boys, crowded into the metalworking shop with Mr. Boswell, who the veteran boys call Boz and who is hard to look at because the lenses of his spectacles are so thick they make his eyes look far too large.

He beckons them to crowd around a compact dynamo with lots of gleaming copper wire wound around a shaft, many attachments hanging from it.

"The simplest form of electrical charge is what we term *static electricity*," he says, taking up two cables that hang from the device, each attached to a kind of hand grip. He looks around, chooses Trouble—

"If you'll just hold these for me—"

Trouble takes the grips in his hands, clearly confused about what is being explained. Mr. Boswell begins to turn a crank on the machine.

"Though it has limited practical use, we can generate this form of charge—"

Smokey realizes that this is some sort of a joke, and knows that Trouble is the wrong person to play it on. Boswell begins to crank harder—

"Don't worry, it won't bite you—"

Trouble's hands and arms begin to tremble rapidly, his hair standing straight out from his head till the boy shakes the grips violently from his cramped fingers with a tiny bolt of lightning crackling from each to his hands, sending him reeling backward to the wall, terrified—

"—though it might *shock* you a bit!"

Half of the other boys laugh and half are equally shaken by the phenomenon. Trouble stares at his hands to see if they've been burned.

"Now if we wish to *chan*nel that electrical energy into a *cur*rent—"

Asa is glad that Trouble is back, but the boy barely looks at him or the other roommates. Asa watches him, sitting cross-legged on his bed, doing something to his nightshirt. Asa wants to go home too, but knows he'll never make it by running.

There are other ways.

Asa lies on his back, checking to see that neither Smokey nor Antoine are looking, then reaches his hand down between the mattress and the springs to find the leather pouch with the buds in it. He only had time to find a few dozen before he was sent away, hiding the pouch in the bottom of the carpetbag he carried on the train. He works his fingers to dig out four, slips them into his mouth, chews, wincing at the bitter taste.

He hears Antoine muttering the prayer he always has on his lips, the only word Asa recognizes, having heard it again and again, sounds like "Hia-watha." Maybe something in Ojibwe, not English.

Asa swallows, waits for it to happen. The thing that carries you grows in your stomach at the beginning, fighting to get out, and when he first ate the buds he thought you had to fight to keep it in. There is a white bowl on the floor next to his shoes, just in case, but he has made this journey before and is rarely sickened by it.

Smokey also mutters, always struggling to read until the bugle makes them turn the lights out. If they ask him to stop he will, but still moves his lips as he works his way across the pages. They are not his family, Antoine, Smokey, and Trouble, not even his friends, really, but they are surviving this together.

And then he is looking down at himself lying on the bed on his back, eyes closed. It always amazes him how when he starts to expand, the room knows to grow bigger—

—as Trouble sits cross-legged on the bed, bending over with the brush he took from the sloyd class in hand, carefully painting a thunderbird on the back of his nightshirt. Antoine brought him the red ink from the room where they make the newspapers, not even asking why he needed it. Tomorrow he will bring the brush back and try to hide a knife or scissors in his pocket so he can cut the shirt shorter and make fringes at the bottom. One of the old medicine men at Standing Rock has a shirt like this, with a thunderbird and stars and a medicine wheel painted on it, but that shirt is made of deer hide. What Trouble is making will never have as much power, but if he wears it beneath his uniform at all times it will help to protect him. He knows one of the songs, taught to him in secret by the older boy who shovels coal, and sings it quietly as he paints—

—while Miss Burgess sits at her desk in the print shop, boys secure in their dormitories, machines at rest. She slants her letters in the opposite direction when she writes, hoping to disguise her hand, though she believes at least young Cato is wise to the true identity of the Man-on-the-Bandstand. This week something laudatory—

The MOTBS reads with pride the reports from the host families of our students in the Outing Program.

—she scribes. Dear Annie writes to her almost daily when she is on her supervisory circuit, complaining mildly of the weight she's gained from too many hearty farm lunches, writes of the progress or petulance of the girls, of her loneliness at night. She spends those nights at the farms if necessary, or at the homes of concerned Friends in the vicinity, saving the school a good deal of outlay. With the shorter days, Miss Burgess has been going to bed earlier.

Steady work, good manners and a cheerful attitude elicit praise and occasional offers of permanent employment. There are no handouts in our modern world—

—and certainly not for never-married women of a certain age. The acceptable professions—teaching, nursing in some areas of the country, domestic work for those of that station—are few, and public opinion, assuming that you are somehow a *failure*, generally harsh. Her mother speaks of the multitude who wore their widow's weeds with no little pride after the terrible culling of the Civil War, the wealthiest even trading their more colorful stones for jewelry fashioned of jet—Mother termed them the Black Legion. This was, of course, almost unheard of among Friends, with so few of their men willing to abandon their principles by picking up a rifle, no matter how strong their abolitionist sentiments. Miss Burgess often thinks of widows as retired military officers—encouraged to sport the uniform but no longer required to serve.

We only regret that our classmates in the field will miss our Thanksgiving festivities. The speakers, the various exhibitions, and of course the marvelous dinner.

Though it is not, literally, a Christian celebration, Thanksgiving is a wonderful way to introduce the least civilized of the students to the holidays celebrated by white America. They play an important role in the story, after all, and she enjoys the annual pageant with a handful of the students attired in bits and ends of Mrs. Pratt's collection of native finery, standing with an equally bronzed and black-haired group of early settlers in pilgrim hats and buckle shoes.

We belong together is the message of the festival, she believes, though she knows in most minds it signifies nothing weightier than a large cooked bird on a platter.

She is encouraged by the subscriptions for *Stiya* that have come in thus far, and is still campaigning with Mr. Ellenbee to have him include it as required reading for his advanced literature students. Her little cautionary tale is not Shakespeare by any means, but with the folly on the reservations exciting national headlines every day, the students can well use a warning about the dangers of returning to the blanket—

We here at Carlisle, sheltered from the hysteria sweeping our Western reservations, have so much to be thankful for.

AGENT ROYER WAS HOPING, if only for the symbolic value, that the next Issue Day could be delayed till Thanksgiving. Perhaps a few of the more progressive Sioux on the reservation, or those who've come back from the eastern training school, could then explain the history of the festival to the hostiles, perhaps even explain the concept of "thanks." Though it may be the weather, a hard, cold wind blowing steadily from the west, the present gathering lacks the festive air that has been described to him by the few holdovers in his service. Yes, many of the incorrigibles have consented to ride in from their camps, with their red wagons and their scrubby little ponies and their scrubbier little children. Yes, there are greetings and laughter as friends and relatives are reunited, though the last Issue was only two weeks ago, Commissioner Morgan weakly conceding to beg, in

Agent Royer's opinion, for peace through provender. But there is a sense of tension beneath it all, tension that has been building since the day he arrived to take over the agency at Pine Ridge. He has made himself extremely visible today, making a short speech that took far too long to translate, a smile on his lips as he nods and waves to sullen groups of his charges, posing for a photograph next to an impressive pile of commodities—it is important that all remember these goods do not just fall out of the sky, and that it is *he* who controls their dispersal—but he has asked Captain Sword to keep a pair of his policemen within sight at all times. The aspect he was not fully aware of till he arrived to take this post, the fatal oversight in policy that he still can barely believe, is that by treaty these savage people have been allowed to keep and carry their weapons.

These are much on display at the moment as the Indians crowd around the government corral, climbing up on the wooden rails, shouting and pointing, adding to the consternation of the long-horned beeves crowded within. Pistols in belts, lever-action Winchesters in hand—even some of the children seem to be armed with knives. Some might explain that this is normal for the beef issue, but Agent Royer believes it to be a conscious attempt at intimidation, the wards hoping to put their new warden in his place.

If so, they have underestimated Dr. D. F. Royer.

Young Humphrey, his good friend Weisbacher's son who he has appointed as the agency quartermaster, is trying to decipher the hieroglyphs of the previous fellow, which are meant to assign a certain number of cattle to specific heads of household. Being new, however, the poor lad is at a loss as to whether Miss Shining Path or Mr. Crockery Face are indeed eligible to collect bounty for the absent Mr. Sings While He Walks. Agent Gallagher, notoriously a pushover, no doubt learned all their blood relations and thus curried favor—Royer plans instead to enforce a system of tightly controlled chits and receipts, and on the future issue days it will be no tickee, no washee.

The first three recipients are announced to a good deal of cheering, as if they have won a raffle, and the sorry spectacle begins. A bar is lifted, a quartet of steers driven out from the corral, and then with much yipping and whooping and raising of dust the animals are chased down on horseback and shot, often by two or three excited bucks at the same time, till they fall in a heap. Then the squaws and unmounted men crowd in with knife and axe, the butchered sections wrapped in bloody hide and loaded onto horseback and wagon. A nostalgic reminder of their glory days upon the plains when the slaughter of bison was the key to their livelihood, but another indulgence he will soon be able to curtail. Captain Sword advised him that ending the custom summarily would incite resistance his small force could not hope to control, so until the military chooses to honor Agent Royer's desperate request for troops, he will have to delay that satisfaction.

What he'd had in mind, what he was just short of promised when he threw his energies into the campaign for Dakota statehood, was registrar of the land office, sure to be a nexus of influence as white homesteaders rush in to settle newly liberated farmlands. But when the worm turned in Washington and prizes were being handed out to the faithful, this was the best he was offered. Not a bad salary, said Senator Pettigrew. You'll be something of a king down there, said the backroom power brokers. Do a good job, whip that bunch of recalcitrant redskins into submission, and you'll be a hero in our new state, not to mention Nebraska—look at the national attention the press is bringing to the situation—and then who *knows* where it might lead you.

Agent Royer throws a glance toward the national press, the layabouts from the Hotel de Finley all here to watch, smoking and cheering the riders and thoroughly enjoying themselves. They are a persistent thorn in his side, and as he does possess somewhat dictatorial powers on the reservation, he has considered banishing the lot of them.

How much easier, he thinks as another terrified steer is hustled out to its doom, to do the entire slaughter and rendering with*in* the corral—some of these bucks could even be paid wages for the service. He has experienced a slaughterhouse in Kansas City, a narrow chute and a Swede with a sledgehammer replacing all this shouting and shooting, this excitement on the very edge of anarchy. Disarming the troublemakers will be no easy task, of course, especially with this ghost dancing insanity, this recrudescence of paganism, infecting so many of his charges. He notes that several of the ringleaders are not present today, no doubt having sent minions to transport their entitlements back to their respective camps.

Much excitement now—one of the bullet-riddled steers, its tongue pulled out and partially severed from its base, suddenly revives and struggles to its feet, managing to hook one of the older squaws and then totter several yards before being brought down a second time in a hail of lead, which, fortunately or not, somehow fails to strike any of the host of enthusiastic spectators. William Cody himself could not have staged a more thrilling bit of Wild-Westing.

And people, mostly easterners, mourn the passing of this "noble" mode of existence.

When I get my soldiers, thinks Royer, we'll have some order here. Let them collect their government handouts—but only in person. Let them refuse to have their children educated—and suffer the consequences. Let them go back to their old ways—with bows and arrows.

And tinned beef might be an option—

THE CELEBRATION IS HELD in the old gymnasium, a huge turkey made of batting covered with real feathers suspended from the rail of the overhead running track, students seated in wooden bleachers with the faculty in folding chairs carried in for the occasion. On the performance platform the Invincibles face off with the Standards, team members alternating in debate. Wesley Cornelius has the podium—

"The red man should not be expected to re*main* an Indian just because he is *born* an Indian," he declares to the audience, "no more so than a man who is born in *sin* should remain a sinner."

Original Sin, thinks Miss Redbird, who had the Catholic faith explained to her during her New York City sojourn. A champion debater herself, she is impressed with the young man's ability to appear so committed to an argument that must repel him.

"Those who wish to preserve him in his present state would shelter a wild, untrained animal, having never been bitten by one."

Or maybe, after eight years of Carlisle, he believes it.

Trouble, absent from the festivities and thankful for nothing, walks into the glow of a streetlight in an unfamiliar part of town, wearing the ghost shirt under his uniform jacket but not feeling invulnerable. Sweetcorn gave him a street name, wrote it on a piece of paper and handed it to him, and whenever he comes to a sign he holds the paper up to see if the writing shapes are the same. He hears music playing in a building across the street. He pauses to study a wooden statue, carved and painted to look like an Indian wearing a feathered headdress, holding a tomahawk in one hand and a small bundle of cigars, also carved in wood, in the other. Three young white men step out of the building with the music and begin to look at him the way he is looking at the wooden statue.

Don't stare at me, he tells them in Lakota.

"What's the matter, chief?" calls one of them. "Can't find your wigwam?"

The Messiah says that if white soldiers come to arrest him he will only have to spread his arms wide and they will sink into the ground. And the ghost shirt, if made properly and given power by the songs, will keep the white man's bullets from breaking his skin.

Trouble turns and walks straight toward the three.

"Aren't you red boys supposed to stay inside the fence at night?"

Trouble makes a fist. He has seen the way they fight, two drunken traders back on Standing Rock making their hands into hard balls and clubbing each other. He punches the closest of the young men in the face—

—as Cato Goforth defends the opposite, pro-Indian view—

"Without the Indian," he says, "the first white men who came to this land would have starved, would have been eaten by beasts or frozen to death in the long winter."

White men's debates, thinks Miss Redbird, never last as long as those in hunting camp or on the reservation. The point here is to tie your opponent's hands and stifle his mouth with your logic, with the precision of your words. Indian debates are conducted so everybody understands clearly what the issues are, which paths are open and what dangers may lie down them. There are not meant to be winners or losers—those who disagree tend to do what they want to, even if the majority stand on the other side of the tree.

"Without the Indian, there would be no Thanksgiving in this country, or Christmas, or New Year, or Independence Day—"

—maybe he made the shirt in the wrong way, or it is meant to stop only bullets. Trouble lies on the ground, covering his head and genitals as best he can as they kick him. They wear hard shoes. He feels something snap in his side and then they stop. He hears shouting, uncovers enough to see, and there is Sweetcorn, throwing the white boys to the ground like they are broken saplings. When they can stand they back into the building with the music, yelling curses. Sweetcorn offers his hand to Trouble—

Stand up, he says in Lakota.

He helps Trouble to his feet, looks across to the building with the music.

We'd better move on.

Clarence Regal speaks last for the Invincibles, able to alter any prepared speech to refute what his opponents have stated earlier. There is a bit of a sneer in his voice—

"Name me one invention of the Indian vital to our age of machinery and progress," he challenges. "What has he given us but to-*bacco*, which rots the lungs and confuses the mind—"

Miss Redbird, close to tears now, knows how the Lakota boy feels. Each of the white man's great inventions, when she first encountered them, both thrilled her and made her vaguely ashamed. There was the steam locomotive—what Indian mind could even imagine such a beast? And the rail that it thundered upon, reaching north, south, east, west, penetrating like an arrow into flesh, carrying the slaughterers of buffalo, the breakers of prairie sod. And the telegraph lines that followed beside the track, allowing men who might never meet to speak together, their words translated into woodpecker taps—

"The Indian consumes but does not produce, copies but does not innovate—"

Kills, thinks Miss Redbird, but does not de*stroy*—

—and now the room that Sweetcorn has taken Trouble to is full of black men. The one Sweetcorn works with feeding the fires, Otis, sits beside them at the long counter, laughing and shouting out to other men he knows who he can somehow see through the smoke in the air. The black man behind the counter brings each of them a third bottle of beer.

"You know it's against the law, servin' Indins," he says. "You got to behave."

"I ever give you trouble?" asks Sweetcorn.

Trouble recognizes his name, wonders what they are saying about him.

"No," says the bartender, pointing at Trouble, "but this one—"

"He be fine," says Otis. "It's *whis*key they can't handle, not beer."

The bartender sniffs and drifts away. Sweetcorn swivels on his stool to look at the bruise on Trouble's cheek, speaks in Lakota.

You should learn not to start a fight you know you're going to lose.

Then we'd never fight at all, says Trouble.

Sweetcorn takes a pull on his bottle, switches to English. "Maybe so. Nowadays."

Leslie John, the photographer's assistant, finishes for the Standards.

"Is it moral," he asks, "is it permissible to exterminate the race who have been the faithful stewards of the land upon which your prosperous government stands?"

Antoine, in his buckskin and single eagle feather, waits to the side of the platform, listening. The other Invincibles have been teaching him about something called rhetoric, which is a weapon that can be used by anyone able to pick it up, used to explain or to confuse, for good purposes or bad. His mother has told him of the treaties her great uncle felt forced to agree to, twisted pathways full of words meant to fool you, to trap you.

"Is there no gratitude?" pleads the Puyallup boy. "Is there no humanity?"

The ground is unsteady. Trouble holds his arms out from his sides, as if he is crossing a stream on a narrow log. Somewhere he has lost Sweetcorn, but he thinks he knows which direction the school lies in, though none of the white people buildings around him are familiar. He wants to do it at the school—

Antoine goes over his lines, his story, in his head, while Lizzie Cloud plays something rolling and stormy on the piano. He is amazed by her, so many of the black and white keys to choose from, the sound the instrument makes able to be high and low at the same time. Not amazed that she is an Indian, who have music in their lives every day, but that *any*body could pull such a complicated song from such a complicated machine.

He can look across the platform, past Lizzie at the big wooden instrument, and see Grace, shifting nervously from one foot to the other in her fringed buckskin dress and moccasins and beads, her hair parted in the middle and twisted into a pair of long braids. When he catches her eye, she puts her hand over her heart and takes a deep breath. He gives her a smile, signs that there is no worry.

Grace is the one who has been on a stage in front of people before, often white people, but she seems more worried than he does. At some point he realized that he knows the story well, that he could tell it in its entirety to anybody he met on the parade ground, so if he forgets a word or even entire lines he will just look at the people and tell them what is happening at that moment. He assumes that nobody watching will know the poem by heart, except maybe Clarence Regal, who told Antoine he played the role three years ago, opposite a Stockbridge girl who has since graduated. And if there is a bad lapse it is not *him* out there but Hiawatha, who is not even really an Ojibwe.

If you can't act you won't survive at the Carlisle School.

Lizzie Cloud finishes and he joins the audience in clapping his hands. It is a strange custom, and at first he didn't understand why the white people couldn't do it in unison—some lack of rhythmic sense in the race, perhaps—and then understood it as a polite response, like many in his life back home. No relative or stranger ever set foot within their cabin without his mother asking if they would like to eat, even if she knew they had just come from a feast.

Six younger boys come out now in blue pants and white shirts, sleeves rolled up, and perform a complicated drill with what the white people call Indian clubs, though they seem useless for any practical purpose, especially warfare. The school's brass band plays something with a lot of huffing tuba and somehow the boy with the cymbals crashes them together exactly when one of the clubs is dropped, as if he had rehearsed it with the gymnasts.

An equal number of girls holding tambourines move up around him at the side of the platform. *The Song* will be right after the tambourines, once the tipi and the trees nailed to flat wooden stands have been placed.

He is a noble huntsman. He is Hiawatha.

He looks across, past the flying, spinning clubs, to see Grace, and realizes that none of the boys will be looking at him.

Hiawatha is in love with Minnehaha.

He looks toward the audience, finds Asa and Smokey a few rows back, Smokey not smiling but waving to him. They both make the sign they have agreed on, Antoine as a question and Smokey as an answer, fists pressed against temples and pushing in—Trouble.

—Trouble, who worries that he'll rip his jacket going over the fence, takes it off, getting it a little tangled on one arm, and tosses it up to snag on one of the wooden points. He sees that his ghost shirt has a bloodstain from the fight with the white boys. He can hear the brass band playing from a building on the other side. A train whistles, passing behind him—westbound, he can tell, and not even stopping at the station. Freight train.

Trouble is still dizzy, and when he reaches up he realizes he can't touch the top of the fence.

And that the moon is full.

It takes a moment to form a plan. Without a ladder, something he has no idea where to find, there is only one way. Trouble backs up, steadying himself, then runs as fast as he can toward the fence, leaping up when he gets to it to grab hold of his jacket, which he can hear tear a bit as he hauls himself up by it and over, wooden points digging into his belly and legs, then awkwardly hanging by his hands before letting go. He hits the ground hard, stays seated with his back up against the wall. Nothing feels broken besides the ribs that were kicked before.

Trouble whoops at the moon—

"*Would he come again for arrows*

To the Falls of Minnehaha?"

—Grace asks the audience, reclining on a straw-covered gymnasium mattress just in front of the extra-wide opening of the Sibley tent that has been decorated like a Plains tipi.

"*On the mat her hands lay idle,*

And her eyes were very dreamy—"

Cato Goforth, unable to hide his embarrassment, sits just outside the tent, wrapped in a Navajo blanket to play Minnehaha's father, the ancient arrowmaker.

"*Through their thoughts they heard a footstep,*

Heard a rustling in the branches,

And with glowing cheek and forehead,

With a deer upon his shoulders—"

—and Grace does blush, Antoine having decided to play this moment without his shirt on. The deer, always a problem, is represented by a tan cotton sack stuffed with rolled-up clothing. He mimes his actions as Grace looks toward him, both hands held over her heart now, as if it might fly out of her chest with excitement—

"*Suddenly from out the woodland*

Hiawatha stood before them."

Miss Redbird is smiling. Though she is no admirer of the poem, which the author could only have written satisfied that its protagonists were safely lost in the mists of time, the boy and the girl are clearly smitten with each other. She has seen this developing during her chaperone duties, fascinated to watch male and female patiently reveal themselves to the other without the traditional intermediaries. Her own troubled courtship, with an Indian physician presently working in the far west, has been variably aided and thwarted by the national postal system—

"At the feet of Laughing Water,

Hiawatha laid his burden," says Antoine, letting the sack slide to the floor in front of Grace—

"Threw the red deer from his shoulders—"

"And the maiden looked up at him," Grace interjects,

"Looked up from her mat of rushes

Said with gentle look and accent,

You are welcome, Hiawatha!"

She pats the straw beside her, and Antoine steps into the tipi, ducking his head slightly—

"Very spacious was the wigwam," he says—

"Made of deer-skins dressed and whitened,

With the Gods of the Dacotahs

Drawn and painted on its curtains—"

Given the current frenzy of superstition in the West, thinks Miss Burgess, there might have been more supervision of the tent's decorations. She recognizes an eagle, some horselike figures, and either a crescent moon or a hunting bow, all applied in red, the color of war. Other designs, though seeming rather abstract, might have sinister meaning for some of the students present, and thus do not belong in a ceremony meant to attract them to the path of peace and civilization. And then the young brave baring his torso—if this story is enacted next year it should be by less physically mature students.

Antoine has taken to one knee, pleading with the ancient arrow-maker, who frowns with arms crossed beneath his blanket—

"After many years of warfare

Many years of strife and bloodshed,

There is peace between Ojibways

And the tribe of the Dacotahs."

The Ojibwe aren't dancing, Clarence has heard, at least not yet. They have never had open war with the U.S. Army, and have lost considerably less territory than the combined bands of the Sioux. Not dancing, perhaps not so desperate—perhaps an explanation for LaMere's ability thus far to bend with school rules without breaking under them—

Antoine turns to face the audience now, arms held out wide, addressing them directly—

"*That this peace may last forever,*
And our hands be clasped more closely,
And our hearts be more united,"

—then turns again to Grace and Cato Goforth—

"*Give me as my wife this maiden,*
Minnehaha, Laughing Water,
Loveliest Dacotah woman!"

He says this last line looking into Grace's eyes. Lizzie Cloud, back in the audience, sighs out loud, several of the girls in the row echoing her.

The door of the stable is forced open with a cracking of wood. Trouble squeezes in, jams the door shut. His favorite of the horses swings its head over the top of its stall.

Don't look at me, says Trouble in Lakota. He moves to where they keep the ropes and harness leather—

—while an Arapaho chief stands on the platform in ceremonial buckskin and feathers, directing his speech to the students as the interpreter who has traveled with him translates into English.

You are not at home, he says. You are at the white man's school to learn of the white man's ways. Listen to your school father, Captain Pratt. Obey those who teach you. Work hard, learn all you can. The campfire of the red man is very low—it gives smoke, but very little warmth.

The chief takes a long moment to meet the eyes of all the students. You young ones must not let it die.

Trouble, with the rope over his shoulder and noose already tied, climbs the slats of the hog pen, the pair of black Berkshires inside raising their pink snouts with vague interest. Though still unsteady from the beer, he thinks he can manage to lean out and tie off on the lowest overhead rafter, then jump and swing his legs out—

—as Grace, still tingling from the performance and the applause it garnered, is waiting just on the other side of the standing screen the male performers change costume behind, excited conversation and scraping chairs heard from out front. She beams when she sees Antoine coming—

"You were the perfect Hiawatha!"

She kisses him, quickly, but on the lips, and hurries behind the scenery to the girls' side. Antoine is still a bit stunned when Smokey appears.

"You seen Trouble?"

"Wasn't he in the audience?"

"No."

"Maybe he's hiding out in the room—"

"He ask me in the morning if you can ride alla way to Dakota on one horse."

Antoine hurries to button his shirt. "How many horses do they keep in that stable?"

Asa has joined them by the time they reach it, finding that the door has been forced. Trouble is swinging from a rope over by the hog pen, his legs pumping as if he's trying to run up a hill. Antoine rushes to get his shoulders under Trouble's feet, grabbing his ankles in case he starts to kick, as Smokey runs to grab the axe hung by the hay rakes, tossing it up to Asa, already balanced on the top rail of the pen. Three strokes of the axe and Trouble falls, Antoine going to the floor with him.

By the time they leave the barn the grounds are full of students and instructors, talking in small groups, full of Thanksgiving turkey. They can see Mr. Skinner planted between them and the dormitory, loudly regaling two well-dressed town merchants with his favorite story.

"They take the train all the way to Washington to see the Great White Father," he says, "not one of the chiefs who's ever slept in a four-poster bed before, and they check into the hotel they've been told about, and go upstairs, four to a room. Only one of them really speaks English, and nobody at the desk thinks to explain the *gas* lights in the rooms to them. So one of the chiefs, when it's time to sleep, thinks 'Well, I guess it's time to blow these lamps out—'"

"They thought they were oil lamps?"

"Whatever they thought, he somehow manages to get the flames out, but doesn't pay any attention to the hissing sound that's still going on—"

Antoine has one of Trouble's arms over his shoulder, nods for Smokey to take the other, and they half carry Trouble toward the dormitory.

"*Beautiful dreamer,*" sings Antoine, repeating one of the ballads Lizzie Cloud had thrilled the audience with earlier in the evening, "*wake unto me—*"

Smokey joins him singing, and Asa, following along, hums in tune.

"*Starlight and dewdrops are waiting for thee—*
Sounds of the rude world, heard in the day
Lulled by the moonlight have all passed away—"

"Is he all right?" calls the disciplinarian as they pass near him.

"Too much to eat," Antoine calls back.

"*Beautiful dreamer, queen of my song—*"

Trouble helps them a little bit getting up the stairs, pushing with wobbly legs, his face slowly resuming a proper color, and they get him laid out on his bed, Asa stashing the torn jacket and severed noose in Antoine's footlocker. Smokey studies the designs on Trouble's ghost shirt.

"So that's it, huh?" he says quietly. "That's the thing they're up to."

There is a knock on the door. Antoine hesitates, steps over to open it a crack. Clarence Regal stands outside.

"Open," he says.

Maybe Clarence is the Man-on-the-Bandstand, thinks Antoine. He misses nothing.

Clarence steps in, signaling Antoine to close the door behind him. He goes over to Trouble, takes up the one burning oil lamp to hold it close enough to examine the rope burns on the boy's neck. He grabs a chair, sits on it beside Trouble.

"Look at me."

Trouble looks at the master sergeant, angry and ashamed and not at all drunk anymore. Clarence speaks to him in Lakota—

Hanging is no way for one of us to die! Think of the shame it would bring your parents.

He thumps his own chest—

You have murder here. I know how that feels. But we have to fight with our wits now. Learn what you can here, then go home and be a warrior for our people!

Clarence stands and looks around at the others.

"Not a word of this to anyone."

He steps out. The oil lamp, left on the floor, throws their shadows high on the walls and ceiling.

Asa moves to the side of the bed then, touches the palm of his hand to the Lakota boy's chest and then to his own.

"*Hermanos*," he says. "Brudda."

Antoine gives Smokey a look, and then they both step in to put a hand on each of his shoulders.

"Brother," says Antoine.

"Brother," says Smokey.

"You're not alone here," Antoine tells him.

"That's right," adds Smokey. "We're a *tribe*. Carlisle Indians."

Trouble, trying manfully not to weep, looks to them and slowly brings his index and middle fingers up to touch his lip, making the sign—

Brother.

THE BOYS IN THE BOXCAR have five candles lit now, and have arranged a comfortable space for themselves, sitting on and surrounded by crates. After-hours in the dormitory at Carlisle they'd roll a blanket up and stuff it across the bottom of the door, keeping their voices down. Here in the freight car Antoine and the white boy speak over the dull rumble of the train and the clack of rails beneath the floor.

"So this Trouble fella is—?"

"Lakota. You call it Sioux."

"Like at the Custer massacre."

"His father was at the battle."

"Jeez—"

"On the winning side. Along with the Cheyenne, Arapaho—"

"There's a big difference?"

Antoine looks the white boy, Jimmy, over.

"Where your people come from again?"

"Poland."

"The Cherkowski tribe."

Jimmy grins.

"Any difference between you and the Italians?"

"Hell yeah—guineas drink vino, we drink beer. Well—my old man always *starts* with beer, then it's whatever he can find that'll knock him on his ass. Can't hold their firewater, the Polish."

They ride in silence for a moment.

"So," says Jimmy, "you headin' home, or what?"

"I don't know," says Antoine. "Maybe. I'm a fugitive from the government."

"You mean you're playin' hooky from school."

"If you head straight back home, they wire ahead and catch you. I been working some places, begging handouts—"

"Whattaya mean, they catch you—"

"We're not citizens."

"Sure you are."

Antoine shakes his head.

"Wards of the state. Like crazy people they lock up."

"But you were here first."

Antoine shrugs.

"Crazy," says Jimmy, then pulls a soiled handkerchief out from his pocket, unwrapping it to reveal a hunk of corn bread. He offers half to Antoine—

"Here."

Antoine hesitates, then nods and accepts the food. Each boy tries to eat slowly, staring at the candle flames—

"Ice will be breaking up on the lake now," says Antoine when he's finished. "People at home fix up their canoes, get out after the fish. Sometimes we'll go out at night with torches, spear them in the shallows—"

"I got no home."

Jimmy's statement hangs in the air, and then they notice that the rhythm of the clacking has changed—they're slowing down.

Jimmy quickly grabs a rag and begins to douse the candles, sticking them back into the crate they came from.

"Get behind something."

Antoine arranges a wall of crates with just enough room for him to crouch behind as the last candle is snuffed out.

Darkness.

Banging of the couplings as the train comes to a halt.

Voices outside, then suddenly the rumble of the side door being hauled open. A flashlight beam stabs into the darkness and for a moment Antoine can see Jimmy only a few feet away from him, trying to hold his breath. The light beam twitches around the interior, Antoine hoping there is no hanging smoke left from the candles. The boys lock eyes just before the beam swings away and the side door is banged shut.

Darkness again. Voices, fading.

"So," comes Jimmy's voice in a whisper, "the Sioux kids hangs but he don't die—"

DECEMBER

IT IS THE THIRD FUNERAL THIS MONTH. ANTOINE STANDS AT attention, picked for the honor guard for reasons he is not aware of, staring into the red, creased back of the neck of Father Dolan from St. Patrick's as he half-sings the Latin—

"*In manus tuas, Domine, commendo spiritum ea*—"

The girl's coffin is slightly bigger than the last one they stood witness to. When they gave Antoine his footlocker it reminded him of what his cousin Terese's little boy who drowned was put in, only that had been decorated with crosses and angels by her people.

"*Omnis chorus Iustorum, orate pro ea*—"

A Cherokee boy died last month, but his parents had the money to have him sent home for burial. Antoine's A Company was chosen to walk as the honor guard after the ceremony in the auditorium, Carlisle students lining both sides of the road as the boy's coffin was carried to the train station and the band marched behind playing a dirge. Clarence says they put the coffin in a car on the mail train and make sure to keep track of it. He says if it's going west of the Rockies, they put it in a refrigerator car. Antoine looks past the priest and over to the line of older girls—

"*Omnes sancti Innocentes, orate pro ea. A poenis inferni, libera eam, Domine*—"

Grace has tears streaming down her face. She told him she knew the girl from her nursing, an Apache girl who barely got off the train before she was in the infirmary, her parents, if still living, obviously too poor to send for her body. The oldest graves are scattered at the bottom of the hill behind the shop buildings, most of the crosses and tablets made of wood, some of them fallen over. There is a new cemetery area started, the graves in a more orderly line, and plenty of space left to be filled.

"*Per gloriosam resurrectionem tuam, libera eam, Domine. Requiem æternum dona ei, Domine, et lux perpetua luciat ei.*"

Captain Pratt watches from the rear of the small boys with Marianna Burgess by his side. Funerals at the school are always bad, and there are too many of them. Early on he made more of a protest to the Indian agencies for sending children who were already afflicted, but has come to believe that the medical care offered on the reservations is most likely far inferior, whether through lack of funds or criminal neglect, to that here at the school, so why not give them a better chance at survival? But soon more land will have to be dedicated to the cemetery. He thinks of the little boneyards at each of the military posts where he has served, filled mostly with private soldiers who may well have enlisted under invented names. He had one artful dodger at Fort Gibson who had signed on and deserted at least three times, enjoying the government meals and relative lack of fighting every winter, then gone with the spring. The tribes Captain Pratt is acquainted with are very serious about death, of course, each with their particular mode of mourning, not shy of self-mutilation or taking foolhardy risks to retrieve a slain comrade from a battlefield—

"The Romans," mutters Miss Burgess as the priest begins to make gestures over the coffin with the ornate cross in his hand. "Dazzling their followers with colorful vestments and elaborate theatrics—"

"Yes," agrees the Captain. "They do love a ritual."

"*Requiescat in pace. Amen.*"

The brass band eases into Chopin's *Funeral March* then, and the various companies begin their march back to their dormitories as one of the groundsmen and, if Pratt is not mistaken, the overgrown Sioux boy, Sweetcorn, who has been such a disappointment, wait to carry the box to the school cemetery. A fire had to be set on the spot to thaw the earth enough to dig a grave.

The band acquit themselves remarkably well with the sonata, solemn without becoming dreary, trumpet, trombone, and tuba a slow-flowing river of sorrow above the rattle of the snare drum.

Lord knows they've had plenty of practice with it this year.

It is always a pleasure to meet somebody who is passionate about trains. The Sioux boy has just helped him shoe the gelding, stroking its head and cooing to it in a language he probably shouldn't be speaking, even to a horse, when he saw Drayton's railroad map of the country on the table they use to lay out harnesses to teach the young boys how to hitch a team. Went to it like a housefly to buttermilk.

"Now, when I was a boy," says Drayton, turning the map so north is at the top, "there wasn't even a *wag*on that could take you crost the country. Nowdays, seventy, seventy-five dollars, railroad'll let you off right at your doorstep in—where is it? Your home?"

"Stannin Rock," says the Sioux boy.

"*Stand*ing Rock. You'd get the CVRR—that's the Cumberland Valley Railroad—right here from Carlisle to Harrisburg"—the boy watches intently as Drayton traces the route with his finger—"then switch to the Philadelphia, Harrisburg, and Pittsburg road—"

The boy, Trouble something, has a real knack for the horses and does a good job mucking and feeding. You get the feeling there's a story going on in his head though, a story he's keeping to himself—

"—then on to the Pittsburg, Cincinnati, Chicago, and St. Louis—

that's the PCC and St. L—get off in Chicago, and from there you got the Chicago and Northwestern all the way to Pierre in the Dakota Territory—though it's states out there now, isn't it?"

The boy puts his thumb on Pierre, then slides his index finger up from the Missouri River to where the Standing Rock reservation is marked, as if calculating the walk—

"If you got the train fare," says Mr. Drayton, "we're practically neighbors."

The cover of the book is the most upsetting thing, a photograph of poor Evangeline, though the character is named Stiya and is a Pueblo girl.

"No, mother, I have not become a white woman," Grace reads out loud. "*Talking Indian as fast as they could they tried to help me from the train*—"

There are a dozen girls seated around the reading room, as well as Miss Burgess, the proud author, and Miss Redbird, sitting solemnly beside her.

"*My father took my valise and my mother threw her head upon my shoulder and cried for joy.*"

Grace usually loves reading out loud, trying to match her voice and emotion to the characters portrayed. But this she tries to speed through—

"My *father?* My *mother? cried I desperately within. No! Never! I thought, and actually turned my back on them. I had forgotten that home Indians had such grimy faces*—"

Grace lowers the little book away from her face. "I'm sorry, Miss Burgess, I'm feeling a little shaky."

Concern from Miss Burgess. "Are you ill?"

"No, just feeling a little dizzy on my feet. I didn't eat much today—"

"You girls, worrying about your figures. Sit then, and Lizzie will pick it up. Lizzie?"

Lizzie gives Grace a hard look as they change places, then finds the page and reads in a flat, colorless tone—

"I had forgotten that my mother's hair looked like she'd never passed a comb through it, that she wore such a short, queer-looking buckskin bag for a dress. 'My mother!' I cried, this time aloud. I rushed frantically into the arms of my school-mother, who had accompanied me this far, threw my arms around her neck and cried bitterly, begging of her to let me get on the train again. 'I don't want to live in a filthy place like this,' I cried, 'I cannot go with that woman!'"

Miss Redbird stands abruptly. "I'm sorry, but she doesn't look at all well to me," she says, stepping to Grace and extending her hand. "I'm taking her to the infirmary."

"Very well. You go ahead, Lizzie—and don't read in such a hurry—"

They are halfway across the parade ground before Grace speaks.

"It's not anything like that when I go home! My mother dresses as well as anyone, and we live in *houses*!"

"Miss Burgess says it's based on her visits to the Pueblo."

"I'd never treat my mother that way."

"I should hope not. White people"—Miss Redbird struggles with her thought—"When they look at us, they only see what they want to. Even here—"

"Save the man, kill the Indian."

"Sometimes I fear we're only doing the second part of the task."

Grace stops walking, rubs tears from her eyes. "I'm not really sick, you know. I just couldn't—"

"You gave me a good excuse to get out of there. I thought I might scream."

This confidence stops Grace in her tracks. "You've done so well in their world."

"Treason has its rewards," mutters Miss Redbird, veering off toward the teachers' quarters. "I'll tell Burgess you took a bromide and went to lie down in your room."

Jesse Echohawk, healing well, has developed a quick forward gait with the crutches, swinging his body between them and landing on the foot of his good leg, the other boys having to hurry to keep up with him.

"I don't even play football," calls Antoine as he trails the group.

"That's why we need you," Jesse calls back. "This should be pure logic. The Captain loves oratory, and you represent the school body—"

"I wouldn't go that far—"

"Better than that, you can remember a load of talk."

"That poem took me weeks."

"Then let's go over the argument again."

Antoine closes his eyes for a second, then recites—

"Football is the all-American game—"

In Captain Pratt's office their order is reversed, Antoine standing to the fore, and Jesse between two of the bigger boys so his crutches are less prominent.

"As rough a game as it is, when people think about football, who do they think of? Harvard, Yale, Princeton, West Point—"

The Captain listens without expression.

"It's where the elite young white men in this country show their discipline, their courage, their willingness to tackle adversity."

Antoine feels like it's sounding too rehearsed, tries to hit a more common note—

"Gosh, if us Indians are gonna compete in their world, why shouldn't we be allowed to compete in their most cherished sport?"

"'*We* Indians,'" corrects the Captain.

"Sorry. Sure, there's always a risk of injury, a risk of failure, but like you always tell us, Captain Pratt, nothing worthwhile comes easy."

Antoine, out of ammunition, holds his hands out pleadingly, feeling like what Clarence Regal would call a sap.

The Captain takes a long moment to consider.

"Aptly stated, young man," he says finally. "Let me make a bargain with you boys—" and here he looks past Antoine to Jesse Echohawk. "Football, including matches against outside schools, will be reinstated on two conditions—first, you must never *slug.* This has become a lamentable part of the game, and when white players do it, it is merely considered football. If *you* slug your opponent it will be taken as a confirmation of the inherent savagery of the red man."

"We can manage that, sir," says Jesse.

"Very well. The other condition is that you must promise me that within the very near future you will *beat* the football squads of Harvard, Yale, Princeton, and West Point."

The boys are stunned. They can barely stand up to the Dickinson students from across town.

"We'll do our best, sir," says Jesse.

"No, you must promise that you will de*feat* them. Best intentions don't get the job done."

Jesse smiles manfully. "We'll run them off the field, sir."

"That's the spirit! I'm only sorry that the season has ended."

Captain Pratt waits till the boys have given their thanks and gone before he begins to chuckle. Harvard, Princeton, Yale, indeed. Though no devotee of the sport, he knows those august institutions are apt to lower their academic expectations to bring in some dreadnought to run the fullback position, that Yale's Pudge Heffelfinger is rumored to tip the scales past two hundred pounds, while his reservation boys, though often sprightly athletes, would be as delicate antelope before a charging buffalo herd should they ever venture forth against a real college eleven.

But give them something to strive for.

And who knows, he thinks then, what with a real coach who understands the game—

SATURDAY AFTERNOON, the Carlisle streets busy with white people who have places to be and affairs to attend to. Even if the mere thought of it didn't make her palms sweat, Miss Redbird doubts if any of them would be able to direct her to an immigrant luthier's repair shop if she did stop them to inquire.

They're looking but not staring. It is a skill Miss Redbird appreciates, having been sufficiently scrutinized since adopting what they call "civilian dress." She is slight enough and young enough to be mistaken for a Carlisle student, but students are not allowed to venture this far from the train station when not in uniform. A fixing and holding of their gaze at her just a tad longer than necessary, something akin to "Do I know you?"

But this is "What *are* you?"

In the Southwest, perhaps, she could pass for a Mexican woman and be ignored if she wasn't also carrying the violin case. That is the second flick of the eyes, and then they pass by, wondering.

Let them wonder.

The curiosity is natural, she knows, as they don't see people who look like her in their everyday lives, and are too polite to come straight out and question her provenance. In the Dakotas or Nebraska there would be anger behind many of the stares, and she once experienced a man vehemently objecting to her being allowed in the same train compartment with him. The conductor, to his credit, politely escorted the man to a seat in the next car.

Miss Redbird pauses to look at the little map that Dennison Wheelock, a student who is all but running the school band, has drawn for her. She has passed Blumenthal's Clothing Shop and the Flickenmeyer Bakery, has marveled at the imposing stone prison, so like a picture-book castle, and there realized she had somewhere taken a wrong turn. The white people step around her as she attempts to puzzle out where she is at the moment, and she senses that it is more than skin color that sets them apart.

They be*long* here.

And Miss Redbird, virtuoso musician, erstwhile debate champion, paragon of her endangered race, has nowhere to call home.

She walks on, lost, till she sees a sign ahead for Pitt Street, which is on her little map with an X marking the music shop location. She steps to stand beneath the sign, looks both ways—it is a very long street—makes a guess, and turns left.

In New York she was treated like a rare and valuable animal, interesting to look at but not to be trusted out of sight, and therefore escorted everywhere she was to perform or be shown off. She tends to become disoriented when surrounded by buildings, always relieved when there is a river in sight to anchor her position. At what used to be her home you could literally see for miles, each substantial hill and creek bed with a story attached to it. In these cities, loaded horse carts and carriages full of people working their way around each other, men under hats, women carrying umbrellas even when it isn't raining, she struggles not to despair. She can't imagine ever being a part of it, any more than she can imagine herself again living on the blighted reservation with her mother.

And now the people staring at her are colored.

It happened very suddenly, and though they are not dressed so differently, there is not a white face among them. She has seen plenty of black men before, soldiers at the fort when she was a small girl, the men who lift baggage at the train station, but she has never been this close to the women.

Now, she fears, she is staring back.

The women's hair, what she can see underneath their hats, is so different, and they are in fact all different colors. She wonders if they venture from these few blocks around her, if they walk alone in the white city. And, shamefully, she wonders if she is safe here.

Then there are young men stepping up in front of her from Briscoe's Oyster Cellar, in this season advertising pigs' feet, turtle soup, Yuengling beer, but NO SHELLFISH. Three young Negroes, and then a young man she recognizes from school, though he is dressed as colorfully as the others. They pass in the opposite direction, talking and laughing, seeming to be having far too much fun this early in the day. She and the student, who she has heard stories about from the other faculty, look through each other as they pass.

Sweetcorn. His name is Sweetcorn and he is Sioux and restricted to the school grounds.

I am a music teacher, thinks Miss Redbird, not a prison warden.

And then, in the window of a narrow wooden building with paint peeling on the outside wall, is a hand-lettered sign.

GIOVANNI DiVINCENZO
FIX ALL INSTRUMENTS

The sighting by the music teacher doesn't worry Sweetcorn. He's already packed a satchel for his trip to Philadelphia. If he can shovel coal at school he can do it in the big city, and be paid for it. Otis has been there and says a man can breathe, can live in a neighborhood no white man dare enter, can write his own ticket. Independence—isn't that what the Captain has always wanted for them?

The farm woman has offered Miss Ely tea, which she sips between filling in the visit form.

"She's been attending church with you?"

"She's a good girl," says Mrs. Hauptman. "Minds what I say, does her chores well—though she does mope a tad on laundry Monday—very polite at the table. My girls just dote on her."

Wilma stands just back from the door to the kitchen, hidden from their view, ready to bustle away with an armful of sheets if they get up—

"And you've been monitoring her—you know—?"

"Oh, she's been having her courses, just like clockwork. I see it in the wash."

"And her health otherwise?"

"Excellent, excellent. She has a hearty appetite—I'd swear she's gained ten pounds since she came to us."

Wilma has taken to wearing an apron all day but leaving it untied in the back. There is something going on in there, she can tell, and wonders how long it will remain her secret alone.

"General cleanliness is acceptable?" asks Miss Ely, checking boxes on the form. "No nasty habits?"

Saturday night features a cakewalk. There is even cake, several different sizes and shapes and flavors of icing, laid out on the tables near the entrance to the gymnasium. Lizzie Cloud plays a 2/4 march on the piano as Carlisle boys in their uniforms and Carlisle girls in their nicest dresses move in opposite directions, the boys making a squared pattern as the girls weave through them. Lizzie hits the chord to signal and the boys one by one take a corresponding girl's arm and promenade down the center of the square, Antoine pushing two small boys past him to end up with Grace, who smiles as she offers her arm to him.

They promenade together, passing the phalanx of instructors by the punch bowl. Miss Burgess, appeasing the Captain's nostalgia for the few elaborate officers' balls he has attended, has organized the evening, hoping that the positive effect of the required gentlemanly behavior toward the young ladies, something she found sorely lacking in her Pawnee Agency experience, will outweigh any worry that the boys and girls will "pair off." There is no face-to-face dancing in a cakewalk, which will be followed by a sedate square dance or two, the farrier, Mr. Drayton, set to call the figures. Miss Redbird, though touted to be a virtuoso on the violin, has declined to serve as fiddler, and so a fellow from out in the county has been engaged. Miss Burgess notes that the Captain and his wife seem pleased, and the young people, segregated by sex except in the classroom, appear to be enjoying the opportunity.

Trouble and Asa, among those judged still too sluggard in their comprehension to hazard on the dance floor, watch from the west wall bleachers. They are accustomed to the white people's music by now, but this random pairing of male and female seems to them slightly scandalous, and wonder if the girls' parents, should they still be alive, know what goes on here at Carlisle. If there is a *rea*son for this dancing, a message to the spirits or even a celebration of a victory, they have not been told what it is.

Later, Grace and Antoine sit at one of the small tables set out on the floor as ice cream and cake are served, acutely aware that fellow students as well as chaperoning adults are watching them, and trying to appear more lighthearted than their conversation.

"If you pretend for long enough," she says, "maybe that's who you become."

"But you like it here. That's not pretending—"

"I don't like everything about it."

Antoine nods, then waves to Jesse Echohawk, just off his crutches, who is making the sign for "pretty girl" across the room to him.

"Back home they tell me I'm not Indian enough cause my father is half white," he tells her. "Here I'm not white enough cause I still think like an Indian."

"You do?"

"Everything I do here, I got to think, What's gonna make them happy? What's gonna keep them off my back?"

"I just do what seems right at the moment."

"Your people been around them a lot longer than mine have."

"Maybe. My brothers went here—they made it sound important. So I wanted to be part of—you know—"

"The Carlisle tribe."

She smiles. "Yes."

"Sometimes I feel like the Old Ones are watching me—talking about me in Ojibwe. They don't approve."

"They lived in a different world."

"They were never a*lone*. Back home, I come inside and find my mother—nobody else is in there—and she's talking to the Old Ones, or to the animal spirits—"

"Do you miss your home?"

"Only when I think about it."

Grace laughs. She sees Miss Burgess heading across the floor toward them—

"But if I didn't come here," says Antoine, "I wouldn't have met you."

Grace has only an instant to be thrilled.

"Grace," calls Miss Burgess, speaking as she drifts past their table, "young ladies are meant to *cir*culate and be lovely, dear, not set up camp. Like butterflies."

SNOW FALLS ON CARLISLE in the first week of December. Sweetcorn, expert with a shovel now, is tasked to help clear the wooden boardwalks laid out on the parade ground, and the students' feet flatten the drifts where they muster in the mornings. The Man-on-the-Bandstand takes note—

Winter's downy mantle hugs our school grounds once again, and it is a joy to see our students taking full advantage. The skaters and sledders are in their glory—

—as Antoine trots along pulling little Tecumseh Starr behind him on a slider improvised by the carriage-making apprentices, and as he listens to the swoosh of the runners he thinks of his brothers out on the lake, ice fishing—

Meanwhile the Messiah craze continues its deadly grip on the superstitious minds at our Dakota reservations—

—and Trouble imagines his westward odyssey, train by train, as he curries the gelding in the freezing stable, the steam from his breath and that of the horse mingling in the air—

But there will be no Messiah, no Great Flood, no opening of the earth's surface—

—Clarence Regal reading these words in *The Indian Helper* as he sits in a club chair in the large boys' library—

Thousands, perhaps, of your people will suffer and many will be killed before they get their eyes open. Boys and girls, if you were there you could not help them.

General Assembly.

Captain Pratt understands that the best antidote to barracks fever is preemptive intervention.

"I know you are aware of the reports from Rosebud and Pine Ridge," he says. "I believe them to be greatly ex*ag*gerated. These ghost dancers are more a figment of the overheated imaginations of avaricious eastern correspondents hoping to whip up war fervor, so that they might have something to spill their ink on, than exemplars of a true spiritual movement among the Indians!"

He takes a moment to meet the eyes of his solemn, tightly packed students, then addresses the faculty section, front left, hoping to remind them of their true mission.

"Teachers—we cannot sit idly on the sidelines and watch as a quarter million of our fellow citizens"—he pauses for this to sink in—"for I do firmly believe that they should be *grant*ed that status—remain chained to the socialism of the tribe and the reservation, and be crushed by the whims of ancestral oligarchy."

He notes that Marianna Burgess isn't in her usual seat, and Skinner is absent from his vantage at the back of the aisle—

"We'd have dismissed the boy," says the disciplinarian as he and Miss Burgess move down the girls' dormitory hallway, voices muted, "but he disappeared last night. Lit out to the east from what we can tell—"

"A scoundrel."

"If he were still here he'd be facing an F and B."

"Pardon?"

"Fornication and banditry—it's still a crime in Pennsylvania, no matter what your race."

"Oh dear."

"And I'm afraid he's one of those who regularly snuck into town to worship at the altar of Venus. Dr. Hazzard examined the boy on Tuesday—some concern about his lungs becoming contaminated in the boiler room—and reported he'd acquired a little souvenir."

"Are you implying—?"

Skinner nods gravely, enjoying the drama. "The young lady is not only in a delicate condition, she may be diseased."

"Do we tell her this?"

"To what end? Our wire will arrive at Crow Agency before she does."

Miss Burgess, truly distressed at losing another of her charges to sin, shakes her head. "She was a poor student, but so willing to *try*. And doomed now to be only another camp girl—"

—while in their room Grace helps Wilma, betrayed by a week of vomiting and a doctor's visit, gather her possessions and arrange them in a cardboard suitcase. It feels like they're about to attend another burial.

"You'll get to see your mother and father," offers Grace.

"They'll be ashamed of me."

They speak English together so easily now, Wilma having very little when she first arrived, but through their years of rooming together it has progressed to where the Crow girl no longer thinks in Absaroke.

"They'll be thrilled to have you back."

She knew Wilma was sneaking out to see the Sioux boy—really a man by now—but had no idea it had gone this far. She feels a bit hurt not to have been confided in.

"I think I'm supposed to leave all the school clothes," says Wilma, laying a folded uniform dress on the edge of her bed. "They don't fit me now anyway."

She turns to the wall to take down a color advertisement for Old Sachem Bitters and Wigwam Tonic, featuring a drawing of a handsome, idealized warrior, looking it over and then adding it to the pile in the suitcase.

"I was just a little girl when I came here."

Miss Redbird, given the word by Lizzie Cloud, the other roommate, hurries across the slippery boardwalk between the snowbanks to the dormitory, arriving just in time to relieve Skinner and Miss Burgess of their escort duties.

"I'll take over from here," she tells them.

Such a tiny thing, thinks Miss Burgess as she nods her assent, but fierce when she wants to be.

Miss Redbird takes one of Wilma's arms and Grace, carrying the cardboard suitcase, takes the other. It is snowing again, big wet flakes on a nippy wind, and Miss Redbird was in too much of a rush to throw on her heavy coat. She waits till they're far enough away from Burgess and the disciplinarian to speak.

"I'll write to the agent at Sweetcorn's reservation—"

"I doubt they'll pay much attention," says Grace, "with all that's going on."

"He doesn't want anything to do with me!" says Wilma in a teary burst. "He never wrote once while I was on Outing."

"If he did, his letters were likely kept from you."

The girls slow to look at Miss Redbird, shocked.

"Even if he went to a postbox in town, they have an agreement with the school. The school acts *in loco parentis*—as if you're literally their children—just as the government does with all of us. And they do what they can to avoid scandals."

"Or just to keep them quiet after they happen," says Grace, brooding.

Two cadet guards, a dusting of snow on their caps and shoulders, open the gate to reveal a one-horse cab waiting, the driver standing beside it. Wilma turns to hug her roommate—

"If it's a girl I'll call her Grace."

"I reiterate that civilization and savagery are *habits*," states Captain Pratt, "which can be learned and unlearned. And the first step for the Indian in that learning process is to hold his own land as an indi*vid*ual."

The Captain drills his eyes into those of the older boys, the ones who might soon be going back to allotments created through the Dawes Act. All this carping about Indians selling their land to whites—it is theirs to do what they wish with. The free man, the citizen, takes responsibility for his actions—

"And let that individual thrive upon it by the sweat of his brow, or lose it and sink into penury."

Do you wish me to take the earth, my mother, thinks Clarence Regal standing at the back of the hall, recalling Red Cloud's response to the farmer sent to demonstrate the plow to the Oglala, *and cut into her flesh? Do you wish me to break her bones?*

"This Messiah business, this ghost dancing, is a mere distraction and will soon fade away," the Captain reassures them. "Believe me."

AGENT MCLAUGHLIN SAID to bring a wagon, but a rattling wagon will wake the whole camp up. The plan was originally to wait till Saturday, when most of the people, even the ghost dancers, will be in at the agency to pick up their issue. But then Bullhead saw the number of horses, fast-riding horses, increasing by the medicine man's cabin every day and warned McLaughlin, and the arrest was moved forward.

The ride from Bullhead's house to the compound by the river is only a few miles, the road between well traveled enough that they can move swiftly even in the dark. It is bitter cold, ground frozen under the horses' hooves making a hollow, metallic sound as they ride, two companies of Indian police and a few volunteers, at an easy trot. Bullhead has gone over the strategy with them all at his house—who will go into the cabin, who will bring the riderless horse they're stringing along up to receive the prisoner, which men will dismount to form a protective perimeter, which will remain mounted. More and more of the ghost dancers have been gathering around the cabin, some even coming up from Cheyenne River and Rosebud and camping out in the cold, but this early they should still be asleep.

If he'll cooperate it should go smoothly.

Agent McLaughlin says it might only be for a serious talk, and if Sitting Bull will change his mind, agree to stop stirring the people up, they'll escort him back home. But if not—he has said several times that he is ready to fight, ready to die—and the Messiah says those who die now will have a short journey and not wait long before they return to the land as it was before the whites arrived. If that's what he wants, Bullhead is bringing forty men to help him on his way.

When they see the first canvas tents and tipis, ghostly white in the darkness, Bullhead prods his mount into a canter and the others follow. Get it done before the people can object. It will be good to be well on the way back to the agency before the detachment from Fort Yates reaches them. The ghost dancers have been told that their ceremonies have bewitched the white soldiers, made it so their bullets lack the power to break an Indian's skin, and some fool is sure to want to see if this is true—

Bullhead and his men are not white soldiers.

Forty-some mounted men pull up outside the cabin, plenty of dogs barking but no people about yet, and deploy, Bullhead leading Sergeant Shavehead, Little Eagle, High Eagle, Warrior Fear Him, and Red Tomahawk in through the unbarred door.

Sitting Bull is in bed with one of his wives. He is pulled to his feet while a rifle beside his bed and one from the wall are taken.

You are under arrest, Bullhead tells him. You'll be taken to the agency, where Major McLaughlin wishes to talk with you.

He can come here to talk, says Sitting Bull.

My orders are to bring you to him. Get dressed.

Sitting Bull considers this for a moment. He is surrounded by policemen holding rifles. He turns to his wife.

Make us some coffee.

There won't be time for that, says Bullhead.

What is the hurry? Am I fighting you?

Get dressed.

Sitting Bull's son Crowfoot, more than a boy and not quite a man, steps in then from another room, looking upset.

What do they want?

They've come to take me away.

Only to the agency, says Bullhead. Those are my orders.

You've come to kill my father.

If that was true he would already be dead.

Crowfoot looks to his father.

Are you going to go?

Sitting Bull is dressing, very slowly.

You see how many rifles they have.

And there are more outside, Bullhead tells him.

You'll kill him on the way, says Crowfoot. You'll lie and say he'd tried to escape.

You can help, Bullhead tells the young man. As we leave, you can tell the people here not to follow us, not to cause trouble.

Shoots Walking steps in from outside.

People are coming, he says. All around us. It's too dark to see their faces.

Sitting Bull, dressed now, sits back down on his bed.

When the ground opens up and the white men sink into it, he says, you'll be buried too. That metal on your chest will be your doom.

Bullhead touches the tin badge pinned to his vest.

You don't really believe that.

I have had the vision myself.

Then what do you have to be afraid of?

I'm not afraid. I'm deciding whether I'll allow you to take me away or not.

You're going to the agency, says Bullhead, one way or the other.

He can tell the old man is stalling, giving his followers time to gather. There is shouting outside now, both men's and women's voices. High Eagle and Warrior Fear Him have their rifles leveled at Crowfoot.

You can walk out the door like a man, Bullhead continues, or be carried.

The old man is thinking. Even Red Cloud, a greater warrior in his time, has made a peace with the whites, accepting that the Sioux are outnumbered, they are outgunned, that to fight more is to starve, is to see the young ones die, is to end as a people. But Sitting Bull is a medicine man who claims to have visions, who, maybe, even believes that the Creator of All Things is ready to deliver them from the prison of this reservation—

Sitting Bull stands.

We go now.

They start for the door, Bullhead leading, Little Eagle and High Eagle each taking one of the prisoner's arms, Sergeant Shavehead just behind them. Crowfoot follows them all, taunting.

You're the white man's dogs, he says. He throws you a scrap of meat and you lick his hand.

When they reach the door, Lieutenant Bullhead turns to Sitting Bull. If there is bad trouble, he says, you'll be the first man we shoot.

When they step out the darkness has thinned enough to see shapes if not recognize faces. Bullhead sees the backs of his policemen forming a rough rectangle that they move into as quickly as possible, and beyond them the angry followers, shouting out insults and threats, pressing in, maybe three times more of them than there are of his own men. The people, torn from sleep, have not dressed for the cold, most with only a blanket thrown over their shoulders.

Blankets can hide weapons.

Afraid of Soldiers is trying to pull the horse meant for Sitting Bull forward, but it sulls and fights him, eyes rolling, frightened by the shouted oaths, sharp as gunfire in the cold, dark morning. And now the medicine man, still strong, is doing the same, digging in his heels and calling to his people.

Don't let them take me! he calls. They have no power here!

Tell them to back away, orders Bullhead, reaching for his pistol. He hears the rifle shot before he feels it—

THE STUDENTS ARE IN THEIR FREE TIME, dozens of boys pelting each other with snowballs as Miss Burgess crosses the parade ground with her brother.

Eddie is grinning like a wolf, as always.

"Quite a battle. You think it's one tribe against another?"

"The Sioux, because of their number here, can form a bit of a clique," she tells him. "Not something we encourage."

She feels self-conscious walking with him, though doesn't know why she should. At least he's not in one of his ridiculous costumes.

"Doesn't look like it will lead to bloodshed," he says, flinching away from an errant throw. "Good to get it out of their systems."

"They're given sports for that."

"Any notable riders?"

Eddie has become an expert at lassoing running livestock from horseback, paid to exhibit this skill in popular frontier-themed entertainments around the country.

"I wouldn't know. Riding is not in the curriculum."

Eddie laughs. At the agency, both in Nebraska and in the Territory, he was always off with the wilder Pawnee boys, hunting rabbits and birds, catching and riding horses not their own, though always returning them in short order. "If you don't ride them," he'd explain to their disapproving father, "they'll go wild."

"I had a boy in the Mormon play," says Eddie. "Comanche boy, younger than some of these fellows, who could ride full-tilt hanging on the side of his mount, no saddle, just holding on with his knees and a handful of mane."

"Why would one wish to do such a thing?"

"Ride past your enemy that way, he can't even *see* you, much less shoot you."

"And this boy portrayed a Mormon?"

Eddie turns to back up in front of her, surefooted on the frozen boardwalk, eyes glowing. His enthusiasm was always infectious, though the objects of his passion—

"*May Cody, or Lost and Won.* Written for Bill Cody by Major Burt, the Indian fighter. May Cody—this is an actress, now—plays Bill's long-lost sister, who has been boarding in a house in New York City, till turned out into the streets by her landlady, whose son has fallen in love with May—"

"Very few Comanches in New York, I'd presume—"

"Oh, he comes in later. May is being romantically pursued not only by the landlady's son, but by the Mormon bigamist, John D. Lee—"

"Wasn't he recently—?"

"Executed by firing squad. Took him to the scene of his depredations, stood him on a coffin, and shot him down."

"But then how can he be—"

"The play is set in the recent *past.* Like, what—*Uncle Tom's Cabin.* Slavery has been gone for decades now, but people still thrill to see Eliza dashing across the ice floes with her babes in arms."

"It is a very moral play," says Miss Burgess.

"As is this—just listen. Bill finds his sister, May, and with the landlady's son, Stoughton, attempts to bring her back with him to California. But they are pursued by Lee, who when they reach the Utah Territory, kidnaps her and takes her to Salt Lake. But there his superior, Brigham Young, takes a fancy to her and announces that *he* will take her as one of his many brides—"

"And they consider themselves Christians."

"The wedding is proceeding in their special endowment house, when Bill, Stoughton, and some native allies, all dressed as Ute warriors, break in and spirit her away. That's one of the scenes the Comanche boy—his name was Broken Spear, or at least that's how he was listed in the program—is in. He's also one of the attackers at the Mountain Meadow massacre."

"There is a *mass*acre onstage?"

Eddie throws his hands out. "How else is Brigham Young to get Lee out of Salt Lake so he can wed poor May?"

"And you appeared in this—?"

"In several roles. I was a Mormon, I was a Ute Indian, I was in the Baker-Fancher party that is slaughtered, and in the added attractions after the play I did some roping and riding."

"*Horses* onstage?"

"Of course—people paid a *quar*ter to see this show."

"And gunplay, I suppose—"

"Not during the story—we'd just shoot off blanks then—lots of noise, lots of smoke. The live rounds are saved for Bill's shooting exhibition."

"When he executes several Latter-day Saints."

Eddie laughs again. He and his brother Charley, raised so far from the Friends' Society, were wont to doze through the Quaker meetings at the agency, and grew up believing their responsibility in life was to have *fun*.

"He's an incredible sharpshooter. A potato—actually a series of potatoes—is balanced on the head of the actress who plays May—"

"Ah, the life of a thespian—"

"And Bill shoots them off—sometimes one little piece at a time. Straight on, ducking his head through his legs, back turned to her and looking in a mirror—"

"Nobody killed in the wings?"

"There's a bale of hay just offstage to soak up the lead. Then for the finale one of our Indians, Cha-sha-cha-o-pogo, lights up a cigar and Bill shoots the lit end off of it from the other side of the stage."

"You had several Indians?"

"A dozen in that show, more in *Life on the Border.* You probably remember a few from the agency. They're my responsibility on the road, while Charley is in charge of the bear."

"A bear among the Mormons?"

"Bill puts the bear into every show. When they wrassle it really looks like an attack. Women faint."

"I shouldn't wonder." They have reached the print shop, and Miss Burgess unlocks the door. "I take it you two are currently at liberty."

The worst was when the dime novel was published and circulating. Edwin Burgess or *Yellow Hair, the Boy Chief of the Pawnees*—a pack of fabrications that would have her brother, just in his teens, kidnapped by the Sioux, living as their slave for a spell, before escaping to warn his friends the Pawnee of an imminent attack, which he helps to repel and is rewarded by being named their youngest chief. Oh, and a fight with a cougar along the way, his knife triumphing over tooth and claw.

"Oh, we'll be Wild-Westing soon enough," he smiles. "I'm helping to put a combination together for Pawnee Bill."

They step in and Eddie takes a deep breath.

"Ah—that smell. Like every one of Father's news dens."

After he was forced to resign as agent, their father had returned to his former trade, serving as editor and business manager of the *Intelligencer,* the *Gazette*, the *Leader.* Marianna had learned the mechanics of it before they left Pennsylvania, when he ran the *Wyoming Republican* in Tunkhannock—

"Linseed oil and turpentine, in the ink," she says. The shop has been left clean and organized, something that always pleases her upon first sight. "I assume Pawnee Bill is another army scout turned showman."

"You know him," grins Eddie. "It's Gordon Lillie."

"That *boy*?"

Marianna knew him as a teen boy who followed them from Nebraska to the Territory, even helping to build the new agency house on Black Bear Creek, becoming fluent in Pawnee and even teaching at the school for a spell after her father had been bullied out of the service. He would go out hunting and trapping with her brothers and the Indians, but was no leathery frontiersman.

"He helped Bill Cody recruit some Pawnee for a show and served as their interpreter and chaperone, where he caught the bug. He's putting together Pawnee Bill's Historical Wild West Indian Museum and Encampment. Folks are ripe for a Western show again what with all this ghost dancer business—"

"Courtesy of that old murderer Sitting Bull."

"Who Bill Cody paid a fortune to just to mount up and ride around the ring a couple loops at the beginning of the festivities. The first night he asked me why the people were mooing like cattle. 'Those are boos,' I told him, 'from the people who don't like you.' And he makes a face which is as close as he ever come to a smile and says, 'Good. I don't like them either.'"

"Is there room for another Bill to be gallivanting around the country, pretending to shoot redskins and subdue grizzly bears?"

"Sure. Lillie—Pawnee Bill—is quite celebrated now. Mr. Ingraham, who wrote that book about me, has done a couple on him. *The Prairie Shadower, The Buckskin Avenger*—"

"You've seen my book?" she asks, holding up a copy of *Stiya* from a crate.

Eddie grins. "Read it twice."

"And—?"

"You always could sling the words around. Hey, I'm one of your regular subscribers—I get back to San Francisco there's always a couple issues of the—what's it called?"

"*The Indian Helper.*"

Eddie winks. "You're that Bandstand fellow, right? I recognize the tone—'a gentleman does this, and proper young lady does that—'"

He is booked at the Mansion House Hotel, so she won't have to offer him lodging at the school. If possible, the Captain, with his undisguised loathing for Cody and his ilk who celebrate the Indians' regrettable past rather than their hopeful future, can be avoided during this visit. Eddie is well dressed at the moment, if a bit flashily, and can't be here to borrow money—

He pulls a slip of paper from his pocket. "Actually, it's the *Helper* I came to talk to you about. I'd like to purchase an advertisement."

"We don't run advertisements—"

"This is more of a Help Wanted notice. Read it—"

The text has been roughed out in pen and ink—

> WANTED—Young men, tribe not important, yearning for adventure, good pay. Must be proficient with bow and arrow, excellent horsemanship. Inquire H. E. Burgess, care of this periodical.

Marianna is aghast.

"You expect me to help lure Carlisle boys to join this perverted circus?"

"Twenty-five dollars a month." Eddie grins. "More if they bring their own horse. They get to ride, shoot arrows, whoop it up, see the country—maybe see the *world* if the show does well."

Marianna was born here in Pennsylvania, of course, before she traveled with her parents to Nebraska and then the Indian Territory. Her father took her to the Philadelphia Exposition—you could climb onto a platform to see the arm and torch for the proposed Statue of Liberty. But Eddie and Charlie have been *everywhere*, sending her letters and postal cards from places she has to search for on the pull-down map in the geography-and-history classroom.

"Absolutely out of the question," she says, then lowers her voice as a few of the print boys enter, preceding the bugle call by at least five minutes. "That's exactly the sort of behavior we're hoping to stamp out."

"But it's pre*tend*."

"It is a *trave*sty—"

"Where, honestly, are these fellows going to make that kind of money once they've left here?" Eddie waves the boys over.

"Wherever it is, they won't be making a mockery of themselves."

The Ojibwe boy who so ardently rendered Hiawatha and the little office boy approach.

"Gentlemen," booms Eddie, thrusting out his hand, "a pleasure to meet you."

The boys shake, uncertain.

"This is my brother, Henry Edwin," Miss Burgess tells them. "Visiting us from the West Coast. This is Mr. LaMere and Mr. Starr."

Eddie brightens. "Related to the Cherokee deputy marshal?"

"He was my father," says the boy.

"A terrible loss. I met him in Tahlequah shortly after he broke up the Dick Glass gang. You can wear that name with pride."

"Thank you, sir."

"My brother is just passing through," says Miss Burgess, folding the paper with Eddie's advertisement on it. "I've been showing him the school."

She is relieved when Cato Goforth steps in and motions for the boys to join him by the rollers.

"Love the uniforms," says Eddie. "Makes them look like regular little soldiers."

"Captain Pratt is still a commissioned officer. We have regular drill, student-led court-martials—"

"I've seen the boy give that bugle a working over. You must have some Pawnee here—"

"One of our finest students is Jesse Echohawk—"

"Whose father was the trader at the Genoa agency—?"

"He's become a master sergeant here, leading the other boys."

"Sounds like he could take over my job."

Marianna sighs. There is a line between irrepressible and obnoxious—

Cato makes sure Burgess isn't looking at them before he hisses it in a whisper.

"They killed him! Right in front of his house!"

"Killed who?" asks Antoine.

He holds the folded copy of the Carlisle *Sentinel* up for them to read, the headline in 24-point font—

SITTING BULL SHOT DEAD!

OLD CHIEF KILLED DURING ARREST ATTEMPT

Little Tecumseh looks up to the older boys.

"What's going to happen now?"

The students from the Plains tribes, most fluent in sign language, spread the news.

Hands held close to the temples, index fingers partially curved while the thumbs and other fingers are closed, then raise the hands above the head and push them slightly forward—then bring the right hand down to the center of the belly, extending only the index finger out and upward—

Horns and a penis. A buffalo bull—

Close the right hand and bring it in front of and almost up to the right shoulder, turn the back of it to the right then move the hand down several inches—

A buffalo bull that sits—

Bring the right hand back near shoulder height, ball of the thumb pressing against the second joint of the index finger, hand nearly closed and wrist bent so the knuckles are higher, then strike quickly forward, down, and a little to the left in a sharp twisting motion with a slight rebound when the hand stops suddenly—

Killed.

Captain Pratt is for once well behind his students while he shepherds a new group of potential donors around the school grounds, blissfully unaware of the incident as they approach the classroom used for advanced English study—

"—and of course we manufacture much of what we wear and consume here at the Carlisle School—uniforms, shoes, mattresses, dining utensils, milk and butter—"

He slows as they reach the open door of the classroom, touching a finger to his lips and lowering his voice—

"You can peek in at some of our most successful students, a few of whom will graduate this year—"

The visitors tiptoe to look in past the Captain, seeing a tall boy with master sergeant's stripes on his uniform sleeves, standing to face another with a captain's bars on his shoulder, reading roles in *The Tempest* out of their books—

"*For this, be sure*," says Captain Cornelius with some venom, "*to-night thou shalt have cramps!*

Side-stitches that shall pen thy breath up. Urchins

Shall, for that vast of night that they may work

All exercise on thee—"

"*This island's mine*," snaps Master Sergeant Regal in response, "*by Sycorax, my mother!*"

He pauses for an instant, noting the white faces in the doorway, Captain Pratt looming behind them.

"*Which thou tak'st from me. When thou cam'st first,*

Thou strok'st me and made much of me, wouldst give me

Water with berries in't, and teach me how

To name the bigger light, and how the less,

That burn by day and night—and then I loved thee,

and showed thee all the qualities o' th' isle—"

Pratt has seen Clarence recite classic texts before, but never with such passion—

"—*The fresh springs and brine pits, barren place and fertile*—"

He turns from Cornelius to look to the visitors. "*Cursed be I that did so! All the charms*

Of Sycorax—toads, beetles, light on you!

For I am all the subjects that you have,

Who was once mine own king!"

Clarence spreads his arms to indicate the classroom, then wider, to encompass all of the Carlisle School. "*And here you sty me,*

In this hard rock, whiles you do keep from me

th' rest o' th' island!"

The Sioux boy and the superintendent stand staring at each other for a long moment, then Captain Pratt begins to clap, a few of the lady visitors tapping their gloved hands together in agreement.

"Clarence Regal, you have taken classic verse and given it wings! Very impressive! We shall leave you to the Bard—"

The Captain leads the visitors away, Clarence watching, then speaking almost to himself, completes the outburst—

"*You taught me language; and my profit on't*

Is I know how to curse."

GENERAL BROOKE ISN'T five steps out of the tent before the War Scare Department are upon him, firing questions he has no intention of answering.

"Who ordered the killing?"

"Who fired the first shot?"

"Have they attacked the agency staff up there?"

It is these fabricators who have led to the veiled reprimands in the statements by General Miles that have undermined his authority over his troops and no doubt caused serious unrest where there was only religious fanaticism.

"Was his son armed when he was shot?"

"Are the renegades in the Bad Lands on the warpath?"

"Did he have any dying words?"

He doesn't deserve this. Nearly killed at Gettysburg, spotless record of service, and then to be dragged into this—this in*san*ity. It's not even his department—General Ruger handles Dakota, both of them under Miles, and it is a constant puzzle as to which of them needs to be informed first of new developments. The agent is a ninny and the Indians—well, they are besotted with this Messiah craze, and when they get a notion, however strange, into their heads—

"Has McLaughlin asked for more troops?"

"Is there an outbreak at Cheyenne River?"

"Is it safe for us to travel to the Stronghold?"

It is the youngest of them, Kelly, who asks this, not the worst liar among the pack. Brooke is tempted to assure them they are in no danger and let them get their worthless hides perforated by Kicking Bear's wild young bucks—serve them right. But he'd be blamed for that as well.

"If I were you, gentlemen," he snaps as he continues toward Royer's office, "I'd stay in the hotel and make up your stories there."

Inside, he first sees Sword, the most sensible man on the agency payroll.

"I need a party of the respected men to go out to the Bad Lands and talk to those people," he tells him. "Who do you suggest I get to head it?"

The police captain considers this. Something is being hammered on in the Indian agent's office.

"I'll tell Plenty Buffalo Chips to come see you," he says. "He might do it."

"What do you think happened up there?"

Again Sword ponders before he answers. The hammering is insistent.

"Sitting Bull lost power over people when he was up in Canada," he says finally. "And when Bullhead and them come to get him, he must have been ready to die."

In the office, Agent Royer stands watching one of his carpenters nail boards over the window.

"I've already called all my people in," he says when General Brooke enters. "Sword has some of his men out at the mission to protect Father Jutz and the nuns—"

"The students have been sent away?"

"They stay locked in there till this is over. The hostiles have already stolen part of the herd and they're terrorizing the Christian Indians, taking their food—"

"Who will no doubt be coming here for shelter. We can supply some tents."

"I've wired to General Miles for more troops—"

"Half the United States Army is already in the department."

"This is my responsibility—"

"It's in *our* hands now," says General Brooke. The carpenter stops hammering. It is dark in the room, a single oil lamp on the desk between him and Royer. "I think you've done quite enough."

Outside there is a cheer from the reporters as Charlie Seymour and R. J. Boylan pull up in a one-horse carriage.

"We thought you were gone for good!"

"So did we," says Boylan, climbing down. "'Not enough action,' says my editor, 'Fold your tent and come back to the paper.' But we roll into Rushville—"

"That wagon didn't *roll*," comments Seymour, tying the lathered horse to the porch rail. "It's like it had square wheels—"

"—and you know Rushville, if the railroad didn't stop there it'd be a prairie dog village—"

"I had no idea they had that many two-legged humans in the town, and here's every one of them in a panic, packing up their belongings to run south, 'cause they've heard *per*sonally from our Agent Royer that the whole Sioux nation is up in arms and looking to murder some white folks. Only took us a minute to hear about Sitting Bull and to know we'd better hightail it back here, only the jasper who'd brought us in the wagon just snapped his reins and lit out for Oshkosh."

"How'd you manage to snag this rig?" asks the Professor.

"Well, there was a great deal of con*fu*sion. New troops were coming in off the train—they'll be here once they get organized—and like Charlie said, people are all in a panic, so we were able to sort of *bor*row it—"

"Horse thievery is a serious offense in Nebraska," says Tibbles.

"With savages on the hunt, I doubt anybody will be coming up here to look for it. What's Royer up to?"

"Preparing for a siege, from what we can tell. Hate to tell you this, but a couple fellas from Sioux Falls already took your room."

"Hell, that don't matter," grins Charlie Seymour. "We're back in *bus*iness!"

ON THE FRONT PAGE of *The Indian Helper*, right-hand column—

> Mr. Henry Edwin Burgess, of San Francisco, visited his sister at our school on Tuesday. Mr. Burgess has had considerable experience among the Indians of the Plains, his father having been agent for the Pawnees during the boyhood days of the first named. Mr. Burgess speaks the Pawnee language with the fluency of a native, and can carry on an intelligent conversation for hours with any of the tribes of the Southwest in their interesting sign language. In 1875 he was intertribal interpreter for the Cheyennes, Arapahoes, Comanches, Kiowas, and Pawnees, being employed by the Government to assist in adjusting the deal which the latter made for the Pawnees with the tribes of the Southwest, at the time the Pawnees bought their present reservation. He was struck with the gentlemanly bearing and demonstrativeness of our boys and girls in contrast with the taciturn Indian youth he is used to see hanging around the reservation agencies.

—and just inside the second page, the Man-on-the-Bandstand weighs in—

> *According to the Dakota medicine men, the world as we know it was supposed to have ended today—but the Man-on-the-Bandstand notes no apocalypse. Poor Sitting Bull is dead, however, and nobody weeps.*

Makes-Trouble-in-Front continues to wear the ghost shirt he has made under his uniform. The white teachers still look at him, speak to him, but their eyes and words no longer pierce his skin—

His is a woeful legacy—born in ignorance, steeped in treachery and violence, died in confinement and obscurity—

—while Clarence Regal sits alone on a seat in a passenger car of a westbound train ready to pull out of Carlisle station. The conductor takes the ticket from his hand, glances at it, hesitates—"Heading home, are we?"

Clarence lifts the folded letter he has forged, gives the man a sad smile. "Death in the family," he says.

The conductor punches the ticket, slips it into the loop on the back of the seat in front of the boy. "I'm sorry to hear that," he says.

GRACE FEELS FLUSHED today, despite all the other girls complaining about how cold it is in the girls' dormitory. "Sweetcorn is gone," they joke, "and there's nobody left to pick up his coal shovel."

She lies back on her bed, exhausted though it is only just after supper, looking up at the photographs she's pinned to the wall. Evangeline, scissored from the cover of Miss Burgess's book, the rest of it thrown in the garbage bin in the kitchen in a moment of pique, and Wilma, a shot of her taken by Mr. Choate when she first arrived from the Crow Agency, procured for Grace by the Puyallup boy who serves as the photographer's assistant. Little Wilma, in a simple cotton dress with a blanket thrown over her shoulders, looks scared and defiant at the same time.

"Seems kind of empty without her," says Lizzie Cloud, collecting a book from her footlocker.

"We'll get used to it."

"Are you all right?"

"I'm fine."

Lizzie starts out the door. "We're practicing in the library."

They have been taught all the Christmas carols in English, and the tradition has become for the older girls to sing them from the balcony on the holiday morn. Grace sighs. "I'll be right down."

The short days are part of the problem, of course, and the cold, so much more oppressive here somehow than it ever is in Green Bay. And the news from Dakota. She will graduate this year, like her brothers before, and should feel more excited about that. But she will miss so many people when it's over, the girls from tribes all over the country, her sisters in the Longstreth Society—and Antoine, he'll have to stay here for his people to keep their enrollment—

Grace wills herself to her feet, crosses to the mirror on the wall they share, checks her hair, frowns. There is some kind of rash beginning on her face and neck.

If they weren't all in their flannel long johns, the four boys would make a picture of the sort printed on the postcards the school sends to solicit donations—Antoine, Smokey, and Asa sitting on their beds, staring into open books, while Trouble sits at the desk, pencil in hand, intent on his task. He is drawing a kind of pictogram escape route—lengths of railroad track, one leading to the next, with the letters he has learned from the blacksmith's map—CVRR, PCC St. L, GN—letters that will be on the sides of the train cars, so he can choose the right one to climb onto.

What their School Father, Pratt, says is true—to equal the white man you have to learn his ways.

Jesse Echohawk throws their door open, calls inside—

"La Merde! Downstairs!"

Antoine and the other members of the debate team have been marched into the large boys' library and stand facing Captain Pratt and Mr. Skinner. It is cold in the room, cold inside everywhere for the last week.

"I cannot believe he would not have shared his plans with at least one of you," says the Captain, standing close enough to tower over them.

"He wouldn't want to compromise us, sir," says Jesse Echohawk.

"Did he seem discontent?"

"No more than usual—I mean to say, he was full of moods, Clarence. And some of them were very dark."

"He was awful worried about this ghost dance business," Antoine volunteers. Antoine saw Clarence only once after the news of Sitting Bull's murder broke, the master sergeant passing by him with no hint of recognition in his eyes.

"But he doesn't be*lieve* in any of it," blurts Jesse.

"We're all of us upset about the ghost dancing," says Captain Pratt. "It is a desperate, pathetic—"

"Those are his people," says Antoine.

Antoine has seen the headlines every day as Cato brings them in to share with the print shop boys, the newspapermen at Pine Ridge obviously enjoying the drama if not the locale—

ON WITH THE DANCE!

—then—

STARTLING STORIES

—then—

GEN. MILES ALARMED

Captain Pratt is giving Antoine a hard look. "*His* people? I wouldn't think so, not after all his education, his accomplishments—"

"Maybe not, sir."

"In any case, he won't be gone long. Every train depot between here and the Dakotas has been contacted to look out for Clarence Regal—"

"War Eagle," says Jesse.

"Pardon?"

Jesse is staring straight ahead, standing at attention, the obedient master sergeant.

"If you remember, sir," he says, "his name was changed at the blackboard. When we first came here, he was War Eagle."

There was a choice in Minneapolis between the Great Northern road and the Northern Pacific, and Clarence had a premonition that they'd be checking for fugitives at Sioux City. So he is reboarding the NP westbound, newspaper folded under his arm, from the platform in Aberdeen. The passenger cars are only half full and he easily finds an empty seat. He'll have to change once more in Pierre, now the capital of a state that didn't exist when he first left for the school. The conductor shouts his litany, then the train snorts and spits and lumbers into motion.

The *Saturday Pioneer* is published in Aberdeen, just off the press, and Clarence is hoping for some news of what may lie ahead of him. But he can't get past the editorial, written by one L. Frank Baum. "Sitting Bull, most renowned Sioux of modern history, is dead," it begins:

> He was not a Chief, but without Kingly lineage he arose from a lowly position to the greatest Medicine Man of his time, by virtue of his shrewdness and daring.

The line from *Macbeth* comes to Clarence—*Nothing in his life / Became him like the leaving it.* Savages, he has learned, tend to grow nobler the longer they've been dead—

> He was an Indian with a white man's spirit of hatred and revenge for those who had wronged him and his. In his day he saw his son and his tribe gradually

> driven from their possessions; forced to give up their old hunting grounds and espouse the hard working and uncongenial avocations of the whites. And these, his conquerors, were marked in their dealings with his people by selfishness, falsehood, and treachery. What wonder that his wild nature, untamed by years of subjection, should still revolt? What wonder that a fiery rage still burned within his breast and that he should seek every opportunity of obtaining vengeance upon his natural enemies.

When Clarence first left for Carlisle, Sitting Bull had just led his people back from their Canadian exile. It was still the Great Sioux Reservation then, easier for a red man to shift from one area to another, and the famous medicine man's movements and pronouncements did not take long to be known of down at Pine Ridge. His imprisonment at Fort Randall, his return to Standing Rock, even the crazy rumor that he had converted to Catholicism were all discussed and debated. Clarence's first years at the school coincided with Sitting Bull's sojourn with Cody's Wild West show, Captain Pratt extremely vocal in his disapproval, citing a lack of both dignity and foresight in the notorious leader's actions. Until the dance reached the Dakotas, Clarence regarded him as a relic of the past—

> The proud spirit of the original owners of these vast prairies inherited through centuries of fierce and bloody wars for their possession, lingered last in the bosom of Sitting Bull. The nobility of the redskin is extinguished, and what few are left are a pack of whining curs who lick the hand that smites them. The whites, by law of conquest, by justice of civilization, are masters of the

> American continent, and the best safety of the frontier settlements will be secured by the total annihilation of the few remaining Indians. Why not annihilation? Their glory has fled, their spirit broken, their manhood effaced; better that they die than live the miserable wretches that they are.

It is not hot in the passenger car, windows frosted with rime and impossible to see through, but Clarence has begun to perspire under his suit. He thinks of the Thanksgiving debate, and that the Invincibles could have recruited Mr. L. Frank Baum to argue their position. He has heard that the new state of South Dakota is offering a bounty for killing wolves, which is mostly done with strychnine. Perhaps in the next issue of food staples on the reservations—

> History would forget these later despicable beings, and speak, in later ages of the glory of these grand Kings of forest and plain that Cooper loved to heroism. We cannot honestly regret their extermination, but we at least do justice to the manly characteristics possessed, according to their lights and education, by the early Redskins of America.

Clarence does not feel honored as a king of forest and plain. A man in a checkered vest sitting across the aisle from him flicks his eyes from the open newspaper to Clarence's face.

"You can read that?"

It will not be a long ride to Pierre, but there is no telling if the man will be a fellow passenger on the next leg of the journey. Clarence folds the newspaper carefully.

"After a fashion, yes."

The white man grins. "What do you think of them killing your man?"

He knows this means Sitting Bull, no more "his man" than President Harrison. He decides to engage the fellow.

"Sitting Bull was Hunkpapa," he says. "My people are all Oglala."

"That's still Sioux, right?"

"Yes."

"And that's which reservation?"

There is always the chance that the man is a railroad detective, tasked to sniff out suspicious travelers.

"I'm currently on a mission from the ERA," Clarence tells him.

"That's an organization?"

"Early Redskins of America."

"Ah," says the man in the checkered vest, attempting to make sense of this information. "And you're heading for Standing Rock."

"Pine Ridge."

The man makes a face. "Likely you're heading into a hornets' nest."

"Perhaps."

The man seems a bit flummoxed, as if he's encountered a talking dog.

"So what do you think of this ghost dance business?"

In point of fact Clarence has not thought much about the dancing, or even the armed troops that have flooded into the area, surrounding the agencies, scouring the Bad Lands for Short Bull and Kicking Bear's runaways. What has preoccupied his mind during the journey is his shaky ability to recall the Lakota tongue. He can't remember what year he actually began to *think* in English, but it has happened, and there are things he has forgotten how to express in Lakota.

"I think I'll have to see it with my own eyes," he says.

CHRISTMAS DAY IS SUNNY but still cold. Grace joins the others on the balcony of the large girls' dormitory, dressed in their heavy coats, the other students ranged below them on the parade ground in their companies—

"God rest you merry, Gentlemen,
Let nothing you dismay,
Remember Christ the Savior
Was born on Christmas day—"

Feeling dizzy, she has to hold tightly to the rail—

"To save poor souls from Satan's power
Which long time had gone astray
Bringing tidings of comfort and joy!"

—they sing until the bells of St. Patrick's begin to chime in town, and then the girls who are in the chorus join the Catholic students, not marching but hurrying to be ready at the church by nine o'clock. Grace goes back to her room to lie down.

The chapel at St. Patrick's is decorated with evergreen boughs. The Carlisle chorus sing to the students gathered for the special service—

"Adeste Fideles læti triumphantes,
Venite, venite in Bethlehem,
Natum videte,
Regem angetorum—"

Antoine recalls how when he was very small he thought Latin was just the language God and Jesus and the angels spoke with each other, and that somehow Père Etienne had learned it—

"Venite adoremus,
Venite adoremus,
Venite adoremus, Do-ominum!"

—and later, in the large girls' library, Miss Burgess pushes colored glass slides into the new magic lantern Miss Longstreth has bought for the school, throwing images of the Holy Land onto a sheet hung over the wall.

"A view of Jerusalem, taken from the north," she says. "Some of these buildings were no doubt standing in the early Bible times. And now *here*—"

She has become adept at operating the device, smoothly pulling one scene out and sliding the next in—

"—here we are in the narrow streets of Bethlehem. Imagine, children, that His feet may have trod upon these very stones—"

Grace feels flushed and swoony. She thinks of Christmas, which her parents and most of her relatives celebrate, at home. She wishes she was there—

"And this is the Sea of Galilee, where Peter's faith was tested and found wanting—"

Religious services over, the students congregate in the gymnasium, also bedecked with evergreen, a tall tree hung with ribbons and strings of popcorn standing in the center of the floor. Miss Redbird and Miss Noble supervise as the small boys and girls empty their stockings, filled with oranges, nuts, combs, pencils, and fresh popcorn.

Trouble sits with the large boys, curious. There was a white people mission church on the reservation, run by the Black Robe Craft, but he never set foot in it. Trouble understands Christmas by now, the story being explained over and over here, knows that the baby grew up and then spoke as the Messiah Wovoka has spoken, but was captured, was tortured and killed by his enemies. What he doesn't understand is why worship such a weak man, who allowed himself to be nailed to a pole without raising a hand to defend himself?

The small boys are disappointed to find no marbles in their stockings.

But shortly after, they are entranced by Fannie Noble, small boys and girls sitting cross-legged on the floor around her as she tells them a story from a book, now and then showing them drawings in it. In the story a cruel man who loves only riches is visited at night by spirits that warn him of his future—

—while at the sociable that night it is the school custom that for once the boys are the servers. The mess hall has been decorated lavishly, a small manger with cardboard figures representing Mary and Joseph and the Wise Men propped up on the hay, and a haloed baby doll made by the sewing girls placed in the cradle. Lizzie Cloud and Miss Redbird play a piano/violin duet while the older boys wait on the long tables.

Captain and Mrs. Pratt sit at the head table, smiling and chatting with a few of the most loyal benefactors to the school. Fifty-three turkeys have been obtained to feed the children, the Captain knows, having had to mount a last-moment campaign to avoid settling for pork-and-veal pie this year, Congress proving as stingy and suspicious as always, and one of the school's Philadelphia stalwarts dying intestate. He makes sure to smile as he looks out over the gathering, though feeling weary and disappointed. The Regal boy, with all his bright potential, absconding and still unaccounted for, the troop movements on Rosebud and Pine Ridge—

Antoine carefully carries two pitchers of eggnog from table to table. For the sociable the students are seated with girls on one long side and boys on the other, and he finds Grace at one end.

"Eggnog here! Straight from the chicken and the cow!"

The first girl nods that she wants some and he pours, serving from the left, then moves on to Grace.

"No, thank you," she says, smiling wanly. She doesn't look right, with some kind of rash on her neck.

"Are you all right?"

"I'm fine," she says. "Just tired from all the preparations. Is it really warm in here?"

CLARENCE SITS on a wooden bench in the drafty office waiting to see the Indian agent. He has come down from Cheyenne River, riding in a sutler's wagon that skirted around the Bad Lands, passing several small detachments of cavalry moving about in a hurry. His first encounter on arrival was with the gang of correspondents who seem to have taken over Finley's little three-bedroom hotel near the agency offices, sitting out on the vine-covered front porch teasing each other and cooking up stories. Fascinated, he stood to stare at them, the newsmen assuming he understood none of their jibes and exaggerations.

"And what do you think about it, chief?" the boldest of them would ask every now and then, to the great amusement of his fellows, eventually pushing it beyond tolerance.

"But what they reserve for special occasions," he said, a grin on his face, "and I'm talking about very important guests—is puppy *soup*. Wouldn't you agree, chief?"

Clarence fixed him with an appraising look. "You must be Cressy."

The others looked amused, the journalist uncomfortable. "And wh-who are you?"

"Only a long-haired, blanket-swathed musk bag," he said, quoting the *Bee* correspondent. "Or perhaps an ocher-covered memento of a fast-vanishing race."

He was halfway to the agency office, the other pressmen still laughing, when intercepted by Yankton Charlie, one of Cody's barnstorming Indians who have returned and signed on with the Pine Ridge police force. Claiming not to know any of Clarence's relatives and maintaining that nobody from here could speak Lakota so badly, he escorted Clarence inside as a "trespasser" and told him to wait. It is a long, one-story barracks building tacked together with flimsy cottonwood boards, fine dust sifting through the cracks to form little drifts on the bare floor, the police quarters and the reservation doctor's dispensary and living space stacked beyond the agent's office like cars on a passenger train. Pine Ridge looks worse than when Clarence was last here four years ago, though some of that may be the bleak winter and the obvious tension among the different factions. The sutler who gave him a ride, a half-white man named Sturgis, said that the Christian Indians are afraid of the ghost dancers, and neither group is happy to have the government troops here.

The cavalrymen camping just south of the agency enclosure are black and wear heavy buffalo-hide coats and muskrat fur hats with earflaps. Even closer there are white infantrymen in rows of white tents, and even an artillery unit, their cannon lined up and pointed out toward the clusters of tipis that have been thrown up since the agent ordered all the so-called friendlies to come in where they can be "protected."

A bluecoat lieutenant steps out from Agent Royer's office and an impatient captain, who has remained standing and tapping his leg with a riding crop, steps in. Clarence can read their ranks from their bars, but is not close enough to divine which units they serve in. A dark-skinned Indian in a corduroy riding suit and new, thigh-high boots steps in, and the agent's assistant tells him to sit at the bench. He offers a hand to Clarence and speaks to him in Lakota.

It is good to meet you, he says, sounding like he might be a Santee, the people from the East. I'm the new doctor here.

Clarence has never met an Indian with a medical degree.

"You're working for the bureau?" he asks in English.

"You're educated!"

The man has a wonderful smile. The people here might trust him, even if he is an outsider.

"Eight years at Carlisle."

Dr. Eastman smiles again. "Lucky for you. I moved around quite a bit—but finished up at Dartmouth and Boston Medical College. I arrived here only two weeks ago, and it has been—well, you'll meet the agent."

"A politician?"

"Back in Alpena he was postmaster, city treasurer, chairman of the board of education, and county coroner—as well as a trained dentist. I taught Sunday school at his church."

"And somehow he's landed here."

Eastman sees the captain step out and switches back to Lakota.

He's afraid the ghost dancers want to kill him.

Perhaps they do, says Clarence.

The new doctor considers this for a moment.

My father became a Christian while he was in prison, he says. Now he believes that someday heaven's army will come to earth, that all people will be judged, and the good will live forever in paradise.

The captain hurries outside and there is a blast of cold air.

"The Book of Revelation," says Clarence. "And what do you believe?"

Dr. Eastman is not smiling now. "I was raised to be a hunter and a warrior," he says. "Raised as an Indian. I lived in exile in Canada. I have never seen our people in a sorrier state."

Clarence nods. "It used to be only the Loafers who stayed close to the agency."

"Everybody has been ordered in. A lot of the Christians left solid log cabins and are now stuck freezing in canvas tents. I've been busy fighting la grippe."

"What can you give them?"

"Cod liver oil in alcohol is very popular," he says. "I'm not supplied with much else."

"*You,*" calls the young assistant, pointing to Clarence. "Stand and spread your arms out."

Clarence stands, as does the doctor.

"He's a Carlisle student."

"We're taking no chances. Spread your arms out wide."

The assistant nods to an Indian policeman who has been half dozing in a wooden chair, leaning against the wall. The man only pats the pockets of Clarence's coat and pants, then nods to the assistant. The assistant points to the door to the agent's office. "He'll see you now."

If I'd had a weapon, thinks Clarence, I could have killed the assistant first—

We'll talk later, says the Indian doctor in Lakota. Welcome home.

Agent Royer has a red face and wears a mustache. He glances up from his desk, annoyed.

"What are you doing here?"

"I live here."

Royer has only been agent since October, replacing Gallagher in the election shuffle.

"You're supposed to be back east at Carlisle—"

Clarence has prepared a half dozen lies, banking them for the occasion. "There's an outbreak of the Russian fever there," he says. "Half my dormitory is in the hospital and they've sent the rest of us away."

The man appears too overwhelmed with crises to bother telegraphing the school. He scowls—

"Try to stay out of trouble," he says with some finality.

"I shall," says Clarence. "Thank you, sir."

They love being called sir.

He steps out and waves to Eastman in passing, choosing his words in Lakota carefully.

You could be very useful here.

Outside, Clarence buttons his coat and heads for the stables, hoping, with the little money he has left, to be able to rent a horse for a few days. He has heard that his uncle Strong Bow is living up by Wounded Knee Creek, and though no kneeling Christian, the man wears citizen's dress and has a logical mind.

If spirits do exist, Strong Bow has always said to whoever will listen, they abandoned us when the white people came.

Clarence has always been struck by how lonely the government buildings look, scattered here on the frozen, barren prairie. They appear no less lonely fenced in now with barbed wire and surrounded by the little tipi camps of refugees, and the new obscenity of rows of white Sibley tents.

There was game here on the White Clay Creek when his father was a boy, but it was hunted out before Clarence was born, and the people went south to chase buffalo and kill Pawnees. Now, he thinks, it is land fit only for ghosts.

He approaches the government warehouse, remembering vividly the Issue Days of his boyhood, pack horses and lumber wagons crowded together, women dressed in their brightest calico, men already making bets on the horse races that would follow the give-away. Out at the government corral the scrawny longhorns would mill uneasily till family names and their beef allotments were called out by the issue clerk, then a warning cry sent children scampering away from the rail as the beasts were driven out, one or two at a time, gleefully chased and shot from horseback. A thrilling few minutes of sport before the younger women joined with knives and axes in hand for the butchering, camp dogs nervously eyeing the process, ready to swarm and fight over whatever was left in the grass.

Here is our Lakota nation, he remembers Uncle Strong Bow saying as he pointed to the yipping curs. We are to the white people as the dogs are to us.

Nobody was pleased to hear this, but Strong Bow had been a brave warrior, and is still a good man who does what he can to help his family survive, even serving on the Indian police until Agent McGillycuddy was forced to leave.

A group of young men, dressed the old way and staring sullenly at the infantry tents, sit on the loading dock of the warehouse. Clarence recognizes a familiar face.

Hello, brother, he says.

The young man came to Carlisle at the same time he did, a Brulé known on the Rosebud reservation as Plenty Horses, which the school changed to Plenty Living Bear after his father, with the teachers eventually naming him Guy, and the other boys just calling him Plenty.

Plenty takes a moment to recognize Clarence.

You ran away, he says.

I didn't run. I rode in trains.

One of the other young boys laughs.

He sounds just as bad as you do, he says to Plenty. They made you both stupid at that school.

He was always a big, quiet boy, in A Company with Clarence, and struggled in the classroom. The last couple years before he left they sent him on Outing for months at a time, often a sign that they've given up on you ever learning English.

What have you been doing since you came back? Clarence asks him.

Nothing, says Plenty. There is no work here, only waiting for the Issue to come. And now they've sent the solders to kill us.

The white people are worried.

Good, says Plenty. I hope they are afraid to sleep at night.

The other young men laugh. Clarence notices that one of them has a pistol tucked into his belt.

You were so good at being white, says Plenty. Why have you come back?

Because I am Lakota.

Not anymore, says Plenty Horses. Believe me.

NURSE TUCKER WALKS down the long row of feverish Carlisle girls with Dr. Hazzard. She can't tell if he's been drinking again or if he's only missed even more sleep than she has.

"As much water as you can get them to drink," he says. "Change the bedding when it gets too damp, cold rags to the forehead—just keep it all at arm's length."

Nurse Tucker knows that arm's length is no protection from a disease as infectious as scarlatina, and has been ordering her staff to check each other's temperature with a mercury thermometer every few hours.

She sees the boy's face pressed to the glass of the door at the end of the corridor again.

"Excuse me," she says to the doctor. "I have to deal with this."

She sympathizes, but they are a people, like the Italians who are crowding into her native New York, who believe that sickness is a family affair.

She opens the door and feels the chill immediately.

"This ward is *quar*antined, do you understand what that means?"

The boy is an Ojibwe, very well-spoken in English, but annoyingly persistent.

"People have fevers, and if you're exposed to them we'll have to keep you here!"

The boy tries to look past her to the patients.

"Will you tell Grace Metoxen I came to see her? My name is Antoine—"

"Write her a note and I'll see that she gets it. But do it out*side* of the hospital!"

IT IS ONLY FOUR MILES from the agency to the mission school and church, the mule slow but steady, Clarence pleased that he is able to ride it without a saddle. One of the policemen stationed outside, who Clarence remembers as an older boy named Fish, seems glad to see him.

They keep all the children locked up inside, he says in Lakota, even at night. So the ghost dancers won't get them. Or maybe so their parents can't take them away.

Do you know where Strong Bow has his lodge now?

Fish points to the East. Go that way till you reach Wounded Knee Creek, he says. Then follow it north.

Clarence points to the young man's badge, pinned outside his heavy coat.

Do they pay you enough to wear that?

Fish grins. For now, yes. If people start shooting, maybe no. He points at the mule.

Is that what they ride at your school?

We don't have horses, he answers, embarrassed. We ride on the train.

It is another hour on the animal's back before he encounters a dozen people carrying their babies and their household possessions in their arms.

The ghost dancers took our horses, says the oldest of the men. They took the food we had left and told us to leave our cabins, told us we could either follow them to the Stronghold or go beg at the agency with the other cowards.

The Stronghold is in the Bad Lands, and there is little water there, and less to eat.

They are staring at the mule. It is one thing to lead a mule, and another to ride one.

There are many of our people living close to the agency, Clarence tells them, and many soldiers there. But for now it seems safe from fighting.

They look hungry and he feels bad that he has nothing to give them. They wish him luck in finding his family.

Clarence reaches the creek, and less than a mile to the north are three roughly built cabins, smoke coming from the chimney of only one of them. Inside, crowded around a government-issue woodstove, are his mother and his uncle Strong Bow and several of his cousins.

Why have you come now? asks his uncle, who as eldest of the lodge can be direct. Better to return when this Messiah wind has blown itself out, when war has been put back in the bag.

We're not at war, says Clarence.

The shouting has begun, says Strong Bow, and bullets always follow the shouting.

They give him the seat closest to the stove, his mother avoiding his eye, as if he is a stranger whose intentions she does not trust. Half the people sitting around the smoky fire with them are in civilian dress, so it isn't his clothes.

Maybe the reasonable people will keep that from happening, he says.

Strong Bow laughs. You even think in the white man's language now.

It is true, but Clarence thought his Lakota might come back to him the moment he set foot on Pine Ridge. He finds himself struggling to remember the subtleties, struggling to make the proper sounds—

We aren't allowed to speak Lakota.

They do this at Red Cloud's school as well, says his uncle. As if forgetting their own tongue will make them white.

The Holy Rosary Mission was still being built when Clarence came to see his father's grave, Red Cloud himself petitioning President Harrison to allow the Catholic priests and the Sisters of Penance and Christian Charity freedom to proselytize for their faith on his reservation.

At least those children live close enough to see their families, he says.

This is only allowed on the days of the government issue, says Strong Bow, making a disgusted face. Women and children weeping when they are parted.

Clarence can tell that all in the cabin are disappointed that he has come empty-handed, assuming that he must now be wealthy and powerful, full of the white man's magic. But arriving on the mule—all that was available for rental at the agency—has somehow brought the Bible story of Mary and Joseph in Bethlehem to their minds, and three cousins have asked for reassurance that he has not become a Black Robe. His mother places a bowl of *wohanpi* in his lap, and he eats slowly, hoping not to be offered another portion. A little boy, looking far too thin like all the others, can't take his eyes off the food, and Clarence's mother has somehow fished out the one chunk of government beef left in the pot to give to him.

When will you return to school? his mother manages to ask him, stirring the pot that has almost nothing left in it.

I don't know, he answers honestly. I don't know if I will.

This does not please her.

This is not a place you should be. Not now.

He looks to his uncle. Strong Bow stares at the flames in the open belly of the woodstove for a long moment. Clarence has forgotten how impolite it is considered among his people to answer a serious question without taking time for serious thought.

Short Bull and Kicking Bear and their followers, his uncle says finally, are drunken with the idea of the Messiah, but these are not people who will ever be content. They have run off to the Stronghold, where there is no game to hunt, and no agency to hand them food. So now they must either starve or come back and surrender to the white man's soldiers.

Who are afraid of them, says Clarence.

How can they be afraid, says Strong Bow, when there are five of them to every Lakota who can raise a weapon?

The wind is cold and sharp on his ride back to the agency, Clarence declining to add himself to Strong Bow's burden in the overcrowded cabin, assuring him that the deteriorating shed he is staying in with Plenty Horses and his friends is shelter enough. His overcoat is not nearly warm enough, and his uncle's parting shot has put him in a sullen mood.

It is fitting that you ride on a mule, he said as Clarence mounted to leave. Neither horse nor donkey.

He has a pass from Captain Sword of the Indian police, which he will either reveal or hide depending on who he encounters, and wonders if he should buy a weapon. He is nearing the Holy Rosary Mission when a white man on a jittery bay stallion overtakes him.

"*Hau, kola!*" the man calls as he rides up from behind.

Clarence is tempted to answer that he does not know the man, and certainly isn't his friend, but holds his tongue. As the man pulls up alongside, he can see a heavy metal crucifix and some kind of military medal hung conspicuously outside of his overcoat. He remembers that it is Sunday, and that he didn't even think of attending Mass.

"Catholic?" he asks in English.

The man grins. "How'd you guess?"

"White Robes wear a cross, but nobody has been nailed on it yet."

"Father Craft," says the man, shifting reins to offer his hand. "Black Robe."

Clarence warily shakes his hand, glad that his mule is at least as tall as the priest's bay. "You run the mission school?"

They are passing near the modest building now, with even the police guard inside dodging the cold wind.

"That's Father Jutz—Austrian fellow. Of course the sisters really rule the place. I'm more of a traveling apostle."

"Is that allowed?"

Father Craft laughs. He is youngish, handsome, strong-looking, and an American, unlike the Catholic priests Clarence has met at Carlisle.

"I'll let you in on a secret," he says, leaning toward Clarence and lowering his voice as if there is a human in sight within a mile of them. "I'm on a confidential mission, in the secret service of the War Department."

Clarence eyes the gold medallion. "You look like a soldier."

The priest smiles, pulling the medal over his head and handing it to Clarence to examine. A bit of colored ribbon holds up a golden oval with thirteen stars on a blue background around it, a minuteman carrying a long rifle etched on one side and a profile of George Washington on the other.

"Sons of the Revolution," says the priest. "General Greene was on my mother's side of the family."

Clarence hands it back. The chiefs who go to Washington to be condescended to by government officials always return laden with decorations, copper and brass popular for their heft, which they proudly wear along with the eagle feathers and other tribal honors they've earned for important ceremonies.

"If you travel alone here," he advises the priest, "you don't want to look like a soldier."

Father Craft only smiles. "I was one, in another life. I fought with the Chasseurs d'Afrique against the Prussians, fought against the Spanish in Cuba with the *insurgentes*—"

"A soldier of fortune—"

"A revolutionist, in that case. Of course I was trained as a medical man, like my father—with those I can't cure, I can at least administer the Last Rites."

Clarence wonders if the man could be sporting with him.

"You fought in wars and then you had a—what is it called? Visitation? Revelation?"

"Vocation. I wasn't born into the True Faith, I con*vert*ed—as have many of your brethren, some of them three or four times. I'm afraid the devil is extremely active here."

"No more than anywhere else."

Craft gives Clarence a careful look. "You've been away, I gather."

"Carlisle."

"No stranger to the bugle's call."

"Our rifles are never loaded."

"For the safety of your instructors, no doubt. I've crossed swords with your Captain Pratt a few times. He was at Rosebud on a recruiting trip, explaining his credo through the interpreter, when I stood to inform the gathering, in Lakota, that shipping children thousands of miles from home to educate them might not be necessary."

"That must have gone over well."

"He and Agent Wright and the big chief of the Episcopals had me banished from Indian country. It took me a year to be reinstated up at Standing Rock."

Clarence has heard the story of the great Brulé chief Spotted Tail, coming to Carlisle to visit the children and grandchildren he allowed to be brought there and being horrified to discover they were being assigned menial trades and disciplined like soldiers instead of merely learning the white man's language. Threatening to take the entire Rosebud group, which then was a substantial portion of the student body, back home with him, it required considerable pressure from Pratt's supporters in Washington to limit the chief to removing only his own close relatives, with the added insult that he was required to pay for their transportation home.

"Captain Pratt," says Clarence, "has a whim of iron."

"How long have you been back?"

"A few days."

"But you've heard of our situation here? The ghost dancers?"

"It's in all the newspapers."

"I attended one of the ceremonies hosted by Short Bull, over on Rosebud. Very intriguing."

"Dangerous?"

"Only if one attempted to interfere, something I'd caution against at a Baptist tent revival. What struck me was how open to religious ecstasy your people are—there is an enormous opportunity here to win souls."

"You think so?"

"They've merely chosen the wrong messiah to follow. The Sioux remind me of the ancient Israelites—though they have not degenerated as fully as that execrable race."

A Black Robe unafraid to offer his opinions, thinks Clarence.

"So do you think we need all these bluecoats?"

Father Craft considers this. "Allowed to fester unbridled till the spring, when the believers were promised they'd be up to their eagle feathers in buffalo, the craze would have disappeared *par levibus venti.*"

"Like the swift winds."

Father Craft raises his eyebrows. "They must have loved you at Carlisle. Trotted out to impress the Quaker ladies, no doubt—has Pratt sent you here to spread his gospel?"

"I came on my own. I'm Lakota."

The priest laughs at this.

"Is something funny?"

"I've never seen a Sioux *hu-bo* ride a mule before."

Clarence scowls, embarrassed. "It's all they had at the stable."

"All they *said* they had. Our friend Royer must have put out the word on you—an Indian agent is something of an emperor."

"Especially when he's got half the federal army at his disposal."

"They have a debating society at Carlisle, as I remember. Your command of the language—"

Clarence feels his blood come up. "I can read a treaty, if that's what you mean."

Father Craft looks at him shrewdly. "Well enough, I hope," he says, "to never sign one."

Clarence can't help but notice the bulge at Father Craft's hip, the kind a pistol in a holster would make. He feels as if he's being tested.

"So whose side are you on?" he asks.

Craft grins. "I am but a lieutenant in the service of *God*, through the Sacred Heart of Jesus."

"Does Agent Royer know that?"

Father Craft waves his hand dismissively. "Indian agents, army generals, politicians—they are as *fleas* to the King of Kings."

The first Pine Ridge agent Clarence remembers was McGillycuddy, known as Little Whiskers for his drooping mustache, and then for years the less volatile Gallagher. A Lakota needs the agent's permission to travel off the reservation, to build or take down a structure, to slaughter his own cattle. The Indian police are the agent's disciplinarians, though family ties and fear of reprisal make them less imposing than the men who bear the rod at Carlisle.

"Interesting times here," says the renegade priest. "Apocalyptic. I wouldn't miss it for the world."

They are approaching the agency, riding past the most recent arrivals, Seventh cavalrymen jockeying a quartet of cannon mounted on huge wheels to point out toward the clusters of tipis recently thrown up.

"Hotchkiss guns," says Craft, nodding to the cannon. "Woefully impractical for raid-and-run warfare, but they make a big noise and lots of smoke—very persuasive."

"People think the army is here to kill them."

Craft's expression darkens. "Troublemakers, mostly white, spreading lies."

Clarence thinks of the editorial he read on the train. Extermination. How much easier for them it would be to just sever the root right here and forget having to drill their overcomplicated language into the heads of sullen Indian children—

"It doesn't matter what's true," Clarence says. "It's what people bel*ieve*."

"The line between faith and superstition," smiles the priest. "Very narrow indeed."

They reach the agency compound, Dr. Eastman stepping out, troubled, from his dispensary as they dismount.

"The very man I want to see," calls the priest, "If I could trouble you for some camphor, I have an incipient toothache."

Eastman ignores the request. "Word just came in that they've got Big Foot's band," he says.

"Was there a fight?"

"Apparently not, thank God. General Brooke is sending four more troops up to meet them all at Wounded Knee Creek."

Father Craft frowns as he considers this information. "I know the bunch of incorrigibles from Standing Rock who've joined him," he says. "I should be there."

"They're likely to be afraid for their lives," calls Eastman to the priest, already pulling his recalcitrant horse toward the cavalry tents. "I'd be careful—"

"I've survived the Franco-Prussian War, the Cuban Insurgency, and three years among the Jesuits," he calls back, eyes shining with excitement. "A handful of deluded pagans can't scare me off!"

They watch him hurry away.

"Not your average missionary," mutters Clarence.

"He's—he's very ex*cit*able—"

"He's in*sane*."

"Very likely," says Eastman. "He's been accused of baptizing children *after* they're dead."

"And Big Foot?"

Eastman shrugs. "He packed up and left the Cheyenne River Agency with his people after Sitting Bull was killed, and others have been joining him. He keeps changing direction."

Clarence hoped to speak about the situation with Red Cloud, still the most respected chief among the Oglala, but the old man, not wishing to be drawn into the troubles, has shut himself away in the big wooden house the government built for him, visible just beyond the Army tents.

"How many people with Big Foot?"

"They say a few hundred. But they're already outnumbered by Major Whitside's detachment, and then with this new bunch heading out—it's a lot of fuss over nothing, if you ask me."

Dr. Eastman sounds like he's trying to reassure himself.

Soldiers have appeared to take the wheels off the Hotchkiss guns now, the cannon tubes loaded onto the backs of Army mules, and there is a bugle call that sends a mass of cavalrymen scurrying. One thing Clarence was looking forward to away from Carlisle was a respite from horns cutting the days into pieces and telling you what to do.

The bugler repeats the call. *Boots and Saddles.*

THERE IS SO MUCH left to discover. Even when the methods of transmission are somewhat understood, the origins of the diseases remain unclear. Despite strict adherence to Captain Pratt's edict that filth, foul air, or polluted water never be the culprit at Carlisle, the children continue to sicken and die. Dr. Hazzard steels himself, steps into the isolation ward.

It is an assault on the ears, more than a dozen hackers and honkers at it in concert, with a handful either asleep with exhaustion or enjoying a period of respite. These few are mostly in the area where the Vapo-Cresolene lamps have been set up in between beds, the open kerosene flames heating black liquid in the metal dish above, the fumes hopefully a tonic for their severely compromised lungs. As Dr. Hazzard subscribes to the modern idea that the infection may be spread in fine droplets of sputum expelled by the sufferers, the whooping cough victims have been housed together, boys on one side of the aisle and girls on the other. As the great majority of them have not yet reached their teens, there has been no suggestion of impropriety from the puritans among the faculty. Dr. Hazzard fixes an all-purpose smile on his face and breathes, shallowly, through his mouth, vaporizing coal tar not his favorite perfume. He walks down the very center of the aisle, chin up—adults are not immune to the affliction—and waves vaguely to the children who catch his eye.

It has not been termed the "hundred-day cough" for nothing, some of his patients on their third visit to the ward—a few days without symptoms apparently not long enough to judge that the body has won its battle. Acute diseases merit symptom medications to relieve suffering and prevent complications while waiting for the disease to run its course. Once diagnosed—no great feat in this case—his only involvement is to declare the patient fit to rejoin his or her classmates, or to fill out the death certificate.

The rest is in the hands of his nurses.

The sheer number of children and the vast array of pathologies they exhibit as they pass through the school have, without doubt, afforded him the opportunity to make some well-founded observations, even to perform some experiments. In his experience, belladonna does indeed lift the stigma of bedwetting from the unfortunate piddlers, but the concomitant dizziness and blurring of vision is not worth its prescription. Ergot is somewhat effective against migraines but induces bizarre mental apparitions and a burning sensation in the fingers and toes, *nux vomica* is a poor restorative after excesses of food or drink, and yes, asafetida combats poor digestion and flatulence, but there is no human capacity to tolerate the odor of it as either a liquid or a gum.

Dr. Hazzard ducks around the barrier of blankets they have hung to dampen the noise coming into the next section of the infirmary—hard walls would seriously hinder the circulation of air so vital to the overall health of the patients—and finds Nurse Tucker waiting for him, already fixing him with that accusatory gaze. Why aren't you *do*ing something? it seems to ask, and he has no useful answer. She is rightfully distressed, so many of her "girls"—her nursing hopefuls—now down with scarlatina that the afflicted boys and students with other sundry ailments have been moved to temporary quarters in the old gymnasium.

It is an unsightly and debilitating disease, a painful redness beginning on face and neck, then spreading outward on the body, angry spots in most places, solid welts under the arms and between groin and thigh, then the fever itself—

"Have we lost any today?"

Dr. Hazzard has been gone since the first bugle call, consulting on an outbreak of la grippe in town. It has been a difficult winter.

"No. But three are in very bad condition."

His nursing staff has been stalwart during this crisis, the changing and sanitizing of sweat-soaked linen alone a Sisyphean effort—the sheets and pillowcases are carefully transported and washed in a special superheated run at the laundry. One of the older boys' companies has volunteered to bring buckets of snow to the back door every morning, a cold douche behind the neck an excellent tonic to start the day for girls who are burning up. Keep them hydrated—lemonade or buttermilk proffered depending on the acidity of the stomach—cod liver oil as a restorative, salicylic acid to reduce fever and inflammation, a calomel purge for those with sluggish bowels, and chloral hydrate, now that the stock of laudanum has been used up, to induce sleep.

What more can be done?

Sponge baths of course, cold to the forehead, tepid vinegar and water on the palms of the hands and soles of the feet. Besides the cooling effect and stimulation of the blood, the children are being *handled*, which, though there is no medical literature dealing with it, is a vital part of the palliative care.

He wishes one of his ladies in white would rub his temples.

The migraine, if that's what it is, began in the carriage on the way into Carlisle, an ice pick just behind his right eye, then the undulating waves of pain and feeling of nausea. He has given up alcohol twice before without anything more than a week of jittery mornings and a dragging depression, so this may be something new, and, he fears, chronic. Doctors must not become ill, and if they do, they must grin and bear it.

Nurse Dantley is wielding her array of oral thermometers, taking and recording temperatures. With scarlatina, 105 degrees is the breaking point—let it rise above that and hopes of recovery are pointless. As the most effective antiphlogistics and antipyretics he knows of come with alarming counter-effects, the treatment they can offer is principally nonmedical—the sort of cosseting any good mother could do at home.

He counts eighteen girls in the beds. It might make sense to dispense with nightgowns and tent their top sheets to avoid contact with their inflamed skin, but these Indian maidens are much too modest. Dr. Hazzard is undecided on the theory that they are a doomed race, physically unfit to bear up to the infectious challenges of modern life, much as white citizens would be if condemned to dwell in the jungles of Honduras or Africa. The Apaches, lately, have been arriving already suffering from consumption, but he imagines that is the fault of their agency accommodations rather than a congenital weakness. The Sioux here at Carlisle have certainly endured hard winters before, and those from the Eastern tribes have often already survived rubella—

One of the girls suddenly disgorges, the vomitus spilling out over her chin and chest as she jerks upward and then begins to convulse, her eyes rolling up in her head. Nurse Dantley is at her side immediately, grasping her shoulders to keep her on the bed, and then there is Nurse Tucker on the other side, a pitcher of the cold meltwater in hand. She looks to Dr. Hazzard—

"Proceed."

He doesn't need to be there, of course, but it is proper to be consulted. Tucker dumps the chilled water on the girl's head and it has an immediate effect, her eyes swimming into focus and her body ceasing to twist and arch.

"Grace?" says Nurse Tucker calmly as she bends close to speak. "Are you with us?"

The girl nods.

"We're going to clean you up now, and change your nightgown. Do you think you could eat anything?"

The vomitus is mostly yellow bile, acid-smelling. Her face is drawn—feeding is always problematic.

"Thirsty," whispers the girl.

Nurse Tucker smiles. "We'll get you something to drink right away. Can I help you sit up?"

A change of gowns is the doctor's cue to leave. He pauses by the door, giving his usual valediction to the nurses.

"I thank you, ladies. Carry on."

The cold drives sharpened icicles into his brain as he steps out onto the parade ground, quickly buttoning his coat and pulling up the collar. The migraine, if that's what it is, is near to overwhelming now, and here is Miss Burgess, handkerchief already pressed over her nose and mouth as she arrives for her daily review of the school's ailing and infected—whether to sympathize or gloat he has never decided.

She produces muffled sounds from behind the handkerchief.

"I'm sorry, I can't understand you."

She pulls the handkerchief away.

"How are they faring?"

"As well as can be expected." A phrase he uttered a dozen times this morning in town.

"We lost two already this week."

"Yes—I'm afraid we did."

Miss Burgess shakes her head. "I believe there is a principle of *will* involved," she says. "Some of them just aren't *try*ing."

And with that passes into the infirmary.

He'll make his round of the students in the old gymnasium and then, having forfeited breakfast, see what the hospital kitchen can muster for him. Sleep has become a problem, the room spinning a bit when he lays himself flat in bed, the day's frustrations and failures—for what is a doctor's life but failure—dogging him, and then the sharp pressure in his skull. How can one sleep?

With his nightly alcohol tonic off-limits and the cupboard rather barren of hypnotics—the mere thought of paraldehyde making him wince—it is difficult to prescribe a remedy.

Cannabis indica perhaps, fired and ingested through an inhaling tube—

AT POINT-BLANK RANGE you keep your rear sight pushed down flat—that much he knows. The rest of it is a mystery, and just his luck that he wasn't settled at Fort Riley a full week before they get sent off on this detail. As for telling the redskins apart so you know who to shoot, the "friendlies" camping back around the agency, even the ones who dress almost white, look pretty damn hostile themselves.

Though nothing compared to this bunch sitting and squatting in the council ring—

"The painted-up ones, those are your ghost dancers," says Sergeant, who by good fortune is standing right next to Potter in the K Troop line, carbines leveled at the sullen Indians. "They been told if they sing their songs and wear these magic shirts, our bullets will just bounce off of 'em."

Potter wonders why they don't just ask for a volunteer to prove or disprove this theory and have it done with. He also wonders why, if orders are to make all the bucks hand over their Winchesters and Navy pistols, it wasn't done last evening when they came up to reinforce Major Whitside's troops. He might have slept some in that damn freezing tent instead of worrying all night what they were up to. Barely time to boil coffee this morning, awake before sunrise and into formation—his K Troop making a picket line facing the council ground just to the left of the wall tent they had the old chief sleep in—word is that this Big Foot is down with the ague and might not last the trek to the agency—with B Troop stretched out at a close right angle to them, the Indian tipis with the squaws and squallers just up behind them on the north edge of the ravine, some of the squaws already gathering ponies and packing up. A and I Troops are dismounted as well, strung out in a line that starts by the ravine behind the Indians' herd, then loops around behind the council ring all the way to Wounded Knee Creek. On a knoll off to the left and behind these troopers, maybe a hundred yards away, is Captain Capron and the Hotchkiss guns, which are aimed at the tipi village. What doesn't make sense is that right now, Colonel Forsyth and Major Whitside, along with some captains and lieutenants, the doctor, the Catholic priest fellow, and a couple news correspondents are all standing on the other *side* of the hostile bunch, and behind them the A and I troopers, right in Potter's line of fire should he miss nailing a redskin.

"Hit 'em right here," Sergeant told him and Johnny Rounds, tapping right over his heart. Only Potter has never shot at anybody before, in fact only fired his carbine ten times at a target back at Fort Riley, and Johnny, the numbskull who talked him into coming along to enlist, is in the same boat. Potter has one cartridge ready in the chamber and three more tucked and ready between his fingers like Sergeant taught them, knows how to flip the trapdoor open and load again if it comes to that, and has the hammer half-cocked just like Sergeant. But they've been standing for a godawful long time and his legs are getting shaky—

It's mostly been palaver, Colonel Forsyth speaking out, then the interpreter, who is some kind of half-breed, then one or another of the Indians, and then they had maybe twenty of the bucks go back in between the B and K Troop lines to the tipi village, told to bring their weapons out for collection.

So far this has produced a pair of muzzleloaders that might have belonged to Daniel Boone.

Colonel Forsyth is getting steamed, but these redskins aren't his soldiers, they're enemy hostiles and Potter supposes you maybe got to sweet-talk them some to get their cooperation, even though they're sitting like fish in a barrel, outnumbered four to one at the least with mounted troops waiting on all sides, and all the while there're spectators watching by their wagons on the high ground and a bunch of Indian schoolboys still in their gray uniforms playing tag just behind their firing line, like it's some damn picnic.

"Strip them blankets off the bucks and you'll find plenty rifles," says Sergeant.

"It's cold."

"Not so cold they won't dance around naked if the spirit moves 'em. I'll bet there's a couple dozen twelve-shot Winchesters in that crowd."

Sergeant, one of the few left in the Seventh who was there to see the Custer fight, doesn't have much use for the redskin, male or female.

"And the women will carry weapons for the men," he tells them. "So don't turn your back on no squaw."

Potter trades a look with Johnny Rounds, three men down from him on the firing line.

Sergeant has already explained to them how the Hotchkiss guns can fire exploding shells or grapeshot, and Potter wishes they weren't pointed so close to where he stands. Colonel Forsyth now orders a handful of soldiers to go into the tipi village and see what they can find, one of the newsmen tagging along. This doesn't sit too well with Big Foot's bucks, one of the painted characters standing now and hopping about in little circles, making high-pitched noises with a little bone whistle and seeming to spit curses at the sitting and squatting Sioux. Every now and again he'll bend down and toss some dirt in the air.

"That a ghost dance?"

"Naw," says Sergeant. "He's just trying to rile up them warriors."

"And those other men moaning?"

"Maybe singing their death songs. Getting ready for a bad fight."

"How can Colonel let them do that?"

Sergeant's answer is to pull the hammer of his Springfield all the way back. Potter and the rest of the men on the firing line do the same.

The interpreter is trying to tell the yipping ghost dancer to sit down and be quiet when the troopers come back from the tipi village with only a few more old pieces and a bag full of knives and hatchets. The ghost dancer makes a final circuit around the sitting bucks, then sits moodily beside old Big Foot, who is wrapped in a couple blankets and barely watching the show. Forsyth barks something at the interpreter and then orders B and K Troops to step forward three paces, while the men who just came back search the Indians squatting right in front of them and then there is the ghost dancer throwing dirt in the air and some wrestling and a shot and the squatting men throw off their blankets and turn to aim right at Potter and there is a roar of gunfire and smoke in the air and he realizes he has already fired and is backing up, trying to get the next cartridge into the chamber as the bucks come screaming at him, firing and chopping with axes, Potter getting the breech closed and ramming the barrel of his carbine against the chest of the Indian attacking him and trying to pull the trigger but he hasn't cocked it and he is smacked on the head with something hard, driven to his knees and cocking the hammer and firing into the groin of another man trying to run past and the Hotchkiss guns are blasting away now, troopers from A and I stepping forward to fire over his head at the scattering bucks and he sits up, feeling blood seeping through his scalp, hat gone, looking back to see the little tipi village and Big Foot's wall tent blown apart, Indians running in every direction with mounted troopers and troopers on foot in pursuit, the bugle blowing and officers shouting orders he can't understand, Sergeant kneeling to examine his wound and clap him on the shoulder—

"You're done for the day, private. Just stay put."

And then there is hanging smoke and the gunfire more scattered, more distant, and a circle of bodies—some Indian, some soldier—laying on top of each other where the council ring had been. Potter looks to his left and there is Johnny Rounds laying on his back, a hatchet sticking out of his forehead. There is movement in the circle of bodies lying in front of him, and Big Foot struggles to sit up but is immediately shot several times by men behind Potter, then his daughter, a sturdy, grown woman, runs out from the ruins of the wall tent and there's a rifle crack and she goes down on top of the others.

Potter looks down in his lap and sees the rifle is still in his hands, two unused cartridges stuck between his fingers—

Cut Nose, from one of the Loafer bands, is trying Clarence's mule in the wagon harness when they hear the Hotchkiss guns firing to the north.

I knew it, he says. They're going to kill us all.

And then he lashes the mule into a gallop, his wagon rattling up the road toward the Catholic mission as Clarence steadies the spotted pony he was trading for. The vast collection of tipi camps scattered on the plain and ridges around the agency, tranquil only a moment before, are suddenly swarming with activity—horses and wagons loaded, tents pulled down or simply abandoned, people grabbing what they can and hurrying west toward the Bad Lands.

Plenty Horses and his friends are already gone when Clarence reaches the shed they've been staying in. The pony is skittish, adjusting to a new rider, and the continued booms of the distant cannon and the bugles and rushing troops of cavalrymen across from the agency buildings have it thoroughly spooked. Clarence considers following the soldiers, then can't imagine what his role will be if he does.

He finds Dr. Eastman in his dispensary, packing medical supplies.

"If that's as bad as it sounded," says the doctor, the cannons finally silent, "there won't be enough room here for everybody. You can help me get ready at the Holy Cross church."

Reverend Cook, a Yankton Sioux, runs the Episcopal mission, and helps them tear out the pews and stack them against the walls. Miss Goodale, a young white woman who supervises schools on the reservation, arrives to help, and seems to be more than familiar with Eastman.

"They're engaged to be married," the reverend tells Clarence as they wait for word from Wounded Knee Creek. "I've been asked to preside over the service."

Captain Sword of the Indian police comes by with the first rumor.

"The rider said it was a big fight, lots of people killed on both sides," he tells them. "Agent Royer got us protecting his buildings, so you're on your own out here."

The Christmas tree is still standing in the chapel, ropes of evergreen hung along the walls. Clarence helps cover the floor with hay and quilts, then is sent back to the agency to wait. As he rides he looks up at the ridges, empty now of white canvas, and again wishes he had a weapon, though still not sure as to who he would turn it on. He is not challenged as he passes the military encampment—soldiers frantically digging a trench around the periphery, a large medical tent being filled with cots and operating tables—and ties his pony to a post at the warehouse, then sitting on the loading dock and considering his options. He envies Eastman, a doctor able to help his people and somehow absolved from choosing sides in the conflict. But the idea of more years of schooling in the white man's world, the suspicion that he has no affinity for biology or chemistry, make that seem an unlikely path. Working for the Indian Bureau is openly treasonous, and farming—even the desperate Swedes and Germans, famous for their tolerance for drudgery, have despaired of and in many cases already abandoned their stolen homesteads on this blighted soil.

And he won't be asked to teach at the Carlisle School.

It is nearly dusk when the first of them come in, three mule-drawn wagonloads of dead and wounded soldiers, two more packed with dead and dying Lakota. There is sniping at the agency buildings now, "hostiles" firing long-distance from the hills, the Indian police dug in behind the breastworks raised around the buildings returning fire when they can see something to shoot at, but Clarence is able to guide the wagons to the church unharmed.

Others have come to help, white and Indian, including the former agent McGillycuddy, here as a representative for the new state of

South Dakota, but also trained as a doctor. Clarence climbs into the wagon to help hand people down, lifting them under the arms while Reverend Cook takes their legs. Most are women and children—a few are already dead.

Inside it is hectic work at first, bleeding to be stopped, a quick appraisal to discover who needs care most urgently. An Army physician, sent over by General Brooke, approaches one of the women, who begins to wail at the first glimpse of his uniform.

"Sorry," he says to Dr. Eastman, "I don't think I can help here."

"Can you send Father Craft over? I think they'll trust him—"

"We've got Craft on the table," says the Army doctor. "He was stabbed in the back."

Clarence does whatever he is asked, moving people as gently as he can, holding arms or legs down while Eastman pulls bullets and shards of canister out of torn flesh. The quilts, from a pile Mrs. Cook's sewing group was hoping to sell, are quickly soaked with blood. He kneels to check on an old woman holding a screaming baby that has twisted metal from a Hotchkiss gun shell stuck in its bare legs, four other grandchildren sitting beside her, both of their parents killed in the first minutes of the slaughter.

We were inside the tipi, she tells him. And then it was gone.

He helps a white man named Tibbles, a reporter who left the camp shortly before the shooting began, pull off the rings from a young woman's fingers. She has been shot through both thighs and her wrist is broken, wrist and hand swelling so badly that her fingers are blue above the rings. Clarence presses the rings, once free, into her other hand.

Squeeze on these, he tells her, when it starts to hurt too much.

Another woman refuses to let Dr. Eastman cut off her leg, torn and shattered beyond repair.

If you take my leg, she says, my friends in the next world won't know me.

You'll be there soon, Clarence says to comfort her.

Dr. Eastman, saw in hand, seems relieved to walk away.

Shot in the head, shot in the face, shot in the leg, shot in the back, shot in the back, shot in the back—

The wounded call for water and Clarence checks with McGillycuddy or Dr. Eastman before bringing it to them. Cheyenne scouts bring in four more, men this time, one shot through the lung and coughing blood. Clarence loses sense of time, Miss Goodale giving him a small mirror to hold under the noses of those who seem to be asleep. Somehow nobody dies right away. He feels dizzy, exhausted, splashes cold well water on his face.

Hours pass and nobody sleeps. Clarence recognizes a son of American Horse who has come over from the agency with a basket of apples, giving them to the children, who were desperately hungry even before the battle. They meet over a boy sitting naked except for a blanket he holds around himself with his bone-thin arms, eyeing the apple longingly. His throat has been mostly shot away.

I don't think he can eat that, Clarence says to the son of American Horse, and goes to get the boy a bowl of the gruel Mrs. Cook has heated up. The boy takes the bowl in both hands, the blanket sliding down his back, and swallows as best as he can, gruel mixed with blood slithering out the ragged throat wound and onto his shoulder.

It is cold enough in the church that steam rises from the badly wounded as they struggle to breathe. A soldier comes to tell them that the day school has been burnt down, that the colored troops saved a detachment from the Seventh caught in an ambush near Father Jutz's mission, and to request that Reverend Cook come to officiate over the burial of the thirty troopers who were killed at Wounded Knee. There will be a solemn march, holy words, but no rifle salute that might give anger a focus.

When he steps out with Reverend Cook to get a breath of air, Clarence realizes that a night and a day and another night have passed, that it is morning, with a blizzard roaring in from the north—

IT IS BLACK NIGHT and Grace is on a boat on the lake with all the other boats lit up, fishing with torches—but her boat is on fire, burning and sinking and the flames blister her skin but the black water rising from below is so cold, freezing cold, as if it's winter but why would everybody be out in boats in winter and for some reason she can't cry out, she can only burn or freeze, drown or burn, shivering in a sweat and the firelight so beautiful reflecting off the black water but she burns and she worries is Antoine in the boat too, he said his people did the same fishing at night with torches, but Antoine will survive, he knows how to swim, he is slippery like an eel, like an eel she can wrap her hand around his body thick and hard but not cold to the touch, no, it's warm and alive and she's burning, freezing, drowning then she shudders awake with a cry and pushes her body up to see—

No nurses in the room, the electric lights turned off, a pair of lanterns turned low, throwing patterns on the ceiling.

Night.

She turns to ask the Klamath girl in the next bed how long she has been gone, but there is nobody there, the mattress rolled up on top of bare springs. Grace is tired, so tired, she lays down flat and it feels like ice on her back, she has sweated through her nightgown and the sheet and even the top blanket is damp, laying heavy on her chest, so heavy, like she's at the bottom of a lake full of freezing black water—

A crust of snow armors the parade ground now, the leafless trees black and sinister. Crows mob the branches in the early mornings, though there is never anything for them to eat. Antoine walks toward the hospital, breathing through his nose so his teeth won't ache, and sees a pair of cadets carrying a body down the back stairs on a stretcher. He panics, runs till he catches up with them as they head toward the training buildings.

He pulls the thin sheet down to see the face of the dead student.

It is a smallish boy, not one he knows. The cadets stare at him over the linen masks they've tied over their mouths and noses.

"Sorry," he says, and covers the boy's face.

"We put them in the shed behind the metalworking shop," says one of the boys. "There's two there already."

Nurse Tucker, her face drawn with exhaustion, has stepped out onto the stairs for some air, seemingly oblivious to the cold. Antoine crosses to hand her the note he's written.

"Another one."

"You'll give it to her?"

The nurse wearily accepts the folded paper. "If she wakes up."

"She's still sleeping?"

"She's un*con*scious, Antoine."

Antoine feels like he's been hit with a club.

"Please don't forget."

He is halfway across the parade ground when the Walla Walla boy blows *Assembly* and students come streaming out to form ranks. Jesse Echohawk runs A Company alone now that Clarence is gone, and Elmer White Shield, a fellow Invincible, has been made a corporal after Antoine turned the honor down.

"An officer is supposed to set an example," he told Jesse, "and I don't even want to be here."

Smokey whispers without looking to Antoine as he takes his place.

"Soldiers kilt lotsa ghost dancers, lotsa Lakota."

"Where?"

"The *Sentinel* says at least two hundred dead," mutters Cato Goforth from behind him. "On Pine Ridge."

"Where Clarence come from," adds Smokey.

Antoine has been so fixed on Grace, held like a prisoner in the infirmary, that he hasn't thought much about the news from the west. Lakota business. Sure, everybody here has to deal with some Indian agent back home, has had the white people's army steal land from their tribe, but what does he really have in common with, say, the Apache boys here who barely utter a word and catfoot around like ghosts in blue uniforms?

Though maybe he is starting to hate white people as much as they must, people who will infect you with a disease they have no idea how to cure—

"Is it a war, then?" asks Antoine as he looks down the line to see Trouble, a Sioux like Clarence. The boy's face is set in an angry glare.

"Hard to say yet," hisses Cato. "The paper says it's freezing there—"

"Eyes front, mouths *shut*!" barks Jesse Echohawk, then begins the roll call.

There are news scribblers from as far as New York and Boston, men disappointed to have missed the carnage in Dakota but here hoping the Captain will let slip an utterance worthy of his crucifixion. Eight of the jackals crowd his office, Pratt standing in front of the wall he has covered with before-and-after photographs early this morning, anticipating their arrival. They have asked his honest opinion, and he is determined to give it to them, with both barrels.

"It's a case of damn poor soldiering, if you ask me! If General Miles had been at the reservation I can guarantee you there would have been no discharge of weapons, much less a so-called massacre—"

"But the ghost dancers have been on the warpath," states the fellow from the risibly christened *Scranton Truth*.

"The dances," he says, "though rooted in savagery and fueled by the ingestion of peyote, are re*li*gious rather than military in nature. This labeling of everyone who doesn't care for you as a 'hostile' is witless and destructive!"

The men scribble on their pads. The sage from Pulitzer's *New York World*, a man who has likely never ventured west of the Hudson River before today, weighs in.

"Are any of your former students involved?"

Pratt fixes the man with a withering look.

"Even a year at Carlisle," he says, "would have cured them of such delusions."

JANUARY

THE WEATHER CLEARS ON THE THIRD DAY. THE AGENCY HAS offered a contract for the burial of the Indian dead at the site where they were killed, two dollars a body, to be placed in a common trench. No one steps forward to fulfill it—too many roving bands still out for revenge—but Clarence joins American Horse and his son and nearly a hundred people, mostly Lakota, packed in wagons heading north on the road to Wounded Knee Creek to look for their friends and relatives. Dr. Eastman rides at the front on a big, white American gelding.

"There might be some survivors," he says to Clarence.

"They'll have frozen to death."

"Then we'll see they're given the proper ceremony," says the Indian doctor.

They ride past the Holy Rosary Mission, Father Jutz waving from the steps, sun glinting off his spectacles. A squadron of infantry has been picketed around the building since the killing, all hundred or more boys and girls locked inside till the troubles are over for good. Red Cloud, too old and too blind to fight anymore, has let it be known that the school is under his protection, and such is the respect he still inspires that the soldiers have not been needed. Dr. Eastman waves back to the priest.

"They're safe in there," he observes.

"They heard the cannon firing like everybody else," says Clarence. "And don't know if their parents are dead or alive."

They are at least two miles short of Wounded Knee Creek when they come upon the first bodies. Stiff and twisted, a thin dusting of snow on top of them. A photographer who has come with the newspaper people sets up his camera. Clarence helps load bodies onto a hay wagon, the first woman he handles shot in the back of the head with an eye gone where the bullet came out. The group spreads out to search for more, Clarence struck by how gently the seekers brush the snow from the faces of the dead, and then the wailing and death songs begin as people find their lost ones.

There are dead children, shot, run down. There are babies frozen in their mothers' arms. In what is left of the tipi village Eastman finds a baby, wrapped in several layers, still alive and crying out with hunger under collapsed canvas. There are at least thirty bodies of Lakota men, including that of their chief, sprawled in a circle at the center of it all, their faces bluish gray, looking like so many piles of rags left out in the snow. Clarence walks his pony around them.

"However it started," says Eastman, "they just shot down anybody wrapped in a blanket."

Scattered among the bodies here are crates of soldiers' rations, some of them broken when they were thrown off the army wagons to accommodate dead and wounded bluecoats. Food, in this starving country, but nobody stops to touch it.

There is enough wailing and crying out angrily in Lakota that the white people from the agency and the reporters are getting edgy, men on horseback appearing up on the buttes to the west now, watching them. As Dr. Eastman has the fastest mount, he is tasked to ride back to the agency for an escort to bring them all home.

Clarence kneels to roll over one of the dead warriors, and finds that the man is still holding a Winchester rifle. He manages to pull it free from the death grip, his fingers sticking to the metal barrel in the cold. He mounts the spotted pony, holding the rifle in his left hand, and turns the horse toward the ravines to the west, where people are crying out that they've found another body, and another, and another—

Clarence thinks of the graduation ceremony at Carlisle last year, the handful of students on the stage beaming in their caps and gowns, Reverend Lippincott, the local Episcopalian minister, invited to speak on the occasion—

"I offer you my warmest congratulations," he said, turning at the dais to address the honorees. "You have struggled and you have succeeded. You must remember, though, from this day forward, that the Indian is *dead* within you."

Clarence rides toward the watchers on the butte.

AT CARLISLE THE SIOUX ARE TALKING, and in their own language. Miss Burgess sees what they're up to, drifting together in twos and threes, jumping their places in line to stand with each other, eyes shifting, growing mute when they see her approach. And the signing, as if not being audible it isn't still forbidden. The two girls she caught lingering outside the sewing room were jabbering away at full volume, bold as brass, just staring at her when she asked them what they thought they were doing.

And now Miss Redbird in the stairwell, blocking her way.

"Both of them have relatives who were killed," says Miss Redbird, as if accusing her of pulling the trigger.

"And they are both fully capable of discussing that in the English language."

Girls' punishment is meted out in a room on the top floor of the dormitory, where Miss Burgess has just left them to cool their heels till a judgment of their peers can be arranged. And since that Yakama girl last year, ill-spirited and mentally deficient, set a fire during her incarceration, a matron will be required to keep them company.

"Have you seen those photographs?" challenges Miss Redbird.

"I understand that they are quite disturbing."

"You under*stand*?"

Miss Burgess stares back down at the defiant young woman. "When I was just about your age," she says, "my mother and I treated the survivors from a hunting party of Pawnee who were massacred by the Sioux—*your* people, if I'm not mistaken, Miss Redbird—at least half of them women and children. Treated the wounded and helped to prepare the dead, many of whom had been horribly mutilated, for a decent burial—I *know* what a massacre looks like—"

"But your people—"

"My people, my *tribe*, if you will, are Quakers. We take some pride in not killing anybody. If you'll excuse me—"

Miss Redbird steps aside, stone-faced, and Miss Burgess continues down the stairs. The most difficult task, she thinks, is to save them from themselves—

CAPTAIN PRATT WOULD be proud of him. The School Father's pitch, especially among the Sioux, has always been that their children will be taught English in order to help the tribe understand white man's ways, white man's law, and avoid being cheated in future treaties. Plenty Horses seems to have forgotten much of what he learned of it, and Red Cloud's son-in-law Pete Richard, who the men call Rishaw, speaks English haltingly and with a heavy French accent, and does not read it well. Which has left it to Clarence to be the conduit for white people's news at No Water's camp.

> The New York papers cede us the sensible advice. "Give the bucks plenty to eat and take away their guns." But if that is to be one of the planks in the Democratic platform,

> explanation is needed as to why we should "give" the lusty Indian bucks "plenty to eat." Why not give them plenty of chance to work or starve, and to be peaceable or get killed, just like white folks?

Clarence finds it very difficult, given his years away, to convey sarcasm in the Lakota tongue. He translates the article as simply as possible, then adds—

They say this mockingly.

Red Cloud, nearly blind and having difficulty walking, is here to talk with the renegade leaders, so far advising them to try to control the younger men, that there are so many bluecoat soldiers now around all the agencies that open warfare is senseless. The old chief listens with no expression as Clarence interprets the articles, the young man aware that though most of the authors have never been to Pine Ridge, their words are like the lightning that starts a prairie fire—

HOSTILES GATHERING THEIR FORCES
FOR ANOTHER BATTLE

—reads the headline on the latest *Yankton Press and Dakotan*—

RED CLOUD AND LESSER CHIEFS
HAVE JOINED THE WAR PARTY

—with an opinion piece appended to the list of Seventh Cavalry soldiers killed or wounded in the slaughter.

> The Indians must have been mad to have attacked the number of soldiers who were gathered about them, there being only 120 bucks. The treacherous deed, coming at the time it did, was a surprise, and our correspondent

> doubts if any of the Indians will be left alive to tell the tale when the soldiers get through with their work.

This is what I believe, says Crow Dog. They mean to kill us all.

Crow Dog, who murdered the great Brulé chief Spotted Tail and walked away with only a payment of blood money and ponies to the grieving family, who has been one of the leaders of the ghost dance on both Rosebud and Pine Ridge.

Army generals read the newspapers, Clarence dares to offer, unsure of his status among these older men, but they do not obey their words.

The whites always have more soldiers than we do, and they bring more powerful weapons, muses Red Cloud. But what they don't bring with them is their wives and their children. This has always been our weakness. When they make war, they only risk men who they have no need for. When we make war, we risk everything.

There are women and children in No Water's camp, but not as many as would be there during a time of peace. Clarence is staying in one of the abandoned log cabins with Plenty Horses and some of his Brulé friends, everyone with a nose to the wind, wondering which way they'll be blown next. There is no more sending the women in to the agency on issue day, there have been no dances since he arrived—after the massacre at Wounded Knee Creek it is difficult to convince even the most fervid believers that their ghost shirts will protect them.

> The Sioux Falls *Argus Leader* is not an Indian worshipper,

reads another editorial—

> It recognizes the lazy, filthy, immoral and brutal habits of the Sioux. It believes that the rapid extinction of the Indians

> during the past century has been of great benefit to the American people, since it has removed an impediment to civilization. But it believes that justice is above all ends, and particularly justice to the weak. A treaty should be sacred. It is a national disgrace that this is not true of the treaty between the United States and the Indians.

For "civilization" Clarence substitutes "the white man's way." "Justice" is more difficult—he uses *owóthanla*—to be honest, straightforward—and hears Crow Dog snort.

Do they wish to be fair to us or wish us all dead? asks Red Cloud.

They believe we are weak. Crow Dog scowls.

The old chief sighs. Our fire is very low.

When Red Cloud arrived a day ago he asked to see Clarence, peering with rheumy eyes at the young man. Clarence was still in mostly civilian dress, though wrapped in a blanket against the cold.

Why have you left your school? he asked.

I have learned all I need from there, Clarence told him. I belong here now.

That is good, said the Oglala chief, who had fought the United States long before Clarence was born, winning the Powder River country from the Crow in a treaty at the end of his war. It was I who asked your father to send you there.

Clarence has always wondered about this, his father, made lame from a bullet wound in that Powder River war, saying only that he thought it was best to prepare his son to walk the white man's path.

To make war, says the old man, you must always send out scouts. You have returned now to share what you have seen.

What I have seen weighs upon my heart.

Red Cloud nods. I understand, he says. Read more of what they say.

It is from the *Aberdeen Saturday Pioneer,* Clarence's old friend L. Frank Baum—

> The *Pioneer* has before declared that our only safety depends upon the total extermination of the Indians. Having wronged them for centuries, we had better, in order to protect our civilization, follow it up by one more wrong and wipe these untamed and untamable creatures from the face of the earth. In this lies safety for our settlers and the soldiers who are under incompetent commands—

When Clarence is finished translating the men in the cabin are silent for a long time. Red Cloud sits closest to the woodstove, an item given to any Lakota man willing to build a log cabin instead of living in a tipi. No furniture is given, however, and in most of the cabins here at No Water's camp people fold blankets and sit on the floor. They have found a wooden chair for Red Cloud, so he will have less trouble when it is time for him to stand.

Plenty Horses comes in then, with the news that another part of the agency beef herd has been stolen and driven close by, and that men are needed to butcher the cattle before soldiers can come to steal them back.

Please do this, says the old chief. People need to eat.

Clarence joins at least forty of the young men, riding out. A half dozen would be sufficient, but there is little to do in camp and the chance to kill something is welcome. He carries the rifle from Wounded Knee and rides alongside Plenty Horses.

What did the newspapers have to say? Plenty Horses asks after a mile of silence.

"They say they regret that they have to kill us all," Clarence tells him. "And they spell 'extermination' wrong."

Plenty Horses huffs and scowls. His Brulé companions seem to only tolerate him—he wasn't here for the hard years when the Great Sioux Reservation was cut down, wasn't here when Spotted Tail was killed, leaving his band without a clear leader, he was never a killer of Pawnees or a ghost dancer. His father, Living Bear, though respected, is considered tame now, too far down the white man's path to be trusted.

There is a shout and up ahead they see a soldier—a lieutenant if Clarence can make out what's on his shoulder—and two Indian scouts. Somebody whoops and they gallop to surround the men, uneasy to see an enemy, even one so clearly unaccompanied by troops of murderers, so close to their camp.

The uniformed Indian scouts look wary, Plenty Horses signing to Clarence by rubbing his right forefinger over his left—Cheyenne. The lieutenant, who says his name is Casey, seems more casual than he should be, offering his hand to shake. A few of the older men, including Bear Lying Down, who is an uncle to Plenty Horses, and old Broken Arm, who has to use his left, even smile as they do so.

You should not be here, Bear Lying Down tells the lieutenant. You could be killed.

One of the scouts, who seems to understand Lȧkota and speak some English, can only try to translate.

"Danger here," he says to his officer.

Clarence looks to Plenty Horses, who is not volunteering to help, and decides to stay mute himself.

"I'd like to go in and talk with Red Cloud," says the lieutenant. "Can somebody go let him know I'm here?"

Clarence feels, as he often did at Carlisle, like a spy.

He's crazy, says Bear Lying Down, and turns his horse to head back to No Water's camp and inform Red Cloud of the situation.

"You'll have to come in sooner or later," Casey tells them. "Do it now before anybody else is hurt."

Come in, the scout tells them in Lakota. Come in or people will be hurt.

Clarence looks at the faces of the mounted warriors, none of them knowing if this is an offer or a threat. His first years at Carlisle were like this, white teachers making noises while he tried to read their faces, to make sense of the things they pointed to. Many of those around him, he knows, like Plenty Horses or that boy Trouble in his company, just let their minds drift elsewhere, daydreaming themselves outside of the wooden box they'd been trapped in—

"I could ride in," says Lieutenant Casey, "or Red Cloud and the other important men could come here and parlay with me."

The lieutenant does not react when the young men begin to discuss killing him.

He believes he is brave to come here, says one. I think he is only stupid.

He has these Cheyenne dogs with him.

The scout who speaks Lakota, who has said his name is Rock Road, does not react to this.

They should know better than to show their faces here. We could teach them a lesson.

This one is a two bars, says another, leaning forward to gently poke the lieutenant's insignia. That's like a chief.

We're out to kill longhorns, says old Broken Arm. Not soldiers.

About half of the men, bored, ride away toward where the herd is being held.

"If he'd like, I could escort Red Cloud in to talk with General Miles," says Lieutenant Casey.

Rock Road makes the signs for Red Cloud, talk, and general.

Why doesn't the general come here, says a short young man called Hawk. We can talk to him the way they talked to Big Foot.

Big Foot, also known as Spotted Elk, is the man Clarence saw frozen and twisted among the other dead warriors, his body bent as if trying to sit up, hand extended, reaching—

"I don't want to see anybody else killed."

Captain Pratt was like this man when he was still a fighting soldier, thinks Clarence. Sure of himself, rational, a friend to the Indian even as he hunted him down or took him in chains to prison—

"You're probably getting hungry out here," says Lieutenant Casey. "There's plenty of food at the agency."

You're hungry, says Rock Road in Lakota, and the men all laugh. The lieutenant smiles.

"You see that I've come alone," he says. "I only mean to talk."

He's here to spy for them, says one of Plenty Horses's friends as the lieutenant sends Rock Road back to White River on some errand. He's going to tell them how many we are, what weapons we have.

Bear Lying Down returns then with Pete Richard, riding fast.

"Is not safe 'ere for you," says Richard. "Red Cloud, 'e say you go. These young men 'ere is like drunk, is like crazy."

"Could I ride up on the ridge there and get a look at how many people there are left to bring in?"

"Is better you go now. Red Cloud, 'e say 'e come tomorrow, talk General Miles."

Plenty Horses has backed his horse out of the circle of conversation, as if ready to leave. Most of the young men have their rifles held across their laps, only a few with saddles and scabbards like the white soldiers. Clarence sees that Plenty Horses is pulling his Winchester free of the blanket he is wrapped in—

"I'll tell the general to expect him then," says Lieutenant Casey, raising a hand in goodbye as he turns his horse to leave—

Plenty Horses raises his rifle and shoots him in the back of the head.

Clarence has to rein in his spotted pony to keep it from bolting as the warriors immediately scatter, heading in four directions. Plenty Horses waits for the officer to hit the ground before he turns his horse and walks it away, rifle held down by his thigh. The other Cheyenne scout, White Moon, is kneeling over the dead lieutenant now, only Broken Arm, Bear Lying Down, and Pete Richard left there with Clarence. Richard points to Plenty Horses, then signs to the scout—

Why don't you shoot him?

White Moon glances toward the killer, less than fifty yards away, and signs back—

Shoot him yourself.

Clarence decides he should go tell Red Cloud.

ANTOINE STARES at the sheets of *The Indian Helper* as they roll off the press, the clatter of the machines driving thought from his brain as he sees Cato Goforth enter the print shop, casting a wary glance toward Miss Burgess at her desk, then turning to come to Antoine with some new disaster to report—

In the dining hall Mrs. Bakeless rings the bell for the third time and the students sit as one. Antoine keeps his eyes fixed on her as he leans close to Smokey.

"A Carlisle boy killed an army lieutenant on Pine Ridge," he says.

"Was it Clarence?"

"No, but he was there."

Smokey waits a beat for the dining hall monitor to walk by, then turns to pass the information on. Antoine looks to the head of the table, catches Jesse Echohawk's eye. He's already heard. Jesse puts a hand around his throat, cocks his head sideways and sticks his tongue out. It isn't Plains sign language, but Antoine understands.

Lizzie Cloud brings a platter of steaming potatoes to their table. She has been crying.

"Did they let you in to see her?" Antoine asks.

She shakes her head. "She's in isolation."

Isolation is where they put you before—

"Her oldest brother has come and he's staying in town," says Lizzie. "To arrange for the shipping."

CLARENCE IS TOLD to put his hands on top of his head and keep them there as he enters the guardhouse at Fort Meade. He has been searched for weapons by the sentries twice already, the buffalo robe his uncle Strong Bow gave him shaken out, his Carlisle master sergeant's tunic much commented upon, even the fur-lined winter moccasins his mother has made him pulled off and examined, just to be safe. They have him sit in a room alone for a bit, and then a young white man not wearing a uniform steps in. He looks Clarence over.

"They tell me you speak English."

"I do," says Clarence.

The man narrows his eyes. "And they tell me that you were *there*."

"I was."

"What happened?"

"The lieutenant ventured into enemy territory. Plenty Horses shot him."

"He could have picked somebody a lot less popular. Casey's scouts act like they've lost a brother."

"They knew him."

The man sighs, considering Clarence. "I'll need an interpreter."

"Who are you?"

"Well, I *might* agree to be his lawyer."

"You're in the Army?"

The man, who looks like he's just managed to grow his mustache, shakes his head. "They're taking him to Deadwood for a civilian trial. The Army doesn't want to be anywhere near this."

"We were at war."

The lawyer grins. "That's my strategy. The war didn't end till Short Bull came in, and that was at least a week later. You another Carlisle boy?"

"Plenty Horses speaks English, you know."

"Not to me he doesn't. You want to help?"

The prisoner does not stand up from his cot when they enter the cell, tries not to look at the white man.

He wants to talk to you, Clarence tells him in Lakota. He will speak for you in the court if you want him to.

Nobody needs to speak, says Plenty Horses. They know what they're going to do with me.

Unless they say that it was a war, Clarence explains, they have to admit that those people at Wounded Knee were murdered. There's no honor in murder.

It doesn't matter.

"What's he saying?" asks the lawyer.

"He saying he's ready to die."

"Look, he probably won't even have to take the stand. But I need to know a few things."

"I told you, he shot the lieutenant. I saw it."

"Yes, but *why*? Ask him why."

Clarence passes this question on.

Plenty Horses finally looks at the lawyer.

I am Lakota, he says. I was at the Carlisle School for five years, learning the way of the white man. I came back to my home and there was no work, and I had forgotten my own language. People made fun of me, and I was lonely. I shot the lieutenant so that I might make a place among my people. Now I am one of them—the whites will hang me and the Lakota will bury me as a warrior. They will be proud of me.

Plenty Horses sits on the edge of his cot, his arms folded around his sides, unmovable.

I am satisfied.

Clarence still has moments when he feels guilty about running from Carlisle, wonders how white he could have become. Maybe Plenty Horses is beyond these feelings now, or maybe they never managed to put the hook into his heart.

"What did he say?"

Clarence weighs the words before he speaks them. "He says he acted as a Lakota warrior, and is ready to die like one."

"That's the ticket," grins the young lawyer, looking relieved. "We'll ride that right out of the courthouse."

IN THE DORMITORY ROOM, after *Tattoo* but before *Taps*, the boys sit on the edges of their beds, facing each other over a lit candle placed on the floor.

"So Plenty Horses, near as close to the lieutenant as I am to you, lifts up his rifle and bam!" Smokey mimes shooting toward Trouble. "Shoots him right in the head. Then he don't run off or nothing."

Stories from the trial reach Carlisle every day, growing legs as they are repeated and passed along.

"In another time," adds Smokey, "he would have taken his hair."

They ponder this for a moment. Antoine steps to the window to look out at the moon. The nurse says Grace has not been conscious for two days, and it is hard for him to care what is happening on a distant reservation.

"If I could fly," he says, "I'd go home right now."

Asa gets up, begins to rustle through his footlocker—

"Clarence got home somehow," says Smokey.

Clarence has not written to anybody at school, probably figuring his letter would be easily traced. None of the instructors, not even the Man-on-the-Bandstand, have mentioned his name since he disappeared.

Asa pulls a small sack out from under his mattress, dumps the contents out on his bed. The other boys come over to look.

"You eat 'em," says Asa, his English surprisingly good these days for somebody who rarely says a word, "you *fly*."

A dozen peyote buttons lay on the bed.

"How many does it take?" asks Antoine. The idea of staying here, without Grace—

Asa considers, picks up three of the buttons, and hands them to Antoine.

As we at Carlisle enter a new year we reflect upon how far we have come—

—writes the Man-on-the-Bandstand as Miss Redbird sits alone in her little room, looking into a small mirror and using bootblack and rouge to paint her face. She wears the fringed buckskin dress the photographers and portrait artists always request, posing with her violin or fanning a hand over her brow as if scanning the prairie for smoke signals. She traces carefully with her fingers—a red cross on her forehead, red dots from her lower lip to the point of her chin, jagged black lightning bolts on her cheeks. No one is waiting to make a picture of her. She has studied the first printed photographs—bodies frozen in the snow, soldiers in winter gear stacking dead Lakota people in a ditch. Her tears turn black as they roll across the lightning—

—and how far we have yet to travel. We must remember that there is no excellence without great labor—that we must cease to do evil—

—Nurse Tucker brings a damp cloth to the forehead of Moses Smoke, sitting doubled-up in a chair, apparently having eaten something that causes him to vomit spasmically. At least it isn't the scarlatina—

—and learn to do well. That we must keep our shoulders back and minds alert if we are to avoid consumption and the other diseases of indolence—

—Asa, wearing only a pair of knee-length underdrawers, runs swiftly around the perimeter of the tall fence under the full moon, smiling, feeling the crusty snow between his toes—

—That poor dress and posture are evidence of a weak mind—that pluck is for doers and luck is for dreamers—that the road to perdition is paved with good intentions and lackluster application—

—Trouble uses a barrel to help him scale the tall fence and trot away from the school—

—that we can be not what we were born to be, but what we resolve to be—that government rations leave a bitter taste, but bread won through honest labor tastes sweet—

—Captain Pratt, still at his desk and using an oil lamp to save on electricity, contemplates the before and after photographs spread out on his desk—

—that tobacco is the devil's weed and liquor his poisonous blood—

—the earliest of those photographs taken at the fort in St. Augustine, the day Mrs. Stowe of *Uncle Tom* fame visited his prisoners—

—that the fork is used to eat with and the knife to cut with—that bad companions are as leaden weights to a drowning man. We must take stock of ourselves, our lives, our ambitions—

Antoine, standing at the edge of the roof of the large boys' quarters, smiles as he looks across to the lights still on at the hospital. He takes a series of deep breaths, spreads his arms as if he's about to jump—

—while Miss Burgess sits in her nightgown, writing by lamplight and softly reciting the words of her latest decree as Annie prepares to get into one of the two single beds behind her—

"—vigilant to recognize and restrain our baser instincts, building a wall between who we were and who we strive to become—"

—Trouble wanders, intoxicated and disoriented, across the tracks of the Carlisle train yard as a westbound freight rumbles in, the boy pausing under a light pole to look at the much-folded map of the country he has stolen—

—resisting the lures and entreaties of our less fortunate loved ones, who dwell in the darkness of savagery and superstition—

—cross-hatched railroad lines drawn over the states and territories, leading away from Carlisle—

—so that we might regard ourselves in the mirror and honestly report—

—the boy stumbling on a rail, falling to a knee in the middle of the track as the whistle blows, closing on him. He drops the map and covers his face, the headlight of the freighter finding him, the whistle screaming in rapid blasts, then the great beast rolling past on a parallel track—

I AM GETTING BETTER EVERY DAY!

Trouble uncovers his face, takes a moment to decide that he's not dead. He watches the freight train roll through Carlisle without stopping and thinks he sees something.

Or is it only a spirit, mocking him?

The horse looks as lost as he feels. He leaves the map lying on the ground, crunches over the frozen ballast stones to stand staring into the animal's liquid eye, seeing his own reflection. There is a halter rope around its neck, dragging on the ground. He takes it in hand and is on the horse's back in an instant. It doesn't bolt or even shift its feet. He leans forward to stroke its muzzle, speaking softly in Lakota.

Do you know the way?

Miss Burgess turns the lamp down.

Antoine leaps—

ANTOINE AND JIMMY sit in the boxcar, morning light seeping through the cracks in the boards and from the trapdoor above their heads, the train whistle blowing from ahead.

"Coming to a stop. Take on water, maybe."

"So he got away?" asks Jimmy. "The Sioux kid?"

"The newspapers turned on the Army once the pictures of the dead ghost dancers started getting around. And if it's not a war, it just looked like murder," says Antoine. "Which makes Plenty Horses an enemy soldier, and they had to let him go."

"I meant your friend. Trouble."

Antoine shrugs. "Somebody in Altoona maybe saw him on a horse."

"And you run off too."

"I flew."

"Sure you did."

It is how he remembers the night. At some point he left his body still sitting on his bed, alone in his room, and climbed out onto the roof of the dormitory to look at the school. He needed to say goodbye to Grace. He leapt into the air and floated, floated over the bandstand, floated across the parade ground to the hospital, floated in through a window they'd left open and over the beds of the sleeping, dying Carlisle girls, finally settling down next to her in her bed, holding her, Grace burning with heat like a small furnace, till the sky began to lighten and he had to go.

"She's still there?" asks Jimmy. "That Grace?"

Antoine shakes his head no. "They sent her home. On the mail train."

The Polish boy looks stricken. "Gee, that's awful."

It is nearly spring, and Jimmy wonders how the Indian kid can have left Pennsylvania in January and only be this far. The train has slowed, and now the couplings begin to bang together as it comes to a stop. Antoine crosses to the door—

"Careful—"

Antoine listens for a moment, then muscles the door open a few feet, the sudden daylight causing him to squint. When his eyes adjust, the trees look familiar, like something he has always known. He breathes in deeply.

"This is near where I live."

Jimmy stands to look past him into the pine forest.

"How can you tell?"

"The way it looks, the way it smells—"

"You really think so?"

"Just to the north. Maybe a day's walk if I can find a logging trail."

Antoine crouches, hops down from the boxcar, reflexively looking up to the head of the train to be sure nobody is watching. He starts for the woods.

Feeling suddenly panicky, Jimmy thrusts his head out of the door, looks quickly up and down the track, then calls out—

"You're leaving?"

Antoine turns, smiling. "The rice is coming up in the lake."

The white boy, framed in the boxcar doorway, looks very small. There will be stories to invent, thinks Antoine, an Indian agent to avoid or pacify, but he is an Invincible, able to wrestle any side of an argument into his service.

Jimmy waves forlornly from the train.

Antoine is a survivor, he is a Carlisle Indian no less, and it would be bad form to come home empty-handed.

He motions for Jimmy to come along—

"Wait'll you see the canoes we make," he calls as the boy grabs his bindle, hops down, and comes running. "Prettiest thing that ever floated on water."

Acknowledgments

THIS IS A PROJECT THAT BEGAN AS A SCREENPLAY MORE than twenty years ago, and the advantage in that is that my interest in the history never waned- information and connections new to me kept popping up. Barbara Landis, who worked at the Carlisle, Pa. public library for years, has been key, as she first adopted, then organized and digitized the Industrial School records and periodicals that had been uncared for and virtually forgotten for so long, then has continued to help Native people reclaim tribal members who had died and were buried at the school. She has helped so many people explore this history.

Of the countless sources I've benefitted from reading, the first to come to mind is the many writings of Zitkala Sa, aka Gertrude Bonnin, who appears as Miss Redbird in the novel. An honest and forceful writer who taught at the Carlisle school a few years after the events I've covered, she was also co-founder of the National Council of American Indians, which successfully lobbied for Native people's right to US citizenship, and was one of the first to publicize the murder of Osage people for their oil money in the 1920s.

James Mooney, who appears as the Ethnographer, was an observer with a generously open mind for his time, and his *The Ghost-Dance Religion and Wounded Knee* contains some of the most detailed accounts of the massacre I've encountered. Other characters such as Dr. Charles Eastman and Elaine Goodale Eastman wrote useful memoires, as did the Carlisle graduate Luther Standing Bear with his *My Indian Boyhood*. Richard Henry Pratt's *Battlefield and Classroom* provides a good idea as to how the man's mind worked, while Marianna Burgess's *Stiya* is painful to read (Leslie Marmon Silko relates a story of her great-grandmother threatening to burn it in her cookstove) but, along with her Man-on-the-Bandstand writings in *The Indian Helper*, provides a window into her mindset and that of other reformers bent on destroying Native culture. Thomas Foley's *Father Francis M. Craft, Missionary to the Sioux* (yes, he was a real person) contains excerpts from Craft's diaries, and one late chapter is aptly titled *Was Father Craft Insane?*

Newspaper dispatches from most of the journalists who appear as characters in the book can be tracked down, and give a fair idea of the culpability of the press in setting the stage for the massacre, and the excerpts from L. Frank Baum, who later wrote the Oz books, are pretty much as they appeared at the time- a progressive on many issues, including women's suffrage, he was a constant advocate for the extinction of Native people.

I'd also like to cite Dee Brown's seminal *Bury My Heart at Wounded Knee* for jump-starting my interest in history, and *Fool's Crow* by James Welch, one of the best, and saddest, novels I've ever read. The Carlisle School experience was complex, producing notable athletes and activists as well as runaways and suicides, and learning what I have during the long gestation and writing of this book has only increased my admiration for those who survived it.